# DARK APOSTLE

THE WORD BEARERS are among the most zealous and deadly of the Chaos Space Marine Legions, seething with a hatred that is millennia old. When Dark Apostle Jarulek commands his force to lay waste to the Imperial planet of Tanakreg, the assault is absolute and they brutally enslave the population. With the new slaves in their power they set them a mysterious task building a monstrous, kilometres-high tower.

What are the dark visions that drive Jarulek, and can the Word Bearers achieve his vile purpose? Only the forces of the Imperium have the power to stop them, but will they arrive in time?

*More Anthony Reynolds from the Black Library*

MARK OF CHAOS

*More Warhammer 40,000 from the Black Library*

**• GAUNT'S GHOSTS •**

*Dan Abnett*

THE FOUNDING

(Contains the first three Gaunt's Ghosts novels – *First and Only, Ghostmaker,* Necropolis and the short story *In Remembrance*)

THE SAINT

(Contains the next four Gaunt's Ghosts novels – *Honour Guard, The Guns of Tanith, Straight Silver* and *Sabbat Martyr*)

THE LOST

*Book 8 – Traitor General*
*Book 9 – His Last Command*
*Book 10 – The Armour of Contempt*

**• ULTRAMARINES •**

*Graham McNeill*

THE ULTRAMARINES OMNIBUS
(Contains the first three Ultramarines novels – *Nightbringer, Warriors of Ultramar* and *Dead Sky Black Sun*)

**• SOUL DRINKERS •**

*Ben Counter*

THE SOUL DRINKERS OMNIBUS

(Contains the first three Soul Drinkers novels – *Soul Drinker, The Bleeding Chalice* and *Crimson Tears*)
Book 4 – CHAPTER WAR

A WARHAMMER 40,000 NOVEL

# DARK APOSTLE

Anthony Reynolds

*For my brother, Nick, who always believed I could do it.*

**A BLACK LIBRARY PUBLICATION**

First published in Great Britain in 2007 by
BL Publishing,
Games Workshop Ltd.,
Willow Road, Nottingham,
NG7 2WS, UK.

10 9 8 7 6 5 4 3 2 1

Cover illustration by Klaus Scherwinski.



A CIP record for this book is available from the British Library.

ISBN 13: 978 1 84416 507 0
ISBN 10: 1 84416 507 8

Distributed in the US by Simon & Schuster
1230 Avenue of the Americas, New York, NY 10020, US.

It is the 41st millennium. For more than a hundred centuries the Emperor has sat immobile on the Golden Throne of Earth. He is the master of mankind by the will of the gods, and master of a million worlds by the might of his inexhaustible armies. He is a rotting carcass writhing invisibly with power from the Dark Age of Technology. He is the Carrion Lord of the Imperium for whom a thousand souls are sacrificed every day, so that he may never truly die.

Yet even in his deathless state, the Emperor continues his eternal vigilance. Mighty battlefleets cross the daemon-infested miasma of the warp, the only route between distant stars, their way lit by the Astronomican, the psychic manifestation of the Emperor's will. Vast armies give battle in His name on uncounted worlds. Greatest amongst his soldiers are the Adeptus Astartes, the Space Marines, bio-engineered super-warriors. Their comrades in arms are legion: the Imperial Guard and countless planetary defence forces, the ever-vigilant Inquisition and the tech-priests of the Adeptus Mechanicus to name only a few. But for all their multitudes, they are barely enough to hold off the ever-present threat from aliens, heretics, mutants – and worse.

To be a man in such times is to be one amongst untold billions. It is to live in the cruellest and most bloody regime imaginable. These are the tales of those times. Forget the power of technology and science, for so much has been forgotten, never to be re-learned. Forget the promise of progress and understanding, for in the grim dark future there is only war. There is no peace amongst the stars, only an eternity of carnage and slaughter, and the laughter of thirsting gods.

*As Sanguine Orb waxes strong and Pillar of Clamour rises high,*
*The Peal of Nether shakes,*
*And Great Wyrms of The Below wreak the earth*
*With flame and gaseous exhalation.*
*Roar of Titans will smite the mountains and they shall tumble.*
*Depths of Onyx shall engulf the lands, and then exposed shall lay*
*The Undercroft,*
*Death and Mastery.*

*The door shall be opened to he of pure faith*
*Into Darkness two descend,*
*Apostate and he who would be,*
*Into madness and confusion descend,*
*Restless dead and creatures old,*
*The Undying One to face.*

*Master of the cog will come in chains and tattered robes,*
*To become Enslaved,*
*To unleash the Orb of Night and Breaking Dawn.*

*One shall fall, he of lesser faith, he unmarked by godly touch,*
*His fate to remain, trapped eternal,*
*And for one to flee with prize in hand,*
*Gatemaster,*
*He who bears Lorgar's touch.*

# PROLOGUE

MARDUK, FIRST ACOLYTE of the Word Bearers Legion, looked up. His noble, deathly pale patrician features, common amongst those imbued with the gene-seed of blessed Lorgar, were twisted in frustration and anger. Braziers burning within the darkness of the icy mausoleum lit his face, the flames mirrored in his eyes.

'I have read the portents. I felt the truth within the blood of the sacrifices on my tongue.'

He rounded on his silent listener, the ancient Warmonger.

'But this vision fills my head, and its meaning is unclear. I have recited the Curses of Amentenoc; I have supplicated the Great Changer with offerings and sacrifice. I have spent endless hours in meditation, opening myself up to the wisdom and majesty of the living Ether. But the meaning remains unclear.

'I am assailed by the dead, long dead, and they claw at my armour with skeletal claws. They scratch deep furrows into my blessed ceramite, but they cannot pierce my consecrated flesh. I begin to recite from the *Book of Lorgar*, the third book of the *Litanies of Vengeance and Hate*. "Smite down the non-believers and the deceived, and they shall know the truth of the words of oblivion."'

Marduk clenched his fist tightly, servo-muscles in his armour whining as his entire body tensed.

'I shatter their bones with my fists. They cannot stand against me. But they are many.'

'Calm your mind, First Acolyte,' boomed the ancient one. It was the sound of the sepulchre given voice, an impossibly deep baritone that reverberated through the still tomb, deep within the strike cruiser. Each word was spoken slowly and deliberately, amplified through powerful vox-units.

Once he had been a mighty hero who fought at the side of the greatest warriors ever to have lived. As a captain he had led great companies of the Legion against the foes of Lorgar and the Warmaster, and Marduk had studied all of his recorded sermons and exhortations. They were masterpieces of rhetoric and faith, filled with righteous hatred, and his skill at deciphering and predicting the twisting patterns of the future through his ritualised dream visions were astounding. He had fallen fighting against the arch-enemies, the deniers of the truth, those who followed the False Emperor in their ignorance and blindness.

'You fight your visions too hard. They are gifts from the gods, and as with all gifts bestowed from the great powers, you should receive them with thanks.'

The meagre physical remnants of the inspirational leader had been interred within the sarcophagus that lay before Marduk. Though his body was utterly ruined, he was destined to live on within the tomb of his new shell, and become the Warmonger. While the other Dreadnoughts of the Legion had slowly succumbed to madness and raving insanity, the Warmonger retained much of his lucidity. It was his faith, Erebus himself had stated, that kept him from slipping into darkness.

All the anger and frustration flowed out of Marduk, and he smiled. The face that had looked brooding and twisted with anger a moment before was darkly handsome once again, black eyes glinting.

'Pray for enlightenment, but do not be impatient and expect instant gratification,' continued the Warmonger. 'Knowledge and power will come to you, for you are on the path of the devout, and the favour of the gods is upon you. But you must let yourself succumb to the embrace of the great powers; they will buoy you, and only then will the veil be lifted from your eyes. Only then will you see what your vision means. You need not fear the darkness, for you *are* the darkness.'

The Warmonger flexed its huge, mechanical arms, hissing steam venting from the joints.

'My weapons ache for the bloodshed to begin anew,' the dreadnought said, massive weapon feeds aligning themselves in anticipation. 'Do we fight alongside our Lord Lorgar this day?'

'Not today,' said Marduk quietly, recognising that the Warmonger's lucidity was slipping. It was often this way.

'And the Warmaster? Do his battles against the False Emperor fare well? Has he yet dethroned the hated betrayer, the craven abandoner of the Crusade?'

The mention of the Warmaster Horus pained Marduk. He longed for the simpler days of the past, when the victory of the Warmaster over the Emperor seemed like a certainty. The memories were fresh in his mind, and his anger, hatred and outrage burned within him stronger than ever. He wished he had been at the battle of the Emperor's palace on Terra alongside the Warmonger and most of the warriors that made up the Grand Host of the Dark Apostle Jarulek, but he had not. No, in those days he had been but a novice adept sent to serve under Lord Kor Phaeron. It was a great honour, but while he fought the hated Ultramarines of Guilliman on Calth with passion and belief, he longed to be fighting the battle at the palace that would determine the outcome of the long war. Or so he had thought. The war ground on, and would never end until the so-called Emperor of mankind was thrown down, and every cursed edifice that falsely proclaimed his divinity was smashed asunder.

'The Corpse Emperor sits on his throne on Terra still, Warmonger,' said Marduk bitterly, 'but his end draws ever nearer.'

# BOOK ONE: SUBJUGATION

*'From the fires of betrayal unto the blood of revenge we bring the name of Lorgar, the Bearer of the Word, the favoured son of Chaos, all praise be given unto him. From those that would not heed we offer praise to those who do, that they might turn their gaze our way and gift us with the boon of pain, to turn the galaxy red with blood, and feed the hunger of the gods.'*

– Excerpt from the three hundred and forty-first
Book of the Epistles of Lorgar

# CHAPTER ONE

KOL BADAR GLARED across the expanse of the cavaedium. The arena of worship, located deep within the heart of the strike cruiser *Infidus Diabolus*, was large enough to allow the recently swollen ranks of the entire Host to stand in attendance. Its curved ceiling stretched impossibly high, and immense skeletal ribbed supports met hundreds of metres above. The kathartes perched along the bone-like struts, daemonic, skinless harpies that flickered in and out of the warp. But Kol Badar's gaze did not rise to look upon the carrion feeders.

No, his scowling features were focused on the last of the warriors filing into the enormous room. From his vantage point, just one step from the top of the sacred raised dais that none bar the most holy of warriors would occupy, he could see the last of the Host's champions leading their warriors into the cavaedium, to take their places for the coming ceremony. The expanse was almost full. The entire Host had been gathered. Kol Badar let his gaze wander over the serried ranks, glorying in the strength and power that his warriors exuded. None could hope to stand against such a force of the devout, and his warriors would soon prove their worth once again.

*His* warriors. He grunted at his own hubris. They were not *his* warriors. If anything, they were the warriors of the Dark Apostle, though in his words they belonged only to Chaos in all its glory. The Dark Apostle claimed that he was merely the instrument through which the great powers directed these noble warriors of faith, and that Kol Badar was his primary tool to enact the great gods' will.

Kol Badar was the Coryphaus. It was a symbolic title, granted to the most trusted and capable warrior leader and strategos of the Host. His word was second only to that of the Dark Apostle. The Coryphaus was the Dark Apostle's senior war captain, but more than this, he was the voice of the congregation. The mood and opinion of the Host was delivered to the Dark Apostle through him, and it was his duty to lead the chanted responses and antiphons from the gathered Host in ceremonies and rituals. It was also his role to lead the responses within the true house of worship of the dark gods: the battlefield.

The processional corridor that ran down the middle of the nave remained clear as the cavaedium filled. Almost half a kilometre long and laid with black, immaculate carpet consecrated in the blood of thousands, none dared to step upon this hallowed ground, bar those deemed worthy, on pain of immortal torment. There were no seats within the nave; the warriors of the Legion received the word from the Dark Apostle standing, armed and armoured. Dozens of smaller sanctuaries and temple-shrines branched off from the ancient stone walls of the cavaedium, containing statues of daemonic deities, ancient texts and the interred remains of holy warriors who had fallen during the constant, long war.

An almost imperceptible, ghostly chanting whispered around the room. Lazily swooping cherubiox circled in the air, skeletal, winged creatures with sharp fangs set within childlike mouths, each carrying a flaming iron brazier. Odorous incense descended from the tusked maws of daemon-headed gargoyles towards the gathered Host. The clouds of smoke eddied and roiled in the wake of the gently weaving cherubiox.

Kol Badar stepped heavily down the altar steps, the joints of his massive, ornate Terminator armour hissing and steaming. He passed through the gates of the ikonoclast, the spiked metal barrier that separated the altar from the openness of the nave. Its wrought iron frame was decorated with dozens of ancient banners, twisted icons and trophies dedicated to the gods of Chaos, and upon its spiked and barbed tips were impaled the heads of particularly hated foes.

He prowled along the base of the altar, glaring at the warrior-brothers filing into the room, as if daring any of them to dishonour him in any way. The warriors of the Legion stood unmoving once they had taken up their positions. Almost two thousand warriors of the Word Bearers stood in absolute silence, and Kol Badar stalked back and forth along their ranks.

Two thousand was a particularly large number of warrior-brothers for a single Host. The ranks of the Host had swollen a century past, when the warriors of another Dark Apostle had been amalgamated into its ranks after their holy leader had been slain in battle. Ceremonies of mourning had lasted weeks as the Legion honoured the passing of one of its religious fathers. Jarulek had, of course, ordered the execution of all the captains of the leaderless Host for having allowed such a sacrilege to take place. It was deemed by the Dark Council on the revered daemon-world of Sicarus, the spiritual home of the Word Bearers Legion and the throne world of the blessed Daemon Primarch Lorgar, that Jarulek take in the leaderless Host, for he had an apprentice, a First Acolyte who would soon be ready to bear the mantle of Dark Apostle. When, and if, the First Acolyte became worthy of the title of Dark Apostle, then Jarulek would split the Host once more into two.

The thick features of Kol Badar's face darkened at the idea. The very thought of the bastard whoreson Marduk bearing the exalted title of Dark Apostle made Kol Badar's rage and bitterness burn fiercely within him.

The Anointed, the warrior-cult of the most favoured warriors within the Host, stood in neat ranks surrounding the raised pulpit of the Coryphaus, and Kol Badar approached them. The Anointed looked like statues, utterly still and wearing their fully enclosed, ancient suits of Terminator armour. Each suit was a relic of holy significance, and to don the armour was a great religious honour. Once a warrior-brother entered the ranks of the Anointed, he was a member for life, and with lifespans extended indefinitely through a combination of their Astartes conditioning, bio-enhancement and the warping power of the gods of the Ether, the Anointed were only replaced on the rare occasion that one of their cult fell in battle. Many of them had fought alongside Kol Badar and their holy Daemon Primarch Lorgar at the great siege of the Emperor's palace, and he knew of no finer fighting force. Unsurpassed warriors with the hearts of true fanatics, the cult of the Anointed had won countless battles for the Legion. Their glories were sung in the flesh-halls within the temples of Sicarus, and their deeds recounted in the grimoire historicals housed in the finest scriptorums of Ghalmek. Kol Badar stalked through the ranks of the elite warriors and climbed the steps to his pulpit, there to await the arrival of the Dark Apostle.

The Dark Apostle; Jarulek the Glorified; Jarulek the Blessed, a divine warrior who heard the whispered words of the gods, and communed with them as their vessel. One of the favoured servants of the immortal daemon primarch Lorgar, Jarulek truly was a bearer of the word. His furious passion and belief had brought countless millions into the fold. Countless millions more, ignorant and resistant to the words of truth, had been slain in holy war upon his order.

As much as it furthered the cause of the Word Bearers for more systems to be brought under the sway of Lorgar's word, Kol Badar much preferred the worlds that resisted. He enjoyed the killing.

Thin, spider-like limbs extended from the pulpit towards his exposed face. Fine, bladed hooks at their tips emerged and pushed into his flesh, latching beneath the skin. He closed his eyes. A large proboscis uncurled, and he opened his mouth to accept it. It entered his throat, and small barbed clamps latched onto his larynx. The proboscis expanded to fill his throat. His voice, enhanced by the apparatus, would not only carry through the vast expanse of the cavaedium, but also through the entire *Infidus Diabolus,* so that all within the cruiser might intone the correct responses.

He recalled the conversation he had had with the Dark Apostle mere hours earlier, and his face flushed with the thought of the rebuke he had received.

'Speak as the Coryphaus, Kol Badar, not as yourself,' Jarulek had scolded him gently.

Kol Badar had clenched his heavy jaw tight, looking down. 'What would you have me say, Dark Apostle?' he had asked, his voice sounding course and crude in his ears after Jarulek's velvet words.

'I would have you speak for the Host, as the Coryphaus. Does the Host accept him?'

'The Host follows your word without fault, my lord.'

'Of course. Meaning?'

'Meaning that they embrace and revere him, for it is your will for them to do so,' he had said, his voice thick.

'And speaking as yourself?' Jarulek had asked, softly.

'He is an upstart newborn risen beyond his position. He has not been with us from the start. He did not fight at our side as we assailed the cursed False Emperor's lapdogs on Terra,' Kol Badar had fumed. 'You should have let me kill him.'

Jarulek had chuckled at that. 'A newborn, I have not heard you call him that before. He has fought against the False Emperor mere centuries less than you and I, old friend.'

Kol Badar's face had darkened. 'He was not there at the start.'

'No, but a long time has passed since then: ten thousand years in the world of mortals.'

'We do not live in the realm of mortals,' Kol Badar had replied. Time held no sway over the warp; a warrior may spend a month within its unstable boundaries, emerging to find that the galaxy had changed, that countless decades had flown by. To Kol Badar, the siege of the Emperor's palace felt like mere centuries ago, not the staggering ten thousand years that had passed since that time, and his memories of it were strong.

'He has been chosen by the gods,' Jarulek had said. 'Do not struggle against their will, Kol Badar. They are unforgiving masters, and a soul like yours would be an exquisite plaything. You are my most loyal and honoured warrior – do not let your hatred of him be your ruin.'

A mournful, tolling bell echoed across the expanse of the cavaedium. Silence descended, and not a movement stirred through the massed ranks of the Word Bearers. This was the start of the exhortation, and the entire Host stood in silence, awaiting the arrival of the Dark Apostle.

Kol Badar was a warlord, a killer and a destroyer of worlds. But, along with the rest of the Host, he would wait, patient, unmoving and in silence, for the arrival of the holy Dark Apostle. If it took a minute or a week, he would stand immobile. And so he waited.

* * *

'GO,' SAID THE voice over the comm-channel. Reacting instantly, black-armoured figures of the Shinar enforcers stepped out of the gloom of the narrow alleyway. Lieutenant Varnus levelled and fired his combat issue shotgun at the heavy locking mechanism of the rusted door. The sound of the weapon echoed deafeningly, and a fist-sized hole was punched through the metal. Varnus slammed a heavy boot into the door, swinging it violently open, and surged through, the other enforcers close behind him.

The door opened to a refuse strewn corridor, dully lit by humming glow-globes. A man sitting with his feet up on the crude synthetic table looked up, eyes wide, lho-stick hanging limply from his mouth. A second blast from the shotgun threw him backwards, slamming him against the wall in a spray of blood.

'Entrance gained,' said Varnus, opening up the comm-channel.

'All teams have entered the complex. Proceed as planned,' said the captain in reply.

'Yes, sir,' said Varnus. He mouthed an obscenity under his breath once the comm-channel was closed.

Moving in a half crouch up the corridor, he stepped quickly over the scattered piles of twisted metal and broken masonry.

'Smells like a damn sewage pit,' muttered one of the enforcers. Varnus was forced to agree. He indicated sharply to a closed door as he passed it. A pair of enforcers behind him took up positions to either side of it. One kicked it open, and the two of them moved in, shotguns raised. The sharp, focused beams of light from their helmets swung around to locate any threats. The other two enforcers in the team moved up in support of Varnus. He paused at the end of the corridor, and glanced quickly around the corner: another empty, sparse corridor, this one with a single door leading from it. Glow-globes overhead flickered weakly.

Varnus stepped around the corner and moved forwards cautiously, the focused beam from his helmet piercing the dark corners that the weak illumination of the glow globes failed to light. Rodents scurried away from the brightness. The stench was overpowering.

'Who in the Emperor's name would want to hide out here?' remarked one of his team, swearing colourfully.

'Those who don't want to be disturbed,' said Varnus sharply. 'And cut the chatter, Landers. I'm sick of your whine.' The enforcer muttered something under his breath, and Varnus resisted the urge to turn on the big man. Focus, he told himself, and stepped towards the closer of the two doors. He heard the sound of muffled voices, a shout. He swore.

Varnus slammed his heavy boot into the door, and it collapsed inwards, its hinges long corroded. A pair of men were raising a heavy metal hatch in the floor of the room. One, his eyes filled with fear, dropped down into the darkness of the bolt-hole. The other raised an autopistol, face twisted in hatred, and raking fire spat from the end of the stub-nosed weapon. Varnus's shotgun barked, even as the bullets from the pistol ripped across his chest, and the man's head exploded in a splatter of gore.

Varnus fell back from the impact of the projectiles on his carapace armour. 'Get the other one,' he wheezed.

'I can't fit down there,' remarked Landers, shrugging his shoulders. He nodded towards the smallest of the four enforcers, a grin on his face.

'One of you damn well go! Now!' roared Varnus, pulling himself to his feet. The slight enforcer swore, seeing the eyes of the whole team on him. He placed his shotgun on the floor of the room, drew and cocked his autopistol and dropped into the darkness of the bolt-hole. The sound of the man scrambling through a metal duct echoed loudly beneath them.

Still wheezing, Varnus opened up his comm-channel.

'They are running. Undisclosed bolt-holes. Orders?'

Varnus pulled the bullets from his chest-plate as he waited for a response. He could feel the heat from the bullets through the leather of his gloves.

'Captain?' he said with some impatience. 'Did you hear me? What are our orders?'

There was a muffled grunt of pain from the bolt-hole, and then the sound of three gunshots. The enforcer reappeared a moment later. 'Bastard stuck me,' he said, his hand gripped around his left arm, blood seeping between his fingers.

'Hold position. Awaiting new intel,' came the captain's terse response, finally.

'Hold position? They will have cleared out by the time we wait for new intel!'

'Hold your position, lieutenant.' The comm-bead clicked closed in his helmet.

'Frek that,' said Varnus. Yanking the last of the autopistol bullets from his chest plate, he threw them to the ground. 'Right, let's move.'

'Lieutenant?' questioned one of the enforcers.

'The bastards are getting away. We close on the target position, now. If the Emperor wills it, we may yet salvage something from this mission. Move!'

'That's what the captain's orders are, are they?' asked Landers, disbelief clear on his face.

Varnus turned quickly, stepping in close to the bigger man, and slammed a clenched fist into his face. Landers fell back, a cry more of shock than pain escaping his lips.

'I am your lieutenant, damn you, you slimy arse licker, and you will do as I damn well say,' snarled Varnus. 'Now, all of you, let's move out.'

Leading the way, Varnus pushed on deeper into the stinking, crumbling complex. He heard the others falling in behind him, and heard Landers muttering to himself. He grinned. He had wanted to punch that man for months.

The enforcers moved on, covering each other as they ghosted through the corridors and down corroded metal stairways. Varnus heard running footsteps ahead, and raised a hand, crouching low. He turned off the light on his helmet, the other enforcers following suit, and they plunged into dim, semi-light. A figure ran lightly around a corner, and Varnus reared up, slamming the butt of his shotgun into the figure's head. There was a crunching sound, and the figure dropped. Clicking his light back on, he saw it was a woman, her hair clipped short. Her eyes were open and staring, and blood seeped from her head where Varnus had struck her. An autogun was clasped in her dead hands.

'We are close,' said Varnus.

Carefully descending another flight of metal stairs, the enforcer team could see a flickering of orange light coming from below. The stink of promethium filled their nostrils.

Reaching the landing below, the team was faced with a single, heavy door standing slightly ajar, its plasglass window smashed through. Flames could be seen on the other side.

'Quickly,' hissed Varnus, and the enforcer team entered the room. It was a large, square space, and one of the glow-globes in the ceiling exploded as flames touched it. Couches and chairs were ablaze, as was a low table covered in papers and documents. The walls were lined with bunks and desks, and a makeshift kitchen had been constructed in the eastern corner. The figure of a man, oblivious to the sudden appearance of the enforcers, was liberally upending the contents of a metal can across a table on the far side of the room.

Varnus hissed, motioning for his team to lower their weapons. 'Take him, no guns,' he mouthed to Landers. The enforcer nodded, the confrontation of minutes earlier forgotten, and moved swiftly towards the figure. Feeling the presence behind him too late, the man turned just as Landers's thick arms wrapped around his neck, locking him firmly. He was dragged back across the room, and slammed face first onto the floor, his arms held painfully behind his back. The man struggled in vain, and Landers dropped his knee into the man's back, pinning him in place.

Varnus ran across the room and picked up one of the sodden papers that covered the promethium doused table. It was a detailed schematic map. He swore as he saw what it detailed.

'Get these damn flames out now! This whole place could go up at any second!' Varnus hollered. He opened up his comm-channel. 'Captain, this is Lieutenant Varnus. You need to get in here. Now,' he said, moving back towards Landers and the captive.

He knelt down beside the pinned captive and turned his face roughly towards him. The man's features were twisted in hatred and pain.

'What in the Emperor's name were you planning here?' Varnus said quietly.

The captive spat, eyes blazing with fury.

'What do you make of these, lieutenant? Gang markings? I don't recognise them,' said one of the enforcers.

Varnus looked to where the man motioned with his head. A crude tattoo was visible where the captive's dark brown overalls had been torn at his left shoulder. Ripping the heavy cloth fully away from the man's body, he gazed upon the emblazoned design: a screaming, horned daemon head surrounded by flames.

'I don't recognise it either, but it looks like some kind of damn cult marking to me,' said Varnus. He swore silently to himself.

# CHAPTER TWO

BURIAS WALKED WITH a warrior's grace as he stalked through the dark, musty smelling halls of the *Infidus Diabolus*, impatient for the slaughter that was soon to come. His armour was a deep, bruised red, edged in dull, brushed metal. It was an exhibit of exceptional craftsmanship, each heavy ceramite plate fitting perfectly over his powerful, enhanced body.

He could not recall a time when his sacred armour had not been a part of him. He had laboured over every coiling engraving covering the auto-reductive armour plates, had painstakingly whittled the words of blessed Lorgar along the burnished reinforcement bands that circled his forearms, and had carved the words of the gods themselves around the rim of his heavy shoulder plates. The sacred Latros Sacrum, the symbol that represented the Word Bearers Legion was embossed on his left shoulder. A bronze, stylised representation of a roaring, horned daemon surrounded by flames, it represented all that the Legion and Burias stood for, all that they believed in and all that they killed for.

He wore no helmet for the upcoming exhortation. His vicious, deathly pale face was unmarked by scars, a rarity for a warrior who had fought in as many campaigns as he had, and it was framed by long, oiled black hair.

With each step, the heavy butt of the icon that Burias held in his left hand slammed into the polished, black-veined, stone floor, the sharp sound echoing around him.

The icon was a thick staff of spiked, black iron. It was almost three metres tall, taller even than him, and loops of heavily ornate bronze encircled its shaft. These loops were inscribed with litanies and epistles, sacred words of the Daemon Primarch Lorgar. It was topped with a glistening, black, eight-pointed star, the points of the symbol of Chaos barbed and sharp. In the centre of the star was a graven image of the sacred Latros Sacrum.

Burias had received the honour of becoming icon-bearer with great pride, and he had the privilege of walking before Marduk, the First Acolyte, and Jarulek, the Dark Apostle, leading them to their positions in the ceremonies of worship and sacrifice. He had performed this sacred duty for many years, and the esteem he had earned from his warrior-brothers as a result was great.

He paused before he began his ascent up a grand set of curving stairs. The staircase was wide enough for twenty Space Marines to walk side by side, and its curving balustrades were highly ornate and picked out in bronze, crafted by some unknown hand countless aeons past. Two intimidating statues glared at any wishing to climb the steps, monstrous, coiling daemons said to strike down those with unworthy hearts.

Raising his head high, Burias began the long climb, his footfalls on the cold stone echoing up into the gloom of the arching ceiling hundreds of metres above. Ghostly chanting flowed down upon him, the sound of dozens of servitor eunuchs, forever ensconced in hidden pulpit-casings, intoning the canticles of blessed Lorgar in never-ending cycles.

Reaching the top of the grand staircase, Burias continued on towards a pair of gigantic, arched doors on the opposite side of a long gallery. Huge, stone tablets lined the walls of the gallery, each more than twenty metres in height and covered in intricate, precisely carved script, just a part of the Book of Lorgar, said to have been carved by the Dark Apostle Jarulek.

At the far end of the gallery, at either side of the great doors, stood a pair of warrior-brothers, the two chosen to act as the honour guard accompanying the First Acolyte to the exhortation. Each wore long robes of cream over their blood-red armour, and stood static in their positions, bolters held clasped across their chests. Tall curling horns extended from the helms of the warriors, and the pair made no reaction as Burias crossed the gallery to stand before the great doors.

A partially hidden side door clicked open, and a shuffling, robed figure emerged. Bent almost double, the figure's face was obscured beneath its hood, and it bore a brazier upon its back from which strong smelling incense smoke wafted in thick clouds. Sickly thin, grey-fleshed, shaking hands clasped a metal lidded bowl, and as the awkward figure hurried towards him, Burias raised his arms out to either side. The attendant lifted the lid on the bowl, revealing a stiff brush sitting in oil. Burias stood impassively as the shuffling figure daubed his armour with the sacred cleansing oils, stretching to reach his arms. Its duty done, the figure turned and retreated back within the sanctity of its den. Idly, Burias wondered for how many centuries the pathetic creature had performed this duty.

He pushed such thoughts from his mind as he strode forwards and placed a hand upon one of the great doors. Perfectly weighted, it swung open noiselessly at his light touch. Without pause, Burias entered the sanctum of the First Acolyte, the door sliding shut behind him.

The entrance room was sparsely decorated, with little ornamentation. Arched doorways led off to other parlours and rooms of worship, and on the other side of the large room hung a curtain of bone beads, leading to a smaller antechamber. Burias was always intrigued by the floor when he entered this room, and he stared down at it in awe. The entire floor space had been constructed in a clear, glass-like material, and beneath it was a gigantic stone-carved, eight-pointed star. Around the star, a red liquid writhed and boiled with a life of its own, and as he watched, faces and hands appeared within the viscous substance, clawing at the smooth glass beneath him. He grinned at the pained and angry expressions of the beings within. He imagined that they looked at him jealously, walking freely without containment as he was. Once, he had asked Marduk what they were. Are they daemons trapped within, he had questioned? Marduk had replied that they were, in a sense. He called them the Imaginos, and he claimed that they were but reflections that mirrored the inner daemons of those that looked upon them. A face manifested itself right beneath Burias's feet, and ripped its smiling face open, revealing a snarling and spitting visage beneath. Burias laughed softly, and snarled back at the creature.

'Is it time already, Burias?' asked the powerful voice of Marduk, the First Acolyte, from behind the curtain.

'It is, First Acolyte,' Burias replied. He could just make out the shadowy form of his master behind the beaded curtain, a large, dark silhouette kneeling within the slightly raised small room beyond.

'A shame. I was experiencing some most lucid dream visions. Most enlightening,' said the voice. 'Come closer, Burias.'

Obeying his master's order, he strode across the room. Up close, he could make out the details of the bone beads, seeing that they were tiny skulls. Were they real, shrunken with sorceries? he wondered, as he had done a million times before.

'Surely the exhortation will be such that any regrets as to its timing will be soon forgotten,' suggested Burias.

'Sometimes I think you should lead the sermons, such a golden tongue you have,' said Marduk. The shadow of the holy warrior rose to its feet and rolled its shoulders, loosening muscles that had been immobile for long hours of prayer and meditation. He angled his neck from side to side, producing cracking sounds, and turned around. With an imperious sweep of a gauntleted hand, the First Acolyte brushed the beaded skull curtain aside and stepped down into the room. Burias instantly lowered his gaze respectfully. Coiling smoke followed in Marduk's wake, and Burias could taste the dry, acrid incense in the back of his throat.

Eyes downcast, he saw that the Imaginos had fled. He could feel the closeness of the First Acolyte: the charged air, the electric taste of the gods that hung upon him. Truly, he was chosen of the gods, and Burias relished the sensation.

'You can look up now, Burias, your reverential obeisance has been witnessed,' said Marduk, a sarcastic tone tingeing his words.

Burias raised his gaze to meet his master's flinty, cold eyes. 'Have I angered you, First Acolyte?'

Marduk laughed, a harsh, barking sound.

'Anger me? But you are always so careful with your displays of respect. How could you have possibly angered me, Burias?' Marduk held Burias's gaze, dark humour in his eyes. 'No, you have not angered me, my friend,' he said, turning away. 'My mind is... occupied. The dream visions are coming to me more frequently since leaving the Maelstrom, the closer we draw to the planet of the great enemy.'

'Your power grows, First Acolyte,' said Burias, looking at Marduk's strong profile, his skin so pale it was translucent.

'And yours with it, my champion,' Marduk growled.

Burias grinned ferally. 'That it does.'

Marduk's head was ritually shaved, except for a long, braided length of black hair that sprouted from his crown. A network of criss-crossing, blue veins pulsed beneath his flesh. Cables and pipes pushed through the skin at his temples, and his teeth had grown into sharp fangs over the centuries. He was truly a terrifying warrior to look upon, and his armour was bedecked with honorifics and artefacts of religious significance. Burnished metal talismans, tiny shrunken skulls and Chaos icons hung from chains on his ornate, deep red armour. A scrimshawed bone of the prophet Morglock was strapped to his thigh with padlocked chains, and extracts from the Book of Lorgar, scratched upon human flesh, hung from his shoulder pads.

'And how is Drak'shal today?' asked Marduk, looking deep into Burias's lupine eyes.

'Quiet. But I can feel he is... hungry.'

Marduk laughed. 'Drak'shal is always hungry. It is his nature. But I am glad he is not strong today; today is no time for him to come to the fore. Keep him in check. His time will come soon enough.'

'I look forward to it. He so likes to kill.'

'Yes, he does, and he does it very well. But come now, we must not keep the Dark Apostle waiting.'

The pair left the sanctum, Burias leading the First Acolyte in silence, the icon held out before him, reverentially clasped in both hands. The honour guard fell into position a step behind. They walked through twisting corridors and up further flights of stairs until they came to a great, golden door, details picked out in relief. Once there, all four of the Word Bearers warriors dropped to one knee and bowed their heads. They waited in silence for several minutes before the doors before them were thrown open.

'Arise,' said a dangerously softly spoken voice.

Raising his eyes, Burias looked upon Jarulek, the Dark Apostle of the Host. Bedecked in a black robe that covered much of his ancient, blood-red armour, he was neither particularly tall nor broad for one of the Legion. Outwardly, he projected none of the sense of brutal power that Kol Badar exuded, nor the potent vitality that Marduk possessed. Nor did warriors fear him for the lethal savagery that Burias knew lurked only barely beneath the surface of his own demeanour.

It was perhaps the confidence of one who knew that the gods themselves sanctioned his actions that made warriors tremble before him, or perhaps it was the absolute belief in what he did, the fire of faith that burned within his soul or whatever of it was left, for it had long been pledged to the ravenous gods of Chaos. Whatever it was, Jarulek inspired fear, awe and devotion in equal measures. His words were spoken softly and deliberately, but on the battlefield his voice would rise to a powerful howl that was terrifying and inspiring to hear.

Every centimetre of Jarulek's exposed pale skin was covered in the hallowed words of Lorgar. Tiny, intricate script was inscribed perfectly across his flesh. Litanies and catechisms ran symmetrically down each side of his pale, hairless head, and his cheeks, chin and neck were sprawled with passages and curses. There was not a place upon him where you could place a data-stylus and not be touching the hallowed words of the great daemon primarch. Devotions, supplications, orisons, they extended over Jarulek's lips, inside his cheeks and across his tongue. Not even his eyes had been spared, citations of vengeance, hate and worship scribed on the soft, glutinous jelly of those orbs. He was a walking Book of Lorgar, and Burias was in awe at his presence.

'Lead the Dark Apostle forth, Icon Bearer,' intoned Marduk. Six additional guards of honour stepped into place around Marduk and the Dark Apostle, and together with the pair accompanying Marduk they represented the eight points of the star of Chaos.

'First, we worship,' said Jarulek. 'Then we kill a world.'

'I RISK MY men in there, and I am told to forget all about it?' spat Lieutenant Varnus. 'There is some kind of cult organisation operating in Shinar, perhaps across the whole of Tanakreg. We are just getting close.'

Varnus glared across the plain metal desk at Captain Lodengrad. The captain looked of middling years, but it was hard to gauge. He could have been forty, or a hundred and forty, depending on how much augmetic surgery he had been subjected to. Certainly he didn't appear to have aged in all the time Varnus had known him.

There were no features within the blank walls of the interview room other than the desk, the two chairs and the door. One wall was mirrored, and Varnus stood glaring at his tired and angry reflection. He knew that a trio of conjoined servitor twins stood beyond the mirror, recording and monitoring every movement made and every word spoken in the room. His heartbeat, blood pressure and neural activity were being analysed and recorded on a spooling data-slate, the details noted down by fingers ending in needle-like stylus instruments.

'Sit down, lieutenant,' said the captain.

'You seriously want me to go back on patrol and just forget everything I saw in that damned basement?'

'No one said anything about you going back to work, lieutenant,' said the captain. 'You disobeyed a direct order, and you struck a fellow enforcer.'

'Oh, come on! If I had obeyed your direct order, *sir*, the whole place would have gone up in flames. And Landers is a loudmouth cur. He was questioning *my* order. And he reports directly to me, if I recall correctly.'

'Sit down, lieutenant,' said the captain. Varnus continued to stare at his own reflection. 'Sit *down*,' the captain repeated, more forcefully.

'So what, are you going to kick me out? Send me back to work the damnable salt plains? Like before you recruited me?' Varnus sat back down and folded his arms. 'You knew what I was when you gave me this job. If you didn't want that, then you should never have pulled me out of the worker-habs in the first place.'

'Forget about all that, lieutenant. I'm not getting rid of you just yet. I'm just telling you to forget everything about what you saw in that basement. It is no longer our concern.'

'Not our concern?' exclaimed Varnus. 'That was no group of isolated, small-time, hab-gangers, captain. The information they had was highly classified material: maps, plans, schematics. They had plans of the damn governor's palace, for Throne's sake! You know what would happen if they managed to get explosives within the palace? They could knock out the entire city's power in one go, and what would happen then, captain? It would be bedlam: rioting, looting, murder. It would take a lot more enforcers than you have to put all that down. The PDF would have to be brought in. It would be absolute bedlam.'

'Are you quite finished, lieutenant?' asked the captain.

'Um, let me think. No. No, I'm not actually.'

'Well, hold onto those thoughts. There is someone here who may be able to answer them,' said the captain, rising to his feet. Varnus raised an eyebrow. 'I'm sick of listening to you, lieutenant. I'm going to get some caff. Wait here.'

The captain walked to the door and knocked twice. The door opened a moment later, and he left the room.

Varnus pushed his chair back and placed his feet on the table. He closed his eyes. He was so damn tired.

The door opened a few moments later. Varnus didn't bother to open his eyes. He sighed dramatically.

'It's Varnus, isn't it? Lieutenant Mal Varnus.' The voice was hard, and the lieutenant dropped his feet from the table, standing to look up into the face of the newcomer.

The man was big, bigger even than Landers, and he was dressed in the severe black uniform of an Arbites judge.

Throne above! An Arbites judge!

The blood rushed from Varnus's face, and he licked his lips.

The judge walked around Varnus and sat down in the seat recently vacated by the captain. His jaw was thick and square, his nose flat against his face and his brow heavy and solid. In all respects the judge looked hard and unrelenting. His intimidating physical presence was further enhanced by heavy ablative carapace armour and by the severe black uniform he wore over it.

'Sit down, lieutenant,' he ordered forcefully, his eyes cold and dangerous, his voice deep.

Varnus sat down warily.

'What you discovered, it is not within the jurisdiction of local enforcers. It is within the jurisdiction of Imperial law, Arbites law.'

Varnus frowned darkly.

'However, I have been reading your record,' continued the judge. 'It was... interesting reading. The Arbites could use a man like you, lieutenant.'

Varnus's raised an eyebrow and pushed himself back in his chair. 'Huh?'

The judge pushed something across the table towards him. It was a heavy round pin, embossed with the aquila. He stared at it, and then looked questioningly into the eyes of the Arbites judge.

'Tomorrow, come to the palace. I have matters to attend to there, but at their conclusion I wish to speak with you. Present this.'

And with that, the judge rose to his feet, huge and imposing, and left the room.

Varnus sat still for long minutes. Then he picked up the pin. He stood, and turned to leave, halting when he caught a glimpse of his own reflection. He snorted in amusement and left the room.

THE INFIDUS DIABOLUS left the roiling, familiar comfort of the warp, the realm of the gods, and burst into real space. Crackling shimmers of light, colour and sheet electricity ran along its hull as the last vestiges of the Empyrean were shaken off. The strike cruiser shuddered, its immense length creaking and straining as the natural laws of the universe took hold of it once more.

Deep within the belly of the cruiser, Jarulek's grand Host of the Word Bearers Legion joined together in worship of the gods of Chaos. It was a requiem mass, a celebration of the death that they would soon deliver, a promise of souls. It was a prayer in the darkness, a pledge of faith, an honouring of the very real, insatiable deities of the warp.

The huge mass of the *Infidus Diabolus* was tiny and insignificant in the vast, cold darkness of the galaxy. But to the doomed world that it ploughed silently towards it was death, and it closed towards the blissfully unaware planet unerringly.

# CHAPTER THREE

THE PALACE OF the Governor of Tanakreg was a sprawling fortress bastion that perched on a long dormant volcanic outcrop overlooking the city of Shinar, the largest industrial city on the planet. Shinar rolled out to the west of the fortress. Any other approach to the palace was impossible, for sheer cliffs hundreds of metres high dropped down from the bastion walls into the blackened, acidic oceans that dominated the planet's surface.

Varnus held onto the railing tightly as he stared out of the vision slit of the fast moving tri-railed conveyance. The compartment was packed with adepts of the Administratum whose access level allowed them to move around the city freely rather than confining them to their workstations. Soft-skins, he thought derisively. They were uniformly scrawny, wide-eyed and pale-faced, weakling specimens of humanity.

Their faces and hands were unlined and soft. Most of the citizenry had a wind-blown harshness to their craggy faces, and eyes that were practically hidden from squinting against the salt winds for years on end. Indeed, most living on Tanakreg succumbed to salt-blindness by the time they reached forty standard Imperial years of age. Their skin generally looked like dried, cracked parchment, the moisture slowly sucked from their bodies by years of exposure to the harsh, salt-laced air.

Varnus was full of scorn for the privileged soft-skins able to avoid the harshness of the land. Most of them had probably never felt the touch of the wind upon their skin. He glared at them occasionally, enjoying the uncomfortable shuffling it caused amongst the robed adepts. Though the compartment was densely crowded, the adepts left a good amount of space around Varnus, intimidated, he imagined, by the enforcer uniform. He was glad of the additional room. Shinar spread out beneath him as the tri-railed conveyance began its ascent to the palace.

He marvelled at the view. From this angle, the city almost looked attractive. Throne above, but it was an ugly bitch of a city from every other angle, he thought. From here, the angled sails were just rising. The winds were coming. Every building within Shinar was constructed with a metal sheet sail that would slide out to protect the building from the worst of the salt winds. Those winds were devastating. They could reduce a newly constructed building to dust within years if not adequately protected. Even as it was, most of Shinar was crumbling away. But then, it was cheaper to build anew on top of the ruins of the past than to properly maintain what was already built. He had never understood how that worked, but he accepted it nonetheless.

From his viewpoint, as the tri-rail climbed ever higher, the vision of a million sails rising in perfect unison was a deeply bizarre one. As the light of the blazing orange sun caught the sails, it looked for a moment as if the whole of Shinar was burning. Varnus shivered.

Shinar spread out like a growing cancer, each week encroaching further out into the salt plains, clawing its way ever closer to the mountains, hundreds of kilometres to the west. Varnus was thankful that he did not still work those damnable salt fields. He was certain that he would have been long-dead, a dried, desiccated husk had he not been picked out from amongst the other hab-workers.

The tri-rail came to a shuddering halt. A giant, tentacle-like satellite clamp reached out and fastened to the exterior of the conveyance, and the doors hissed open amongst blasts of steam and smoke. The adepts surged from the carriage, their reticence to be near Varnus apparently gone as they bustled and pushed past him, shuffling down the long corridor within the middle of the tube-like tentacle.

Filing along amongst the bustling crowd, Varnus was half carried to a great, domed reception hall. Around a hundred other tentacle tubes spilled out their cargo of humanity into the vast hall. It was seething with people, almost all garbed in robes of various shades, from grey to dark brown, and every variety of off-white and puce in between.

Looking up through the transparent dome-top, he could see the mighty walls of the bastion fortress, beyond which stood the palace proper. Those walls were immensely thick, some fifteen metres worth of reinforced plascrete. He could see half a dozen massive turrets, huge batteries of heavy calibre cannon pointing towards the heavens.

Thousands of workers, Administratum adepts, politicians and servants were joining long queues. Bored palace guards armoured in regal blue semi-plate oversaw the masses as they filtered past servitors processing their data passes. Only once through the checking station could they pass on into any of the hundreds of offices, temples, shrines or manufactorums that were located in the volcanic rock beneath the palace. It was a city within a city. And built far beneath all of this were the giant plasma reactors that powered all of Shinar.

With a sigh, Varnus joined the queue that he thought looked like it was moving quickest, though he knew it would doubtless turn out to be the slowest. He prepared himself for a long wait.

'You are certain that the traitor will succeed?' growled Kol Badar, his critical gaze watching the Legion's warriors in the vast bay below. Led by their champions, hundreds of Word Bearers marched in orderly squads up the embarkation ramps and entered the bellies of the transport craft. Most were Thunderhawks, their hulls the familiar clotted-blood red, some were older Stormbirds, but there were dozens of others that had been salvaged or claimed by the Legion on their many raids from the ether. More than one had been discovered adrift in the warp, their crews slaughtered by the denizens of the realm when their warp fields had failed. The *Infidus Diabolus* had no need of such warp fields, the Word Bearers embracing the creatures of that unstable realm.

'He will succeed,' stated Jarulek flatly.

'If the traitor fails then the enemy's air defences will be fully operative. The Deathclaws will be annihilated.'

Jarulek turned towards the towering form of his coryphaus, his eyes flashing.

'I have said that the traitor does not fail. I have seen it. Board your Stormbird. Go kill. It is what you do well.'

GOVERNOR THEOFORIC FLENSKE sighed and fingered the sugared sweetmeats on his tiny, porcelain plate. They were his favourites, and they normally gave him small moments of joy in his otherwise long, drawn out and exhausting days.

He had always known that being governor of Tanakreg was going to be a stressful and thankless task, and was quite comfortable with that. He knew that he was admirably suitable for the role, and that he had best served the Emperor by taking on the position. He was utterly devoted to the Imperium, and was very happy to serve it as best he could. But this accursed bickering! It was going to be the death of him! He popped a sugar-coated nut into his mouth and closed his eyes briefly. It was a moment of escape. He crunched down on the nut, the sound echoing loudly in his head. He opened his eyes quickly, flicking his gaze around the table to see if anyone had noticed.

Dozens of advisors, PDF officers, politicos, consultants and members of the Ecclesiarchy were sitting around the long table. This was a gathering of the most powerful individuals on Tanakreg, but for all their importance and rank they argued like children, and Governor Flenske felt a headache building behind his eyes.

'Some cool water, my lord?' asked a quiet voice at his ear. Flenske nodded his head, thankful as always for the attentiveness of Pierlo, his manservant and bodyguard. Each of the people sitting at the council table had a small team of aides standing to attention behind their high-backed, velvet seats, though these little coteries were each distinctly different from one another. Behind the colonel and his majors of the PDF were stern-faced adjutants, their uniforms crisp. Behind the jabbering politicos, bureaucrats, adepts and ministers were servitor lexographers that recorded their words, long mechanical fingers scratching their masters' diatribes onto tiny rolls of unfurling paper, and punching holes in data-coils. Lesser priests and confessors stood behind the high ranking members of the Ecclesiarch, their eyes downcast. Kneeling at the side of the cardinal, who was sweating in the full regalia of his office, were a pair of shaven-headed women, their mouths sewn shut. They wore the aquila upon their chests, and bore seals of purity stitched into their pale robes.

Sitting quietly at the table amongst the throng was the scarlet-robed Tech-Administrator Tharon. He wore a twelve toothed cog upon his breast, the symbol of the Adeptus Mechanicus, and his right eye had been replaced with a black lens piece that whirred softly as it focused.

The Arbites judge stood with his back to the proceedings, looking out through the tinted, floor to ceiling plex-windows over the city spread out below. His arms were folded and he made no move, nor any comment, as the items on the agenda were discussed. Barring his helmet, he wore his full suit of carapace armour beneath his heavy black coat. A large autopistol was holstered conspicuously on his hip; there was no one within the palace with the authority to claim his weapon. His immobile presence made Flenske sweat, and the governor dabbed at his forehead, glancing over at the judge's back every few moments. The presence of a member of the Adeptus Arbites spoke of serious matters indeed, but he had no idea what it was that the judge sought in his cabinet meeting.

'Friends, please,' he began, his trained and subtly augmented voice carrying out over the din. Despite his unease at the unexpected appearance of the judge, his voice was self-assured and practised. 'Adept Trask, please summarise your point concisely. Leave out the rhetoric,' he said, a generous smile upon his face. 'It seems to irritate the colonel.'

Polite laughter greeted his comment, and Adept Trask rose again to his feet, clearing his throat. He lifted a slate and began to read from it. The governor coughed markedly, interrupting the dull voice of the small man, who looked up from his slate expectantly.

'A *summary* of your point, minister,' said the governor, still smiling, 'as in one that you can say out loud in less than an hour of our precious time, perhaps?'

The adept did not know whether to be insulted or not, but seeing the governor smiling at him still, he gave a nervous smile of his own and flicked through the thick wad of papers on his slate. Moron, thought Flenske.

'In... in summary,' the adept began, 'there have been seventy-eight raids across Shinar in the last three weeks, and two hundred and twelve insurgents have been detained by the enforcers. The situation is under control.' The adept sat back down quickly.

'Under control? Are you of sound mind, adept?' asked a robed, skeletally thin bureaucrat. 'We are overrun with riots and demonstrations, all linked to insurgent activity, and getting worse every week! Situation under control? I beg to differ. The enforcers are unable to control Shinar any longer. I mean no slur against them, but they do not have the resources or men to contain the insurgents.'

The aging Minister for the Interior, Kurtz, raised his hand to speak. He was a stocky, powerful man despite his age, but he had lost the use of his legs decades earlier and was confined to his powered chair. Once he had been an officer in the PDF and a captain of the enforcers, before he had been deprived of the use of legs. He was a tough old fighter, renowned among Flenske's ministers for his stubbornness, and most considered him a crude man with none of the refinement that came from proper breeding. The governor sighed as he saw the thick pile of documents that Kurtz held in his hand.

'The honoured Bureaucrat of the Third speaks the truth. I have been reviewing the various reports that show the activities of these so-called insurgents. They are far more organised and widespread than any here give them credit for.'

There were snorts of derision from around the table, and the governor fixed his gaze on Kurtz.

'What is this evidence then, noble minister?' he asked, flicking a glance towards the judge.

'Extensive details of Shinar and the Shinar Peninsula. Focused map work showing the valleys and paths that lead through the mountains.'

There were more snorts of derision around the table.

'You mean the enforcers found some *maps*, minister?' asked the governor. 'They needn't have raided insurgents just to find *maps*, man. I'm sure that our cartographers could have loaned them some.'

'They have detailed layouts of your palace, governor, including,' Kurtz said firmly, looking down at a map layout in front of him, 'the location of passages that show up on no unclassified map of the palace. Passages leading into your bedchambers, for instance.'

The governor swallowed whole the nut he had been gumming, and several of the figures at the table stood, their voices raised. He felt his manservant Pierlo lean in close behind him.

'Shall I go and change the combinations on the access passage to your personal chambers, my lord?' he asked quietly.

The governor nodded, and the man slipped out of the room.

'From the evidence garnered by the enforcers,' continued Kurtz, raising his voice over the clamour in the room, 'it is my belief that these covert groups are coordinating acts of rebellion and sedition that threaten the stability of Shinar. These are not isolated groups of rebel salt workers that are trying to avoid paying taxes. This is a well supplied and armed group of organised insurgents that have integrated covertly into the institutions of Shinar and beyond.'

He held up a schematic map.

'This shows unsanctioned construction of a considerable size in the Shaltos Mountains, not three hundred kilometres from where we sit. I believe this is a staging post, a training facility perhaps.'

'Minister, these documents, I would like them to be studied by my own people. Please pass them on to my aide once this meeting is concluded.'

'Governor?' said Kurtz, his face incredulous. 'You... you do not wish to act upon the information I have gleaned immediately?'

'I will act, minister, when and if I deem it to be appropriate to do so,' the governor said forcefully.

'Now,' he said. 'Colonel? I hear that the PDF is having some problems at the present?'

'I regret that that is so, governor. The Commissariat has been forced to execute a number of officers for... various infractions. And as for the *insurgents*, I recommend that we pull more of the PDF ranks into Shinar. I believe the popular unrest can be stemmed with a martial presence.'

'Popular unrest?' burst the minister of the interior. 'This is coordinated cult activity, governor, not *popular unrest*,' he spat. 'It is my belief that these insurgents are worshippers of the Ruinous Powers, and that...'

'That is *enough*, minister!' hollered the governor. He felt the pain behind his eyes increase, and he took another sip of water. 'I will not have such talk bandied without irrefutable proof!' He took a deep breath. 'Thank you, colonel,' he said. He turned towards the sweating cardinal. 'And the Ecclesiarch? Holy cardinal, what do you say?'

'More citizens are attending the sermons than ever, governor. I attribute it to the nearing conjunction of planets. Scaremongering propaganda has been spread through the lower hab-blocks claiming that it signals the end of the world. The superstitious salt farmers are afraid.' The cardinal shrugged his thick shoulders, 'Ergo, more citizens on pews in the daily hymnals.'

The governor grunted. 'It certainly seems to me that this rise in insurgency, the riots, the scaremongering, it all relates back to the conjunction. It's just a damn planet passing, for Shinar's sake! Why under Throne is it such a big deal?'

'The red planet of Korsis circles our system in an aberrant, elliptical orbit, and on occasion it passes extremely close to Tanakreg. On very rare occasions, Korsis passing us coincides with a conjunction of sorts, when all the planets in our system are aligned. The last time this happened was ten thousand, two hundred and ninety-nine years ago. Such a conjunction will occur in less than three months time,' said a bespectacled, robed man.

'Thank you, learned one,' said the governor sharply. The pain behind his eyes was becoming almost unbearable.

'If it pleases you, governor,' said the tech-administrator, 'I would like to return to the substation. I was in the process of blessing the machine-spirits of the turbines when your request for my presence came through.'

'Fine, fine, go,' said the governor, waving his hand.

The Arbites judge turned around, his face emotionless. The room went deathly quiet, and the severe figure let the silence grow. The governor felt his stomach knot.

'I have heard enough,' the judge said finally, the sound of his voice making Flenske flinch.

VARNUS WAS BORED. Once he had finally been filtered through the checking facilities on the sub-ground floor, then the third floor, the eighteenth and finally the ground floor of the palace proper, he had been subjected to a rigorous security check from the regal, blue-armoured palace guards. They had requested his weapons, and he had realised that he would be denied access if he refused to give up his side arm and his power maul. With some reluctance he handed them over. He had even been forced to relinquish his helmet – 'comm security', apparently.

He had been directed to a small alcove, there to await the Arbites judge. It was a small corridor space linking two grand galleries, and there were dozens of other plaintiffs and officials already sitting there, their eyes glazed. He took a seat at the far end of the corridor alcove.

It had been hours, and he was deathly tired of the whole thing. There was an impressive staircase on the other side of one of the grand galleries that the alcove opened onto, and he watched it with boredom. A heavy guard presence prevented anyone from climbing the stairs. Those that even began to approach backed away after seeing the guards. At the top of the stairs was a massive pair of double-doors, with another set of guards holding tall, high powered las-locks, vertically to attention. They didn't move, and their faces were stoic. They must be as bored as he was, he thought.

With a click he saw one of the large doors open briefly, and a man exit. The guards barely looked at him as he lifted the hem of his red robe and quickly descended the stairs. Some tech, he thought, as he saw the Mechanicus symbol on his chest and the bionics of his left eye. The man looked flustered, and he hurried to the bottom of the stairs, looking left and right frantically. A man that Varnus had not noticed before stepped out to meet him, and the tech began to talk animatedly. The other man shushed him, and Varnus recognised him as the one who had exited the same room earlier. The enforcer instantly disliked him; he looked like yet another arrogant, officious noble. The pair hurried off, and Varnus sighed.

THE GOVERNOR LICKED his lips and a bead of sweat rolled down the side of his face as the imposing Arbites judge stared across the room at him, his face a cold, expressionless mask.

'The local enforcer units have been sapped of resources and manpower over the last decade as a direct result of the policies of the governorship, and as a result it is unfit to deal with the insurgent threat. This speaks of gross and inexcusable incompetence.'

The accusation hung in the air, and none around the table dared make a sound. Governor Flenske felt his world contract and heat rising up his neck. His eyes flicked around the table before him. No one met his gaze except Minister Kurtz.

'I'm... this... perhaps we... misread the severity of the... the situation. Nothing that cannot be rectified, I assure you,' said the governor, his voice sounding hollow and weak in his own ears.

'Shinar risks falling into anarchy and rebellion. The security of the city is compromised, and this is an unacceptable situation. The time for bureaucratic pandering is over. Governor Flenske, I find you in contempt of your duties. You are to be replaced by a stewardship until a more suitable governor can be instated. I am locking down Shinar in a state of martial law until the insurgency has been eliminated and the city secured.'

The governor's face paled, and he felt his chest tighten. He tried to speak, but he couldn't find the words, and his mouth flapped open and shut in rising panic.

The judge pulled his large, black autopistol from its holster and pointed it at the governor. Never before had a weapon been levelled at him, and Flenske felt rising warmth in his trousers. He realised that he had soiled himself, and he felt shame as he stared in horror and panic at the barrel of the pistol.

'With the power vested in me by the Adeptus Arbites I hereby remove Planetary Governor Flenske from his position.'

'No, no…' began the governor.

The autopistol barked loudly. Three rounds punched through Flenske's forehead and the back of his head exploded. His body was thrown backwards to the ground as his chair overturned beneath him. Three empty shell casings fell to the marble floor with a musical, tinkling sound, and smoke rose from the barrel of the gun before it was smoothly replaced in its holster.

The judge walked around the table, his boot steps echoing loudly across the room. Giving the governor's body a push with his heel, he righted his chair and sat down at the head of the table.

'I want all local PDF units retracted to Shinar,' he stated to the pale-faced group of individuals staring at him in shock and horror. 'I want a lock down of all traffic into and out of the city, and I want armed checkpoints set up along all main thoroughfares. I want an indefinite curfew instated; any individual found on the streets after curfew is to be shot. The palace is to be secured; I want no one coming in or going out without my say-so. Contact the twin cities and order their local PDF units to be recalled within the city boundaries. Tell them to be ready for potential hostile activity.'

He glanced around the table, his gaze hard.

'We have a lot of work to do, and I am not here to play your little political games. I am here to bring this city back to order in the name of the God-Emperor. I am here to avert disaster, if at all possible.'

Governor Flenske's blood pooled out beneath his body. There was shocked silence around the room. No one dared move. The acrid smell of the gun's discharge was mixing with the stink of blood.

'Tanakreg teeters on the brink of destruction,' said the judge. 'This group is its only possible salvation.'

Then the room exploded, turning into a roaring inferno. Everyone in the chamber was instantly slain as the force of the detonations ripped the room apart. The marble floor exploded into millions of tiny shards and the synth-hardened plex-windows shattered outwards. The force of the blast rocked the entire palace and oily, black smoke billowed from the rising ball of flame that burst from the shattered windows.

* * *

VARNUS WAS THROWN back through the alcove corridor from the force of the blast that smashed aside the huge doors, throwing them off their hinges and hurling the guards through the air like rag dolls. Varnus was thrown back over ten metres, flying clear of the corridor and smashing to the gallery floor, amid a tangle of burning rubble and flesh. Dimly, he heard blaring alarms, and then he heard nothing.

# CHAPTER FOUR

KOL BADAR GLARED around at his warriors, all members of the cult of the Anointed. The most vicious, faithful and dangerous warriors within the Host, he had wanted them to accompany the Dark Apostle on his drop assault, but Jarulek would not hear of it. Their Terminator armour was too bulky for a lightning assault on the palace, he had said, and Kol Badar had reluctantly agreed with him. It just did not feel right, though. He had always fought at the side of the Dark Apostle with his elite brethren.

The horned helmets of the Anointed looked daemonic under the glowing, red lights within the cramped hold of the Land Raider, and Kol Badar knew that he too looked like some malevolent daemon of the warp in his ornate battle-helm. Barbed tusks protruded like monstrous mandibles from his ancient helmet, which was crafted in the likeness of a snarling, bestial visage. The massive tank roared across the plains of the planet Tanakreg, hauling its deadly cargo ever closer to the central battle lines of the pathetic Imperials.

He was disappointed with the enemy, but then, he could not expect any more from them. The Imperium had grown weak.

The Host was borne from the *Infidus Diabolus* in scores of smaller vessels, angry hornets swarming from their nest towards their foe. They had landed on the planet surface as the harsh, orange sun was setting and stormed the first defensive line, taking it within an hour. The Anointed, borne within the belly of revered Land Raiders, had assaulted up the steep embankments to take the most heavily defended sections, slaughtering all in their path.

The enemy artillery was next to useless against the powerful tanks, and the remainder of the Host rampaged through the breaches carved by the Anointed and set up their own heavy weapon teams atop the earthworks, raining death upon the Imperials mustered beyond. They marched relentlessly through the trenches, killing and mutilating, and taking bunkers and strong points at will. Kol Badar had been disgusted to see hundreds of the Imperials flee before the Legion, seeking the false safety of the second defensive line. That second line had fallen almost as quickly as the first, once its emplaced guns had been silenced. The third line broke almost as swiftly.

There remained only the last line, the one closest to the city. The glow of the Imperial city could be seen over the horizon. This last defensive line was the shortest of the four, and had more emplacements than the first. Kol Badar hoped that it would prove somewhat more of a challenge.

So far there had been little satisfaction in these battles; they had been nothing short of massacres. The estimate was somewhere in the realm of fifteen thousand enemy troops slain, and around five hundred tanks, aircraft and support vehicles destroyed. The losses amongst the Word Bearers had been minimal.

The lascannon sponsons of the Land Raider screamed as they fired. The tank did not slow, and hit a slight rise at speed. There was a moment of weightlessness as the front of the tank became airborne before slamming back down to the ground. Dull explosions and detonations could be heard, the sound muffled by the roar of the engines and the screaming of the lascannons. The vehicle rocked as explosive shells struck its thick, armoured hide, and Kol Badar growled.

The Land Raider began ploughing up a steep incline, and Kol Badar knew that they were at the earthworks. High calibre rounds pinged off the exterior but the powerful machine had carried the Word Bearers across much deadlier battlefields on a thousand worlds, transporting them safely against far worse than these weakling Imperials could muster.

A glowing, yellow blister light began to flash, and Kol Badar pulled off the hissing coupling that held him to his seat and flexed his power talons.

'In the name of the true gods, Lorgar and the Dark Apostle,' he roared. 'Anointed! We kill once more!'

The elite cult warriors roared back, and the assault ramp of the Land Raider slammed down as the immense tank drew to a sudden halt near the top of the incline, steam hissing out into the cold of night.

After the muffled dullness within the belly of the Land Raider, the noise of the battlefield was deafening, as cannons boomed, boltguns thumped rhythmically and the screams of dying Imperials echoed across the salt plains.

Kol Badar led the Anointed onto the field of war, roaring like a primeval god. His archaic combi-bolter, its muzzle sculpted to resemble the fanged maw of some fell creature, coughed fiery death as he strode heavily forwards. His first shots ripped a grey uniformed soldier in half, and dozens more were torn apart by the gunfire of the Anointed.

The night was lit up as thousands of weapons fired, and Kol Badar could see the immense enemy bulwark stretching from horizon to horizon. Tens of thousands of uniformed PDF troopers stood along the defensive line, and hundreds of tanks and armoured units added cannon fire to the barrage.

He had chosen this place to attack the enemy for it was their most heavily defended point along the bulwark. A decisive strike that shattered their defences here would demoralise them completely.

Streaming las-fire lit up the night as the Imperials tried desperately to drop even a single one of the Anointed. The hulking Terminator-armoured figures strode to the top of the bulwark, walking straight through the frantic gunfire. Their own weapons ripped through the cowering ranks of the lightly armoured PDF troopers, the protection of their dug-in positions rendered useless.

A score of Land Raiders disgorged more of the Terminators at the top of the earthworks, and the butchery began in earnest. Kol Badar dropped down heavily over the lip of the corpse-strewn defensive position and raised his bolter to mow down a team of men working to reload an artillery piece. They were ripped to pieces, blood spraying.

Reaper autocannons roared along the line of the bulwark, the rapid firing, high-powered weapons tearing through the lines of reinforcements rushing to stem the breach in their lines. The high velocity rounds from the potent weapons tore up the defensive line and reached a battery of artillery pieces. The guns were instantly engulfed in a huge explosion as the armour piercing autocannon rounds ignited stacks of high-explosive shells. The fireball rose high in the sky, and further explosions answered it as other Anointed warriors struck further gun batteries.

'Warmonger, lead the Host forward,' growled Kol Badar, opening a comm-channel to the Dreadnought. 'Come join the slaughter, my brother.'

'SIR! WE ARE being massacred! They won't die! Emperor save us, they just won't die!'

Captain Drokan of the 23rd Tanakreg PDF cursed and licked his dry lips as he ordered the comm-channel closed. What could he do? There must be a way to salvage something out of this disastrous engagement, but he was damned if he knew what it was. He turned to his adjutant, who looked absolutely terrified, his face pale and his eyes staring.

'Val! Anything from the colonel? From any of the damn officers?'

The pale-faced adjutant shook his head, and Drokan cursed once again.

There had been no warning of the attack. The Emperor alone knew what had happened to the listening posts that skirted the system; a sudden attack like this just should not have been possible!

But it was happening, and it was all too real. And somehow Drokan had found himself the most superior ranked officer, cut off from the upper echelons. Him, Anubias Drokan! Never a dedicated student of tactics or strategy, he had risen to the rank of captain more because of his family's status and his own skill with a sword than through any real competence. It was only the PDF, damn it! Father had wanted him to join the ranks to give him a bit of hardness about him, he had said. A few years of service; he had never expected to be on the front line of a full-scale planetary assault!

Think, man. Think! What should he do? He had four companies of the 23rd with him here (dying here, he thought), but what other regiments were close by? There was the 9th and the 11th, but his adjutant had been unable to contact them on the comms. He assumed they had already been engaged and destroyed by the enemy.

He had to get the other nearby regiments to pull away from the last line, pull back to Shinar. That's what his superiors would do, he thought. Shinar, the palace, the governor; they were what needed protecting. Feeling slightly buoyed, Drokan turned to his adjutant once more.

'Put out a blanket message to all Shinar PDF regiments. Tell them to pull back to the city. The 23rd will hold them here for as long as we can. We will buy them as much time as possible.'

The adjutant gaped. 'We are to hold here? That's suicide!'

'Pass the damn message! Shinar is more important than the 23rd!'

With shaking hands, the adjutant began to relay the message. The captain shouted to the driver of the Chimera to head towards the battle. The man gunned the engines and the vehicle roared across the salt plains.

The men of the 23rd had never seen active service. War had never come to Tanakreg, and the only time the PDF had been required to use live ammunition had been to quell a minor insurgency within Shinar some four decades earlier. Most of the PDF soldiers had never fired on a live target.

Still, Drokan felt clear-headed suddenly. Yes, he would hold the enemy here. He pulled his laspistol from its holster. Just like his men, he had honed his skills on the target field, though he had never fired a shot in anger or defence. But I am a renowned swordsman, he told himself, patting the ornate chainsword at his hip. He had fought in countless tourneys, and had won several medals.

'Ca... Captain Drokan?' said his adjutant. 'The other regiments... they are not responding. Not one of them. I... I think we may be the last regiment within a thousand kilometres of Shinar.'

The captain frowned. 'Ah,' he said, 'I see.' He felt strangely calm. 'Well, pick up my family standard. We go to fight alongside the men.'

The adjutant gaped at the captain.

'Come on, boy!' urged Drokan. The younger man unclipped his safety harness and scrambled across to the other side of the command Chimera. He opened a stowage compartment, and removed a long black case. He struggled with the ornate clasps, but finally popped them open, and pulled out the captain's family standard. It was furled tightly around a telescopic pole. With a nod, the captain leant back in his seat as his Chimera took them into the maelstrom of battle.

KOL BADAR STRODE along the fortified line, gunning down dozens of terrified PDF troopers, their puny bodies torn apart by the force of his combi-bolter. Reaching an enclosed bunker emplacement, he ripped the sealed blast door from its hinges and stooped to enter. It housed half a dozen men and three, rapid firing heavy bolters that were pumping fire into the advancing lines of the Host.

Kol Badar gunned them all down, the walls of the emplacement splashing with their blood as he raked them with fire. Ripping another blast door from its housing, Kol Badar exited the emplacement and began killing once more.

Looking down over the plains beyond the last defensive line, he saw scores of APCs moving forwards in a desperate last-ditch attempt to hold back the Word Bearers. Salt dust kicked up behind the approaching vehicles, and lascannon fire and krak missiles streamed towards the Imperial vehicles from the heavy weapon teams that had gained the bulwark. Several of the advancing vehicles exploded spectacularly, spinning end over end as fuel lines were penetrated.

The Chimera APCs roared to a halt, and over a thousand PDF reserve troopers emerged, las-fire stabbing towards the Word Bearers. Smiling, Kol Badar strode down to meet them.

He knew that subtlety and strategy were not needed, just killing and more killing. It was what his warriors excelled at.

He strode onwards through the hail of gunfire, spraying boltrounds left and right. The salt plains were turning a deep red colour as the porous granules soaked up the gore.

'TANAKREG 23RD!' SHOUTED PDF Captain Drokan. 'Drive them back!' The soldiers screamed as they ran, their lasguns firing and bayonets readied. The captain's adjutant found himself shouting along with them. Hefting the captain's unfurled banner in one hand he began firing his laspistol, even though he could not yet see the foe.

Suddenly he saw the enemy, and he wished that he had not. They were huge, making the PDF soldiers look like children.

They were all going to die, he realised.

KOL BADAR RAISED an eyebrow within his fully enclosed helm as he saw the soldiers running towards him, an officer at their forefront brandishing a roaring chain blade. The towering warlord didn't even bother to raise his combi-bolter, and he began stalking towards the fools running at him and his Anointed warriors. Lasrounds thudded uselessly into him as the distance closed. The officer lifted his chainsword high, his face defiant. Kol Badar almost laughed out loud.

The warlord swatted the blade away dismissively with the back of his power-talon, breaking the man's arm in the process, and clubbed the officer down into the ground with a blow from his combi-bolter. He stamped down heavily on the mewling wretch, and the man's skull shattered like a pulverised egg.

The Anointed cleaved into the PDF troopers, ripping limbs from sockets, tearing heads from bodies. The Coryphaus saw Bokkar drive his chainfist into the body of the diminutive PDF standard bearer, lifting him up into the air before the whirring blades cut the boy in half. The Anointed warrior turned his heavy flamer on the fallen standard, the fabric consumed instantly under the intense heat.

Las-fire sprayed across his back, and he hissed in pain and anger as one of the beams caught him in the back of his knee-joint. He turned and gunned down one of the PDF troopers before they disappeared beneath an inferno of flames, screaming horribly. Kol Badar nodded his head towards the Anointed warrior Bokkar, who acknowledged the Coryphaus with a nod of his own, before his heavy flamer roared again, engulfing another group of soldiers.

Heavy footsteps made the ground tremble, and Kol Badar turned towards the huge form of the Warmonger, the Dreadnought dwarfing even him as it walked through the carnage, potent cannons pumping fire towards enemy vehicles in the distance.

'It is good to crush the enemy on the field of war once more, but this is no battle, Kol Badar,' the ancient war machine boomed. There were few within the Host that would dare call the warlord by his name, but the Warmonger was amongst them. They had fought at each other's sides for millennia. Indeed, Kol Badar had been the Warmonger's Coryphaus when the warrior had been Dark Apostle.

'The enemy is weak,' agreed Kol Badar. 'How I yearn to face a worthy foe,' he added, turning his gaze up into the void of the heavens.

'You think Astartes will come?' boomed the Warmonger hungrily.

'No, I think not,' sighed Kol Badar. 'As much as I wish to face them once more. The Dark Apostle has said that in none of his dream-visions did he see any Astartes come to this world to do battle with us.'

'But minions of the Corpse Emperor will come, will they not? They will come to do battle?'

'Oh, they will come, my friend. They will be marshalling their forces even now.'

'But not Astartes?'

'No, not Astartes.'

'Bah,' snorted the Warmonger. 'It will be just mortals then.'

'Yes, mortals,' said Kol Badar, still staring up into the night sky, as if he could pierce the heavens with his angry gaze. 'One can only hope that they will come in force. At least then there may be a worthy battle.'

The Warmonger stomped off, its cannons firing once more. He saw the daemon engines clawing over the bulwark, multi-legged and spitting great gouts of flame from their maws, while others busied themselves tearing apart enemy tanks with contemptuous ease.

Kol Badar began to follow the Warmonger, to rejoin the battle once again. No, he reminded himself, this was not battle. This was a slaughter.

* * *

VARNUS COUGHED, CAUSING a searing, sharp pain in his side. Smoke was all around him, and bodies. No, not just bodies: body *parts*. He pushed himself to his feet, gasping at the pain that seemed to erupt all over his body, and his head reeled. He put a hand to his forehead and felt wet blood there, but the worst pain was in his side. It was slick with blood, and he winced as he loosened the clips holding his chest-plate in place. He hissed as he pulled out a long shard of metal that had pushed up under the body armour and into his side. He dropped the bloody shard to the floor. Still, he was alive, which was more than could be said for the others splayed out on the chamber floor.

The blast had ripped through the palace, and smoke and dust rose from piles of rubble. The walls were blackened in part, and ancient wall hangings were ablaze. Many of the bloody bodies strewn around him were also on fire, and the stink of burning flesh and fat almost made him retch. Varnus coughed painfully and he felt the floor beneath his feet shake as another blast somewhere else in the palace detonated.

The sound of shouting reached him, and he staggered towards it, away from the inferno that was blazing behind him. A trio of palace guards ran past along an adjoining corridor, and he hurried along in their wake. He felt another explosion rock the floor beneath his feet and increased his pace, wincing against the pain. He had to get out of this part of the palace.

Staggering along through the smoke that seemed to be thickening around him, he followed the direction that he thought the guards had taken. He limped through a half open door, entering a service corridor usually closed to those frequenting the palace. He passed a palace guard lying dead on the ground, a gunshot wound in the man's head. He leant down and picked up the guard's long-barrelled las-lock. It was heavy and unwieldy in his hands, but it was a weapon none-the-less.

Rounding a corner, Varnus saw a pair of palace guards standing over a fallen man. He wore a plain, cream coloured robe, identical to any number of anonymous bureaucrats that worked within the palace. Seeing him, the guards shouldered their weapons. Varnus held up his hands.

'I'm an enforcer. What the hell is going on?' Varnus managed.

'Insurgents,' said one of the guards. 'Our commander has called us out onto the upper battlements. You had best come with us, enforcer.'

Varnus nodded his head and hurried along after the guards as best as he could. Through winding passages they passed, through hissing blast doors that their pass-cards gave access to. They climbed a set of steel stairs, and finally passed through a heavy door to emerge upon the high battlements of the palace bastion. The door slammed shut with grim finality behind them.

It was night. No, it was almost dawn, Varnus realised. How long had he been unconscious?

He saw masses of PDF soldiers garrisoned along the battlements and smaller groups of blue-armoured guards. They were rushing all over the bastion, the whole area seething with soldiers. Many were firing over the battlements at unseen foes on one of the multiple lower terraces of the bastion, and streaking lasgun fire answered them. Men crouched behind other sections of the battlements as rocket propelled grenades struck the walls, and they were raked by heavy gunfire. Men were shouting, and with the cacophony of gunfire and explosions, it seemed to Varnus that he had escaped the burning section of the palace only to enter a hell of a different kind.

Pain lanced through his side and Varnus grimaced, holding his hand to the bleeding wound.

'I'm fine,' he wheezed as he saw the guards accompanying him hesitate, caught between aiding him and joining the gun battle.

'Go,' he said, making the decision for them.

Floodlights lit up the battlements as if it were daylight, and Varnus, leaning heavily on his salvaged las-lock, staggered across the open area to take cover below the thick crenellations. He risked a quick glance down towards the sprawling, ugly city.

There was a series of lower terraces below the battlements upon which he stood, but beyond them he could see dozens of fires burning all across Shinar, and he could hear a steady thump of explosions coming from all over the city. From over the horizon, he thought he could see dim flashes.

'Emperor preserve us,' said Varnus quietly as he crouched back down behind the crenellations.

He started as one of the enormous air defence turrets along the battlements suddenly came to life, hydraulic servos whirring as the massive cannons rotated, the barrels angled high. What next? thought Varnus, as more of the turrets rotated their giant cannons heavenward.

The floodlights that lit the whole area flickered suddenly, then died. The lights of the entire palace turned off as the potent plasma reactors beneath it went dead. A fifty-block radius around the palace went black instantly, swiftly followed by the rest of the city. Las-fire and tracer rounds flashed through the darkness.

The air defence turrets went off-line.

Without the glare of the lights, crouching, as he was in pitch darkness, Varnus could see what the turrets had been turning towards before they had died.

They looked like stars at first, but they burnt bright orange, and they were getting larger. What the hell were they? Meteors?

Whatever they were, they were approaching the palace with sickening speed. Varnus could almost feel the heat of the objects as they plummeted from the heavens.

Death rained down upon Shinar.

# CHAPTER FIVE

Marduk smiled, exposing his sharp teeth as the Deathclaw drop-pod hurtled down through the atmosphere of Tanakreg. The First Acolyte felt savage joy as the g-forces pulled at him. Burias grinned back at him like some feral beast from across the other side of the plummeting attack transport. Marduk pulled on his helmet, hearing the hiss as it slid solidly into place around his gorget, and breathed in the recycled air of his power armour deeply.

He savoured these moments, the thrill just before battle commenced. He knew that Borhg'ash, the daemon bound within the archaic chainsword at his side, felt his anticipation for the bloodshed that was soon to erupt for the weapon was vibrating slightly. It too hungered for battle.

Warning lights flashed, and Marduk felt the powerful retro-thrusters scream as they kicked in. He howled, the vox amplifiers fitted to his ornate helmet further enhancing the potency of the daemonic sound. The other Word Bearers joined in with howls of their own as their systems were filled with a sudden rush of adrenaline administered by their power armoured suits. Marduk relished the sensation of the combat drugs flooding his system.

'Into the fray once more, my brothers!' bellowed Marduk. The other nine warriors strapped into the Deathclaw roared their approval. 'We are the true bearers of the righteous fury of the gods!' Another roar. 'And in their name, we kill! Kill! And kill again!'

With that the Deathclaw struck, smashing into the ground with bone jarring force, stabiliser claws embedding deeply. Infernal mechanics grinded as the drop-pod was lifted up on its four claws, and the bladed arcs of the circular floor slid back with a hiss.

Marduk was first out of the Deathclaw, his heavy boots slamming hard onto the cracked plascrete, the booming of his vox amplifiers sounding out over the barking of his bolt pistol.

'Hate the infidels!' he roared, his pistol kicking in his hands as he fired. 'Hate them as you kill them! Hate them with your bolter and hate them with your fist!'

The towering hulk of the Deathclaw had slammed into a crenellated, terraced balcony on the upper face of the palace. Other drop-pods screamed down from above, their hulls glowing with the heat of the rapid descent. Seeing the enemy around him and feeling the fear emanating from them, Marduk licked his lips.

He thumbed the activation rune blister on his chainsword and it screamed into life. He could feel it trembling in his hand with barely suppressed hunger, and he gritted his sharpened teeth as he felt the weapon bond with his flesh, tiny barbs piercing his armoured palm.

There were uniformed soldiers all around them, scattered across the cobbled open area atop the crenellated defensive structure. Not that it was any defence against enemies that landed in their midst, thought Marduk as he fired his bolt pistol into the soldiers. They were falling away in terror from the Deathclaws that were landing with titanic force all around them.

'Death to the False Emperor!' he roared, charging into the midst of the foe. He carved left and right, hacking and rending flesh with his screaming chainsword. Blood sprayed out as he tore through the PDF troopers.

Blood and brain matter sprayed across Burias's twisted visage as he swung the heavy, barbed icon two-handed into the face of a soldier, and Marduk knew that the change would be upon him shortly. Good, he thought. Let the mortals see the face of the daemon and know that hell beckoned them.

The Word Bearers ripped though the PDF troopers, and Marduk saw a group of blue-armoured warriors standing together, long lasrifles held to their shoulders.

'With me my brethren!' he roared as he raced across the blood drenched cobblestones towards them. The soldiers fired, and las-fire streaked past Marduk's head. With a roar of animal fury he was amongst them. His chainsword ripped flesh and armour apart with ease, and he felt that the beast bound within the chainsword was pleased at the bloodshed. It pulled at his arm, urging him to seek more death for its whirring teeth. It has been too long since you tasted the blood of the heathens, he thought.

Blood welled in the carefully designed catchments of the weapon and was sucked eagerly into its inner workings. Veins pumped and throbbed along the length of the chainsword as the beast within fed. Power surged through Marduk, flowing from the daemon weapon as it grew in strength. He cleaved Borhg'ash into the chest of another victim, its sharpened teeth ripping apart flesh and ribs in a shower of gore.

The change came over Burias suddenly. His face seemed to ripple and shimmer like a mirage on a horizon. His features flickered back and forth between his own and the horned, bestial face of the daemon Drak'shal. He opened his mouth wide as his lips curled back, exposing sharp fangs and a long, flicking, bruised purple tongue. His bolt pistol dropped from his hand and was instantly retracted to his hip, the length of chain linking the weapon to his belt withdrawing automatically. His index and forefingers fused into thick, bladed talons, and he gripped the icon two-handed once more. Burias dropped into a low, bestial crouch, even as he seemed to grow in stature as the daemon's power increased.

With a roar that was at once his own and the daemon's, Burias-Drak'shal leapt from his crouch, launching straight at a terrified PDF soldier who ineffectually fired off a frantic las-blast at the creature. Burias-Drak'shal smashed the icon down onto the man's head, killing him instantly. Nevertheless, the daemonically possessed warrior punched his fist through the man's chest and raised the dead body up into the air, letting out an ungodly roar that made the substance of the air ripple with warp spawned power.

'The gods themselves send us their aid to smite the infidels!' roared Marduk. 'Behold the majesty of their power!'

The battlements were almost clear. A blast from a lasrifle struck Marduk's helmet, and his head was jerked to the side. Snarling, he turned to face the attacker that had dared to shoot him.

VARNUS SWORE AS he waited for the las-lock to re-power. Though they fired powerful single bursts of energy, the weapons were painfully slow between firing. Still, the shot had done little more than irritate the towering monster that was leading the power armoured killers, so one more blast would be unlikely to do anything but stall the inevitable. Varnus knew that death had come to Tanakreg and that he had but moments left to live. Emperor protect my soul, he prayed.

The palace guard were being slaughtered. He saw one man explode as a bolt-round detonated in his shoulder, spraying blood around him like a mist as he fell to the ground, the entire left side of his torso missing. He saw another die instantly as one of the enemy clubbed him in the head with a bolter, the force of the blow crushing his skull as if it were glass.

The hulking fiend he had shot rounded on him, stalking through the melee, and Varnus swore. The monster towered over him. Varnus was in no way a small man, but he barely came half way up the beast's chest. With a hum, the las-lock re-powered and he fired again at the huge Chaos Space Marine. The shot was taken in haste and was not on target. Nevertheless, it struck the beast in his wrist, and his accursed bolt pistol dropped from his hands.

SNARLING IN ANGER, Marduk cleaved the long lasrifle wielded by the infidel in two, and reached out and grabbed him around the throat with his empty hand. He felt blood seeping from his wrist where the wretch had blasted him, but it was already congealing. His hand almost encircled the man's entire neck, and he could feel the pathetic fragility beneath his fingers. Tendons and ligaments strained as he exerted pressure.

Lifting the man into the air, his feet kicking uselessly half a metre from the ground, Marduk drew him close to his helmeted visage.

'That hurt, little man,' he said, the vox amplifier booming his words into the face of the wretch, 'but this is going to hurt a lot more.'

With that, he hurled the man off the battlements.

'Your weapon, First Acolyte,' said one of the Word Bearers, and Marduk turned to accept his bolt pistol, held reverently in the warrior's hands. Without a word, he took the weapon.

Looking out over the battlements, Marduk saw scattered fighting on a lower tier of the bastion some fifteen metres below, where the broken body of the infidel he had hurled had landed. He could see fighting down there, but no Word Bearers. Curious, he thought.

'Warriors of the IV Coterie, with me,' he ordered. The rest of you, cleanse this level of the Imperial filth.'

'Burias-Drak'shal!' he roared, and the daemonically possessed warrior turned from his killing, gore dripping thickly from his icon, arms and mouth. 'With me.'

The twelve warriors of the IV Coterie extricated themselves from the killing, and jogged towards the First Acolyte. Burias-Drak'shal stalked along with them, breathing heavily.

Marduk launched himself over the edge of the battlements, dropping down towards the lower terrace. He landed in the midst of a firefight, and cobblestones cracked beneath his weight. He rose up to his full height as his brethren landed around him.

'Death to the False Emperor!' he roared. The shout was repeated by several dozen of the Imperial garbed warriors. Marduk saw that most of those that had shouted had ripped their clothing to expose a crude, tattooed representation of the Latros Sacrum on their shoulders, the sacred screaming daemon symbol of the Word Bearers legion.

He began laying around with Borhg'ash and his bolt pistol, carving flesh and planting bolt-rounds through bodies. He didn't pay too much attention to those he killed, and doubtless he and the warriors of the IV Coterie slew as many of their cult followers as the Imperials, but it mattered not – the souls of both would be welcomed by the gods of Chaos.

The gunfire suddenly ceased, and the remaining men dropped to their knees, gazing up at the towering Chaos Space Marines with awe and reverence. Several had tears in their eyes. The Word Bearers held their killing in check, waiting to see the First Acolyte's reaction.

All except for Burias-Drak'shal, who stepped forward and smashed the icon into the head of one of the cultists. The man's skull crumpled and he fell without a sound.

'Burias-Drak'shal,' said Marduk quietly, and the daemon warrior looked up, snarling. His entire body trembling, Burias-Drak'shal stepped back and dropped into a half-crouch, staring hungrily at the humans. Marduk too felt the urge to step forward and slaughter the weaklings, but he knew that they had their uses. Borhg'ash trembled in his hands, wishing to kill more.

'Which one here speaks for you?' asked Marduk. The cultists looked around at each other, and finally one man stood and stepped through the other cultists to approach.

'I do, lord,' said the man, his head held high.

Marduk raised his bolt pistol and shot the man in the face. Pieces of skull, brain matter and blood splattered over the remaining kneeling cultists.

'Lower your eyes when looking upon your betters, dogs, or I shall ask Burias-Drak'shal here to remove them,' Marduk snarled.

'Now, who here speaks for you?' he repeated.

A shaven-headed woman in beige robes stepped forwards, her gaze lowered. 'I do, my lord,' she said in a shaking voice.

'What is the fourth tenant of the Book of Lorgar, dog?' asked Marduk dangerously, fingering the trigger of his bolt pistol.

The woman stood in silence for a moment, and Marduk raised the pistol to her head.

*'Give up yourself to the Great Gods in body and of soul,'* she said quickly. *'Discard all that does not benefit their*

*Greatness. The First thing to be discarded is the Name. Your Self is nothing to the Gods, and your Name shall be as nothing to You. Only once you have reached Enlightenment shall you Reclaim you Name, and your Self. Thus spoke Great Lorgar, and thus it was to Be.'*

Marduk kept the pistol raised to her head. 'What is your name?'

'I have no name, my lord,' the woman replied instantly.

'If you have no name, what then shall I call you?'

The woman faltered for a moment, biting her lip hard, acutely aware of the bolt pistol held a centimetre from her forehead.

'Dog,' she whispered finally.

'Louder,' said Marduk.

'Dog,' said the woman. 'My name to you, lord, is dog.'

'Very good,' said Marduk, lowering his pistol. 'You are all dogs, to me, and to all of my noble kind. But perhaps one day, with faith and prayer and action, you will rise in my esteem.

'Arise, dogs. Gather your arms, and prove yourselves. Walk before your betters. Joyfully take the bullets of our enemies, so that not a scratch need mar the holy armour of the warriors of Lorgar. Such is a noble sacrifice. Lead forth, dogs.'

JARULEK STEPPED CAREFULLY through the carnage, the script covered orbs of his eyes taking in all the details of the slaughter wrought by his warriors. Bloodied and broken corpses lay sprawled throughout the palace. The fortress-like was enormous, and every living soul within it had been slain or was in the lower atrium on the ground level in shackles. He had sent the cultists out into the city, to spread panic and misery amongst the populace, and to hunt down the last remnants of resistance. He didn't care if they succeeded or not; Kol Badar and the bulk of the Host were fast closing on the city, and they would smash any final resistance utterly.

The Dark Apostle was pleased with the attack. The palace had been taken with few casualties and the kill-count was exceptional: a good sacrifice to the gods.

Picking his way carefully up the nave of the heretical temple, he felt hatred as he raised his gaze to the towering, granite statue of the aquila that dominated the back wall. Both of the heads of the two-headed eagle had been smashed by his zealous warriors, and the tips of the wings reduced to dust.

Dozens of clergy members were nailed to the defiled aquila, thick metal spikes driven through their flesh and bone, and into the stone.

The First Acolyte, Marduk, stepped forwards to greet him. He joined the fingers of both hands together, making the stylised sign of Chaos Undivided, and bowed his head. When he raised his head, he was smiling broadly, exposing sharp teeth: the row of smaller, razor sharp incisors in the front and the larger, ripping teeth behind.

'We left them alive, mostly, Dark Apostle,' he said. 'I thought that might please you.'

Jarulek too smiled. The intense hatred that the Word Bearers had for the Imperium of man was as nothing compared to the exquisite hatred that they reserved for members of the Ecclesiarchy. He stepped closer to the debased aquila statue, looking up at the priests, who were groaning in agony. Rivulets of blood ran down the statue, funnelled by the carved eagle feathers, and Jarulek placed a finger in the crimson liquid. He raised the finger to his inscribed lips and licked it with the tip of his script covered tongue.

'It does please me, First Acolyte,' he breathed. He stepped back, hands on his hips, as if he were appraising and admiring a favourite piece of artwork. 'Yes, it pleases me very much indeed.'

'Then there is this pair,' said Marduk. Two men were dragged forward and forced to their knees with heavy hands upon their shoulders. They both kept their eyes low, not daring to look up at the Word Bearers around them. One wore a red robe, his bionic eye buzzing softly as the lens rotated. The other, the larger of the two, wore a robe of plain cream. Both had exposed their left shoulders, showing the leering daemon face of the Latros Sacrum tattooed upon their flesh.

'The one on the left disabled the air defence turrets,' said Jarulek, not taking his eyes off the priests impaled upon the statue. Marduk looked at the man. His left eye had been replaced with a mechanical augmentation.

'While the other,' said Jarulek, 'ensured that the Cultists of the Word gained access to the palace. I believe that he was the bodyguard of the governor of this backwater planet. Was that not so?' he enquired, turning his face towards the man.

He nodded his head, wisely not speaking out loud.

'I have seen your faces in my visions,' remarked Jarulek. 'And in my visions of what is yet to come, your face is there, treacherous adept of the Machine-God. But I regret to inform you, bodyguard,' he said calmly, 'that yours is not. It would seem that your part in this venture is complete.'

The man stiffened, but did not raise his head.

'But you are not yet to be made a sacrifice to our gods. No, you are not yet worthy of that honour,' said Jarulek in his velvet voice. 'Take him down to the atrium to join the slave gangs. He can spend the last weeks of his life in service to the gods, aiding the construction of the Gehemahnet.' The man was dragged away.

'You, administrator, you are to stay close to me. But first, you must remove that abomination that you wear upon your breast,' said Jarulek, pointing at the twelve toothed cog upon his chest. The man instantly removed the metal plate from around his neck and held it in his hands, not sure what he was meant to do with it now that it was removed.

'First Acolyte, take the accursed thing and see that you perform the Rituals of Defilement upon it,' said Jarulek. Marduk took the metal emblem, his face curled in disgust.

'It is no god, you know, that your erstwhile brethren pray to,' remarked Jarulek conversationally.

'My... my lord?' questioned the administrator. Marduk paused as he was turning to leave, a snarl on his face for the man daring to speak in the presence of the Dark Apostle. Jarulek raised a hand to halt the blow that Marduk was about to deal the cowering man.

'They are coming, you know, coming here, your erstwhile brethren,' said Jarulek, almost to himself, seeing the waking vision as it overlapped with his surroundings. 'Yes, they come soon. They fear that we will succeed where they failed.'

Jarulek came out of the vision, and saw that Marduk had paused, looking at him. That one's power is growing, he thought.

It was sometimes possible for one of powerful faith to experience, albeit considerably weakly, the visions that another experienced. How much had he seen? he wondered briefly, before discarding the thought.

It mattered not. What was to come was to come, and nothing could change the prophecy.

# CHAPTER SIX

DAYS AND NIGHTS blurred together into one long, nightmarish, pained existence. Varnus was plucked from death and his wounds had been tended by the horrific chirurgeons that served the Chaos Legion, even as he fought against their administrations.

They had borne him from where he had lain after the Chaos Lord had hurled him off the battlements, and placed him on an icy, steel slab. He was restrained with thick binding cords of sinew. Bladed arms had cut into him, and long, needle-tipped proboscises had plunged into his flesh. He screamed in agony as the skin and muscles of his shattered leg and arm were peeled back, and the splintered bones reset before being sprayed with a burning liquid. His veins burned with serums, and his eyes were held open with painful spider-legged apparatus, for what purpose he knew not, unless it was for him to witness the infernal chirurgeons at work.

The skin of his forehead was delicately peeled back from his skull, and a burning piece of dark metal in the barbed shape of an eight-pointed star was inserted there before the skin was returned to its position and stapled back into place.

A collar of metal the colour of blood was wrapped around his neck and soldered shut, and he was taken to join the tens of thousands of other slaves that the Chaos forces had rounded up once the occupation of Shinar had been completed. Heavy, spiked chains connected Varnus's collar to two other slaves. They too bore the mark of Chaos beneath the red-raw flesh of their foreheads.

He had found that within a few days he was able to walk, albeit with considerable difficulty and pain. He was made to work day and night, his efforts directed by horrifying, hunched overseers, garbed in skintight, black, oily fabric. The faces of the overseers were, thankfully, obscured by the same black material, though how the creatures were able to see was beyond him. Grilled vox-blasters were positioned where the creatures' mouths should be, and their fingertips ended in long needles. Varnus had felt the pain of those needles when he had stumbled one night, and the pain that they caused was far in excess of what he imagined a slaver's whip would deliver. The overseers stalked along the lines of slaves, their hunchbacked gait bobbing and awkward.

But far more terrifying than the overseers were the Chaos Marines. Whenever Varnus glimpsed one of them he was overwhelmed by the scale of the monsters and the pure aura of power and dread that they exuded.

The sense of oppression never lifted. For days, the sky was largely obscured by the immense shape of a titanic Chaos battle barge hanging in low orbit, plunging most of the city into darkness. Enormous landing craft were in constant movement between the Chaos ship and the ground, ferrying Emperor-knew what down to the planet. Then one day it was gone. Not being able to see the battle barge of the Chaos forces in the atmosphere was a small blessing amid the horror that was Varnus's existence.

The great red planet of Korsis could be seen both day and night, getting increasingly larger as its orbit drew it ever closer to Tanakreg and the time of the system's conjunction of planets.

Varnus had watched as an area somewhere in the region of a hundred city blocks was levelled by heavy siege ordnance. In a short flurry of brutal devastation, hundreds of buildings had been demolished with ground shaking force. Dust had rushed across the landscape for hundreds of kilometres all around, Varnus guessed. He no longer knew if it was day or night, for the air was thick with dust and foul, heavy, black smoke that left a residue on every surface.

Giant, smoking, infernal machines had been brought in to push aside the debris of the demolition, and along with thousands of slaves, Varnus had been forced to follow in the wake of these mechanical beasts, clearing away the smaller rubble that the machines missed. His hands had bled, and chirurgeons moving through the lines of chained Imperials had sprayed them with a dark, synthetic coating, stemming the bleeding, but not the pain.

Monstrous, polluting factories, foundries and forges were constructed, vast, vile places filled with acrid black smoke, heat and the screams of those being 'encouraged' by the overseers and their needle hands. Titanic vats of superheated, molten rock were fed with the rubble of the demolished buildings, and what looked like bricks, though bricks on an insanely large scale, were being created in gigantic, black, metal moulds.

The corpses of those killed in the defence of Shinar were dumped in giant, stinking piles, and more bodies were pushed there by huge bulldozers, black smoke belching from racks of exhausts. Varnus thanked the Emperor that he had not been assigned to one of the slave gangs forced to strip those corpses naked before they were deposited in vast silos. He had no wish to learn what abhorrence the enemy had planned for the bodies.

Other worker teams were busy in the centre of the vast open space that had been cleared, working with smoke-belching machinery, drilling down into the earth, creating a vast hole over a kilometre wide that sank lower into the planet's crust with every passing day.

The destruction of the city was not, it seemed, complete, and on what Varnus guessed was his second week of hell, more demolitions began. The rubble created from the demolitions was brought to the smelteries in cavernous vehicles and upon the backs of thousands of slaves. Varnus completely lost track of time as he dragged and hauled twisted metal, chunks of rockcrete and stone to the vast smelteries, there to be turned into ever more giant blocks.

A sudden weight pulled at the collar around Varnus's neck and he was hauled back a step, almost dropping the chunk of rock he was bearing. He tried to keep moving, but there was a dead weight on the chain attached to his collar, and he glanced around fearfully, trying to see if there was an overseer nearby. Seeing none, he turned around and saw that the man behind him had fallen. Swearing, Varnus dropped the stone he carried to the ground and hobbled to the fallen slave, trying to pull him to his feet.

'Get up, damn you,' he swore. The punishments exacted upon the entire worker gang if one of their number slowed their progress were harsh. The man didn't move. 'By the Emperor, man, get up!'

Sudden, wracking pain jolted through his nervous system, and he heard the rasping voice on an overseer. There was a slight delay as whatever fell language the overseer spoke was translated into Low Gothic by its vox-blaster.

'Speak not the name of the accursed one!' rasped the overseer, and slammed another handful of needles into Varnus's lower back. He had never felt such pain in his life, would not even have been able to conceive of such agony. He convulsed and jerked on the ground. Abruptly the pain ceased, leaving him feeling numb.

The overseer called out something in its own rasping dialect, and another of its kind stepped forwards with a las-cutter, as Varnus shielded his salt-sore eyes from the white-hot light. The chains connected to the collar of the man who still lay unmoving on the ground were cut, and Varnus felt his own chain go slack for a moment. Then he was pulled violently to his feet by the chain, as the severed links were fused together.

The slave was dead, or close to it, and was dragged away.

Two sharp notes were blown on a whistle, and Varnus quickly picked up his dropped rock and shuffled to the side of the ruined street with the other slaves of his worker gang. A detachment of blood-red armoured Chaos Space Marines marched past, and the other slaves kept their gaze lowered, as did the black clad, hunchbacked overseers.

The familiar burning feeling beneath the skin of his forehead itched, but Varnus resisted the urge to scratch at it. He had seen other slaves claw at the eight-pointed star symbols beneath their flesh, and terrible, painful welts had erupted.

A Discord, one of the floating monstrosities that accompanied every slave gang, blessedly silent for a moment as the Chaos Marines had walked by, began once again to blare its cacophony of unintelligible words and hellish sounds from its grilled speaker-unit. It hovered limply half a metre off the ground, dragging behind it an array of mechanical tentacles as it moved ponderously up and down the line of slaves. The sound was sickening, making Varnus's insides twist with nausea.

A long, drawn out whistle sounded, and Varnus once again dropped his stone and lowered himself painfully to the ground. An overseer walked along the line of seated slaves, holding a muddy brown bottle with a straw out to each of the men in turn. When it came to his turn, Varnus leant forward and sucked deeply from the tube. He almost gagged on the foul, thick liquid, but forced himself to swallow. He had no idea what it was that the bastards fed them, but it was the only form of sustenance that they were allowed.

'So, what were you before?' asked a low voice in a conspiratorial whisper, after the overseer had moved on.

Varnus glanced surreptitiously at the man next to him. They were now chained together, since the poor soul who had been chained in between them had just been dragged off. He thought that he recognised the man from somewhere, but he couldn't place the face.

'Enforcer,' said Varnus quietly.

'You got a name?' whispered the man.

'Varnus.' A whistle blew, and the slave gangers pushed themselves to their feet. 'Yours?' he risked, whispering.

'Pierlo,' said the man quietly.

MARDUK WAS FIRST off the Thunderhawk, striding purposefully down the assault ramp as it was lowered from the stubbed nose of the gunship. He removed his helmet and breathed in deeply. The air was thick with pollution, smoke and the taint of Chaos, and he smiled. Much had changed since he had left the city of Shinar.

For the past weeks he had been engaged against various PDF armies far from the city, ensuring that there was no military power upon the planet with the strength to launch a counter-attack against the Word Bearers. While there were still dozens of areas of resistance scattered across the planet, there was no single force that would prove a threat.

The skies were scarred with dust and smog, and the first cautious rumbles of thunder rolled across the marred heavens. The fires of industry were burning fiercely in the city below.

The palace had changed. The spires and towers that had once formed the silhouette of the bastion had been ripped down, replaced with brutal spikes and barbed uprights, and corpses were strung up all over them. Marduk saw that the skinless forms of the kathartes, the daemonic, cadaverous furies that accompanied the Host, were perched amongst the corpses. The vicious harpies screeched and fought amongst themselves for the prime perches. The powerful air defence turrets had been returned to activation, and they scanned the heavens. That was good; it would not be long before the Imperial fleet arrived.

Purple-red veins pulsed beneath the surface of the once plain, pale grey, plascrete walls of the upper bastion, and Marduk was pleased to see the symbols of all the great gods of Chaos artfully painted in blood on the walls of the galleries he passed through.

He nodded to the honour guard flanking the vast glass doors, and walked past them out onto the large, opulent balcony. Jarulek, surveying the ruin of a city below, did not acknowledge his approach.

Marduk strode to the Dark Apostle's side and knelt down beside him, his head lowered. After a moment, Jarulek placed his hand upon the kneeling warrior's head.

'The blessings of the dark gods of the Immaterium upon you, my First Acolyte. Rise,' said the Dark Apostle. 'You return having accomplished that which I requested,' he said. There was no hint of a question in the remark, since there would be no need for Marduk to return had he not completed the task appointed him.

'There is no fighting force upon Tanakreg that can interrupt the preparations, my lord,' said Marduk. 'I bring with me near to five hundred thousand additional slaves to aid in the construction.'

'Good. The slaves of this planet are weak. More than a thousand of them perish every day.'

'The Imperials are all weak,' said Marduk emphatically. 'We will smash those soon to arrive, as we smashed the pitiful resistance on this planet.'

'I have faith that you are correct, we will smash these new arrivals. Individually they are weak, yes,' said Jarulek, 'but together, they are not so. It is only through division that we weaken them. This is why we must always propagate the cults. When the Imperium fears the enemies within its own cities, that is when it is the most vulnerable.'

'I understand, my lord,' said Marduk, 'though I do not believe that your Coryphaus sees it so?'

'Kol Badar does not need to. He is the warlord of the Host, and he fulfils that role perfectly. Rarely has the Legion seen such a warrior and strategos,' he said, turning his disconcerting gaze towards Marduk for the first time since they began speaking. 'He brought in well over a million slaves from his attacks against the cities in the north, you know,' said Jarulek softly, watching his First Acolyte carefully. 'He is and always will be a better warrior than you.'

Marduk tried to remain composed, but his jaw clenched slightly. He saw the dark amusement in

Jarulek's eyes. The Dark Apostle kept watching him, seeming to Marduk to enjoy making him feel uncomfortable, as he always did.

'You still feel the shame, don't you?' asked Jarulek, cruelly.

'I could have beaten him,' said Marduk, 'if you had given me the chance.'

Jarulek laughed softly, a bitter, cruel sound. 'We both know that is a lie,' he said.

Marduk clenched his fists, but he did not refute the Dark Apostle.

Jarulek placed a forceful hand on one of Marduk's battle-worn shoulder pads and turned him towards the view over the ruined city.

'Beautiful, is it not? The first stones of the tower have been laid, the ground consecrated with the death of a thousand and one heathens, and the blood mortar is setting. The tower will breach the heavens, the gods will be pleased, and this world will be turned inside out.' He turned towards Marduk, a hungry smile on his scripture covered lips. 'The time draws near. "*As Sanguine Orb waxes strong and Pillar of Clamour rises high, the Peal of Nether shakes, And Great Wyrms of The Below wreak the earth with flame and gaseous exhalation. Roar of Titans will smite the mountains and they shall tumble. Depths of Onyx shall engulf the lands, and then exposed shall lay The Undercroft, Death and Mastery.*"'

The First Acolyte's brow creased. There was not one of the great tomes of Lorgar that he had not memorised in its entirety, nor any of the scriptures of Kor Phaeron or Erebus that he did not know word for word. As First Acolyte, he was expected to know the words of the Legion as well as any Dark Apostle did. Any time that he was not killing in the name of Lorgar or aiding the Dark Apostle in the spiritual guidance of the Legion was spent in study of the ancient writings, as well as the required ritualistic penitence, self-flagellation and fasts. He prided himself on his knowledge of the Sermons of Hate, and the Exonerations of Resentment, as well as thousands upon thousands of other litanies, recitations, curses, denunciations and proclamations of the Dark Apostles through the history of the Legion. He had spent countless hours poring over pronouncements, predictions and prophecies witnessed in ten thousand trances, visions and dreams. Marduk had even studied the scrawled recollections and scribed ravings of those warrior-brothers possessed by daemons, words straight from the Ether, seeking the truth in them. And yet he had never before heard the prophecy that Jarulek quoted.

'It is not written in any of the tomes within the librariox aboard the *Infidus Diabolus,*' said Jarulek, seeing the look on Marduk's face. 'Nor is it written anywhere within the great temple factories of Ghalmek or the hallowed flesh-halls of Sicarus. No,' said Jarulek smiling secretively, 'this prophecy is scribed on only one tome, and it resides in none of those places.'

Marduk felt his frustrations grow.

'A fleet of the great enemy draws close,' hissed Jarulek, his eyes narrowing.

'I have felt no tremor in the warp indicating their arrival,' said Marduk, knowing that he was particularly sensitive to such things.

'They have not yet left the Ether. But I feel their abhorrent vessels pushing through the tides of the warp. They will arrive soon. I have sent the *Infidus Diabolus* back to the warp.'

'You do not wish to engage the enemy fleet as it emerges?' asked Marduk.

'No.'

'You do not seek to engage them in the warp?' he asked, somewhat incredulously.

'No, I have no wish to risk the *Infidus Diabolus* in a futile battle of no consequence.'

'No battle against the great enemy is of no consequence,' growled Marduk. 'So Lorgar spoke, and so it is to be.'

'Speak to me in such a tone again and I will rip your still beating twin-hearts from your chest and devour them before your eyes,' said Jarulek softly.

Jarulek held Marduk's gaze until the First Acolyte could look no longer and dropped to his knees, his head down.

'Forgive me, Dark Apostle.'

'Of course I forgive you, dear Marduk,' said Jarulek softly, placing his hand upon the First Acolyte's head.

Marduk felt a sudden lurch. By the way that the Dark Apostle withdrew his hand, he knew that he had felt it too. He had felt that same feeling countless times, though much stronger in intensity, as the *Infidus Diabolus* dropped out of warp space. Jarulek stepped away, and Marduk stood.

'The great enemy,' said the Dark Apostle, 'has arrived.'

# CHAPTER SEVEN

BRIGADIER-GENERAL ISHMAEL Havorn of the 133rd Elysians crossed his arms over his chest as he surveyed the flickering pict-screen. The image was hazy at best–at worst, nothing could be made out at all. He shook his head.

'Your pict-viewer is of inferior quality, Brigadier-General Ishmael Havorn,' said the techno-magos. His voice was monotone, and barely sounded human at all. 'The level 5.43 background radiation of the planet c6.7.32 and Type 3 winds disrupt its capabilities.'

'Thank you, that is most helpful, Magos Darioq,' Havorn replied.

'You are welcome, Brigadier-General Ishmael Havorn,' said the techno-magos, clearly not registering the sarcasm in the middle-aged general's tone. The large form of Colonel Boerl, the commander of the Elysian 72nd and Havorn's second in command smirked.

The techno-magos, one of the pre-eminent members of the Adeptus Mechanicus of far distant Mars, was a massive, augmented being. It was hard to know where the human ended and the machine began. No features could be discerned underneath the low hood, just an unblinking red light where an eye had once been.

From the back of his red robe, two huge, mechanical arms extended over his shoulders like a pair of vicious, stinging tails of some poisonous insect. Another pair of servo-arms extended around his sides. Formidable arrays of weaponry, heavy-duty machinery, power lifters and hissing claws were constructed into them. The staff of office of the techno-magos was incorporated into one of the servo-arms, a long-hafted, double-bladed power axe topped with a large, brass, twelve-toothed cog, the symbol of the Machine-God. Dozens of mechadendrites hovered around him: long, metallic tentacles fused to the nerve endings of his spine. They were tipped with dangerous looking, needle-like protrusions and surprisingly dextrous grasping claws.

The man's organic arms were wasted, useless things that he held crossed over his chest. It looked like they lacked the strength to grasp anything any longer, and they were held immobile. Clearly they had been made redundant by the hovering mechadendrites and servo-arms.

A diminutive, robed figure the size of a child stood before the magos, though nothing could be seen of its form within its deep hood. It appeared to be connected to the Mechanicus priest by cables and wiring. A floating servo-skull hung above the techno-magos, mechanics covering the right-hand side of its cranium. Its unblinking, red eye watched the goings on within the command centre unerringly.

With a slight shake of his head, Havorn squinted at the pict-screen again. Bleary images flickered across the viewer of massed bulk carriers sinking slowly through the atmosphere of Tanakreg, with escorts of gunships flying in figure-of-eight patterns around them. It was hard to make out, but Havorn had seen scores of similar landings, and he could see exactly what was occurring in his mind's eye.

Imperial Navy attack craft, a variety of interceptors, fighters and assault boats, would have swarmed from their launch bays aboard the twin Dictator Cruisers, the *Vigilance* and the *Fortitude*, like a cloud of angry insects. As the first of the mass transports detached from the cruisers and began sinking slowly through the atmosphere, it was these Imperial Navy craft that were its first line of defence.

As the atmosphere was broken, vast bay doors on the descending transports would retract, and flights of Valkyries would emerge like circling buzzards, descending towards the surface of the planet in advance of the wallowing mass transport ship. Thunderbolts and Lightning fighters would scream from the still-descending transport to ensure air superiority. The Valkyries would sweep low over the ground and the first Elysians to step foot on the world would rappel swiftly from the gunships to secure the landing zone.

A wide perimeter would be quickly secured, the rapidly deployed Elysians establishing strong points along their line with quickly dug-in heavy weapons.

More troops would rappel to the surface and smaller, breakaway transports would detach from the massive bulk of the main ships on the descent, dropping in heavier support to bolster the perimeter defences: rapidly moving Sentinel walkers and Chimera infantry transports bearing cargos of specialist Elysians.

Havorn had no doubt that the landing was proceeding smoothly and as planned, and a glance at the data-slates being updated every few seconds with fresh information confirmed this. The perimeter had been established well within the usual expected time-frame, and Sentinels were already scouting beyond the landing zone, seeking out possible threats invisible from the air.

The pict-image flickered again, but it was clear that the last of the mass transports had landed. Dust rose around the ships as their immense weight was lowered onto the earth. Havorn could imagine the rumbling beneath the feet of the men already on the ground as the ships landed and their titanic cargo-doors dropped open.

He raised a hand to his long, greying moustache. Landings were always stressful; the mass transport ships were such tempting targets. He was pleased, though somewhat surprised, not to have had any sightings of the enemy. That was a blessing. A shudder of revulsion ran through him as he thought of the foe that his soldiers would soon be facing.

Chaos Space Marines, the most dangerous and hated of foes: traitors and betrayers who had turned their backs on the light of the Emperor and sold their souls to devils and eternal damnation.

The Space Marines, were the most elite warriors of the Imperium, each genetically modified to become giants among men, perfect machines of death with bodies created to withstand wounds that would kill a lesser man ten times over. In every respect they were superior to regular warriors. They were stronger, tougher and faster. Add to that the awesome protective and strength enhancing properties of their power armour, their unparalleled training and the best weapons that the adepts of Mars could construct, and you had the most powerful fighting force in the galaxy, and the most dangerous.

The Space Marines were meant to be the warrior elite of humanity that brought stability to the galaxy with bolter and sword in the name of the God-Emperor of mankind. But more than half of their number had turned their backs on the Emperor, embracing the sentient darkness and malice of the Empyrean.

The Elysians were soon to face these accursed traitors on this dead-end planet. His men would be fighting the genetically modified monsters, the results of a deadly experiment gone horribly wrong when they turned upon the Emperor. Havorn had fought alongside loyalist Adeptus Astartes many times, and their involvement in those wars had ensured that tens of thousands of Imperial Guardsmen had lived, but he would never trust them as he would trust any of his men.

Why are we on this accursed planet? he fumed, his face impassive. He was not one to question orders from the Lord General Militant, but he resented being left in the dark as to the reasons.

Still, it mattered little. The enemy was here, and wherever it raised his treasonous head, the snake must be cut down. It was just that Havorn knew that this world must be of some hidden importance for the 133rd and the 72nd, in their entireties, to have been drawn off from the Ghandas Crusade to retake it; important, but not important enough, it seemed, to have drawn one of the loyalist Space Marine Chapters to the world.

Tanakreg was a backwater planet dominated by black, acidic seas. There were only two main land-masses on the world, and only one of those was inhabited. An inhospitable and desolate land dominated by salt plains and high ranges of mountains, it seemed to Havorn to be a planet that the hated forces of Chaos could damn well keep if they wanted it so much.

The Planetary Defence Forces had been overwhelmed contemptuously quickly, a fighting force of two hundred thousand soldiers, defeated within days by a force that could not have been more than three thousand. But those three thousand were Astartes, he reminded himself, and he surmised that traitors on Tanakreg had aided them. It sickened him that people could turn on their own like that.

'Brigadier-general,' said Colonel Boerl, 'the perimeter is secured and primary bulk transports landed. The secondary perimeter is being established and will be operational at any moment.'

'Thank you, colonel,' said Havorn. He turned to the representative of the Mechanicus.

'Techno-Magos Darioq, you may order your own transports to descend, if you wish,' he said.

'Thank you, Brigadier-General Ishmael Havorn,' replied the magos in his mechanical monotone. 'I will leave you now to return to my ship, to oversee the landing.'

Gyro-stabilisers hummed as the magos turned to leave. His footsteps were slow and heavy, clanking loudly on the metal-grilled floor plates of the command station aboard the battleship. Clearly, his legs were either augmented or had been completely replaced with bionics in order to bear the colossal weight of the harness. Mechadendrites floated freely around him, and a small, wheeled contraption, joined to the Tech-Adept by ribbed cables and wiring, trailed behind him. The floating servo-skull hovered in the room briefly before following its master from the command station.

'A word, before you leave, Tech-Adept,' said Havorn. The red-robed, towering figure turned around slowly.

'Yes, Brigadier-General Ishmael Havorn?'

'I am intrigued; what is it about Tanakreg that interests the Mechanicus so? It is rare to see such a gathering of Martian power.'

'The Adeptus Mechanicus supports the armies of the Emperor in all endeavours, Brigadier-General Ishmael Havorn. The Adeptus Mechanicus wishes to support the battle against the enemy on this planet c6.7.32.'

'You bring with you a force the likes of which I have never seen on a battlefield before; why is it that this place, of all the planets in the galaxy, is of such particular interest to the Mechanicus?'

'The Adeptus Mechanicus supports the armies of the Emperor in all endeavours, Brigadier-General Ishmael Havorn. The Adeptus Mechanicus wishes to support the battle against the enemy on this planet c6.7.32.'

'That does not explain a thing and you damn well know it,' said Havorn, his voice rising. 'What I am asking is *why?*'

'The Adeptus Mechanicus supports–' began the techno-magos, but the brigadier-general cut him off.

'Enough! Leave my command station and my ship, and see to your damned landings.'

'Thank you, Brigadier-General Ishmael Havorn,' said the techno-magos.

The brigadier-general's face was hard as the Adeptus Mechanicus priest left. Then he swore loudly and colourfully.

THE CHAOS INFESTED, polluted atmosphere was killing him. The foul smoke from the infernal machines spewed into the skies, and Varnus's breath was heavy and wet with fluid. Several times he had thought he had felt *things* crawling within his lungs, and he had hawked and coughed until blood had run from his tortured throat. Then the cursed, black-clad overseers had inflicted pain on him, stabbing him with their needle claws, and he had writhed with agony.

His eyes were weeping constantly, and a painful, mottled rash had developed around his neck and wrists. The eight-pointed metal star beneath the skin of his forehead pained him, and he imagined that the hateful thing was fusing to his skull, becoming a part of him. The thought was sickening.

The broken bones of his arm and leg had healed well, however, and though they still pained him, he had almost regained his full range of movement.

He wiped the back of his mortar encrusted hand across his eyes as another layer of immense stone blocks slammed into place, the sound booming out over the ruined city of Shinar. The tower was being erected at a ferocious pace, one layer of the huge bricks at a time. Giant, insect-like cranes swung around and lowered their cables to the ground to grasp the next round of blocks in their barbed claws, belching smoke and dripping oil.

Varnus stared into the booth of the closest crane with his sleep deprived, exhausted eyes. The pilot of the machine may once have been human, but was far from that now. It hung suspended within its cabin prison by dozens of taut wires and cables hooked painfully through its skin with vicious barbs. Ribbed pipes extended from its eye sockets and from its throat. Its legs had atrophied to a point that they were little more than withered stubs protruding from its torso, and with long, skeletally thin fingers it plucked at the wires suspending it. He tore his eyes away from the foul sight.

A sharp note sounded across the worksite, and black-garbed overseers prodded thousands of slaves forwards, off the scaffolds and onto the top of the stone slabs. Varnus and Pierlo stepped onto the wall of the round tower, and waited for the mortar hose to swing in their direction.

Other slave teams within the shaft of the Chaos tower toiled far below. Though the tower was only around thirty metres from ground level, the inside of it had been drilled down into the core of the earth twice that distance, and Varnus felt a surge of vertigo pull at him. Every time he looked over that edge, he had an impulse to hurl himself over, but he resisted these urges. He would fight death for as long as he was able; he wanted to be alive to see the Chaos forces utterly destroyed. He believed fervently that help would come to deliver Tanakreg from this hated foe.

Other slaves had not been able to stop themselves leaping from the walls of the tower, but it gained them little. The chains that linked around the slave's necks were bolted to the scaffolds at intervals and those slaves that slipped, or hurled themselves off the edge, seeking an escape from their hellish existence, ended up dangling against the inside wall of the tower. Normally, they would drag a handful of other slaves with them. It was not usually enough to kill them. The only chance a slave had was to throw himself with as much force as he could muster and pray that his neck snapped. Still, if he survived, the punishments at the needle-clawed hands of the overseers were severe, and meted out not only to the instigator, but to all those who were dragged over the edge with him. Such was the fear of these punishments, that any slave that looked as if he might try to end it all was restrained by his fellow captives and forced to continue with his servitude.

The thick weight of the mortar hose swung into position above Varnus with much hissing and steaming of pistons, and Pierlo and he reached up, pulling the hose across so that it hovered above the middle of the stone block. Thick, gruel-like mortar began to emerge in congealed lumps from the end of the hose, slowly at first, then faster, piling in the centre of the stone block. A deep pile of the foul substance was deposited before the hose, clanking and steaming, swung away from them to a pair of neighbouring slaves. Varnus and Pierlo dropped to their knees to spread the mortar evenly across the surface of the stone with their hands.

The mortar that held the stones in place smelt foul and was a sickly shade of pink. Varnus tried not to look too closely at the disgusting substance after he had found human teeth in it some time earlier.

That was where the dead of Shinar ended up, he had realised with horror. They were ground up into a thick paste, bones and all, and turned into this foul blood-mortar.

He was smeared in the stuff, from head to toe, and he tasted the hateful, metallic tang of it on his tongue, and smelt its repugnant stink in his nostrils.

A Discord hovered nearby as the slaves worked, its tentacles hanging limply as it blared a hellish cacophony of sound from its grilled speaker. An evil collection of voices chanted something in a language that Varnus hoped never to understand amidst the garbled, daemonic sounds, bellows and sibilant whispers that blasted from the infernal thing. *Varnus,* he imagined a voice whispering sometimes amidst that din, his quietly spoken name almost hidden beneath the garbled, Chaotic roars and screams. Not a moment went by when the slave's eardrums were not assaulted by the insane sound. *Kill him,* he heard a reasoned voice say, in amongst the jumbled shrieks, horrified moaning, ceaseless chanting and the drone of static that was emerging from the Discord.

Varnus and Pierlo finished smearing the blood-mortar across the top of the stone slab just as another sharp note rang out, and they hurriedly stepped back onto the scaffold. Shrieks of agony rang out from those slaves that had been deemed too slow as they were disciplined by the overseers.

The slaves held onto the metal spars of the scaffold as it shook. The outside wall of the tower was not perfectly smooth, but rather was slightly stepped, each block overlapping the one below by half a hand-span. After every twenty layers of stones were laid, the mechanical scaffold would climb those narrow steps, pistons steaming as the spider-like legs of the framework pulled it further up the growing structure. It was an ingenious creation, Varnus had been forced to admit, though he hated it to the core of his being.

Varnus squatted atop the shuddering structure, holding on tight. Pierlo grinned at him, his eyes lit up feverishly. He guessed the man was losing his mind, for he almost seemed to be enjoying the hellish work. It took almost ten minutes for the framework of the scaffold to reposition itself, and it was the only real break that the slaves got until the shift rotation. The Discord blared its hateful sound.

'So what was it that you did before?' whispered Varnus. He knew his fellow slave's name, knew that he had lived his entire life in Shinar and that he had fathered no children. But he did not know what the man had done before the occupation. It was almost as if the man had been avoiding the subject, and Varnus had been waiting for this moment to ask him directly.

The blood-mortar smeared man looked away. 'What did you do?' whispered Varnus again, more forcefully. *Betrayer,* he thought he heard amidst the horrific sounds blaring from the speaker of the Discord.

'I was a manservant and bodyguard,' Pierlo said, his eyes flicking left and right madly, and it suddenly clicked where Varnus had seen him before.

'I have seen you before,' he said. Pierlo looked around sharply, his eyes blazing with unnatural heat. He shook his head vigorously.

'No, I have,' said Varnus, 'in the palace, right before the explosion.' *Kill him. Betrayer.*

Varnus shook his head and held his hands over his ears, moaning, trying to get the sound of the voices out of his head. This place and that damned Discord were driving him insane. Pierlo was not the only one losing his mind.

'You okay?' he heard Pierlo ask dimly, and he nodded his head.

'Someone will come,' Varnus said to himself. 'Someone will come to liberate Tanakreg.'

Pierlo giggled hysterically, shaking his head. 'No one will come. We will die here and our souls will join with Chaos.'

Anger filled Varnus suddenly, hot and quick. 'Don't say such things! The Emperor's light will protect us in the darkness.'

'Chaos calls us, brother. Can't you hear its voice?'

The Discord blared its monstrous sound.

*Kill him.*

Varnus closed his eyes tightly, and rocked back and forth slightly, trying to blot out the hideous din.

'Someone will come,' he said to himself. He felt the hated symbol embedded in his forehead writhe. He imagined that feelers from the vile thing were pushing through his skull, entering his brain.

He prayed to the Emperor, his mouth moving silently, but the harsh, discordant babble of the Discord seemed to get louder. The sound of the deep voices chanting within the noise pounded at his eardrums.

Someone will come, he thought. They had to.

A HISS OF PAIN emerged from Marduk's pallid lips as the chirurgeons removed the vambraces of his power armour from around his forearms with their spider-like, long, metal fingers. Patches of skin were ripped from his flesh as the curved armour plates were removed, and pinpricks of blood covered the areas of the skin that remained. Tiny, barbed thorns lined the inside of the vambrace; Marduk and his sacred armour were slowly becoming one. It was not uncommon amongst the Legion.

The hunched chirurgeons scraped and bowed before him, and shuffled off to place the bloody pieces of ceramite armour on a purple, velvet cloth alongside his gauntlet and under-glove. Marduk clenched his fists before him, looking at the translucent, bloodied and pockmarked musculature of his arms. They seemed almost unfamiliar to him.

Kol Badar led the morbid, monotonous chanting of the Host, and it carried across the open ground, accompanied by the pounding cadence of giant, piston driven hammers striking great metal drums. The roars and hellish screams of the heavily chained, restrained daemon engines mingled into the din of worship. Throughout the city, the sound of the ritual would be blaring from the daemon amps that accompanied the slave gangs.

Jarulek stood atop the altar, his blood-slick arms raised high as he rejoiced in the sound of worship washing over him. Burning braziers lit the altar and thick clouds of incense rose from the maws of bestial, brazen gargoyles. In the distance behind him was the Gehemahnet, the tower rising at a rapid pace. A hundred slaves knelt along the front of the altar, adding their own music to the cacophony of sound. They were restrained, their wrists bound to their ankles behind them, and they stared out at the gathered congregation of Word Bearers, their faces twisted in terror, anguish and despair.

Jarulek walked behind the line of kneeling slaves. He grasped the hair of one, pulled his head back and slashed his throat with a long, ceremonial knife. Already, hundreds of throats had been cut with that knife that day. The slave gasped, a wet, gurgling sound, and his lifeblood sprayed from the wound. He was pushed off the front of the altar by a pair of Word Bearers honoured to have been chosen for the duty, and the bound, dying man fell amongst the bloodless bodies piling within the metal trough at its foot. Hunched overseers dragged another slave forward to take his place, and Jarulek stepped to the next victim, swiftly cutting his throat, and he too was pushed from the altar.

The blood of the sacrifices ran down the inside of the trough and drained into a catchment where it pooled before being pumped through a twisted pipe that extended out to a large basin positioned before Marduk. It bubbled as it was filled with the warm lifeblood, and he dipped his bare arms into it.

Kol Badar was the first to step forward, still chanting, and Marduk reached up to the warlord's forehead with a bloody hand. He drew the four intersecting lines that formed the Chaos star in its most basic form across the Coryphaus's brow with his thumb. The huge warrior then closed his yellow, hate-filled eyes, and Marduk placed a bloody thumb mark on each eyelid.

'The great gods of Chaos guide you, warrior-brother,' Marduk intoned, and Kol Badar wheeled away. The next in line was Burias, the warrior's vicious, handsome face framed by his slick, black hair. He dropped to his knees before Marduk, an aspect of the ceremony that Kol Badar had been unable or unwilling to perform in his bulky Terminator armour. Marduk drew the star of Chaos upon his forehead and placed his thumbs to his eyelids.

'The great gods of Chaos guide you, warrior-brother,' Marduk intoned, and Burias filed away. The entire Host was to be marked, blessed by the gods before they entered sacred battle once more.

He felt the daemon stir within the chainsword at his side as blood dripped from his gore-slick forearms onto the hilt. Marduk smiled as he applied the blood to the face of a towering Anointed warrior. Soon, dear Borhg'ash, he thought.

Over the course of the next hour, Jarulek slashed the throats of hundreds of slaves, their sacrifice offered up to the glory of the gods of Chaos, and the stench of blood and death was strong. The droning chants of the Host continued unabated, and the last warrior-brother was blooded.

Jarulek descended imperiously from the altar, drenched in blood, and stepped lightly down the stairs, his long, ceremonial skin cloak flowing behind him. The entire Host dropped to one knee as the Dark Apostle reached the ground, and even the raging daemonic engines were cowed by the powerful figure. He walked towards Marduk, and the Dark Apostle raised the First Acolyte's head with gentle pressure under his chin. Jarulek drew the lines of the Chaos star upon Marduk's forehead and placed his bloody thumbprints against the skin of his eyelids.

His skin burned where the blood was smeared, pulsing with energy and potency. Opening his eyes, he saw that colours appeared more vivid than before, and he could clearly see a shimmering aura, the power of Chaos, surrounding the Dark Apostle like a ghostly, gossamer shroud. That power could always be felt when in Jarulek's presence, but it was rarely seen.

'The great gods of Chaos guide you, warrior-brother,' intoned Jarulek, his voice silken. Marduk rose to his feet and followed Jarulek as he strode back in front of his gathered warriors towards the altar steps. Kol Badar fell into step alongside Marduk, and without missing a word, Burias took over leading the ponderous chant of the Host.

Solemn and in silence, the Coryphaus and the First Acolyte followed the Dark Apostle back up the altar stairs. The Dark Apostle turned to face the gathered Host, and the pair stood a respectful distance back from him.

A chirurgeon shuffled forwards, accompanied by hunched, robed figures dragging a stepped platform behind them. The platform was placed before the Dark Apostle, and the chirurgeon climbed awkwardly atop it. Hissing steam, the platform rose until the robed figure stood at chest height to the Dark Apostle.

The chirurgeon then set to work, the blades and needles of its fingers piercing the flesh of Jarulek's face. Biting claws gripped the skin, holding it taught as the black robed figure sliced through Jarulek's pale flesh, cutting a neat strip from first one cheek, then the other. Blood ran freely from the wounds, before its flow was staunched by the tainted cells within its make up. The chirurgeon bowed and handed the two strips of flesh to the Dark Apostle.

Jarulek stood, holding the two rectangular, bloody ribbons high in the air for all to see. The pounding of mechanical drums ceased and Burias led the chanting of the warriors to a close.

'I honour these two warriors with passages from the Book of Lorgar, carved from my own flesh,' Jarulek said, his voice carrying effortlessly across the gathered mass. Already the red-raw rectangles on his cheeks were healing. Within a day the skin would be smooth and unmarked: two small patches of pale skin amidst a sea of scripture.

Marduk stepped forwards in front of Kol Badar, smirking at the flash of anger in the Coryphaus's eyes, and the skin of his left cheek was cut away by the chirurgeon. Speaking a blessing, Jarulek placed the scripture carved from his own skin upon the wound. There was a tingling, painful sensation as the flesh of the Dark Apostle knitted to his own. Bowing his head, he stepped aside.

'Go forth, my warrior-brothers,' said Jarulek once the second scripture had been fused to Kol Badar's cheek. 'Go forth, and kill in the name of blessed Lorgar, and know that the gods of Chaos smile upon you!'

# CHAPTER EIGHT

ICY WINDS WHIPPED at Marduk as he stood silhouetted atop the mountain ridge watching the approach of the Imperial scout vehicles below. The two-legged walkers, each manned by a single crewman, were climbing along a rocky ravine, making far faster progress than could be achieved by a man on foot. Clearing over three metres with each step, the walkers were making good progress, stepping easily over cracks in the rocky ground that fell away beneath them for hundreds of metres.

He had no concern about being spotted. A mere human eye would be unable to pick him out at such a distance, and the rocky terrain and gale force winds would make the crude sensors of the sentinels almost completely ineffective.

'Shall we gun the fools down?' asked Burias. 'The havocs of the VI Coterie have lascannons trained on them.'

'No, let the dogs down there take them,' said Marduk, indicating with a nod towards the figures waiting in ambush.

The three sentinels continued along the ravine, completely unaware of the cultists waiting in the rocks. A screaming rocket streamed through the air, slamming into the exposed cabin of the rearmost walker, which was annihilated in the billowing explosion.

The cult warriors wore pale cloaks as camouflage against the densely packed rock salt that was as hard as any stone, and they billowed out behind the men as they peppered the sentinels with las-fire.

The Imperial walkers began to edge backwards and returned fire, strafing the rocks with autocannons. Several of the cultists fell back as bullets ripped through their cloaks, but they had chosen a good place from which to launch their ambush and the rocks took the brunt of the fire.

One cloaked figure sprinted across the lip of the ravine, bullets spraying at his heels, and threw himself from the high rocks. He landed sprawled atop the roof panel of a sentinel and rose to one knee, a long blade appearing in his hand.

The sentinel crewman leant from the cabin, an autopistol raised, and fired off a quick burst across the rooftop of his cabin. The cultist grabbed the man's arm, pulling him further out of the cabin, and plunged his knife down into the man's neck.

The autocannon on the last sentinel went quiet as a lucky shot slammed into its pilot's head.

'Not bad,' grunted Marduk, as he began the descent towards the victorious cultists.

* * *

Karalos looked up sharply as he heard the shout. Brushing his long, unkempt hair back behind his ears with his blood-splattered hand, he sheathed his knife and stood atop the motionless Imperial sentinel. The mutilated, bloody corpse of the Imperial soldier was forgotten as he shielded his eyes to see what the commotion was.

His jaw dropped as he saw the two colossal, red-armoured warriors walking through the ravine towards his band of the faithful.

'Get everyone together,' he ordered. 'The Angels of the Word have come, as the Speaker foretold.'

The cultists' base of operations was high in the mountains, hidden from view from the sky by pale tarpaulins that draped over the low structures. Every member of the cult within Shinar had spent some time at the Camp of the Word, the old Speaker had told Marduk.

The Speaker was a withered man, the flesh all but wasted from his almost skeletal frame. He was blind, his vision long lost to the biting salt of Tanakreg. To Marduk he had looked pathetic.

'Bring me a hundred of your strongest warriors,' he had ordered the old man, 'and send the rest of your cultists out into the passes. The enemy will be soon be upon us.'

He had grown bored as the old man had babbled on, and had eventually put a bullet through his head. The one hundred men on their knees before him had not made a move as the shot had rung out, and Marduk had seen that Karalos had smiled as the old man was slain. Marduk liked the man; he had the soul of a true warrior of Chaos, even if he was just a wretched mortal.

'You men are blessed indeed,' Marduk said, 'for you have been chosen to receive a great gift, a boon of the great majesty of the warp. It is the Calling, and you are to be the hosts.'

Marduk began to chant, his voice effortlessly mouthing the difficult, unearthly language of the daemon. He felt the creature Borhg'ash within his chainsword stir at his words.

The kneeling men were surrounding by dozens of burning blood-candles, the light of their flames the only thing holding the darkness of the room at bay. They flickered as Marduk continued his incantation, the flames straining in towards the First Acolyte.

Whispers could be heard, flittering around the dark edges of the room, and Marduk welcomed them, for they spoke of the arrival of the Kathartes. The flickering of the candles increased, and a howling sound began to circle the gathered group as Marduk's voice rose.

The blood of the Speaker, pooling out on the floor of the room, began to bubble, and Marduk knelt and placed both hands in the rapidly heating liquid.

Marduk continued to speak the words of the Calling and stepped towards the kneeling figure of Karalos, placing a bloody hand on either side of the man's head. He held onto his head firmly, feeling the skull compress beneath his hands, and continued his complex incantation.

Karalos began to writhe and twitch, but Marduk did not release his grip, holding tightly to the man's head. The cultist's eyes began to bleed and blood seeped from his ears, but still Marduk continued to chant and clasp the man. He could feel the power of the warp opening up, its strength pulsing through his hands into the boiling brain of the man beneath him, but Karalos made not a sound, silently welcoming the beast that was emerging within his flesh.

With a final barked stream of daemonic words, Marduk pushed Karalos away from him. The man stood for a moment twitching, blood streaming from his eyes, before he fell to the ground, writhing and convulsing. A flickering blur seemed to overlap the thrashing figure, flashing between the body of a mortal man and the insubstantial form of something distinctly *other*. His tongue bulged from his mouth and he arched his back unnaturally, before breaking into severe muscle contractions that threw his body across the floor. Bones broke under his exertions and his spine twisted horribly, tendons and sinews tearing and ripping. The other men stood hurriedly and backed away from the wildly jerking man, horrified fascination and devotion on their faces.

The man's flickering flesh bulged unnaturally, as if things held within were trying to burst free, and he scratched frantically at the skin of his face, ripping bloody rents. The bones of his fingers lengthened and pushed through the skin of his fingertips, curving out into sharp talons, and he ripped at his skin and clothes, tearing them off in bloody strips.

He rolled over and over on the ground, ripping and tearing at his flesh frenziedly, every muscle of his body straining. Blood vessels bulged on his neck and at his temples, and he lacerated his skin with his long talons as he continued to spasm and convulse soundlessly.

His teeth lengthened into fine points and he bit into his own shoulder, ripping off chunks of meat.

Marduk smiled and crossed his arms over his chest.

The thing that had been Karalos entered even more frantic convulsions, ripping and tearing at its flesh, until it finally went still. It lay for a moment, bloody and broken, before it picked itself up from the ground and crouched, its skinless face turned towards the First Acolyte, staring at him with eyeless, bloody sockets. Almost its entire bloodied musculature was displayed, and only patches of raw, red skin clung to its frame. The hazy flickering still overlapped the creature, blurring its image slightly and hurting the eye.

An extra, backwards bending joint had formed in the lower leg of the daemon creature, in the manner of a bird, and long talons emerged from its toes. With a sickening, wet cracking sound, a pair of long, skeletal wings unfolded from the monster's back, sheets of bloody skin hanging limply between the bloody bones.

Opening its sharp-toothed, lipless maw wide, the daemon creature hissed hollowly at Marduk, like some newly hatched chick crying to its mother for food. He smiled broadly, the flickering candlelight glinting in his eyes.

'Karalos is no more,' spoke Marduk. 'He gave up his mortal vessel selflessly that this katharte might come into existence.'

The gathered men stared at the daemon with wide eyes. The air tasted electric; like the taste of Chaos.

'Now, all of *you* will selflessly give yourselves up to Chaos as good Karalos did,' said Marduk, 'for that is what I wish, and through my words you hear the desire of the gods themselves.'

The gathered men glanced warily at each other

'Well,' said Marduk to the daemon clawing at the floor in front of him, licking itself with a long, barbed tongue, 'call the flock.'

The men in the room fell to the ground as one, blood running from their eyes and ears, and they began to convulse.

'IT'S NOT RIGHT,' said Sergeant Elias of the 72nd Elysian storm troopers, hotly. 'We are the damned *elite*. We are not meant to be the grunts of the Imperium, plodding through the mud and crap getting gunned down in droves. We ain't that kind of regiment. We are...'

'The glory boys?' suggested Captain Laron wryly. The captain was a big, blond haired soldier, born of pure Elysian stock. Brash, strong and proud, he was the perfect captain for the brash, strong and proud storm troopers of the 72nd. If any other soldier or officer had spoken to him in such a way he would have had the man disciplined, but Elias had been his comrade for decades. He had fought alongside the man long before he had been captain, or even sergeant.

'Damn right we are!' said Elias with considerable passion. 'It's the job of the other regiments to grind mindlessly up the centre. We are the elite, fast in and fast out.'

'I'm sure the camp women appreciate that, sergeant.'

Elias laughed at that. 'But you know what I mean, sir. We don't have the sheer number of men or tanks to fight a conventional frontal assault, not against this enemy.'

'Who said we would be fighting a conventional frontal assault? The brigadier-general is not a damn fool.'

'I know that he is not, sir, but... I still don't know why we didn't just drop on Shinar and have this whole thing over with as soon as possible.'

'We do that and the entire damn regiment would be slaughtered. The air defences of Shinar are strong. Don't be thickheaded, Elias. Use your brains for a change and stop thinking with your damn balls!'

Elias grinned suddenly. 'I do have a big old pair of balls though, captain.'

'The sentinels on recon reported yet?'

'Another hour before the next report, sir.'

'Well, keep Colonel Boerl informed. If they see any enemy movement, report in immediately. We must secure those highlands. The brigadier-general says the enemy may be up there already. If that's the case, then without artillery support to make the bastards keep their heads down, we will be weathering the storm trying to land. If they are up there, it is not going to be easy to take it off them.'

'If anyone can take it off them, it'll be the 72nd,' said Elias, turning towards his superior. The captain was looking out across the plains to where the Adeptus Mechanicus battle force was making ready to move out.

'What do you make of them, sir?' asked Elias, indicating the massing Adeptus Mechanicus tech-guard with an incline of his head. Ever more of the disturbing warriors and war machines of Mars were disembarking from the wide-bodied Mechanicus loaders.

Captain Laron curled his lip in distaste. 'Never seen a concentration of them like this.'

The earth boomed as another of the massive cargo-transports of the Mechanicus landed, throwing up a cloud of salt grit. Hulking, slow moving, tracked crawler vehicles emerged from transports that had already landed, each led by a procession of censor waving, red-robed adepts of the Machine-God. From others came more of the pale fleshed tech-guard soldiers, marching in perfect, rectangular phalanx blocks, ten deep and a hundred wide.

Those phalanxes that had already disembarked were arrayed in their rigid formations, standing stone still on the salt plains, awaiting further instruction. Laron was certain that if no instruction came, they would stand unmoving, arrayed as they were until the cursed salt winds buried them. Even then, he supposed that the mindless things would be still, awaiting instruction.

From a distance, they might have been mistaken for regular Imperial Guard infantry platoons, though an observant onlooker would see that they were far too still to be completely human. They stood in serried ranks with lasguns held motionless over their chests, and many of their faces were all but obscured by deep visored helmets.

On closer inspection, many of the tech-guard soldiers looked less like Imperial Guardsmen and more like semi-mechanical servitors.

Servitors existed in every facet of Imperial life, fulfilling all manner of menial, dangerous tasks, but to see so many of them gathered together in one place for the sole purpose of war was highly disturbing to the Elysians. Servitors were neither truly alive nor truly dead. They had been human once, but all vestiges of that humanity had been long lost. Their frontal lobes had been surgically removed and their weak flesh improved upon with the addition of mechanics. These varied depending on the task that they were required to perform. They might have had their arms removed and replaced with power lifters or diamond-tipped drills the size of a man's leg to work in one of the millions of manufactorums across the Imperium, or be hard-wired into the logic engines of battle cruisers to maintain the ships' support functions.

The tech-guard soldiers arrayed upon the plains were created specifically for the arena of war. Amputated arms had been replaced with heavy weaponry, and targeting sensors and arrays filled the sockets where fleshy eyeballs had been plucked. Power generators were built onto the shoulders of some, and they stood immobile beside gun-servitors, cables and wiring trailing between the pair. Others had single, large servo-arms replacing one or more of their removed limbs, giving them an ungainly, limping gait as servos struggled under the weight. These mechanical arms were as easily capable of ripping a man's head from his shoulders as lifting heavy equipment, and some bore oversized rotary blades or power drills that could cut or punch through the heaviest of armour.

Amongst the phalanxes were smaller contingents of heavier, tracked servitor units. The lower bodies of these servitors had been removed so that they had become one with their means of conveyance. These bore heavier payloads of ammunition that spooled into the large, multiple barrelled cannons that replaced the organic right arms of the servitors.

In between the ranks of Martian foot soldiers were tracked crawlers, one for every phalanx. They were Ordinatus Minoris crawlers, and each was the length of three Leman Russ battle tanks. They had two, wide track units, one at the front and one at the rear, and between these was supported the mass of the war machine. Heavy girders and steel struts supported huge weapons, and each crawler had dozens of red-robed adepts and servitors as crew. Steel ladders rose to the control cabins that were offset from the main guns. Laron did not recognise the weapons that these behemoths of steel and bronze bore, but the massive, steaming couplings and humming generators upon their backs spoke of immense contained power.

But these were as nothing to the sheer scale of the crawler that was emerging slowly from a lander of truly giant proportions.

'Emperor above,' said Elias. 'Would you look at the damn size of that thing!'

It bore a resemblance to the Ordinatus Minoris crawlers in the way that a fully grown adult bears a resemblance to its mewling newborn. It rolled forward on what must have been sixteen tracked crawler units, led by a stream of tech-priests. The size of the smaller tracked crawlers were rendered insignificant next to the immense vastness of the Ordinatus machine.

It was the size of a city block and was protected with thick layers of armoured plating. More than ten storeys of platforms rose up around the massive central weapon that the Ordinatus supported, a weapon the size of a small cruiser that ran down the entire length of the immense machine. Criss-crossing lattice works of steel supported gantries running around the circumference of the weapon, and a pair of quad-barrelled anti-aircraft guns rotated atop the control cabin above the highest deck level. Giant, claw-like, spiked arms were held aloft on either side of the Ordinatus, and Laron guessed that the huge piston engines behind them would drive them into the ground when the Ordinatus was readying to fire, to give the machine additional stability. That a thing that size needed stabilising legs was testament to the awesome power that it could unleash.

'Impressive,' said Laron somewhat reluctantly.

The sergeant put a hand to his ear as his micro-bead clicked.

'The Valkyries are ready and waiting, captain. They fly on your say-so.'

'Good. Colonel Boerl will be joining us on the drop.'

'I feel safer already.'

'Cut the crap, Elias,' snapped Laron. Even with Elias, he had his limits. The colonel of the 72nd was a hardened veteran, and he would hear nothing against the man.

'Let's go take those damn highlands.'

HE RAISED HIS crozius before him. Blood hissed along the length of the hallowed staff of office, boiling and spitting under the surging electricity coursing up the haft. Once it had represented faith in the Imperium, belief in the Emperor and the optimistic confidence that the Crusades pushing out from great Terra would bring enlightenment to the galaxy.

Spitting, he sneered at the pathetic sentiment. Now he stood on Terra once more, as the greatest battle in the history of mankind was unfolding.

His crozius was dedicated to beings of far greater power than the deceitful Emperor. It represented faith as it always had, inspiring devotion and fervour in the Legion as it smote the non-believers, but this was a far more pure faith than merely a shallow belief and optimism that looked to a bright future for mankind.

This was *true* faith. The Emperor had been wrong. There *were* omnipotent gods in existence, and they wielded power beyond imagining. No cold, distant deities that watched the plight of their followers from afar, these gods were active and could affect a very real physical presence in the galaxy.

His crozius had been consecrated in the blood of those sacrificed to these great powers, ignorant fools who would not accept or embrace the true powers within the universe.

And now he fought on Terra, alongside holy primarchs, mighty heroes and noble warriors who had embraced the true faith.

The eager young Captain Kol Badar looked at him, passion and fervour in his eyes. His First Acolyte, the clever Jarulek, looked to him for the word to engage. Raising his sanctified crozius of the true faith high into the air, he incanted from the Epistles of Lorgar. With a fiery roar, the Word Bearers of the XII Grand Company launched themselves once more into the bloody fray.

The Warmonger was stirred from his thoughts of battles long past as his receptive sensors picked up faint reverberations in the air from over the horizon to the east.

'The enemy approaches, First Acolyte Marduk,' he intoned via vox transmission. 'The brethren wait in readiness.'

# BOOK TWO: CONTENTION

*'Victory attained through violence is victory indeed. But when the enemy turns on itself – that is the essence of true, lasting victory.'*

– Kor Phaeron – Master of the Faith

# CHAPTER NINE

THE NIGHT WAS lit up with hundreds of lancing beams of lascannons and super-heated streams of plasma. Flames coughed from the barrels of autocannons, and fast burning missiles hissed across the sky, leaving spirals of smoke in their wake.

Storm clouds rumbled overhead, the sound all but drowned out by the din of battle. Rain began to fall over the mountains in driving sheets.

Massive, eight-legged daemon engines strained at the chained restraints locking them in place, each infernal machine overseen by a dozen attendants. They roared into the night sky, metallic tendons bulging, and blazing comets of deep red fire burst from the daemonic hell-cannons built into their carapaces, screaming up towards the Imperial aircraft as they strafed in once more.

Lascannons speared up through the darkness. Flames burst over one of the low-flying Imperial fighters as a wing was shorn off, and it spiralled down into a ravine where it exploded deafeningly. The cockpit of another was ripped apart as lascannons punched through it, and the fighter exploded in mid air, debris and flames raining down along the ridge top. The cover of night did nothing to hamper the warrior-brothers of the Legion, nor the daemons that infused their deadly war machines. The darkness was pierced equally well, whether it was due to genetic modification and acute auto-senses or daemonic witch sight.

A nearby ridge erupted in a series of rising explosions as a stream of bombs struck, and Marduk swore. The enemy had brought in far more air support than even Kol Badar had expected. The fool had not predicted this.

Arcing beams of spitting multi-lasers strafed along the ridge, accompanied by the resonant, barking thud of rapid-firing heavy bolters. Rock and dust were kicked up, and one of the daemon engines was obliterated in a screaming inferno. The fiery explosion rose high into the air, but was sucked back down sharply as the daemon essence of the machine was returned to the warp.

Marduk growled as bullets ripped up the earth less than a metre from where he stood, rocks ricocheting off his ancient, deep-red armour, but he continued to stare angrily down towards the broken ground below his vantage point. While the enemy occupied Marduk's forces, holding the high ground with strafing runs and bombing attacks, other aircraft had hovered briefly beyond the range of the Word Bearer's fire and disgorged their human cargoes. With his targeters at full zoom, Marduk had seen the Guardsmen rappel from these hovering aircraft, disembarking onto the rough ground. He had lost sight of them as they traversed the massive cracks and faults, but he knew that they were climbing slowly towards him in a vain attempt to take the commanding location. Doubtless, hundreds of similar aircraft had dropped their cargoes of Guardsmen all along the rough ground behind the ridges occupied by his warriors, and were even now climbing up. Fools, he thought. No matter how many of them there were, did they really think that mere mortals could dislodge Astartes? Their arrogance was astounding.

'We have engaged the enemy, First Acolyte Marduk,' came the vox transmission from the Warmonger.

'Acknowledged,' returned Marduk as yet another strafing run of aircraft screamed overhead, peppering the Legion with gunfire. 'Take them down, havoc teams,' he snarled into his local vicinity vox.

'Movement,' said Burias, his witch sight keener than the eyesight of the other Chaos Space Marines.

'Where?' barked Marduk, squinting his eyes where the Icon Bearer pointed.

'There, lord. Looks like around... eight Imperial platoons, plus heavy weapon platoons.'

'Bah, the wretches won't get anywhere.'

Burias lowered his head deferentially, rainwater running down his pale face. 'With respect, lord, their mortars could prove... vexing. If they make the rocks there,' he said, indicating a crop of sharp boulders, 'they could lob their shells over the lip of the ridge, and it would be... irritating for us to remove them from the position. And they bear lascannons as well, First Acolyte.'

'You fear their guns, Burias?' asked Marduk.

'No, First Acolyte, I am merely making an observation.'

'It sounded weak to my ears,' growled Marduk, but he saw the sense in what his Icon Bearer had said. 'Choose a small team from one of the coteries. Get around behind those mortars and clear them out of the rocks, if they make it that far.'

Burias's face split into a feral grin. 'I will take members of my brethren, if it pleases you, First Acolyte.'

'Fine. Go.'

'Thank you, First Acolyte,' said Burias, handing his icon to Marduk. Its bulk would merely hamper his mission.

'Take out the guns, and then move to the rear of these weaklings. If there are any of them left,' remarked Marduk.

Burias dropped to one knee swiftly, before stalking off through the gunfire to gather his warriors.

'Good hunting, Burias-Drak'shal,' the First Acolyte said.

CORPORAL LEIRE PYRSHANK held the controls of the Marauder bomber tightly in his gloved hands as he guided the massive aircraft through the darkness. The dark clouds far beneath the aircraft crackled with lightning, and the massive red planet Korsis hung in the black sky overhead, so close that he imagined he could land the heavy bomber there if he wished.

He also wished that he couldn't hear a thing over the roaring drone of the four turbine engines, but unfortunately he could.

'You'd think they were the High Lords of Terra, the way they acted,' said Bryant's incessant voice in his ear. The navigatius operator seemed incapable of remaining silent for more than a few minutes at a time. 'Bit on the dim side, though. All brawn and light on the brain matter. Still, the way they held themselves, looking down on us Marauder crewmen, I was happy to clean them out. The stupid frakker couldn't have had nothin'! But he stayed in. I think it was only 'cos he was a damn glory boy storm trooper, didn't want to fold to the likes of me. He didn't say a word when I won, neither. One of his eyes just sorta twitched, and he stormed away from the table, taking his muscle-bound cronies with him. Five ration packs, a bottle of amasec and five lho-sticks I took off them. Oh, you missed a great game, Pyrshank, a great game indeed.'

'How far to the target?'

'A while yet. Man, it was good. Ended up drinking the whole bottle of amasec with Kashan, you know, that bomber-tech girl from the 64th? Did I show you the scratches she left on my back? That girl,' said Bryant, 'she's really something.'

'How about you cut the damned chatter and concentrate on your screens, huh?'

Bryant merely laughed. 'Thirteen five to target.'

The navigatius operator leant up against the side window of the cockpit and whistled in awe. 'Damn, I'm glad I'm not down there in that mess. I haven't seen a firefight like this since Khavoris IV, and the Guard units there suffered something like eighty per-cent casualties. The whole mountain range is lit up. '

'It happens in times of war, Bryant,' said Pyrshank. 'I can't see a damned thing out here.'

'Just use the nav-screens. You don't *need* to see a damn thing. Ten five to target.'

There was a moment of blessed silence. If you could call the deafening noise of four "ear bleeders" silence. That was when he felt the cockpit rock, as if with a sudden impact.

'What the hell was that?' asked Bryant.

'I dunno,' said Pyrshank. 'Could have been some bird, I 'spose.'

'Pretty damn high for a bird,' replied Bryant. 'Have you seen any birds on this salt heap of a planet?'

'No,' said Pyrshank. The entire breadth of indigenous wildlife of the cursed planet seemed to consist of the brine-flies that thrived in vast clouds along the banks of the salt lakes, and the tiny grey lizards that ate the brine-flies.

The cockpit shuddered once more, and there was a tearing sound of shearing metal.

Bryant released the clips of the harness crossing his shoulders and removed his rebreather mask. He pressed himself against the cold side window, trying to look down the side of the bomber's fuselage.

'What in the Emperor's name was that?' he asked.

'Herdus, can you see anything out there?' said Pyrshank into his comm unit. There was no response from the front-gunner, who sat in the forward facing turret just below the cockpit.

'Herdus, can you see anything?'

Bryant swore, and Pyrshank looked over at him. His eyes widened as he saw the skinless creature grinning in at him from outside the cockpit window.

'Throne!' he uttered, recoiling from the hideous visage. Bryant fell back from the window, a cry of horror and shock escaping his lips.

The creature began scrabbling at the corners of the cockpit window, its long talons scratching at the edges of the clear panels. Finding no opening, it reared its skinless head back and slammed it into one of the panels of the window with sickening force.

Pyrshank swore as he realised he had turned the bomber into a dive, and he pulled sharply at the controls. He saw motion behind him and turned his head to see Bryant, a laspistol in his hand. Before he could shout, the navigatius operator fired, and a neat hole was seared through the window and into the creature. It screamed horribly, but the sound was lost amidst the roaring of the air rapidly evacuating the cockpit. The roaring died as quickly as it had begun and Pyrshank saw that the horrifying creature had inserted a long, bloody talon into the neat hole.

A second later, the entire window panel was ripped clear and the skinless daemon crawled into the cockpit.

Without his harness, Bryant was ripped out of the bomber instantly, sucked out into the icy, airless night. Pyrshank struggled frantically with his own harness, escape from the hideous creature his only thought.

He felt his stomach heave and he vomited inside his rebreather unit. But it didn't matter. The daemon grabbed his neck, talons biting deeply.

With a powerful movement, Corporal Leire Pyrshank's throat was ripped out. As the Marauder bomber began its steep dive towards the gathering storm clouds and mountain peaks below, the katharte kicked away from the aircraft, leathery wings beating hard.

'SHALL WE ENGAGE them, First Acolyte? They are within bolter range,' said a warrior-brother by vox transmission.

'Not yet,' said Marduk. 'Wait until they are closer. Conserve your bolts.'

'As you wish, First Acolyte,' replied the man.

The aeronautical barrage had, if anything, intensified. They were trying to make them keep their heads down as the Guardsmen below advanced, Marduk reasoned. But then moments ago it had ceased entirely, just as the Guardsmen below were almost in position. It didn't make much sense, but then Marduk had long stopped trying to make sense of the Imperium. He would never understand those who chose to worship the shattered corpse of an Emperor whose time was long past rather than embrace the very real gods of Chaos.

From the reports coming in, it looked as if somewhere in the realm of a hundred aircraft had been confirmed destroyed. Around ten bombers had fallen from the darkness of high atmosphere, crashing to earth. Marduk had smiled as he felt the Kathartes kill.

He could see the Guardsmen clearly, their faces all but covered by their grey-blue helmets and dark visors. Sheets of rain drove against them.

Bolter fire barked suddenly, and Marduk turned with a snarl to see which champion had allowed his coterie to open fire.

''Ware the sky,' came a vox from the Warmonger, and Marduk cursed again. He looked up into the heavens to see hundreds of dark shapes dropping like stones. He raised his bolt pistol and began to fire.

COLONEL BOERL HELD his arms clasped tightly to his side as he plummeted through the darkness out of the storm clouds towards the flashes of gunfire marking the target ridge below. Icy cold air and rain whipped at him as he fell, and his heart raced with the thrill.

Forty-two thousand, nine hundred and twenty-seven drops, and over three hundred combat drops, the most of any Guardsman within the 72nd. And still it gave him an adrenaline rush like nothing else he had ever experienced.

He and the other drop-troopers had launched themselves from their Valkyries at extreme high atmosphere, around forty kilometres above the ground, higher even than Marauder bombers operated when unleashing their deadly payloads. It was necessary to jump from such a height in order to avoid detection. Breathing through respirators, their bodies enclosed in tight-fitting jumpsuits beneath their reinforced carapace armour, the storm troopers had been free-falling for well over five minutes, reaching terminal velocity within the first thirty seconds of the drop, and leaving the cracking sounds of sonic booms in their wake as they hurtled towards the ground at phenomenal speed.

The ground was rising up with astounding swiftness and Boerl made ready. The arms of the grav-chute were automatically timed to unfold and engage at the last possible moment, and he watched the click counter in his visor drop as he neared the ground.

Pulling his arms out and splaying his legs suddenly, he slowed his descent fractionally and spun himself expertly in the air. The grav-chute engaged, barely five metres above the ground, and his descent dropped in an instant to a safe speed.

His hellpistol was already in his hand, and Boerl rolled expertly as he hit the wet ground, rising to one knee and blasting the over-charged laspistol into the back of a towering, power armoured figure. With a flick of his hand, he nudged the release button on his bulky grav-chute, and it dropped to the ground behind him. His storm troopers landed around him, rolling smoothly to their feet, and began laying down a blanket of fire with their hellguns. Super-heated air hissed as Sergeant Langer unleashed the power of his meltagun, the white-hot blast scything through the ceramite armour of another enemy.

The other Guard units would be pushing up at the enemy from below, just entering range as the drop-troopers landed. They were well drilled, and he knew that the timing would be perfect. The micro-bead in his ear confirmed this expectation and he made his commands, short and clipped, as he ordered the platoons to converge. The enemy were strong, but they were vastly outnumbered. The Elysians would have the position within the hour.

He was leading one contingent of the 72nd storm troopers, the other two arms of the elite regiment landing at the other main targets.

Tearing the respirator mask from his face, it retracted automatically into the chest unit of his carapace armour. 'For the Emperor and the 72nd!' he bellowed, his powerful voice carrying over the frantic sound of battle.

He drew his power sword in one swift movement as a huge, dark-red armoured warrior lashed out at him with a screaming chainaxe, and he raised his blade to block the swing. The unholy strength behind the blow was immense and he was knocked backwards even as his humming weapon carved into the axe, sparks and shearing metal screaming as chain teeth were ripped apart. The massive brute raised its heavy foot surprisingly fast and kicked Boerl squarely in the chest.

He was knocked back once again, stumbling over the rocky ground. It felt as though a truck had hit him, all the breath knocked from his body. The Chaos Marine loomed over him, savouring the kill. He threw his sparking chainaxe to the ground and raised his bolt pistol to execute the colonel. A blast of las-fire struck his knee joint and Boerl heard a deep, rumbling growl of anger as the Chaos Marine's leg gave out beneath him. Swinging his bolt pistol around, the traitor fired and a storm trooper was killed instantly as the bolt-round exploded in his chest cavity.

His sacrifice was not completely in vain, however, for it allowed the colonel a moment to gather himself, and he surged forwards, slashing his shimmering blade across the warrior's chest, cutting through ceramite easily and scoring a deep wound.

The blow would have killed any lesser man, but the Chaos Marine was Astartes, and he grabbed Boerl around the throat, crushing the life out of him. Frantically, he thrust with his power sword, the blade entering the warrior's gut, sliding easily through his body and emerging from his back. Still the warrior continued to fight, and Boerl began to see stars before his eyes. He managed to raise his hellpistol, pushing it into the Chaos Marine's neck, slipping it between armour plates, and he fired once, twice. Hot blood spurted from the wound, spraying Boerl's face, his skin burning.

The grip around his neck slackened, and he kicked back from the massive warrior, who even on his knees was the same height as the colonel. Still the warrior was not dead, and he raised his bolt pistol. Gathering as much strength as he could muster, Boerl swung his power sword into the warrior's armoured head, the humming blade embedding deep in his skull. At last the warrior fell, the power sword slipping easily from the wound, blood spitting as it boiled on the super-heated blade.

Las-fire erupted as the other Guardsmen arrived, lending the storm troopers additional weight of fire. There was a roar of daemonic fury, and Boerl saw a Guardsman lifted five metres into the air by a pair of immense, mechanical claws before being ripped in half and hurled into the darkness. His eyes widened as he took in the mass of the hellish thing.

It was a massive, eight-legged machine. No, not truly a machine, he realised with horror as he saw the fleshy torso that erupted from the body of the beast. Four times the size of a man, its black skin covered in glowing, blasphemous runes, the beast seemed to blend into the armoured machine that dwarfed it. The metal plates on the infernal thing rippled like muscle, and blood hissed from wounds scored on its armoured hide.

It stepped forwards, its eight metal limbs ripping free from chains that bound it to rune-encrusted stone blocks. Black-clad figures recoiled from the thing, and several of them were instantly killed as it impaled their bodies on spiked claws that unfolded from its legs. Flames belched from its weapon units, engulfing a group of Guardsmen who screamed in agony as the flesh dissolved from their bones.

'Langer!' roared Boerl. 'Take that thing out!'

The Guardsman at his side blasted another searing beam of death with his meltagun and nodded to his colonel.

'Storm troopers, with me!' shouted Boerl, and with Langer at his side, he charged towards the towering daemonic war engine, blasting at Chaos Marines that moved to intercept them. Several of the storm troopers were hacked to the ground by sweeping blows from the massive warriors, and others were torn to shreds by bolter fire. Langer ducked beneath a swipe from a Chaos Space Marine's barbed, short blade, and Boerl carved his power sword through the warrior's leg as he barrelled past, neatly severing the limb at the thigh. Still the warrior did not drop its weapons, despite the horrendous wound, and it fired as it fell, bolt-rounds thudding into the storm trooper beside Boerl, exploding his chest.

A shot smacked into Langer's leg and he screamed in pain as he fell, his leg shattered. A power armoured foot slammed down onto his neck, silencing him instantly, and another running storm trooper was felled by the Chaos Marine's swinging forearm, his neck cracking audibly. Boerl stumbled, a fortunate accident that saved his life as self-propelled bolts screamed just over his head. He fell to his knees before the monster, and a burst of lasgun fire smashed it backwards. Boerl rose from the ground, impaling the Chaos Marine through the neck with his humming blade. The stink of the monster was staggering, and he gagged as he ripped the power sword free.

Dropping his hellpistol and sheathing his blade, Boerl swept up the meltagun from Langer's lifeless hands and scrambled to his feet, continuing his advance towards the towering war machine that was killing his men in droves.

Its back was to him. He raised the powerful weapon, aiming towards the beast's horned head. Wires sprouted from the back of its blasphemous cranium. He squeezed the trigger. The searing, white-hot beam of super-heated energy screamed towards the target, but as if alerted by some daemonic prescience, the creature merely swung its head to one side and the blast passed harmlessly by.

An explosion detonated behind Colonel Boerl and he was thrown through the air, arms and legs flailing. He crashed to the wet ground, still clutching the melta gun, and grazed one of the war engine's spider-like legs. Pain ripped through him as his shoulder was sliced open by the sharp blades positioned on the daemonic machine's leg. Oblivious to him, it took another step, and Boerl found himself directly beneath the massive thing, lying flat on his back as hissing blood-oil dripped down upon him.

Without hesitation he swung the meltagun and shouted wordlessly as he fired it straight into the underbelly of the mechanical beast. The searing beam tore up through the creature, and a splash of hot liquid washed over the colonel, burning his skin and hissing on his armour.

The daemon engine roared horribly and its legs began to buckle. Scrambling frantically, Boerl pushed himself from beneath the monster before it fell. With the roaring, sucking sound of air filling a vacuum, the daemon essence of the machine vacated its host, and Boerl felt himself reel, his head spinning. A blast of energy knocked him from his feet, and all the Guardsmen within a radius of twenty metres of the departing daemon spirit were thrown to the ground. The Chaos Space Marines were buffeted, but retained their feet, and they fired into the prone Elysians, executing them mercilessly with head shots.

Colonel Boerl was spared this fate as a platoon of Elysians swept into the area, las-fire pounding into the Chaos Marines. It took dozens of shots before any of the traitors fell, and they exacted a heavy toll on the Guardsmen, killing more than ten for each one of their own that succumbed to the weight of fire.

'Facing heavy resistance,' came Captain Laron's voice through Boerl's micro-bead. The captain had led one of the other assaults, targeting an area some five kilometres away.

'No shit,' he muttered as he picked himself up from the ground, retrieving a lasgun from a fallen Elysian and firing it into the Chaos Space Marines.

Burias rose from his position and moved swiftly across the rocky ground, running low and fast. He covered the open ground quickly and dropped behind a group of boulders.

Pausing for a moment, he looked out through the darkness that was as clear as day to his eyes. Rain and wind whipped at him, but he didn't care. The other members of his team were all but invisible, even to his eyes, as they moved through the night. They were spread wide and were closing on their prey swiftly. They had fanned out in a wide arc, heading away from the enemy, racing through ravines and massive cracks in the mountainous terrain before swinging back around to encircle the foe.

This was the kind of warfare that Burias lived for, and he excelled at it. He had built a fierce reputation amongst the Host for his hunting and stealth missions, and the Coryphaus would often utilise his particular talents to sow terror and throw the enemy into disarray while the warlord led the main attacking force into the heart of the enemy's battle force.

Burias scrambled on all fours over the rain-slick boulders and ran into a tight ravine that rose up on either side. Water was flowing down through the ravine. He moved swiftly and quietly despite the bulk of his power armour, leaping lightly from rock to rock and stepping easily over cracks that dropped hundreds of metres beneath him.

The walls of the ravine dropped away in front of him suddenly, exposing a massive drop, and without hesitation Burias leapt, clearing the five metre expanse with ease, landing smoothly and continuing his kilometre-eating pace. His mental map of the area told him that they were close. He heard the heavy thump of mortars and picked up his pace, snarling.

He scrambled up a steep, near vertical, rain-slick incline without pause and leapt from the top to a nearby boulder, and from there to another. Up and down the broken, steep ground he traversed, leaping and rolling, always in motion. The mortars thumped again, closer this time, and he leapt onto a steep wall of rock, pulling himself swiftly up. The cliff-face angled beyond vertical, a dangerous overhang with a drop of hundreds of metres. With a snarl, he kicked off the rock face, lunging for a handhold near the lip of the rock. He grabbed it one-handed and hung there for a moment before he secured another handhold and hauled himself over the edge.

Burias paused, crouching for a moment, scenting the air. The rain dulled his senses somewhat, but the taste of meat in the air was strong. Then he was moving again, running along a thin ridge of rock barely two hand spans wide. The drop on one side must have been almost a thousands metres, but he traversed it at a full run before dropping behind some boulders. Glancing down, he grinned and looked back the way he had come, seeing the dark shapes of several of his brethren racing swiftly across the rocks. The thud of mortars was right beneath him.

He leapt from his position out over the drop, landing on a ledge on the other side. He waited for a few breaths, and then launched himself over the edge. He landed behind some large rocks and waited for the heavy weapons to fire once more. As they did, he rose from his position and ghosted up behind the Guardsmen, who were still oblivious to their imminent demise and were quickly reloading the six powerful mortars set on the rocky ground.

Grabbing the first Guardsman from behind by his helmeted head, Burias pulled him violently backwards, ramming his massive knifeblade into the base of his neck. The blade, easily the length of a man's forearm, severed the spinal cord and continued up into the brain. Burias hurled him away.

The other Guardsmen gaped in horror at the red-clad devil in their midst, even as Burias leapt amongst them. He ripped his blade across the throat of one and plunged it into the neck of another with the return, backhand motion.

Another Word Bearer loomed up behind the group, and a further Guardsman died as a bony, bladed arm was rammed into his back. The daemon within that warrior-brother had already surged to the fore, Burias saw, as the possessed Word Bearer ripped the fallen Guardsman's throat out with a tusk-filled, gaping wide maw.

Feeling Drak'shal begin to surface as the daemon responded to the presence of its kin, a jolt of daemonic power and adrenaline shot through Burias's body. He snarled and leapt at the remaining Guardsmen, who had recovered themselves enough to have drawn laspistols, at least those that were not already scrabbling over rocks in a vain attempt to escape.

Las-fire streaked past Burias's head, singeing the skin, and he grabbed the offender's hand, crushing bones as he turned the pistol away from him. Pulling sharply forwards, he ripped the man's shoulder from its socket and drove his blade up into the man's stomach, twisting it mercilessly.

A blast of las-fire struck him from behind and Burias turned, hurling the body of the man he had just gutted into the shooter. The power of the daemon within rose screaming to the surface and Burias-Drak'shal leapt on the man as he tried to rise. He lifted the trooper into the air, holding him by the head and the groin, and he brought his hands together sharply. The man was neatly folded, his back cracking sickeningly under the force.

Other possessed Chaos Marines leapt from the rocks above, crashing down through the rain to land amongst the enemy, hacking and slaughtering, ripping and rending. Blood sprayed the rocks as the Guardsmen died.

Letting the power of the daemon overcome him, Burias-Drak'shal and his possessed comrades slew until there were no more foes to kill. He stood, chest heaving for a moment before leaping off through the darkness on all fours, scenting other enemies nearby. He howled into the night and felt the rest of his pack spread out to either side of him, to encircle the next gathering of meat.

HEAVY BOLTER FIRE tore through the Guardsmen, taking down five men in a screaming burst. Their bodies were ripped apart, bolts tearing through armour as if it were made of paper, and punching through the soft flesh beneath. Blood sprayed out, and Boerl swung his head to see a massive armoured shape turning its rapid-firing guns in his direction. It was at least five metres tall and nearly as wide.

'Emperor above,' swore Boerl as fresh shells fed into the twin-linked heavy bolters of the Dreadnought, and it unleashed its barrage of deadly fire. He leapt to the side, rolling as the heavy bolts tore through more of his men, and came to his feet running.

He blasted a Chaos Space Marine in the head with his lasgun as he moved, the shot striking the warrior's helmet, rocking him backwards but failing to pierce the powerful armour. Ignoring the reeling Chaos Space Marine, Boerl charged towards the towering Dreadnought. He reached to his belt and pulled loose a melta bomb as he neared the hellish machine annihilating his men.

The thing was huge and the ground reverberated with its step, servos whining. Skulls and helmets, rammed upon black iron spikes, adorned the machine's shoulders. There were helmets of loyal Space Marines there as well as dozens of skulls, some human, but many from various xenos creatures.

The Dreadnought swung a heavy, taloned fist at Boerl, flames gushing out from the underslung flamer on the massive, armoured arm. Ducking the blow, the colonel hissed as the flames washed over his back, and he almost fell to the ground as overwhelming pain assailed him. Gritting his teeth, he flicked the activation switch of the deadly melta-bomb and hurled it onto the armoured bulk of the machine. It struck a pitted and inscribed armoured shoulder plate above the heavy bolters that continued to roar, flames spitting from the barrels. It clanked loudly as it stuck fast, the powerful electro-magnets stuck fast to the metal.

Boerl ducked another swinging arm that would have ripped his head from his shoulders and leapt away before the melta-bomb did its destructive work. Rolling to see the results of his handiwork, his heart sank as the Dreadnought picked the grenade off its armoured bulk and flicked it away with its surprisingly dextrous power claw.

Boerl scrambled to his feet just as the Dreadnought swung its heavy bolters around to bear, and dozens of shots ripped through his armour. The Dreadnought continued to pump shot after shot into the colonel long after he was dead, keeping his body dancing in the air for a moment. Colonel Boerl's body was finally torn completely in half, and it fell to the ground, bloody and unrecognizable.

'DEATH TO THE False Emperor!' roared the Warmonger as it stepped forwards. It smashed a mechanical foot down onto the shattered body of the pathetic wretch, grinding it into the wet ground.

Where was this battle taking place? The thought swam through what remained of the Warmonger's ancient mind. Where was Lorgar? He scanned the battlefield quickly, but could see no sign of the revered primarch. No matter. Here were enemies of his lord, and he would allow them no quarter.

The Warmonger opened up once again with his heavy bolters, seeing the weakling men before him ripped apart as he unleashed his deadly salvo. He began to advance once more, death roaring from his guns. One lightly armoured soldier stumbled too close, and the Dreadnought swept him up in its massive power claw, lifting the wretch high, so that all his brethren could see his demise. The Warmonger squeezed, servos in his claw whining, and the man broke. He was hurled to the ground, a bloody and very dead corpse.

'For the Warmaster!' roared the Dreadnought, and continued to kill.

MARDUK CHANTED FROM the *Epistles of Lorgar* as he killed, filling the Word Bearers with fiery hatred for the weakling foe as they slew. He saw the Guardsmen fall away from him in horror, and he imagined that in death they heard the truth in his words: that the Emperor was a false deity, a fraud and a traitor, and that the bearers of the truth were murdering them. They cried out to their fraudulent god for mercy, but his impotence was clear when no salvation came to save them. In death they could see that only the gods of Chaos were worthy of worship.

The sheer audacity and arrogance of the foe astounded Marduk. Against any other foe, a combined assault of air-lifted infantry, supported by heavy weapons and timed to strike in unison with an elite force dropping from the sky, may have worked. To hammer the foe first with barrages from the air, these *were* good tactics against any *other* foe. Indeed, they were tactics that Kol Badar made use of frequently.

But to have the misconstrued belief that these tactics would work against the Word Bearers, Chaos Space Marines, and that these pitiful men could drive them from their positions was beyond the First Acolyte's comprehension.

It was true that the enemy were great in number. Hundreds more troops were dropping through the storm clouds every minute, though they were not as heavily armed or armoured (he scoffed at this even as he thought it) as were the first to land. These men were regular Imperial Guardsmen. But numbers meant nothing against Chaos Space Marines, and Marduk was certain that the battle would soon be over.

The daemon within his chainsword was feeding well. He carved the screaming blade down into the collarbone of another Guardsman, its teeth biting deep, ripping and tearing through armour, bone and soft flesh. His strength was behind the blow, and the eagerness of the daemon drove the whirring teeth deeper. The man fell to the ground, a bloody rent ripped to his sternum.

Marduk swayed to the side and a missile screamed past him. He continued quoting from the Epistles without pause.

'*The favoured son of Chaos, Our lord and our mentor, The bearer of truth. He is with us today, And upon all the battlefields where we strive, Bringing faith to the faithless, And death to the heedless. Always he watches, and lends us his strength.*' he quoted.

'Hear me, my brothers! Lorgar watches us! Make him proud!' roared Marduk, blasting the head from an enemy with his bolt pistol and hacking down another with his chainsword.

The Word Bearers fought with a fury and hatred that had been nurtured for thousands of years, and despite being heavily outnumbered, they were butchering the Imperials that continued to drop in.

The dark shape of a possessed warrior-brother appeared atop a rocky outcrop, and it leapt through the air, smashing into a Guardsman plummeting towards the ground, his grav-chute yet to activate. Other shapes leapt from the rocks to snatch more drop-troopers out of midair, and Jarulek smiled.

Burias-Drak'shal's hunt had gone well.

# CHAPTER TEN

'So, THE ENEMY still holds the high ground. Emperor-knows how many men we lost. A formation of Marauders is missing, presumed shot down, though Throne only knows how. There are at least forty Valkyries either destroyed or needing serious repairs,' snarled Brigadier-General Havorn, his tall, gaunt form trembling with rage. 'And to top it all off, Colonel Emmet Boerl of the 72nd was killed in action.'

Captain Laron stood before the glowering brigadier-general, his gaze fixed forward. Alongside him were the other captains of the 72nd. Laron was the only one of them to have been engaged in the failed attempt to take the mountain highlands. Indeed, he was the only captain to have returned of those who had attacked the mountains, and he felt that most of the brigadier-general's ire was directed at him.

'I ought to have the lot of you executed on the spot, care of Commissar Kheler here,' he said gesturing to a black-clad officer behind him. Laron flicked a glance towards the commissar. The man returned his stare coldly.

'But I will not, as I find the 72nd has a sudden lack of officers,' said Havorn.

He towered over Laron by half a head, though what the captain lacked in height he made up for in brawn. The brigadier-general was a lanky man, and he truly was one of the ugliest individuals that Laron had ever seen.

Where Captain Laron represented physically everything that the Elysians were famed for, the muscular build, the blond hair and the grey-blue eyes set in a handsome, chiselled face, Brigadier-General Havorn was the polar opposite. Tall, thin and dark haired, his eyes were as black as sin and his face was narrow, long and just plain ugly. His hair was clipped to the scalp, and scars riddled his face and head, curling his lip into a permanent sneer. His one extravagance was the long, grey moustache hanging to either side of his scowling mouth.

'Captain Laron, I am instating you as acting colonel of the 72nd,' said the brigadier-general. Laron felt a flutter of pride rise within him, but he tried hard to make sure it didn't reach his face.

'With an emphasis on the word *acting*,' continued the brigadier-general. 'You are only in that position because there is no one better, for the time being. Once we are done with this cursed planet and return to the main crusade fleet, I will request a more suitable replacement for Colonel Boerl.'

The taller man leant down and forward so that he was looking directly into Laron's eyes, his hooked nose only centimetres from the captain's face.

'I don't know you well, Laron, but Colonel Boerl rated you highly. Do not dishonour his memory,' said the brigadier-general quietly, before turning away.

'I am assigning Commissar Kheler to keep watch over you. He has been a trusted advisor of mine for over a decade. His grasp of tactics and morale is strong. If there is ever a moment when it looks as if your arrogance or your pride are going to make you do something stupid that will get good men killed, the good commissar here will take steps to rectify the situation, with a bullet through your head.

'Do I make myself clear, *acting* Colonel Laron of the 72nd Elysians?'

The muscles in Laron's jaw clenched and he felt his cheeks redden.

'Yes, brigadier-general, I understand your meaning perfectly, sir.'

'Good,' said the tall man, turning and walking around his desk before sinking into his leather chair. 'You are dismissed, officers of the 72nd. Not you, acting colonel.'

His face burning, Laron stood motionless as the other men filed out of the room.

'Now,' said the brigadier-general, 'we need to establish how to get a victory after your devastatingly average attack against the highlands.'

THEY HAD AWOKEN him and the other surviving members of his worker team from their allocated two-hour rest break by throwing a bucket of warm water over them. Or, at least Varnus had thought it was water at first, until he tasted it on his tongue; it was blood, fresh and human. The overseers coughed vilely, what passed for laughter amongst them, and jerked at slaves' neck chains to get them to their feet.

The dreams were getting worse. The blaring of the Discord never ceased, and he heard it as he slept, the hideous sound seeping into his brain like a vile parasite, twisting and corrupting within him. It was no release from torment when he closed his eyes and fell into fitful sleep. No, if anything, his dreams were worse than his waking life. He saw a world utterly consumed by Chaos, its sky a roiling miasma of fire and lava. The land was not truly rock or soil, but a pile of skinless, moaning bodies that stretched as far as the eye could see in all directions. For all he knew, the planet was made entirely from these mewling, bloody wretches. Every one of them had a metal star of Chaos bolted to its forehead, the same mark that he also bore. Endless, monotonous chanting filled his head, intoning words of worship and praise. He saw this place every time he closed his eyes, not just when he slept, but every time he even blinked his eyes against the sulphurous, polluted air.

*Praise ye the glory of Chaos* screamed the Discord in his mind, blurred with hateful screams, words and bellows. *Kill him!* they said. *Traitor!*

Varnus stumbled along with the other slaves. He looked around in confusion as they turned off the well-worn path leading towards the tower that rose nearly a hundred metres into the air and headed off in a different direction. He saw his confusion mirrored in Pierlo's wild eyes, his only true companion here in this living hell.

Someone is here already, he said to himself. He could feel it in the air. Liberation was at hand. He prayed to the Emperor, *curse his name*, that his hated captors would soon be blasted from the face of the planet by the force of the Imperium.

He grinned stupidly at the thought.

Dully, he came to his senses to find that the line of slaves had stopped.

'On your knees, dogs,' said an overseer in his grating voice, the translator box over its mouth vibrating.

Without thought, he dropped to his knees. The overseers produced long, rusted metal spikes, and walked behind the line of slaves. They pulled the chains backwards violently, dropping the slaves onto their backs. Standing on the chains to either side of each slave, they hammered the heavy chains to the ground with the thick spikes.

Within moments, Varnus heard screaming from other slaves, but from his position he could not see what was happening. All he could see were the slaves directly to either side of him. On one side, a man cried, his eyes tightly closed as he mouthed the silent words of a prayer. The star upon his forehead was clearly visible, and steam seemed to rise from the skin around it, forming blisters. The stink of burning flesh reached Varnus's nostrils. Needle-tipped fingers plunged into the man's neck abruptly and he convulsed frantically, his prayer forgotten. His head stopped steaming and Varnus realised that it must have been the prayer that had caused the reaction.

Turning to the other side, he saw Pierlo looking at him closely with his crazed eyes.

'What now?' hissed the man. He didn't seem overly distressed to Varnus, but perhaps that was his way of dealing with this horror. He envied the man, briefly. *Kill him,* came the voice within the blare of the Discord.

'What new torture is this?'

The dark figures of chirurgeons loomed over Varnus. They were loathsome creatures, their hunched forms covered in shiny, black material. There was an unholy stink about them that made him gag, and their arms ended in arrays of needles, clamps and syringes.

Something was writhing in the hands of the hateful surgeons and he felt sickness pull within his gut at the sight of the vile, wriggling thing. It was a small, mechanical, flat box that looked somewhat like the translator machines that the overseers spoke through. However, the thin sides of the box were coated in a smooth, black-oily skin that pulsed with movement from within. Four short, stubby tentacles waved from the corners of the box, fighting at the chirurgeon's grasp. His gaze was forcefully removed from the vile blend of mechanics and daemon spawn as a further pair of black-clad chirurgeons pulled his head around.

'Open your mouth,' came the voice of an overseer at his ear, but Varnus resisted. Pain jolted through him as the overseer ran one of its needle fingers along his neck, and he opened his mouth wide in a cry of pain. The chirurgeons darted eagerly forwards with their mechanical hands, whirring power clamps gripping his front teeth. Without ceremony, the teeth were ripped from his jaw. Blood poured from the holes in his gums and he groaned in pain.

Yet the chirurgeons had not finished their brutal surgery. Gripping his head tightly, one of them leant forwards with another mechanical device, and Varnus tried to pull away from it desperately, blood running down his throat and spurting over his chin. He could not escape the attentions of the twisted, hunched chirurgeon, however, and as its partner hit Varnus's lower jaw to close his mouth, the first sadistic creature slammed its mechanical device into the side of his face.

A metal, barbed staple, half a hand-length wide, punched through the bone of Varnus's jaw and cheek, pinning his mouth closed. The metal bit deep into the bone, and Varnus gargled in agony. A second staple punched into the bone on the other side of his face.

That was when the black, tentacled thing was brought towards him. The chirurgeon thrust the fighting thing at his face and Varnus screamed, his jaw stapled shut, in pain and terror. He tried to turn away, but his head was held tight and the box was placed over his mouth.

He screamed and screamed as the four questing tentacles probed his skin, the touch stinging and burning his flesh. The tentacles felt their way across his face, and with horror he realised there was a fifth, thicker tentacle pushing through the gap in his front teeth and into his mouth. No, it wasn't a tentacle, he realised as his tongue touched the vile thing. It was a hollow, fleshy tube, and as it entered his mouth it began to expand and push itself down into his throat, flattening his tongue against the base of his mouth.

Two tentacles latched under Varnus's jaw, burrowing into his flesh to secure a tight hold, and the remaining two leech-like appendages wriggled across his cheeks, probing at the corners of his eyes before burrowing agonisingly into the skin at his temples. He roared in excruciating pain, the sound alien and strangely mechanical to his ears, altered by the thing clamped firmly over his mouth and nose. He breathed in deeply, which was heavy and difficult, and he felt a foul, sickly sweet taste in his mouth and nose.

White-hot pain shot through his head as the tentacles burrowed further into his flesh. They ceased wriggling within him, but the pain remained. His breathing was laboured and the figures above him went hazy, spots of light appearing before him, and he fell into the nightmare of his unconsciousness.

THE WARRIORS OF the Adeptus Mechanicus stepped inexorably forwards, like a seething, relentless carpet, spread out across the hard-packed salt plain. Some amongst them were almost human, though even these were hard-wired into the weapon systems they bore, their brain stems augmented with mechanics and sensors. The Coryphaus had seen their like before. He had fought against loyalist members of the Cult Mechanicus on their Forge Worlds during the advance on Terra ten thousand years earlier. More recently, he had fought alongside those members of the Machine Cult that had long sworn their allegiance to the true gods, the powers of Chaos.

Sheer cliffs rose up on either side of the valley, their tops hidden by dark, brooding, heavy cloud. The rumble of thunder boomed from the heavens and flashes punctuated the dark, threatening sky. The insides of the massed, bulbous clouds lit up as lightning crackled within, arcing, skeletal fingers of electricity that clawed across their surface.

The rain had been falling for almost an hour, hard and driving, lashing down upon the servitors as they plodded forwards at the impulse of their masters. The ground beneath their feet was pooled with salt sludge. The grinding tracks of weapon platforms and hissing crawlers ripped up the ground, creating mires in their wake as they slowly advanced amongst the serried cohorts of mindless and augmented servitors.

Visibility was poor across the open ground, as waves of driving rain were driven into the valley by the fierce winds that were picking up.

Screaming shells descended out of the gloom, accompanied by the constant rumble of artillery that was almost indiscernible from the sound of the building storm. They fell from the high ridges to either side of the valley, obscured by cloud and rain, and detonated amongst the ranks of servitor warriors, sending flesh and mechanics flying in all direction. Red blood and pale, unnatural fluids mixed with the pooling waters underfoot. They made no cries of fear or pain as they were destroyed, though even if they had they would not have carried through the pounding torrents of falling rain.

While visibility was poor for the Word Bearers, who were barely able to see the advancing enemy just rounding the dog-leg of the valley, the wretched slaves that Kol Badar had brought with him were virtually blind. They stood close together, weeping and terrified, shivering in the icy wind and rain that battered at them. They were chained together still, in long lines, clustered in front of the massive Word Bearers, who stood oblivious and uncaring of the hardships they endured at being exposed to the elements.

Kol Badar ordered the advance. Confused and deafened by the sheer fury of the downpour, they looked around blankly. Word Bearers pushed them roughly forward with the barrels of their bolters. A few shots into their midst soon had them moving, and almost five thousand slaves were goaded on through the torrential downpour. Scores of them fell, bustled by their terrified comrades. They were crushed underfoot, many drowning in the pooling, ankle deep water as their desperate companions scrambled over them, their only thought being to keep in front of their tormentors. Their limp, lifeless bodies were forced along with the push of humanity and dragged by the chains secured to their necks.

The Word Bearers advanced behind the seething mass of terrified slaves. They intoned from the Book of Lorgar as they marched through the strengthening rain, while the melancholic phrases recited by those warriors within their Rhino and Land Raider transports blared out from amplifiers on the outsides of the vehicles. Ancient, holy Predator tanks, their mighty turrets and weapon sponsons decorated with scriptures, bronze daemonic maws and icons scrawled in blood, rolled forwards at the wings of the Word Bearers, alongside Defilers and other daemon engines. The howls of the machines rose through the rain that hissed and turned to steam as it neared the infernal hulls of the hellish creations. Dreadnoughts were guided forwards by black-clad handlers, screaming insanely or reliving ancient battles long passed. Kol Badar and his Anointed warriors walked in the centre of the line.

The bombardment from the ridges above continued unabated, but Kol Badar was furious. There should have been more fire coming from above, and he was still angered by his earlier conversation.

'Unacceptable losses against a weakling foe,' he had growled through the vox-unit.

'My warriors hold the ridges still, Coryphaus,' was the snarled response from Marduk, the First Acolyte.

'The barrage will not be as effective as anticipated. Your failure will cost the lives of more of our brethren,' retorted Kol Badar.

'You did not predict an attack of such strength,' snapped Marduk. 'If there has been a failure, it has been yours.'

Kol Badar lashed out in anger towards an attendant daubing fresh sigils on his armour, but pulled the blow just before it connected, and merely clenched the talons of his power fist tightly, instead. The robed figure flinched backwards, then tentatively continued with its work. If the warlord had continued through with the strike, it would have instantly killed the attendant.

'You go too far. One day soon there will be a reckoning between us, whelp,' Kol Badar had promised, before severing the vox transmission.

The slaves stampeded ahead of the Word Bearers, running blindly through the rain. They began to die before they even glimpsed their killers.

A thick beam of white energy surged out of the gloom, cutting through the ranks of slaves. Their bodies burst into blue and white flames that rose fiercely, melting the chains binding the wretches to dripping liquid. A millisecond later, the flames all but died away, leaving piles of white ash in the shapes of the victims. A second later the morbid statues crumbled as they were trampled by the press of bodies that filled the sudden gap in the ranks.

As if the shot was the clarion call announcing the commencement of battle, the gloom was suddenly ripped apart as the guns of the Adeptus Mechanicus spoke. Blasts of plasma screamed through the air, massive rotating assault cannons upon the back of tracked units roared as they began to spin, and salvoes of hellfire missiles were launched.

The slaves surged through the inferno of death, hundreds of them slaughtered within the first second of the barrage. Those at the rear turned to flee from this new threat, but the bolters of the Word Bearers barked, dropping them in droves. And so, the slaves surged forwards once more, running towards those that they would call allies, who were cutting them down mercilessly, killing them in droves.

A barking roar was unleashed as the Skitarii fired. Heavy bolters tore through the flesh of the slaves, and flashes from thousands of lasguns streaked through the rain.

The chained slaves surged towards those who appeared, through the gloom, to be Imperial Guardsmen, clearly not registering that their saviours were to be their executioners.

Kol Badar laughed as the Cult Mechanicus wasted its ammunition. All the while, the Word Bearers marched relentlessly forwards, shielded by the flesh of the Imperial slaves.

The Chaos Space Marines began to fire their own weapons. Lascannons from the lower reaches of the ridge seared down through the gloom, spearing into the heavy weapon platforms grinding along slowly. Predators of ancient, extinct design and Land Raiders daubed with Chaos sigils added their own weight to the fire, and the demented Dreadnoughts and daemon engines roared in excitement, bitterness and anger as they sighted the foe. Battle cannons boomed, autocannons shrieked, missiles screamed through the rain and heavy bolters barked.

The Anointed opened up, cutting down the last of the slaves as they neared the true foe. Striding forwards, Kol Badar saw the approaching ranks of Skitarii through the press of frantic slaves and impatiently shot down those in his way.

The front rank of the foe consisted of heavily augmented servitor warriors with massive shields built into their mechanical arms. These shields shimmered with power as they deflected bolter shots, protecting them and those in the ranks behind. They advanced slowly step by lumbering step, a walking barricade, firing their lasguns through the slaves and into the advancing Word Bearers. The top right corner of each shield was cut down to allow the larger guns of those behind to fire. The two opposing forces were close, and the fusillade was furious. Kol Badar grinned as he powered unscathed through the carnage, the revered plasteel plating of his Terminator armour absorbing the incoming fire.

He had ensured that his most vicious, blood-hungry warriors, those who strayed closest to the dedicated worship of blessed Khorne, were the first wave of Word Bearers to engage the enemy, and they cleaved into the foe with brutal force. The heavy shields of the front line of the enemy were hacked down with powerful blows from chainaxes and spiked power mauls, and bolter fire tore into the flesh of those behind. The shield-servitors were slow and lumbering, though they took a lot of punishment before they stopped moving. Kol Badar saw several of them fighting on, even with limbs hacked off and bolt having removed parts of their skulls.

Lasgun shots peppered off Kol Badar's armour like flies, and he punched his talons through a heavy shield, sparks flying and power conduits screaming as the blow impaled the Skitarii through its neck. With a flick of his arm, he hurled the servitor warrior over his shoulder, and unleashed his combi-bolter on full auto into the packed Skitarii ranks behind. These were softer targets. They had been augmented in lesser ways, not taking them fully down the path to becoming mindless servitors. Targeting sensors had replaced their left eyes, and the left halves of their heads were a mass of wiring and mechanics, but their bodies were easily torn apart by the bolter fire of the advancing Word Bearers.

At a distance, they would be dangerous foes, for many of them carried heavier armaments than a humble Guardsman would be able to bear, but up close they were slaughtered by the brute force and speed of the Word Bearers. The Anointed bludgeoned their way into the heart of the Skitarii formation. It mattered not to these elite killers that the enemy fought on after having sustained wounds that would drop a regular human. The Word Bearers, and the Anointed in particular, were far from regular humans themselves – they were demi-gods of war, and they tore apart the Skitarii with fury and passion.

Within ten minutes, as if a switch was flicked inside the mechanical heads of the thousands of remaining Skitarii, they began to re-form, walking steadily backwards as one, while continuing to lay down their withering fire into the Chaos Marines.

With a surge of his servo-enhanced muscles, Kol Badar pushed forwards into the retreating foe, punching the whirling chainblade that served as a bayonet upon his combi-bolter through the pudgy white face of another foe, and ripping the head and spinal column from another, electrodes and sparking fuses still attached to the vertebrae.

Heavily armoured servitors moved to the fore, stalking forwards between the ordered ranks of the lesser warriors, and Kol Badar was pleased to see that these foes were more to his liking. Around the height of a regular Chaos Space Marine, these were heavily armoured in thick, dark, metal armour. The mechanics of their left arms ended in spinning cannons that roared as they pumped fire from their multiple barrels. Ammo-feeds smoked as fresh bullets were fed to the guns from heavy integrated backpacks.

Concentrated bursts from the weapons were carving through power armour, and Kol Badar hissed in anger as he was rocked backwards by their force, though his Terminator armour was not breached. He fired his combi-bolter, blasting the gun-arm from a warrior in a shower of sparks, but it kept coming at him swinging its other arm towards him in a murderous thrust as the drill-arm began to spin. Metallic tentacles attached to the Skitarii's spinal column reached forwards to ensnare him, but Kol Badar had no intentions of backing away from the machine warrior.

With a backhand swipe of his power talons, he smashed the whirling, industrial drill away and fired his combi-bolter into the chest of the foe. Mechadendrite tentacles latched onto his chest and shoulder plates, and small drill pieces whined as they began to bore neat holes through the ancient suit. Firing his bolter again into the chest of the warrior, he ripped at the tentacles. Their grip on him was stronger than their binding to the warrior's spine, and he ripped them free of the Skitarii's back. Firing again, its armour cracking and shattering, the Skitarii fell onto its back. Kol Badar ended its struggles by slamming his heavy foot down into its head, pulverising the human skull and brain within its blank, metal faceplate.

Ripping off the tentacles still attached to his armour, he saw with pride that not one of his Anointed had fallen to these warriors, though several power armoured warrior-brothers had succumbed to their weaponry. He saw one of the Skitarii warriors torn apart by the fire from the reaper autocannon of one cult member, its chest a ruin of armour, machinery and seeping blood.

The enemy continued to retreat, but the thought of calling off the battle never entered Kol Badar's head. He would push on, deep into the foe, and inflict as much damage as possible, only calling off the attack when the terrain began to favour the Imperials once more. Even then, calling off the slaughter would be difficult, nigh on impossible, for the frenzied Dreadnoughts that were ploughing into the enemy.

One of the insane war machines broke into a lumbering run, smashing aside a warrior-brother in its eagerness to reach the foe. It was roaring incoherently, and gunfire leapt from its twin autocannon barrels and from the underslung bolters beneath its scything array of war blades. Other, swifter warrior-brothers backed out of the way of the charging machine, and it ripped into the Skitarii, its war blades cutting down four of them with one scissoring blow.

The Coryphaus recognised the Dreadnought as housing the corpse of Brother Shaldern, who had fallen against the hated coward Legion of Rouboute Gullimen, the Ultramarines, during the battle on Calth. His sanity had long since abandoned him. Such was the way with those entombed within the sarcophagi of the dangerous war machines, and Kol Badar wondered briefly if he would rather die upon the field of battle than suffer endless torment within one of those cursed engines. Few retained any semblance of rationality. That the Warmonger maintained as much lucidity as he did was a testament to the intense faith and belief that the Dark Apostle had wielded in life, and had taken with him into his hateful half-life.

The machine ploughed through the enemy and a great roar went up from the Word Bearers.

'Forward, warrior-brothers!' Kol Badar bellowed. 'For the glory of the Legion!'

# CHAPTER ELEVEN

Mechadendrites attached to the spinal column of Techno-Magos Daroiq stretched out before him. Needle-like electro-jacks emerged from the tips of these mechanical, clawed tentacles and plunged into circular plugs around the base of the cylindrical device rising smoothly from the floor of the control room. Each of the electro-jacks was around fifteen centimetres in length, and they rotated as the magos connected with the machine-spirit of his command vehicle.

The room was dark and claustrophobic, with exposed pipes and wires lining the walls and twisting across the low ceiling. Eerie light spilled from the screens around the room as lines of data flicked across their surfaces. Hissing steam vented from latticed grills in the floor plates, and thick, ribbed tubing snaked from the grills to climb the walls and disappear amongst the dense, confusing network of conduits.

Pilots and technicians hard-wired into the control room were built into the walls, their forms almost hidden amongst the mass of coiling pipes that engulfed them. Insulated wiring entered the fused hemispheres of their brains through eye sockets, nostrils and ears. They manipulated controls through cables that plugged into the remnants of flesh that remained of their mortal bodies, and from each fingertip spread a spider web of intricate cables, attaching them directly into the holy machine that they were a part of.

Daroiq muttered the incantation of supplication to the machine-spirit and recited the logis dictates that would ignite the spark of connection as his electro-jacks continued to manipulate the inner core workings of the command column. Speaking blessings to the Omnissiah, he tripped the internal switches within his own mechanised form, and his spirit joined with that of his flagship in a surge of images, information and release.

Hovering fifty metres in the air, the bloated airship that served as Daroiq's command centre was as stable as the ground, despite the torrential downpour of rain and the sharp burst of wind that the magos felt buffeting its banded sides. Connected to the huge machine's spirit, he felt the rain and wind on its thick sides as if it were an extension of himself. Massive rotating spotlights that cut through the darkness were his eyes, and endless feeds of information flooded through the multiple logic engines within his construction, filing through the domed hemispheres of his 'true' brain, which then filtered relevant data out into the charged liquid housing domes that enclosed his secondary brain units.

He felt the smooth running engines that powered the mass turbines keeping the hulk airborne, and sensed the holy oils lubricating the cogs and gears slipping through the mechanics, as the dictates required. He could feel the scurrying feet of servitors, Skitarii and priests through the labyrinthine tunnels within the airship's underhull, and the spark of sensation as these servants of the Omnissiah plugged themselves into the vast machine, linking them to him and him to them. He could see through the augmetic eyes of these lesser minions and feel the twitch of their vat-born muscles.

His spirit reached out through the thick, insulated cabling that fed from his control station, travelling through the circuitry and carefully constructed piping that linked the airship to the Ordinatus *Magentus* far below. He linked himself to the intractable spirit of that great creation and whispered a prayer to the shrine-machine as he flowed through its holy workings.

Probing at the plasma-reactor at the core of the *Magentus*, he felt the contained power within, a blessing from the Machine-God. Back in his command station, he felt the vibratory impulse that pre-empted a vox transmissions arrival. An electro-pulse fired within Darioq's true brain and the magos recognised the sensation as irritation. He retracted his spirit from that of the *Magentus* in an instant and returned to his flagship. Though he remained in connection with the airship, he allowed his physical faculties to come to the fore and received visual stimulus through the glowing crystals of his augmetic right eye, and through the blearing, inferior gaze of his left, organic eye.

With a twist of one of his mechadendrites, Darioq turned a function dial on the command pillar and a hololith atop the pillar sparked into life. A three-dimensional image of an Imperial Guard officer sprang into existence, his every feature picked out in the intricate network of crisscrossing green lines. It showed the man's head and shoulders, and extended down to his chest.

'Blessings of the Omnissiah to you, Brigadier-General Ishmael Havorn,' said Darioq.

'Blessings of the God-Emperor to you, magos,' said the green rendering of Havorn, the sound issuing from the speaker box built into the command pillar slightly out of time with the movement of the lips.

'Your tech-guard suffer many losses, my reports tell me.'

'The losses of the servitors and Skitarii units is acceptable, Brigadier-General Ishmael Havorn. The Hypaspists and the Sagitarii units are replaceable. The Praetorians' destruction was necessary to conduct the falling back of the cohorts. The loss of several of the Ordinatus Minoris machines of the Ballisterarii is regrettable, but predicted by my cogitator engine. The Omnissiah has reclaimed their spirits unto the bosom of Mars.'

'And are your preparations for the second push proceeding as planned, magos?'

'The *Exemplis* advances, Brigadier-General Ishmael Havorn, and a larger concentration of cohort units advances beneath its hallowed shadow. My Cataphractarii lead the holy procession.'

'Six companies of the 133rd will accompany your tech-guard. They are advancing as we speak. Alongside them are heavy armour squadrons,' said the image of the Elysian commander. 'Members of the 72nd will re-engage the foe within the highlands to coincide with our combined assault.'

'I will accede to your wishes, Brigadier-General Ishmael Havorn. Your flesh units and heavy armour will accompany the second push.'

The image of Havorn's face frowned darkly, but Techno-Magos Darioq had long passed the point of being able to read facial expressions. He could read more from a blank data-slate or the turning of an engine than he could from the facial contortions of the fleshed.

'Never have I heard of such willingness by the Mechanicus to throw its tech-guard at an enemy, bar one threatening one of the Forge Worlds. You can understand my... confusion, magos.'

'The Adeptus Mechanicus supports the armies of the Emperor in all endeavours, Brigadier-General Ishmael Havorn. The Adeptus Mechanicus wishes to support the battle against the enemy on this planet c6.7.32.'

'Yes, as you have said, magos. I just wish to the Emperor that I knew why.'

'To many within the Cult Mechanicus, the Emperor of Terra and the Omnissiah are one. They would say that the Imperial Guard and the regiments of Mars enact his will equally.'

The image of Havorn raised its eyebrow at a figure off-screen.

'It is usual for brothers in arms to share pertinent information regarding their purpose.'

'The Adeptus Mechanicus wishes to support the battle against the enemy on this planet c6.7.32. That is the purpose of this expedition force.'

'Expedition force? This is a war zone!'

'You are correct, Brigadier-General Ishmael Havorn. Your voice has risen by 1.045 octaves, and my logarithmic codifier indicates that your volume has increased by 37.854 Imperial standard decibels. Are you unwell, Brigadier-General Ishmael Havorn?'

'What?' asked the Imperial commander.

'Your voice has risen by–' began Darioq before he was interrupted.

'Emperor above!' exclaimed Havorn.

'The mnemo strands within my logic engines suggest that some savage cultures within the Imperium believe that the Emperor *does* exist beyond the atmosphere of their home world. Do you believe this, Brigadier-General Ishmael Havorn? Is that why you speak the words "Emperor above"?'

'Are you attempting a joke, magos? I thought such a thing was beyond one such as you.'

'I do not understand the concept of humour, Brigadier-General Ishmael Havorn. My memory functions contain the information pertaining to the notion, but I have erased my memories of such a notion as inconsequential to the Omnissiah.'

The image of Havorn stared fixedly at the inscrutable visage of Darioq. The magos waited patiently for the Elysian commander to speak once more.

'Move the *Exemplis* to the front line. We attack before dawn,' he said, and cut the connection.

Darioq removed his mechadendrites from the command pillar and the image of Havorn, frozen in a scowl when the Elysian severed the connection, disappeared. A ghostly after-image remained for a second before it too faded.

He stood motionless for a moment, his brains alight with sparks of thought. For a few moments the eyelid of his weak, organic flesh-eye flickered as he accessed information stored deep within one subsidiary cortex, and he plunged the blade of the electro-jack on the tip of one of his mechadendrites back into the column.

Another green-lined image sprang up, hovering above the surface of the command column. It showed the rotating sphere of a planet, a stark, rocky and lifeless world. Polar ice-flows spread out across much of the land. Temperature indicators marked the planet as being far below a temperature that was able to sustain life. A light flashed beneath the hovering image of the planet. It was a date, in standard Imperial time, and it indicated that this was the representation of a planet almost two thousand years in the past.

With a twist of his mechadendrite, Darioq caused a second planet to be projected alongside the first. This was a world dominated by water, seas covering the length and breadth of the sphere, bar two continent. With a further twist, Darioq brought the two glowing planets together, so that they overlapped each other perfectly. The mountains of the two images locked together like pieces of a puzzle. They were a perfect, identical match.

He rotated the overlapping spheres and magnified the image tenfold, zooming in on the north-western tip of the larger continent. The mountain plateau above the sea level rose to a point and then dropped off beneath the oceans. The cliff faces were almost sheer and fell into a series of deep undersea valleys, thousands of metres beneath the ocean. He zoomed closer, focusing on one particularly deep, abyssal chasm.

He abruptly retracted his mechadendrite and the green, three-dimensional depiction disappeared. Only the after image of the overlapping planets remained for a fraction of a second, along with a small line of digits beneath the spheres: c6.7.32. A moment later, they too faded.

IT WAS ALMOST midday, though it may as well have been midnight for all the light that penetrated the thick, roiling, black storm clouds. Torrential, blinding rain still lashed the high peaks of the mountains, and ravines and cracks were flooded with streaming water. In the valley below, vast moving rivers of water cut across the landscape, seeking the lower ground of the surrounding flat lands. Even the highly attuned sensors of the Word Bearers were becoming blocked by the high amount of water and electricity that coursed through the air.

The battle raged on, frenzied and devastating, and the bodies of Guardsmen floated through the mire. The wrecked shells of burned out vehicles and tanks were dragged through the rising waters. The Word Bearers strode through the shallower, knee-deep waters, firing into the massed ranks of the enemy.

Experimental weaponry of the Adeptus Mechanicus crackled and roared, ripping apart traitor vehicles and Dreadnoughts, and shells fell among both battle lines, causing torrents of water to explode into the air along with shattered bodies and armour. Coalescing arcs of energy streamed from the weapons borne upon the backs of tracked crawlers that inched forward through the mire of bodies and rain water.

Kol Badar had seen some of those weapons before. Many were weapons developed to be borne by the colossal war machines of the Titan Legions. Without the technology to continue to construct these behemoths of war, many of which were over a hundred metres in height, the Adeptus Mechanicus had clearly deemed it fit to mount these artillery pieces upon tracked crawler units, but the effectiveness of the weapons remained awesome.

Missiles streamed through the rain, exploding in white-hot blasts of super-heated energy. The ground was ripped apart in deep furrows that were instantly engulfed with water as other esoteric batteries fired, throwing warriors and vehicles aside as if they weighed nothing at all. Giant gouts of liquid flame roared through the darkness, engulfing scores of soldiers on both sides and heating the streaming waters of the valley to boiling point.

Casualties were rising, though the Imperials were losing scores of warriors for every Word Bearer that fell. The fervour, or impatience, of the Imperial commanders was strong. Despite their air raids being almost neutralised by the worsening weather conditions, they drove their forces ever onwards in a grinding battle of attrition, desperate it seemed to push the Legion back.

The Coryphaus had ordered the reserve of the Host forward, to reinforce the line of Word Bearers holding the valley. He had also demanded that Marduk leave the command of the ridges to the Warmonger, and for him to bolster the valley. While the lighter Imperial aircraft had been forced to pull out by the buffeting, gale force winds and lightning that had ripped many of their fighters from the air, the heavier Thunderhawks and Stormwings of the Word Bearers were able to remain airborne, albeit for only short flights before they retreated from the heart of the storm.

Marduk had fumed at the condescending tone of the order, but could recognise the danger. Holding the Imperials back was imperative, or the losses that they had already suffered were for nought, and the determined drive of the Imperials threatened to push through the Word Bearers' defence.

Roaring barrages continued to rain down from the ridge-tops, and lascannons and missiles lanced out of the darkness from the cliffs, targeting the tracked vehicles of the Mechanicus and the battle tanks that were rolling into the fray. Soaring missiles and rockets returned fire against the warriors under the Warmonger's command high above, but there was little that could truly reach them, high in the rocks. Nevertheless, it seemed not even to slow the ponderous advance of the Imperials, as ever more troops and vehicles filtered into the valley.

Chimera APCs spat sharp bursts of las-fire from their turret mounted multi-lasers, and strong waves were created as they ploughed through the deeper rivers that flowed across the battlefield. Easily as capable in the deep water as on land, the vehicles churned through the corpse-strewn mire to unload their cargoes of Guardsmen. Smoke-launchers fired, cloaking the battlefield behind white smoke that blocked even the auto-sensors and targeting arrays of the Word

Bearers, but Marduk laughed as the smoke almost instantly dissipated in the gale. Several of the Chimeras were halted in their tracks as missiles and autocannon fire raked their hulls. The men scrambling to vacate the sinking metal coffins were gunned down by bolter fire. Another of the Chimeras was lifted into the air as it reached more solid ground when a Dreadnought struck its side with a massive siege ram before unleashing a flurry of missiles into another vehicle.

A formation of tracked units advanced through the gunfire, bolter fire pinging off their armoured forms. Humanoid upper bodies were integrated into the mechanised units and cannons protruded from the stumps of their arms. Marduk hacked through the metallic torso of a servitor warrior, spraying oil and blood, and broke into a loping run towards the strange, centaur-like creatures.

He felt the presence of Burias-Drak'shal at his side, the daemon soul of the warrior burning hotly. Two coteries of Word Bearers launched themselves forward in support of the First Acolyte and the Icon Bearer, bolters barking as they tore through the Skitarii warriors towards this new enemy,

Their movements jerky, the tracked centaur units fired controlled bursts from their rotating cannons as they rolled forwards. Their bodies were a mass of augmetic, metal body plating, and their heads were almost completely hidden in dark metal encasings, the only exception being the dead, staring left eyes that peered out from white flesh.

The lead unit turned its head jerkily in Marduk's direction and he felt the warning buzz from his auto-sensors as the mass of targeters arrayed over the servitor's right eye fixed on him.

With a snarl, Marduk threw himself into a roll as the mechanical warrior jerked the rotating barrels of its weapon in his direction and bullets began to spray towards him. They clipped his shoulder pad, taking chips out of the thick ceramite plating, and he fired his bolt pistol as he rose. Two bolts slammed into the face of the mechanised warrior, blowing a crater out the back of its head.

The other machines fired into the Word Bearers with short, sharp bursts. Marduk saw the chest of one warrior-brother ripped to shreds and the head of another pulverised.

With a roar, Burias-Drak'shal leapt onto one of the tracked machines as it rolled slowly forwards. He drove the daemon talons of one hand into the side of the Skitarii's head with such force that it punched through metal and bone, and pulverised the fused brain-hemispheres within. A burst of fire slammed into his lower back and the daemonically possessed warrior staggered. With a bellow that came from the pits of the Immaterium, Burias-Drak'shal spun and hurled the icon of the Host through the air like a spear. It slammed into the chest of the tracked creature that had shot him, impaling it on the large spikes that made up the eight-pointed star. Fluids ran from the wound and sparks engulfed the torso of the tracked machine, and it began to twitch convulsively. At a barked command from Burias-Drak'shal the icon ripped free of the malfunctioning machine and flew back to its master's hand.

Marduk launched into the *Catechism of Hate* and raising his daemonic chainsword high into the air, led the Word Bearers forward into the enemy. He pumped shot after shot into the mechanised torso of one of his foes, scoring deep craters across its armour. His chainsword bit through the thick tracks of the machine, and it floundered. Its expressionless face looked down upon him as it brought its weapon to bear, but Marduk moved swiftly around the immobilised machine, holstering his pistol. He pulled a krak grenade from his belt, pressing its igniting rune, and thrust it into the spinning cog-wheels of the damaged track unit.

He drew his pistol again as he charged towards the next machine, and the grenade detonated behind him. Flames washed over another machine, liquefying its flesh, but it fought on, its spinning cannon ripping the legs from a charging warrior at Marduk's side.

The press of the enemy was heavy, as other cohorts moved inexorably to support their kin, and Guardsmen pushed desperately forwards, vainly trying to drive the Word Bearers back. Las-bolts struck Marduk's armour and flames washed over him. Rapid firing rounds from the tracked machines raked him and he hissed in pain as one cracked a chink in the armour of his chest-plate.

His fiery words drove the Word Bearers on and they fought deep into the enemy formations. Blood flowed freely as he carved his screaming chainsword through the head of a Guardsman. A man stumbled towards him, his arm missing from the elbow down, and Marduk smashed him to the ground with the butt of his pistol before putting a round through the back of his head.

He felt savage joy as he slaughtered any who drew near him. He stumbled suddenly as a las-bolt pierced the armour of his thigh, searing the muscle beneath. He shot another man in the chest, his ribs exploding outwards as the explosive bolt detonated within.

An explosion tore the life from a pair of Word Bearers, and Marduk was rocked by the sudden blast, staggering to keep his footing as shrapnel scored across his armour. He saw a battle tank advance, the barrel of its turret smoking.

A heavy blow from his side smashed him to the ground and he felt the blessed ceramite of his shoulder pad compress as it absorbed the force of the blow. A servo-arm clamped around his torso as he tried to rise and he hissed in pain under the pressure. Power assisted pistons hissed as the clamps of the servo-arm tightened, and Marduk felt his ancient ceramite begin to buckle beneath the force.

He swung his chainsword into the neck of the servitor, and flesh and mechanics were ripped apart by the whirling teeth of the weapon. The fused bones of his ribcage strained as the pressure increased and he tried to bring his bolt pistol around for a shot, but the hold the combat servitor had on him made it impossible. Marduk pushed with all the force of his arm, driving his chainsword deeper into his foe's neck, but the crushing force did not relent.

A combi-bolter was placed into one the armature joints of the servo-arm, and bolts tore into the weak point, severing the limb. The combat servitor reeled backwards, the stump of its servo-arm spraying oil and milky liquid as it waved ineffectually, before another blast from the combi-bolter tore the servitor's head from its shoulders.

'One day the pleasure of killing you will be mine, and mine alone,' came a snarling voice. 'None will steal that prize from me.'

Marduk looked up at Kol Badar, standing over him. He could just imagine the smirk on the whoreson's face beneath his quad-tusked helmet, and he rose to his feet quickly, his face burning with shame and fury. His hand tightened around the grip of his chainsword, and he felt the daemon Borhg'ash willing him to lash out at the Coryphaus.

Kol Badar laughed as he turned away from the First Acolyte, his combi-bolter tearing another enemy to shreds. With a swat of his power claw he sent one of the tracked units toppling onto its side, where an Anointed cult member turned its head to molten metal and liquid, burning flesh with a searing blast from the meltagun slung beneath his bolter.

Simmering with anger, Marduk watched as Kol Badar grabbed the track unit of the battle tank in his massive power talons, ripping it clear in a shower of sparks and smoke. As the tank jerked to a halt, the warlord of the Word Bearers clenched his talons into a fist crackling with energy and, with a roar, smashed it into the armoured plating of the vehicle. The reinforced armour buckled under the power of the blow. The second blow punched straight through the armoured hull and Kol Badar wrenched his fist free, tangled metal screeching horribly. Placing the muzzle of his combi-bolter through the hole, he unloaded his clip inside the tank. The bolt-rounds ricocheted around the enclosed space deafeningly and there were screams from within.

As if feeling Marduk's gaze, Kol Badar turned towards him, and pointed at the First Acolyte with one of his crackling power talons. The message was clear: *your time will come.*

I welcome that time with open arms, thought Marduk, flushed with anger and bitterness.

THE IMPERIAL FORCES were being butchered. Despite their efforts to drive against the traitor Legion, they were making no ground. Worse, they were *losing* ground, being slowly pushed back by the fury of the Chaos Space Marines' resistance.

But that was soon to change.

The earth shuddered with each step of the *Exemplis.* It rose out of the gloom like a colossus of the ancients, a towering behemoth of awesome power. The mountains shook to their foundations as thousands of tonnes of metal slammed into the hard, salt packed earth of the flooding valley with each titanic step.

Those legs alone were mighty bastion fortresses, complete with battle cannon batteries and crenellated walls from which soldiers could pour fire into the foe. Within each leg was a demi-cohort consisting of Hypaspists and the elite biologically and mechanically enhanced Praetorians. But the leg bastions were the least of the weapons of the *Exemplis.*

Heaving some of the most powerful weapons ever conceived by the Adeptus Mechanicus, entire traitorous planets had surrendered at the mere appearance of the *Exemplis.* With weaponry the size of towering building blocks, each capable of demolishing cities and laying ruin to armies, the *Exemplis* had been in operational use by the Fire Wasps of Legio Ignatum since the time of the Great Crusade.

The plasma reactor, burning with the contained energy of a sun, roared with terrifying power as a fraction of its energy was siphoned into the giant weaponry of the god-machine.

The *Exemplis* was one of the last remaining Imperator Titans of Legio Ignatium of Mars and was worshipped by the adepts of the Cult Mechanicus as an avatar of the Omnissiah. With thundering steps, it strode to war once more against the traitors that had turned their back on the Imperium of Man.

# CHAPTER TWELVE

THERE WAS SOMETHING distinctly *wrong* about the tower, something far more perverted and unearthly than Varnus could truly conceive. It was almost as if it was a sentient being, that it had thoughts and ambitions of its own, and that these thoughts and ambitions were seeping into the slaves that laboured over its living form.

It was large on an unfeasible, maddening scale, and continued to rise hundreds of metres into the sky with every passing change of shift. It was so high that were it not for the vile, living re-breather masks that had been attached to the slaves' faces, they would start to struggle for oxygen in the increasingly thin air, not to mention the noxious fumes that blanketed the shattered city. The smog fumes seemed inexorably drawn towards the tower, and they circled it lazily.

At times, the tentacles of the creature burrowed deeper into his skull, wriggling and twitching agonisingly. It could not be removed. He wondered if it could ever be removed, even under surgery, and he had seen more than one slave die while trying to tear the thing from their face. They ended up choking to death, blood seeping from their ears and eyes as the powerful, leech-like tentacles burrowed through their brains, seeking solid purchase, and the tubular, living pipes that ran down their oesophagi clenched shut.

The appearance of the slaves was drastically altered by the foul masks; they looked more like devotees of the dark gods than Imperial citizens, and Varnus realised that he too must resemble one of the hated ones.

The work on the tower was never-ending and the slaves were worked at a brutal pace, the overseers viciously punishing those that failed to meet their exacting demands. It was as if the whole operation had gone into overdrive, that there was a looming deadline fast approaching and the tower had to be completed. There must have been around two hundred thousand slaves working atop the walls alone, he estimated, and many more hundreds of thousands working down in the sink-hole that disappeared inside the shaft of the tower, burrowing ever deeper into Tanakreg's crust, down into the depths of the planet. All told, he estimated that there must have been a million slave workers toiling over the construction at any one time. More crane engines had been constructed, and along with thousands of slaves, they were strengthening the base of the tower, making it thicker with additional layers of bricks even as the tower soared up towards the heavens. In addition, they began work on a massive spiralling walkway, wide enough for a battle tank, that coiled its way around the exterior of the tower. It was a mammoth undertaking, but one that progressed at an astonishing pace.

There must have been dire sorceries involved, for the tower had already surpassed the height of the greatest construction that he had ever heard of, and logic dictated that it simply could not rise higher without toppling, or collapsing beneath its own weight. But rise higher it did, defying the laws of the material universe.

Although he loathed the monstrous tower as he hated his overseers and captors, he could not help but have strange paternal feelings over the mass of rock and blood mortar. It was a repulsive moment of self-awareness, but the actions of the other slaves, particularly the ex-bodyguard and manservant, Pierlo, who he was chained alongside, had alerted him to it.

There had been an incident two work shifts earlier. Was that two days past? Two hours past?

The man Pierlo, Varnus had ascertained, was barely holding a grip on his sanity. He had overheard the man whispering to himself, having one side of a conversation that only he could hear. The living, black module that was attached to his face strangely distorted his voice, making it guttural, thick and oddly muted. In fact, it sounded uncannily like the voices of the cruel overseers. Varnus knew that his voice had undergone a similar change.

As he talked quietly to himself, Varnus had noticed that the man was tenderly stroking the stone beneath him, as if he were petting a beloved family salt hound. It was unnerving, but since he heard voices constantly through the blaring cacophony of the Discords, he thought little of it. At least he had so far resisted the desire to talk back to those voices.

As Pierlo stroked the harsh stone, Varnus had heard a wailing cry and had swung around to see the commotion. A block of stone, one of the millions that made up the growing tower, was being lowered into position, but through some mishap, it had not been positioned correctly. It had crushed the legs of three slave workers and was teetering on the brink of tipping off the high wall. One of the spider-limbed cranes strained as it tried to reposition the stone, but it was clear that it would fall. Pierlo and several other slaves had risen to their feet, crying out in horror, and Varnus felt a pang of anguish and terror.

The stone slipped in the claws of the crane and dropped over the outside edge of the wall, spinning and smashing against the stones below. A hundred tonnes of rock, it tumbled end over end, down and down, before disappearing in the low hanging smog clouds. The men whose legs had been shattered wailed, but not in pain. They clawed their way to the edge of the wall, their legs twisted horrifically beneath them, as they watched the descent of the block, eyes already brimming with tears of loss.

Pierlo had fallen to his knees, crying out to the heavens. Varnus's stomach churned, and he felt such a hollow loss within his chest that he thought he would weep. He shook his head as he realised what he was thinking, but the pain remained. All around the tower, slaves cried out in anguish.

He also knew that this was no doubt some further degradation of his sanity, for how else could he imagine that a construction like this had self-awareness? But of that he was convinced. The tower had been distraught when the stone had fallen and the slaves that had tended it had picked up that emotion. It was the kind of feeling a parent has when its child is in pain but cannot be helped.

He hated the tower, but when the time for the shift change came, he found it difficult to leave. The ride down the rickety, grilled elevator that climbed down the narrow steps of the tower on mechanical spider legs was hard, and the pain of separation was strong, even though it repulsed him. Other slaves cried out and wept openly, pushing their hands out through the grill to touch the stone of the tower, often losing a finger in the process.

Sleep was still no respite for Varnus, as every time he closed his eyes he revisited the hellish landscape of skinned corpses. Only now, there were towering buildings made out of the corpses, huge edifices that reached to the roiling heavens. From these buildings came the tolling of bells and the sound of monotonous chanting. He awoke covered in sweat, and instantly the pain of separation struck him; he longed to be back atop the tower, working.

Discords blared and told him that the tower had a name. They told him that it was a Gehemahnet. He did not know the word, but it felt right.

It seemed to him that the Gehemahnet breathed, and that he could feel the pulse of its massive heart reverberating through the stone beneath his touch.

He prayed to the Emperor when he thought such things, but it was increasingly hard to remember the words of worship that had been drummed into him by the priests of the Ecclesiarchy.

He looked at Pierlo as the man worked, smearing the blood mortar across the stone face. The man's robes had fallen open and there was something underneath, a shape on the man's shoulder that even the lumps of congealed mortar could not hide.

'What's on your shoulder?' he hissed, his voice alien to him.

Pierlo looked up in irritation, as if rudely interrupted mid-conversation. He pulled at his tattered robe, covering up the mark, and continued with his work, head down.

Varnus risked a glance around and saw that there was no overseer anywhere nearby. His mind feverish and the din of the Discord blaring, *kill him,* Varnus scrambled over to the slave and grabbed at his robe. Pierlo clawed at his hands, trying to fend him off, but Varnus ripped the robe from the man's shoulder.

There was a symbol there on the meat of his shoulder, a symbol that he recognised, for he had seen it hundreds of times every day. It was embossed on the sides of the spider cranes and it was stamped into the foreheads of some of the head overseers. He had seen it on the shoulder plate of every cursed traitor Space Marine on the planet. It was a screaming daemon's face and he knew exactly what it proclaimed.

'You are one of them!' he hissed. Instantly the pieces fell together in his mind. He had seen the man leave the meeting room in the palace just moments before it had exploded. He was one of the traitor insurgents that had aided the forces of Chaos.

Pierlo's face twisted hatefully as the two scuffled. Dully, Varnus heard the yells of other slaves, but he paid them no heed. All he could hear was the pounding of blood in his head. This bastard was one of those who had opened the door to the invaders. Hatred swelled within him. His hand snapped out towards Pierlo's face, fingers spread like claws.

The man was no stranger to unarmed combat and he grabbed Varnus's hand as it came close, twisting his wrist painfully. Pierlo's other hand slammed into his solar plexus, fingers extended, and all the breath was driven from him. He sank to the stone. Where Pierlo was of high birth, and had clearly been trained in the arts of combat, Varnus had learnt how to brawl on the streets of Shinar, and he knew that fighting as an art form and fighting tooth and nail for daily survival were two very different things. Varnus had suffered countless beatings in his youth as a hab-ganger and had dished out far more. Even when he had tried to go straight and had secured a job on the salt plains, he had fought in bare-knuckle brawls at night to supplement his meagre income. All that had changed when he had been recruited into the Shinar enforcers, but his skills had come in just as useful there.

Varnus surged up suddenly, landing a fierce blow to Pierlo's chin, quickly followed by a vicious swinging elbow that connected sharply with the man's head. He reeled backwards, about to fall off the wall and probably drag Varnus and half a dozen other slaves with him. Varnus grabbed the thick, spiked chain, yanking the man back onto the stone and straight into a knee that he slammed into Pierlo's groin.

As Pierlo bent forwards in pain, the ex-enforcer drove the point of his elbow down onto the back of his head, dropping him to the stone. Pierlo was motionless, but Varnus had not finished there. His hatred suffusing him, he made a loop with the spiked chain and hooked it around Pierlo's neck, placing a foot on the back of the man's neck. He crossed the chains in his hands and strained, pulling on the chain with all his strength. Though Pierlo wore the same blood-red metal collar as all the slaves, the chain bit deeply around his throat, cutting off his breathing as the spiked barbs sank into flesh. Blood ran from the man's throat, mixing with the mortar atop the stone.

Pain jolted him as the needles of the overseers plunged into his flesh, but he didn't care. His muscles bulged as he hauled on the chains one final time before the searing pain the overseers delivered made him collapse, twitching and convulsing, to the stone alongside Pierlo.

In his mind's eye he saw the sky running red with blood. He knew that Gehemahnet was pleased.

He smiled as he looked into the dead eyes of the traitor.

THE EARTH SHOOK, and as Marduk ripped his chainsword from the guts of a Guardsman he raised his head to pierce the gloom. Rain still lashed the bloody battlefield, but he sensed, as much as he felt, something approaching, something *huge.*

Lightning flashed, silhouetting a shape that Marduk had initially mistaken for a mountain. This was no mountain though, for it moved inexorably forwards, and the earth shook as it took another laborious step.

With a curse on his lips, Marduk's gaze rose as the immense shape of the Titan was revealed.

IT WAS LIKE some ancient, primeval god from an antediluvian age that continued to stalk the lands long after its kin had passed into myth and legend.

Its metal hide was pitted and scored by wounds that it had suffered during the battles it had waged over its ten thousand year lifetime. It's leering, dull metal face was fire scorched and scarred, though its eyes still burned with red light. Within that metallic cranium sat the Princeps and his Moderati, psychically linked to the Titan. They felt its pain as their own and experienced savage joy as the behemoth laid waste to everything before it.

Advancing through the press of soldiers and tanks, it dwarfed everything in its path. A multi-towered bastion the size of a walled stronghold sat atop its massive, armoured carapace shell. Siege ordnance and battle cannons, of such size that a small tank could drive through the barrels, were housed within this massive structure, and the pennants and banners that adorned it whipped around in the gale. Scores of symbols were emblazoned on the ancient kill banners that hung from the pair of monstrous main guns that the Imperator Titan wielded in place of arms, marking the enemy Titans and super-heavy vehicles that it had destroyed throughout its long history. The air around the giant war machine shimmered with the power of its void shields.

The siege cannons upon the hulking shoulders of the Imperator thumped as they launched their first salvo, and the air was filled with screaming shells that erupted amongst the Word Bearers. Warrior-brothers were thrown through the air and tanks smashed asunder beneath the barrage, but that was as nothing compared to the awesome destruction that was to come. Super-heated plasma fed into the annihilator cannon on the beast's right arm, filling the air with potent hissing that hurt the unprotected ears of the Guardsmen, and the massive barrels of the deadly hellstorm cannon began to rotate, the wind beating fiercely as it picked up speed.

The hellstorm cannon let loose with a torrent of fire from the spinning barrels that tore along the line of Word Bearers, cutting from one side of the valley to the other, ripping through warriors and vehicles alike. The plasma annihilator cannon flared with the power of a contained sun and a gout of white-hot energy roared from its barrel, engulfing a handful of tanks that were instantly returned to their molten base elements.

The destruction that the Imperator wrought was awe inspiring, and a roar rose from the ranks of Imperial Guardsmen as their god-machine unleashed the power of its weapon systems upon the hated foe.

MARDUK BARED HIS sharp teeth, hissing up at the monstrous, unstoppable beast. Stabbing beams of energy flashed from the mountainside as the lascannons of the havoc squads positioned there targeted the Imperator. The powerful blasts looked like little more than pin-pricks of light as they strobed towards the Titan. Scores of predator tanks, Land Raiders, Dreadnoughts and daemon engines added their fire to that of the havoc squads as they directed their heavy weapons fire towards the towering behemoth. Missiles, lascannon beams, heavy ordnance shells and streaming plasma speared towards the Titan. Its void shields flashed as they absorbed the incoming firepower, leaving the deadly machine unscathed, and it returned fire with dozens of battle cannons situated in the leg bastions.

The ranks of the Imperial Guard renewed their attack, bolstered by the arrival of the Titan that unleashed the power of its plasma Annihilator once more, firing up into the darkness and blasting away a ridge top, causing salt rock, debris and daemon engines to crash down the sheer cliff in a mass avalanche. Its hellstorm cannons smoked as they spun, tearing along the ridge. Rain turned to steam as it lashed against the super-heated barrels of the mega-weapon. Barrages of ordnance continued to pound at the void shields atop the carapace of the Titan, and they flashed with a myriad of colours as they deflected the incoming fire.

Marduk swore again and fired into the press of bodies around him, feeling the shifting tide of the battle turn against his Legion. There was just not enough firepower to take down the Imperator's shields, let alone damage the Titan, not while they were already engaged with the Guard and Skitarii forces.

But to fail in their duty to hold the valley was to face a fate far worse than death. If it was necessary, every Word Bearers Space Marine would willingly give his life in this battle at his word. Though it was Kol Badar's place as Coryphaus and strategos to organise the complex, interwoven battle lines, the carefully planned advance, fire support and overlapping fields of fire, it was Marduk's place, in the absence of the

Dark Apostle, to be responsible for the Host's spiritual leadership. If he gave the order to stay and fight to the death, for that was what the gods of Chaos wished, then his word would be obeyed without question. The warrior-brothers would sell their lives dearly but willingly, taking as many of the enemy with them as they could, before their own life essences were freed from their earthly forms.

But Marduk could not see how a noble sacrifice could be made against this ancient war god. No, there could be no proud last stand. There would be only death and destruction, swift and ignoble. They would not be able to buy the time that the Dark Apostle needed to complete the construction of the Gehemahnet, and that was paramount. If the building work was interrupted then the whole attack against the planet was rendered pointless, and the Council of Dark Apostles upon Sicarus would be most displeased. That was truly something to be feared, for even in death, the Council would reach into the abyss of the Immaterium and seek out the souls of those who had failed them. The endless torment that they would orchestrate was too horrific to even contemplate.

He felt anger build within him and hacked around in a fury, shattering bones and slicing through flesh as he fought in the rising water. Many of the enemy were wading almost to their stomachs through the fast moving flow, and the corpses of the slain floated face down, their blood leaking out like an oil slick. Another blast from the Imperator obliterated a section of the battlefield with the power of its weaponry, and the whooshing sound of water instantly turning to steam was mixed with the roars of the dying and the detonations of the fuel lines and ammo-banks of vehicles.

'We must pull back, First Acolyte,' Kol Badar growled over the vox.

'The great war leader Kol Badar, ordering a retreat from Imperial Guard,' remarked Marduk. 'I can hear them laughing at us already.'

'Let them laugh. They won't have the chance to savour their victory for long.'

'For them to be able to savour any sort of victory against the Legion of Lorgar shames us all,' snarled Marduk.

'You wish to die here, whelp? I will joyfully oblige you if that is what you truly desire. And nobody will save you this time.'

Burias-Drak'shal cleaved his icon into the chest of a Guardsman, splattering blood across Marduk's helmet.

'The battle is good,' he growled, the thick daemon teeth within his shifting jaw making his speech awkward. He was not privy to the private vox transmissions passing between Kol Badar and Marduk. 'Is this the day to give our lives to Chaos?'

Marduk shook his head at the possessed Icon Bearer and snapped a barbed response to Kol Badar.

'The gods of Chaos would curse you if you dared try, warlord. Your failure mars us all.'

'And I will stand with my head held high before my lord and accept any punishment that he metes out. I would not try to wheedle out of it like you, whelp.'

'You admit your failures then, mighty Kol Badar.'

'I listen not to your spineless taunts, snake. As the gods are my witness, I will see that damned Imperator fall. I am still warlord of the Host, and you will do as I command.'

'I look forward to seeing you grovel and lick the ground at the Dark Apostle's feet as you beg for mercy,' snarled Marduk.

'Never going to happen, snake,' said Kol Badar. The vox-channel clicked as it was opened to the champions of the coteries.

'Fighting fall-back,' ordered the Coryphaus. 'Front coteries detach, third and fourth lines lay cover. Second and fifth lines, intersect with the first, overlap and close out. Third and fourth, then detach. And pull back those damned Dreadnoughts and daemon engines.'

Burias-Drak'shal snarled in frustration, ripping a man in two as he enacted his dissatisfaction.

'We flee from these?' he said as he broke the back of another soldier.

'No,' said Marduk. 'We flee from that.'

'Bah! We have taken down Titans before. The Coryphaus is weak.'

'Eyeing his position already, Burias-Drak'shal?'

The possessed warrior grinned ferally before he allowed the daemon within him to reassert itself, and he was transformed beyond being able to communicate. With a roar of animal power, he launched himself back into the fray.

Marduk felt shame and resentment build within him. It was not the way of the Legion to back off from a battle against the soldiers of the Corpse Emperor, though he knew that Kol Badar's orders were the best path of action for the Host.

Still, it would be a pleasure to see the arrogant bastard taken down a peg when the Dark Apostle received word of the setback.

THE WORD BEARERS' retreat was perfectly executed as the lines of coteries fell back in textbook order, laying down fields of overlapping fire to cover those that backed away. Those coteries in turn then planted their feet and covered their brethren. Fallen warriors were dragged back, for to leave them upon the field of battle would have been a gross sacrilege, and in addition, the war gear and gene-seed of the Legion were far too precious to abandon. Vehicles rolled slowly backwards, firing their weapon systems towards the Titan.

Most of the daemon engines and Dreadnoughts were dragged out of the fighting by massive chains hooked to heavy, tracked machinery, though they fought and struggled to rejoin the fray. Several of them turned against their minders, killing dozens of the black-robed humans that strained to rein them in, and tipping over several of the heavy vehicles hauling them backwards. Others ripped free of their restraints and launched at the foe, ripping, tearing and roaring, flames and missiles streaming from their weapons before they were inevitably silenced by the guns of the Imperator.

Kol Badar felt the shame tear at him, but he could not allow the Host to be destroyed. The losses had been high, however, and this day would long be lamented.

He had of course made preparations for a fall-back if it was needed, it was just part of the canon of engagement to be ready for any eventuality, but to order a retreat was not something that he had been forced to do for millennia.

With withering, concentrated fire, the Word Bearers drove the enemy back. The Legion slowly retreated, their bolters creating a swathe of death.

Ground-hugging, eight-legged machines skittered forward from the Chaos Space Marine lines. They were smaller than the towering defilers, and operated by beings that had once been lowly humans. Now they were forever linked to the machines through mechanical hard-wiring and black sorcery, the corrupted flesh of their bodies contained within domed, liquid-filled, blister-like eyes at the front of the constructions.

The bloated abdomens of the machines pulsed as circular mines were excreted from their rears, jabbed downwards through the water and into the earth. They scuttled forward, their oversized bellies shrinking as they laid their deadly cargos just beneath the crust of the hard packed salt rock, placing thousands of the mines across the entire breadth of the valley.

Other, longer legged constructions strode through the deepening water, like perverted, multi-limbed water fowl. They liberally spewed a thick, glutinous, oily liquid across the top of the water flows, spurting it out past the Word Bearers that backed away, out into the no man's land between the two forces.

The Imperials' fire destroyed dozens of the twisted creatures, and entire sections of the valley were still exploding beneath the horrendous force of the Imperator's weaponry, but they were disposable and Kol Badar did not care that they were destroyed. They were performing their allotted tasks and their destruction was of no consequence.

The Titan took another massive step forwards, the huge, multi-tiered metal foot slamming down with thundering force, firing its weapon systems at the retreating Word Bearers. Battle cannons atop the Titan's carapace turned, tracking the Thunderhawks and Stormbirds as they screamed through the storm, veering out towards the ridge-tops.

The words of the First Acolyte rang in his head and his anger grew. Such a victory for the Imperials should never have come to pass and he felt frustration weigh heavily upon his massive shoulders. He had wanted more time to scout out the enemy, to assess its strength and composition, but the Dark Apostle's wishes had been clear, and time had been a critical factor. To properly evaluate the enemy would have meant facing the foe deeper in the mountains, and he had felt that such a strategy would not have been to the Dark Apostle's liking.

'You are too cautious, my Coryphaus,' Jarulek would have said. He had insinuated it before.

His caution would have spared the lives of many warrior-brothers this day, however, for the arrival of the Titan had been an unexpected shock. And now, he was forced to fight a retreat.

Still, he would damn well ensure that the enemy took as many casualties as possible during the Host's withdrawal.

As flames and shrapnel fell upon the thick, oily soup spewed forth by the twisted, long-legged walkers, the valley erupted into tall flames. Burning fiercely, they roared across the entire width of the valley, engulfing dozens of the walkers. They squealed horribly as they perished, legs kicking in agony as flames licked at them. The burning liquid gruel had covered hundreds of mindless Skitarii as they had continued their relentless advance after the retreating Chaos Space Marines, and the flames dissolved their flesh as they marched. Pieces of machinery, having lost the flesh that bound them together, slipped beneath the streaming waters, though they continued to burn, even beneath the surface.

The first tanks reached the mines secreted beneath the salt rock and were thrown into the air as the powerful weapons detonated. Having seen their power, the Imperials would be loathe to continue their advance until minesweepers had been brought forward to clear a path, and the princeps of the Imperator Titan would have no wish to risk his colossal war machine.

He had bought the Legion time, but it was time that he would have to use carefully, to plan and plot the demise of the Imperator Titan. Strategies and ploys were already swimming through his mind. He knew the place where he would face it, having already noted, on his flyover, the narrowing of the valley some five kilometres back.

He raised his bitter gaze to the heavens that were being ripped apart by lightning and falling shells, and repeated the oath he had sworn to the First Acolyte.

'I will see that god-machine fall by my hand,' he swore, 'or may my soul be damned to torment for all eternity.'

Thunder boomed overhead, as if in response to his oath.

He would break the machine-spirit of the beast, and once victory had been achieved, he would stand before Jarulek, the Dark Apostle, and accept whatever punishment he deemed suitable for his failures this day.

THE BATTLE WAS long over, and the intense storm overhead had abated. The waters had receded, flowing further down the mountains, leaving a mire of destruction across the valley. Bodies were strewn all across the battlefield, and burned out vehicles and wrecks scattered the field. Few enemy casualties remained, most having been hauled from the firefight, though Elysians wielding flamers torched those that were left behind. All avoided the blackened hulls of the enemy vehicles and cursed engines, for to destroy them utterly would be too labour intensive. Teams of Elysians bearing heavy arrays of detection sensors inched forward, removing thousands of landmines from the ground. They were far slower than the bizarre minesweeper vehicles of the Adeptus Mechanicus that fanned the ground with great sweeps of mechanical analysis arms. But the orders of the Elysian command were clear: the army would advance as quickly as possible, and every man equipped to detect the mines, whether Elysian or mindless servitor, would be employed.

Under the shadow of the stationary Imperator class Titan *Exemplis,* the adepts of the Mechanicus swarmed over wrecked Imperial vehicles, salvaging precious machineries and supplicating the dead or dying spirits of the vehicles. To Brigadier-General Havorn, they looked like nothing more than clusters of carnivorous ants tearing apart the carcasses of dying prey. The adepts swiftly stripped weapon systems from tanks and Ordinatus Minoris crawlers with focused energy, and loaded them alongside working engines, track-works and control systems onto the backs of hulking hauler vehicles for reuse.

Industrious servitors worked tirelessly, hefting heavy pieces of equipment with servo-arms and harnesses under the watchful eyes of the adepts, and the fallen Skitarii were likewise gathered up and taken to rolling factories that followed in the wake of the main army. There they were dropped onto mass conveyer belts and taken inside for recycling. Havorn was unsure what that entailed. He imagined that the weapons of the tech-guard warriors were torn from the dead flesh of their hosts, but he did not know the fate of the dead flesh. Only when the Techno-Magos Darioq had made a cold entreaty to him had he learnt what happened to those desecrated bodies.

'A request, Brigadier-General Ishmael Havorn,' said the techno-magos in his monotone voice. 'It is my understanding that the flesh bodies of your inactive soldiers are being gathered. Are they to be taken to the reprocessing factorum units of your regiment? I was not aware of the presence of such facilities within your expedition force.'

'Tokens of Elysia will be placed upon the eyes of my fallen soldiers and their flesh will be consumed with cleansing flame. The priests will guide their souls on their way to the Emperor's side,' replied Havorn, unsure of what the techno-magos spoke. 'It is the way of the Elysians. Each man carries with him his twin tokens of Elysia,' he explained, reaching beneath his robe and jangling a pair of round metal coins that hung around his neck, a fine chain running through the holes in their centres. 'This has long been the custom of my people. We specialise in drop attacks, and it is seldom possible to extract our dead, but it matters not where the body lies, merely that the spirit is guided on its way.'

'The dead flesh husks are burned? That is illogical. It is a waste of resources, both of promethium and of the flesh husks. And what of your flesh units that have been rendered inoperative but not yet fully non-functional?'

'My wounded, you mean?' asked Havorn, his voice icy.

'If you wish.'

'My wounded soldiers are removed from their platoons and taken to the medicae facilities within my mass transport-landers. Those with fatal wounds are comforted as much as possible before their spirits are guided on their way.'

'I would make a request of you, Brigadier-General Ishmael Havorn.'

'Ask away,' said the Imperial commander, though he felt wary, not knowing where the magos was leading.

'It is illogical and irrational to dispose of your non-functional flesh units as you do. I would ask that upon the conclusion of your priestly rituals, that the flesh husks are collected for reprocessing by my adepts.'

'Reprocessing into what?'

'Into a semi-liquid, protein based nutrient paste.'

Havorn blinked as if he could not possibly have heard correctly.

'You... you wish to turn the bodies of honoured Elysian soldiers who have fallen in battle against the enemy into *paste.*'

'It is a logical use of limited resources. My Skitarii cohorts are well fuelled, but a replenishment of feed levels would be advantageous.'

'There really is not an ounce of humanity left in you is there, you wretched, base machine?' said Havorn, his voice trembling with emotion.

'Correction. There are exactly thirty-eight Imperial weight units of living flesh and tissue upon my frame, Brigadier-General Ishamel Havorn. I am neither wretched nor base, although their usage in such a context is a new piece of data memory to be stored. And I thank you for calling me "machine", though I am not yet so fully esteemed within the priesthood of Mars as to become truly one with the Omnissiah.'

'Your answer, *magos*,' said Havorn, 'is that you can go and burn in hell before I hand over any of my soldiers to you, dead or alive.'

Seeing no immediate response forthcoming from the magos, he added, 'That means no, you cold-hearted bastard.'

# CHAPTER THIRTEEN

'WE HAVE IDENTIFIED the location from which the enemy has chosen to face us, brigadier-general,' said Colonel Laron.

'Show me,' said Havorn. The large table between the pair lit up at Havorn's word, thousands of twisting green lines of light springing up to show a detailed schematic map of the surrounding area. At Havorn's instruction, the crouching servitor built into the table's base manipulated the rendered image, scrolling it across the surface of the table and zooming in on valleys and ravines. At another word, the densely packed lines began to rise above the table, giving a three dimensional view of the mountains.

Taking a moment to study the detailed map, Laron pointed.

'We advance along this main valley bed here. Our scouts move along the ravines here, here and here,' he said, indicating two thin valleys a few kilometres away from where the main force advanced. 'And our drop-troopers have landed at these points,' he said, picking out a dozen key, strategic high points.

'As you have read in my reports, our attacks to take the high lands up to here,' he said, indicating, 'have been fierce, but a success.'

'The enemy has defended them half-heartedly,' said Havorn. 'Your men took them too easily, and I mean no slur upon them. When they choose their place to stand and fight, then they will face far stiffer competition.'

'My sentiment exactly, brigadier-general, and I believe we have found that place. Early forays to take these points here,' he said, indicating the ridges some ten kilometres into a particularly thin stretch of the valley, 'show high concentrations of the enemy. Our attacks have been rebuffed.'

'And with high casualties, I see,' growled Havorn.

'Indeed, the enemy will not budge. That is where they will make their stand.'

'It is a good place for it. The twisting valley is at its narrowest there. There is not a straight line of fire longer than a kilometre, rendering our ordnance of limited use, but their warriors will excel. It means that the *Exemplis* will have to get close to them to engage, rather than blasting them from five clicks out. It is a cunning place to make their stand. But it could be a ruse. Have you scouted for ambush points ahead of this position?'

'I have, brigadier-general. The valley thins some ten kilometres further up, here. It shrinks to a width of less than a hundred metres at several points; that's a tight fit for the Imperator. That would be the place to launch an ambush, but there are more than forty places where the valley contracts in such a way.'

The brigadier-general grunted.

'Any sign of enemy movement? If we walked into that valley and the enemy had control of those ridges, we would suffer heavy casualties.'

'None, sir. I have sentinels scouring the region, but they have engaged nothing more than cultist outrider vermin that were skulking parallel to the valley. They were all slain.'

'The enemy commander is no fool. If I were him, I would plan something here,' said Havorn, pointing towards one of the narrower areas of the valley. 'The minesweepers have found nothing as yet?'

'No dedicated minefield, only mines scattered every hundred metres or so.'

The Imperial forces had been slowed to a crawl behind the sweeper units. Though no further minefields had been discovered, the traitors had placed sporadic patches of mines down, just enough to force the Imperials into scanning their entire advance.

'A series of cracks riddles the cliff faces all along this stretch. I have ordered flame units to advance along the cliff walls and cleanse any cave systems. Scanner teams are accompanying the flame units, sweeping the area for life-signs and power outputs.'

'Order demolition teams to cave in the larger crevices,' said Havorn.

'Yes, sir.'

'They will wish to wipe the history books clear of the shame they were dealt at the hands of the *Exemplis*,' said Havorn. 'They may well have chosen this place to make their stand against us. If that is so, they will fight to the last.'

KEEN AUTO-SENSORS alerted Kol Badar to the questing machine-spirit of an enemy auspex, and the last systems of his Terminator armour were automatically shut down. He was barely breathing, and his twin hearts beat but once per minute. He had long ago shut off his air-recycling units, and the massive weight of his armour hung upon him as the last of the servos were deactivated.

Dully he heard the muffled thump of detonations, and dust and rock crumbled down upon him as the ground beneath his feet rumbled. Heavier chunks of salt stone broke upon him, but still he stood immobile in his state of semi-suspended animation. It was not the deep slumber that the Legion was capable of, for that would require the attentions of the chirurgeons to reawaken him, and would not allow him to remain at least partially alert for the signal that his prey was near. It was however a deep enough state that any auspex sweep of the enemy should not detect his life signals, particularly while he was shielded behind the thick, insulating plates of his sacred armour.

An indeterminable amount of time passed, and flames washed over him. His heartbeat increased as he registered the brightness of the promethium-based conflagration lapping over him and the sharp rise in temperature. The heat was almost unbearable, the inbuilt heat regulators of the suit having been shut down along with all its other functions, so as not to give off any tell-tale signs of radiation.

The flames lit up the narrow cavern brightly. He could see other members of the cult of the Anointed, immobile as he was, flames licking at them. He saw the external ribbed piping of one warrior-brother's early mark Terminator suit flare brightly as it melted, and the warrior pitched backwards to the cavern floor, his lungs undoubtedly on fire. Kol Badar was pleased to see that he did not cry out as he perished.

As his breathing became more regular in conjunction with the quickening beat of his heart, he began to use too much oxygen, and there was not a lot of that remaining in his suit. He settled his breathing and his heart slowed until once again it almost stopped.

'WHAT WAS THAT? You picking something up?' asked the weary Elysian trooper, looking back at his companion. The half-sphere of the heavy auspex disc was a weight in his arms. Trust him to get stuck doing the lifting rather than the easy job of keeping an eye on the data-screen on the attached feedback unit.

'I thought there was something for a second, but its gone now. Must have been a glitch.'

'Time for us to swap, eh?' he said hopefully. His team member laughed out loud.

'Not a chance. You lost, fair and square. Come on, let's move on. There's nothing here.'

KOL BADAR'S CONSCIOUSNESS was roused as the cavern shook and crumbling salt dust dropped down upon him. There was a pause of almost thirty seconds before there was another booming sound like thunder, closer than the first, and more dust rained down. His yellow eyes flickered and he powered up his suit's basic functions. He reasoned that after the enemy had swept the area and declared it clear there would be little in the way of further scans, so powering up his Terminator armour was but a slight risk. Air began to circulate once more, stale and dry, and he breathed in deeply, flooding his oxygen starved body. His senses came instantly to their full capacity.

His prey was near.

He took in his surroundings, turning his head from side to side as he familiarised himself once more with his situation as his suit's diagnostics ran. The cavern was cramped and demolitions had caused cave-ins in several places, where chunks of rock lay strewn across the uneven floor. Massive blocks leant against several of the Anointed and parts of their blessed ceramite were chipped and dented. Many of his brethren were half-buried beneath the collapse, but it mattered not.

The cavern branched off a deep chasm that split the cliff face of the main valley. He had seen the narrowing of the valley and noted its suitability as a place to face the enemy, but he would never have discovered this cave system in the limited time that he had to prepare the ambush. One of the cultists had brought it to the attention of the Chaos Marines, one of the wretched dogs that doted on the First Acolyte.

Branching off the sheer-faced chasm, the entrance to the cave system was hidden from view, and unless someone knew of its location it would be nigh on impossible to discover. Still, the flames of the enemy's weaponry had found the entrance, even if their bearers had not, and his armoured suit was blackened from the blasts of blazing promethium.

The demolitions that had followed had completely caved in the chasm as the seismic charges shook down rock from above. No exit from the cavern could be accessed by a warrior in Terminator armour. But if the enemy became complacent because they believed their flanks were secure, then all the better.

There was another booming sound and the ground shook. Though the area was most likely not being scanned, it would be too much of a risk to chance vox communication. The First Acolyte whelp should be moving the cultists forwards. If he mistimed the advance, the Anointed would be left terribly exposed to the guns of the cursed enemy. He ground his teeth. Were the whelp to fail in his duty, he and his brethren would almost certainly be annihilated. Not even the upstart Marduk would knowingly leave the Anointed to perish, though he was certain the thought had crossed the bastard's mind.

Still, this was the only chance the Legion had of destroying the Imperator class Titan without the loss of hundreds of warrior-brothers. It was a risky venture, but Kol Badar found a glimmer of excitement at the prospect. He had thought that such battle hunger was long lost to him, faded over the great expanse of time he had been fighting for the glory of Lorgar. He welcomed the feeling like a long-lost comrade.

Dozens of sharp, red lights began to flash against the cavern wall as the ground once again rumbled beneath him. The shifting of rock caused another avalanche of stone and dust to fall, and Kol Badar smirked as he realised that there was every chance that the whole cavern might cave in at any moment, trapping him and his warriors beneath thousands of tonnes of mountain. That would be an inglorious death indeed, and he could just imagine the derision that would be heaped upon him by the bastard Marduk if such a fate was his destiny.

There was yet another crashing impact nearby. He estimated its distance. It was difficult to determine, but he judged that after two more impacts, it would be time to detonate the impact charges.

The red lights of the charges blinked rhythmically in the darkness. They were designed to explode outwards in one direction only, and he had organised their placement carefully. An expert in siege demolitions, he had spent several hours studying the fault lines and angled layers of the rock face so that the powerful explosives would have the desired effect. Just one misplaced charge would bring the mountainside down upon them, and he would allow his fate to be determined by none but himself.

With his savage anticipation building, Kol Badar listened for the heavy impacts that would signal the launch of the ambush.

THE COMMAND CHIMERA rumbled forward slowly in the shadow of the *Exemplis.* No matter how many Titans Brigadier-General Havorn had seen, he was still awed by the sheer scale of them, and this, an Imperator class no less, was amongst the largest Titans ever constructed. From his position in the cupola of his Chimera, he had a good view of the massive war machine as it strode forward. He could understand why the twisted adepts of the Mechanicus worshipped it as an avatar of their god, for it was a powerful, primal thing of epic proportions.

From behind, he could see many of the oiled workings of the god-machine, as its rear was not as well armoured as its front. Pistons the size of buildings rose and fell as the behemoth lifted its huge, bastion legs, and eddies of super-heated smoke and steam blasted from the exhausts in its back. Higher still, pennants were whipped by the bustling breeze atop the arched architecture of the fortress that the Titan bore upon its massive shoulders. Battle cannons and siege ordnance was housed there, along with temple shrines to the Machine-God and mausoleums that held the remains of past princeps.

The narrowness of the ravine made him tense and uneasy. It was more like a chasm than a valley, the sides sheer and close. They seemed to loom in threateningly, and if the enemy moved onto those ridges, they would be able to rain fire down upon the convoy with impunity. Still, Laron's 72nd held those regions and were pushing forwards along the ridge tops ranging out ahead. The point of the Mechanicus forces was moving forward slowly through the ravine and it seemed that the enemy were content to wait for them up ahead. Still, he half expected something to happen, some ploy to be launched, and he had learnt long ago to trust his instincts.

'Rachius,' he called down into the Chimera, 'run another sweep.'

'In progress, sir,' said his communications officer.

The Chimera was outfitted with an array of sensors and powerful vox-units to allow the brigadier-general's commands to be conveyed to his captains, and tall aerials and dishes rose from the rear of the APC.

'I'm picking up faint radiation from the cliff face, sir. The exact position is unclear.'

'Damn it!' he said. He felt his tension rise. This was the critical moment. The diminishing width of the pass had forced the Imperial regiments to spread out in a long, unwieldy convoy. If an attack was launched it would be difficult to bring up support and the rest of the regiments behind would grind to a standstill.

'From the cliff face you say? The demolition teams didn't leave any chasms clear, did they Rachius?'

'No, sir. My reports say that all were collapsed. Could just be geothermals.'

'Try to pinpoint the location. And order the Chimeras to close formation. Tell the commanders to be ready for action.'

The hyperefficient officer swiftly carried out his orders. Donal Rachius was a fastidious man, utterly fixated on his appearance. A crease in his uniform upset him, and he was exact and precise in everything he did. Havorn tolerated his eccentricities because the man was exceptional and his perfectionism, though irritating on a personal level, made him ideal for his role.

The Chimeras behind his command tank revved their engines and advanced, drawing level with his own. There was not room in the ravine for even twenty of the vehicles to advance alongside one another. Still, they kept a wary distance from the Titan. One descending foot of that monster would easily crush a tank flat.

When the attack came, it was almost a relief. But it came at the front of the armoured column, the strongest point in the Imperial line.

He heard scattered bombardments up ahead and saw the column slow.

Instantly, Havorn dropped his lanky frame down through the cupola, swinging his legs around beneath him as the powered semi-lift lowered into the Chimera proper. It was cramped with communications equipment, a small team of officers and a very large ogryn hunched in a specially constructed bucket seat, his head stooped but still pressed against the roof.

'Report,' he ordered.

'The techno-magos informs us that his Skitarii units have engaged the foe.'

'What, the enemy has advanced to meet us?'

'It would seem so, sir. They have rounded the bend here,' said Rachius, pointing to a data-slate with a simplified overhead map that glimmered with points of light that indicated troop formations.

'But that makes no sense. They will be butchered without the support of their bigger guns, which are all positioned back here, are they not?' replied Havorn, pointing along the ridge tops some kilometres around the bend in the ravine.

'They are. We have received no intelligence to indicate otherwise.'

'They want us to engage, halting the column.'

'The Mechanicus have already halted, sir. The *Exemplis* is readying its weaponry.'

'Tell the magos to advance. Tell him his god-machine is in danger,' said Havorn as he climbed once again into the cupola to survey the situation.

He raised the hatch of the Chimera to see the Titan's legs planted firmly, and support pinions locking into place as it readied its weapons. The air was charged with power as its plasma reactors burned hot, making ready to unleash a fusillade of destruction. He lifted a pair of long-range crys-scopes to his eyes, scanning along the cliff walls ahead. There was nothing there, no entrance from which a hidden force could emerge.

'We have enemy movement, sir! They are pushing forward along the ridges! And more of the enemy are moving along the ravine at pace! They are moving for a full attack!'

What the hell are they doing? thought Havorn. They will be slaughtered in their droves by the massive guns of the *Exemplis.* Still, this new development gave him no comfort and his unease rose.

'FORWARD!' ROARED MARDUK. 'The eyes of the gods are upon you and their judgement awaits. Prove your worth before them, and take your hatred to the infidel corpse worshippers!'

The cultists advanced before his fiery oratory, but Marduk despised them, every one of them. The gods were watching, it was true, and they would laugh as these wretches were led to the slaughter to accomplish the goal of the true favoured ones, the Word Bearers.

'Onward, warriors of the true gods! Glory and ascension awaits you! Fear not the guns of the enemy. Embrace destruction, for with your deaths the aims of the gods are accomplished. Give up your mortal bodies unto Chaos, and your souls will soar in the realms of the deities this night!'

Five thousand cult warriors advanced into the tight ravine, towards the waiting guns of the looming Titan in the distance. They screamed their devotion as they marched forward.

Leaving a considerable gap behind the Cultists of the Word, Marduk ordered the remainder of the Host forward, giving up on any further pretence that they were going to wait for the enemy to come to them.

He saw the Imperator Titan plant its feet as the cultists drew within range of its weaponry, just as Kol Badar had predicted. Now was the time for the Coryphaus to act. His gambit needed to work, else the entire Host would be at the mercy of the Titan's guns.

'I still think we should have held back,' snarled Burias. 'Let that bastard Kol Badar face the enemy alone and blast him back to hell.'

'Burias,' laughed Marduk, 'your choler is in the ascendant. You speak these words because you believe they are what I wish to hear?'

'A statement of my feelings, First Acolyte, nothing more. The bastard ordered a retreat against the foe. He deserves death.'

'Maybe, my Icon Bearer, but you would have us abandon the Anointed?'

'The Anointed are Kol Badar's pets. They worship him with nearly as much fervour as they worship the Dark Apostle.'

'And you are bitter at having not been indoctrinated into the cult,' said Marduk. The Icon Bearer made no reaction, save a slight tension in the muscles of his neck, which Marduk observed. He laughed.

'You are an ambitious, black-hearted one, aren't you, dear Burias. And you hold some resentment towards me, is it not true?'

'First Acolyte?' asked Burias in a slightly hurt tone. 'I am your devoted warrior, always.'

'But you blame me for your not having been embraced into the cult of the Anointed. You think it is a subtle insult directed at me from Kol Badar, an insult that you must pay the price for because of our comradeship.'

'The thought... had crossed my mind, First Acolyte.'

'It pleases me that you can at times be honest, Burias,' said Marduk lightly. Before the Icon Bearer could respond, he continued, 'Is it the lure of Slaanesh, your endless desire to raise yourself, to better yourself?'

'It is not perfection I seek, First Acolyte, as you know. I don't need perfection to attain that which I desire.'

'No, you just need to be on the good side of one who would become a Dark Apostle. Do not become complacent, dear Burias. When the time comes for me to take on the mantle of that position, I will choose only the most suitable warrior to become my Coryphaus.'

'My suitability is in doubt?' questioned Burias, trying to keep his pristine, handsome, pale face devoid of emotion, but Marduk saw a flash of Drak'shal's fury in his eyes.

'No, Burias, but nothing beneath the gaze of the gods is certain. Do not allow your hubris to one day shame you.'

'Nothing will bring shame upon me, just as I will never bring shame upon the blessed Legion of Lorgar,' said Burias severely.

Marduk smiled and placed his hand upon the Icon Bearer's shoulder.

'I believe you may be right, Burias, old friend. You said the same words on Calth while we battled the cursed warriors of Guilliman.'

'And you said that one day you would lead one of the grand companies, with me at your side,' said Burias.

'That is true.'

'If this... trick of Kol Badar's goes badly, then there will be too few warriors within the Host to justify splitting it, as the council on Sicarus ordered, especially after the casualties we suffered against the Titan. There will be little need for a second Dark Apostle.'

'That thought had crossed my mind,' snarled Marduk, his mood darkening. 'Regardless, one way or another, I *will* become a Dark Apostle.'

'Always I have fought at your side, First Acolyte, long before I called you such. And I will fight there, always, whatever may come.'

Marduk placed a hand upon Burias's shoulder.

'I would expect nothing less of you, my friend. Now, order the last of the Host to advance. We fight them here, and pray to the gods that Kol Badar succeeds, else we will all be slaughtered and seeing them sooner than expected.'

'What if it is the will of the gods for us to die here, First Acolyte?'

'Then it is their will, but that is not what I have foreseen. The twisting paths of the future are never set, but of the thousands of coiling threads that I have followed in my dream visions, we were slaughtered here in less than half of them.'

'That is of... great comfort, First Acolyte,' said Burias dryly.

Marduk laughed again, his black mood evaporating in the blink of an eye.

In the distance, the Titan's guns flared brightly as they were unleashed, followed half a second later by the cacophony of the barrage as it echoed up the narrow ravine. Hundreds of cultists were instantly slain in the devastation. The timing for the Word Bearers' advance was critical. If Kol Badar timed it wrong, it would result in the destruction of hundreds of the Legion's warriors. If he timed it just right, then the slaughter of the enemy would be great.

Gods of the Ether guide me, he prayed, and he closed his eyes. A waking vision assailed him the instant he closed his eyes, the image sharp and painful, leaving a dull ache in his temples. He wiped a droplet of blood from his nose and watched as it instantly congealed to a dried crust upon his finger. He would need to discuss this vision with the Warmonger at battle's end, for its meaning was obscure and disturbing.

'Come,' he said, 'let us release our anger upon the foe.'

'I'VE GOT A lock, sir!' shouted Rachius. 'Emperor damn them, there are more than fifty of the bastards in there! Vector 7.342.'

Havorn swore and swung his crys-scopes around towards the location that Rachius had indicated. 'Get the Chimeras moving,' he shouted, but the words were lost as a series of detonations ripped apart the mountainside, rocks exploding outwards spectacularly. One sizeable chunk of rock smashed onto the front of his Chimera, denting the thick armoured plate, and others smashed harmlessly against one of the massive feet of the *Exemplis,* no more than thirty metres from the explosion. At such a range its void shields were useless. They were only effective from a certain distance, and anything within them would be able to attack the god-machine directly.

With this thought running through his mind, he swore again and slammed his fist down onto the top of the Chimera as he saw the dark shapes emerging from the cloud of dust surrounding the point of the explosion.

Clattering gunfire erupted from weaponry as the figures stamped heavily through the rubble. They were huge individuals, their armour plate thick and nigh on impervious to harm: Terminators, the enemy's elite.

Havorn banged on the top of the Chimera.

'Go!' he shouted. 'Intercept them! And get some heavy support over here now!'

The engine of the APC roared as the tank surged forward over the hard packed earth. The other Chimeras were already heading towards the foe, and Havorn saw one of them explode, oily, black smoke rising sharply above the orange conflagration.

'Sir, you should come down here,' said Rachius from below, concern in his voice, but Havorn ignored him, instead grabbing the pistol-grip of the pintle-mounted storm bolter. He swung the powerful weapon in the direction of the Terminators and squeezed the trigger.

KOL BADAR ROARED as his combi-bolter barked fire at the enemy. He was in the middle of the foe's colonnade, surrounded, and he saw vehicles and soldiers rushing towards him from left and right. But the true target of his wrath stood before him: the massive Imperator Titan.

Grand steps descended from arched gateways upon the foot of the immense war machine, and he strode towards them. Covering fire from reaper autocannons swept across the approaching vehicles and Skitarii units, and raking fire tore down the enemy infantry that ran across the salt packed rock to intercept their progress.

Nothing would keep Kol Badar from his target, however, and he strode relentlessly forward through the increasing weight of incoming fire, driven on by steely determination and anger. The defensive batteries built into the Titan's leg bastion unleashed their wrath, engulfing the advancing Anointed, ripping through even mighty Terminator armour with the force of their detonations. Air bursting shells exploded overhead, scattering red-hot, scything shards of shrapnel down onto the warrior-brothers and Kol Badar hissed as a shard the length of a man's hand slammed into his helmet, cutting through his armour and piercing one of his eyes. Blood welled and congealed in the wound and he broke off the end of the piece of red-hot shrapnel with a swat of his power talon, leaving the tip embedded in his eye.

Such a wound would not keep him from his prize and he roared wordlessly as he continued his relentless advance.

Arched doors ten metres up the Titan's foot were thrown open and Skitarii warriors stepped out onto the steps, firing their inbuilt heavy weapons down into the terminators. Kol Badar aimed his combi-bolter into the throng of the enemy and strode on.

Enemy Chimeras screeched to a halt and blue-grey armoured Guardsmen emerged, firing their lasguns into the mass of Terminators. Bolter fire ripped through the soft targets and heavy flamers roared as they engulfed swathes of them in deadly infernos. Combi-meltas hissed as they targeted incoming vehicles, and tanks were rendered into burning shells as they detonated, their crews screaming in pain as they died.

A Chimera with arrays of aerials caught the Coryphaus's eye and he recognised it as belonging to an officer of high rank.

'Take it down,' he ordered. Reaper autocannons swung around, spraying bullets from their twin barrels.

Bolter shells struck Kol Badar, knocking him back a step, and he snarled and squeezed a burst of fire from his combi-bolter at the figure manning the pintle-mounted weapon, forcing him to duck back into the Chimera. He swung his heavy head back towards the target. Only twenty metres now. The Skitarii spilled steadily down off the steps of the Titan's foot as more emerged and others advanced around from the limb's three further assault ramps.

'Keep on the target!' he roared, knowing that if the Anointed were held for too long, the Titan would simply walk away, leaving them horribly exposed.

The Skitarii marched straight into the advancing clump of Terminator-armoured warriors, attempting to keep them away from their charge through sheer weight of numbers and the power of their guns. The steps were packed with the enemy and they unleashed a storm of fire upon the Anointed, each tech-warrior firing over the heads of their companions as they stepped slowly forwards.

Rotating cannons tore through more of the Word Bearers, ripping through ancient plasteel plating and flensing flesh from bone.

High above, steam and smoke was expelled sharply from pistons and locking mechanisms ground as they were released. Kol Badar recognised the signs of the Titan preparing to move.

With a roar he smashed into the ranks of Skitarii, battering them out of his path with sweeps of his power claw and ripping through them with his combi-bolter on full-auto.

'Forward, Anointed! For the glory of Lorgar!'

THE CHIMERA SLEWED to the side as it took heavy incoming fire and one of its tracks was ripped to tatters. Armour piercing rounds tore through the shell of the APC and two officers within slumped in their seats, their blood splashing the interior. Havorn slammed his fist onto the glowing rune-plate and the release valves of the assault hatch hissed as the ramp swung down. He was exiting the Chimera even as the ramp was still falling and he flicked his plasma pistol into life.

'Sir, let us at least take the lead, since you seem set on this course,' said Rachius in his concerned voice.

Havorn's ogryn bodyguard emerged from the confines of the Chimera and breathed deeply, its eyes narrowing. It stepped protectively in front of the brigadier-general, shielding him from fire with its muscled bulk.

'We must stop the enemies from reaching the Titan! Why in the Emperor's name hasn't it moved yet?' Havorn shouted.

'Our units are converging on them, sir. You do not need to enter the battle!'

'They are coming too slowly,' shouted Havorn. 'We move, now!'

With that, the Elysian commander pointed the way and the ogryn began loping towards the enemy who were climbing the stairs on the Titan's leg battlement.

They were too late, Havorn thought. The Terminators were already past them and his body was old and slow. He cursed the debilities of age and pushed himself on. Fallen Elysians and Skitarii lay strewn across the ground, as well as the occasional bulky form of a fallen enemy. Few of them were truly dead and they lashed out, grabbing and killing any foe within their reach. Even at the point of death they were more than a match for a Guardsman.

The ogryn raised its heavy ripper gun, a thick finger pulling the trigger. Empty shells scattered in its wake. It did not roar or bellow as it charged. Such base, animalistic behaviours had been erased from its simple brainpan, but no amount of augmetics could improve the aim of the ogryn and the bullets from its ripper gun sprayed the area, hitting nothing.

Havorn snapped off a shot with his pistol, the streaming blue-white bolt of plasma dropping one of the Terminators.

Bolter fire raked towards him, striking the hulking abhuman, who grimaced in pain. Chunks of flesh were torn from its arms and chest, but the three metre creature that dwarfed even the Terminators did not slow. It lowered a shoulder and smashed into one of the enemy, knocking it from its feet. Raising the butt of its heavy ripper gun, the ogryn began caving in the helmet of the fallen warrior, smashing it down onto the prone traitor again and again.

Skitarii and Guardsmen were all around Havorn, filling the air with las-fire and high-velocity bolts. The traitors were on the steps and held a tight defensive formation. More than half of the bastards had been taken down, most from the devastation wrought by the Titan's cannons and the powerful weaponry of the elite tech-guard warriors. It would be but moments before they breached the blast doors that led into the Titan.

'Take them down, men of Elysia!' he hollered, his steely, field parade voice carrying over the din of battle.

Suddenly, victory was snatched away as the Titan raised its massive foot high up into the air, carrying with it the traitor Terminators and hundreds of tech-guard warriors still fighting upon the steps. Many of them were knocked off as the *Exemplis* raised its leg, falling ten metres to the valley floor as the foot was raised higher and higher.

'Damn it!' swore Havorn.

'WE ARE THROUGH, Lord Coryphaus,' reported one his Anointed brethren. The chainfists had made short work of the blast doors that had sealed the entrance to the leg bastion, carving through the thick metal with a minimum of fuss.

'Into the breach!' roared Kol Badar as he crushed the augmented, semi-mechanical skull of a Skitarii warrior and hurled it over the edge as the Titan's leg continued to rise. At his command, the Anointed entered the Imperator class Titan.

# CHAPTER FOURTEEN

FLAMES ROARED UP the spiralling metal staircase, clearing the way. Two abreast, the Terminators had been climbing for what seemed like an age, assailed from above and below by an apparently never-ending stream of Skitarii warriors. Inbuilt defence turrets were stationed at every second level, their hard-wired servitor controllers built into the heavy wall panels of the interior staircase, and they swung their weaponry upon the intruders, filling the cloying, hot air with shells and gunsmoke.

It was hard going, the Word Bearers forced to fight for every step of the mammoth climb up the interior of the Titan's lower leg. Kol Badar's destroyed eye, still with the shrapnel shard jutting from the socket, was throbbing in his head, but he pushed the sensation away as he stamped up the heavy, grilled stairway, blazing away with his combi-bolter.

He was at the front of the line of Terminators, the heavy-flamer wielding Anointed warrior Bokkar at his side. Between the flames of his comrade and the bolts of his combi-weapon, few of the Skitarii could stand against them. Those few that survived were ripped apart by the warlord's power claws and hurled over the railing to fall down the open expanse in the centre of the spiralling stairwell to join a growing pile of sparking, shattered corpses.

The resistance from above slackened. Clearly the last of the Skitarii had been neutralised, leaving just the inbuilt, servitor-guided sentry guns to hamper their progress. The going was unsteady as the heavy Titan foot smashed down into the ground with devastating force and rose once more into the air.

Kol Badar allowed a pair of cult members wielding reaper autocannons to advance past him, for their powerful guns were able to rip through the armoured plating protecting the sentry guns far more efficiently than flame or bolt. It was a torturous task, for they had to advance up through a barrage of gunfire before they could get a clear shot at the servitor housed just beneath the turret, but time was of the essence.

Up and up the Terminators wound, under constant, desperate attack from the Skitarii climbing behind them and the sentry turrets. Ammunition was running low, and with a blast of fiery promethium directed down over the open stairwell to melt the exposed flesh of a dozen enemy machine-warriors, the last of the heavy flamer reloads was expended. Even if they had not a bolt shell remaining, Kol Badar would fight on and succeed. He would die, with all his Anointed at his side, before he would allow the bitch of a Titan to best him once again. He would rip it apart piece by piece with his bare hands if need be.

The noise of turning machinery became increasingly loud as the Terminators neared the Imperator's knee joint. Abruptly, the last sentry gun was silenced, the milky life-blood of the servitor dripping down through the latticed grill to fall upon its brethren advancing from below. At Kol Badar's direction, blinking demolition melta-charges were attached to bulkheads where he indicated, as scattered gunfire roared up from below, shearing through the metal stairs. Scores of charges were placed, four times the amount that were used to blast away the mountainside. Kol Badar was taking no chances.

He nodded as he studied the placement of the blinking charges.

'Commence the descent,' he ordered and the Anointed warriors began to fight their way back down the staircase that they had just fought so hard to ascend.

'We are entering the range of the Imperator, First Acolyte,' hissed Burias. The massive Titan had already blasted every cult warrior apart.

'If he's failed, this war is going to be over very quickly,' replied Marduk.

He climbed atop a rocky outcrop, allowing the ranks of the Host to advance past him. Vehicles rumbled forward slowly, and Dreadnoughts and Defilers stalked across the broken ground. Burias climbed up behind him, planting the icon in the ground at the First Acolyte's side.

The Imperator raised its leg for another step. A series of internal explosions suddenly burst out around its knee-joint. Flames and smoke erupted from the mechanical joint, a mass of detonation within ripping through the thick, reinforced metal. The bastion foot touched down on the floor of the ravine and a secondary flash of timed demolition charges erupted. For a moment it looked as though they had had no effect, until the knee joint gave way beneath the immense weight of the Titan and it lurched to one side as if in slow motion, thousands of tonnes of metal teetering over the battlefield.

Its weapon arms flailed out as if trying to steady the toppling god-machine, but the Titan was falling, gaining speed as its weight bore it down on the ground. There was silence as it crashed to the ground, until the bastion of one shoulder slammed into the sheer cliff face, causing the mountain range to shudder beneath the impact, and an avalanche of rock was sheared from the cliff. Off balance, the impact caused the Imperator to swing towards the ravine wall and the leering head of the great machine smashed straight into the rock face with a resounding crash. The other leg of the Titan, bearing the entire weight of the colossal machine, buckled suddenly with a screeching sound of wrenching metal. The Imperator slammed to the ground with a deafening boom that echoed through the ravine. The impact caused avalanches of rock and rubble, and hundreds of Guardsmen and Skitarii were slain. A rising cloud of dust obscured the fallen, broken Titan.

As one, the Word Bearers roared victoriously at the sight of the mighty war god dying and Burias raised the Host's icon high into the air for all to see.

'Advance and kill!' roared Marduk and the Host descended upon the shattered vanguard.

After killing the traitor Pierlo, Varnus had expected to be slain by his captives, but if anything, his action seemed to have garnered a kind of hateful respect from the hunched, black-clad overseers. Oh, they had hurt him as they prised him off the corpse of the traitor, filling his body with agonising torment as the vile serums that filled their needle fingers assaulted his nerve endings, but he had been expecting far worse.

But no, he had been dragged from the tower and placed on the chirurgeons' familiar, cold, steel slab. There was no Discord there and he felt naked without it speaking to him. There the spindly creatures had prodded and probed him. They seemed particularly interested in the symbol beneath the skin of his forehead, chittering excitedly amongst themselves. They drew blood from him and fed burning black liquid into his veins. Small, black leech creatures with orange patterns on their backs were attached to him and he howled as they burrowed their heads into his skin. They were pulled back out, bloated and fat, some time later.

The joy of killing the man had filled him with warmth. The traitor had turned against the blessed, *hated, False* Emperor and had deserved death. Taking his life had been a great release and it made him feel strong and rejuvenated.

The enemy had taken him back to the tower, transporting him back to the top, now hundreds and hundreds of metres above the ground. He was to work alone. Perhaps the overseers feared that he would kill again if he was teamed up with another slave, and perhaps he would have.

The tower was above the level of the black pollution hanging over the city, and it swirled beneath him. The mighty winds that were building didn't seem to touch the tower; it was as if he stood in the middle of the eye of one of the dust devils that raced across the plains, spinning the salt up in twisting cones of wind. The noxious fumes whipped around the tower and it looked to him like a great, black, whirlpool that stretched out as far as the eye could see.

He felt strange without the cover of the smog overhead. Now he could see the blaring white sun during the day and the stars by night. And always there was the red giant planet Korsis, drawing ever closer. It was so large that it almost filled the skyline and Varnus could see valleys, craters and channels criss-crossing its surface.

The brightness pained his eyes and the lack of oxygen made them heavy and sore. Twice a day he was held down as red-black, stinging drops were inserted into the centres of his eyeballs. He screamed as the sharp needles pierced the aqueous humour of his orbs and injected the substance that squirmed and burned within him.

Tirelessly he worked, doing the job of two men, but the toil no longer drained him as it once had. Indeed, time seemed to pass quickly and he was barely aware of the fall of darkness as the white sun disappeared over the horizon and rose again as he worked, smearing the blood mortar over the stones.

A Discord seemed to favour him, if such a thing was possible, and it hung at his side for hours on end, pounding his eardrums with its blare. He could hear the voices talking to him, teaching him and bolstering him when he felt weak.

Sometimes he shook his head as if waking from slumber and the horror of his predicament washed over him. He would cry out at such times, longing for the Emperor's soldiers to rescue him and his world. He would kick out at the Discord and it would retreat from him. But these moments passed quickly and Varnus would recover himself and be somewhat confused. He couldn't remember why he had been angry and he set back to work with vigour, the feel of the blood mortar familiar and comforting beneath his hands.

The daemon speaker would hover slowly forward until it floated less than a metre from him once again. Sometimes its usually limp tentacles would reach forwards and touch him on the neck or the back as he worked. He would recoil in shock and the thing would retreat once again. Over time, he came to ignore the touch of the thing and in a way he found it almost comforting. He felt a strange, warm, buzzing sensation at its touch, but it was not unpleasant.

The Discord told him many interesting things: what the other slaves were thinking, that the overseers were afraid of him and that his power was growing. It talked of the early years of an ancient hero who had been turned into an immortal godling and lived on in a great palace far away, and the warriors that he had trained to spread his word. He wondered if it was the Emperor, but his head had begun to hurt when that thought had crossed his mind and he quickly dismissed it.

Yet even as he had come to bear his hellish existence, he prayed for release. Not death, no, he had lived through too much to simply perish. He was filled with a new vitality and fervour that made him determined to cling to life for as long as he was able, to see this through one way or another.

He prayed for deliverance and tears ran down his face as he felt himself becoming lost. Had the Emperor forsaken him? Did His light no longer shine upon Tanakreg? Had he been abandoned to his fate? For the first time since the occupation, Varnus felt true despair pull at him. He prayed vainly to the Emperor, but felt no comfort in his soul. No, he felt nothing but emptiness.

The next moment he had forgotten why he had been crying and wiped away his tears in bafflement. Shrugging, he continued his work. The Gehemahnet needed tending.

THE SLAUGHTER HAD been immense and the valley was filled with the dead and dying. A cloying stink rose as the temperature soared, the hot-white sun overhead baking the earth. The wreck of the Titan was like the discarded shell of some giant colossus and scattered debris littered the ravine floor. The battle had been intense. The Word Bearers advanced into the confused Imperial lines after the Imperator's fall, killing thousands of their foes as they tried to realign their battle line and draw support up past the massive frame of the *Exemplis.*

The enemy had inflicted a terrible blow and had retreated once the Imperial reinforcements were brought forward. They had suffered relatively few casualties.

A day had passed and the giant Ordinatus *Magentus* rumbled towards the valley. It was so massive that it was barely able to fit through the ravine and there was no possible way that it would be able pass the fallen Titan. It came to a halt some kilometres back, where the valley was wider.

A dozen, giant, spiked stabiliser legs unfolded to either side of the titanic vehicle, steam hissing out into the hot air as their mechanics were engaged. They reached out to either side of the massive structure and drove down into the ground.

The air tingled with power as giant energy cores were readied and the massive ribbed cone of the Ordinatus's main gun was raised. A sound like a thousand jet engines began to whine, soon reaching a screaming intensity that reverberated through the earth. Elysians within a kilometre of the giant machine clutched hands to their ears as the giant creature made ready to unleash its power.

The air around the ribbed cone-tip of the giant weapon began to shimmer and waver and then the Ordinatus fired.

A deafening, sharp crack like the sound of a planet ripped in two resounded through the valley. Pre-warned, all the Elysians in the vicinity had engaged the sound mufflers within their helmets, but even so the blast of sound was deafening, making Havorn's eardrums vibrate painfully. An ungodly silence followed as if all noise had been sucked out of the valley by the focused blast of sonic energy, and the air between the gun and the valley wall wavered and reverberated.

The effect was astounding. Where the centre of the focused beam of sound struck the wall the rock was turned to dust, exploding outwards in a massive blast as it was shattered down to the molecular level. A wave seemed to spread from the epicentre and the rock rippled as if it were liquid, huge cracks appearing in its wake. Vibrating and shattered, the entire rock face broke apart and fell to the valley floor with a crash that rumbled along the entire mountain range. A huge cloud of salt dust rose up into the air.

# CHAPTER FIFTEEN

THE BATTLE FOR Tanakreg had ground down into a brutal war of attrition. Within five days, the ravine had been levelled by the sheer power of the Ordinatus machine. Its sonic disruptor had reverberated through the mountains, shattering stone to powder and causing vast avalanches that could be felt halfway across the continent. Laron had only ever read about such a weapon and to see it in action was awe-inspiring.

The steep cliff walls had been reduced to dust and the valleys were filled with crumbled salt rock, creating a vast expanse that the Imperial Guard and Mechanicus forces rolled across. The going was difficult, but with the steep ravine walls reduced to nothing, they were able to attack on a wide front. The enemy was unable to contain the sheer number of the Imperial troopers and they were relentlessly pushed back.

The enemy had launched several vicious assaults to destroy the potent weapon, but Havorn had charged Laron with the protection of the Ordinatus and he had coordinated effective battles to stall the attacks. He had used his Valkyries effectively, rapidly redeploying units of his 72nd to launch counter-attacks into the flanks of the foe as they advanced, while the tech-guard of the Mechanicus had taken the brunt of the frontal attack. As he dropped more troopers into the flanks of the enemy, Havorn had directed heavier support forwards. Assailed on all sides, the enemy advance had been quashed time and again. He relished these battles. Now that the terrain had been levelled out, he had found the enemy much easier to deal with.

He snorted, easier to deal with indeed. He had fought the traitor Astartes only once before and they were the toughest and deadliest foes that he had ever encountered in all his days of soldiering. Still, without having to advance up narrow defiles, the small number of the enemy meant that the vast Imperial war engine could grind on. Though their attacks on the traitors became more directed and hate fuelled, they were unable to close on the Ordinatus *Magentus*.

Tens of thousands of Imperial troopers had been slaughtered and, wherever the enemy dug in for a concerted battle, they inflicted horrendous casualties. But it was not enough to halt the never-ending tide of Guardsmen, Skitarii warriors and vehicles. The foe was spread too thin and their flanks were surrounded and overrun. It was simply too wide a front for them to cover and there were too few of them to fight the type of war that suited the massed ranks of the Imperial Guard so well.

Laron had capitalised on this and had ordered hundreds of Valkyries ahead of the main Imperial entourage. Already his storm troopers had assaulted and destroyed several of the enemy anti-aircraft guns emplaced on the foothills of the mountains and he knew that the time would soon come when the Imperials would be able to push forwards and take the fight onto the plains.

Vast lines of siege tanks ground inexorably forward behind the infantry, pounding the enemy with ordnance outranging anything they had.

Slowly the enemy had been driven back, pushed out of the mountains and onto the salt plains that spread out like a rippling blanket towards Shinar. If they could push the foe back to the peninsula on which Shinar sat then they would eventually grind them down and destroy them utterly. Though he saw that the old brigadier-general grieved for every soldier that they lost, he could also see that the Imperial commander was confident of their eventual victory.

It was not the type of war that Laron liked, for it was more suited to the style, or lack of it, of other Imperial Guard regiments. His soldiers of the 72nd were drop-troopers, and in this war of attrition, the unique skills and talents of his units were not being utilised to their full capacity. As soon as the battle reached the plains though, it would be a different matter.

The sheer number of casualties amongst the techguard had been staggering, but ever more of the mindless tech-soldiers marched from the vast factorum crawlers that ground over the earth in the wake of the army.

Laron had seen the mechanised enhancements and weapons of fallen tech-guard servitors being recovered as the Imperials pushed ever forward and he knew that they were used to create more lobotomised, unfeeling soldiers. Brigadier-General Havorn had spoken of what became of the flesh of the fallen tech-guard and Laron had been horrified.

It was like some archaic necromancy, he thought, to reuse the flesh and armaments of the dead to create new soldiers to throw thoughtlessly at the enemy. It was morbid and repugnant, and he tried as best he could to keep his men away from them. What was it that the magos called them? Skitarii? They were unnatural and they made his men uneasy. Hell, they made *him* uneasy. Soldiers that had no notion of fear or self-preservation, he was certain they would all march straight off a cliff to their doom at a word from the magos.

Soldiering was meant to be glorious; heroes were made on the battlefield and the victories of those heroes would be recorded for ever more back on Elysia, recounted in song at the great banquet feasts and balls of his home world. War was a noble act where one could gain honour and standing. There was no such honour or heroism amongst the Skitarii. They were little more than automata, playing pieces of their callous masters. What honour was there to be gained fighting alongside such as them?

He had been fascinated and horrified in equal measures when he had first seen inside one of the mobile factorum crawlers. The motionless shapes of pale-fleshed humans were held in vast aisles of bubbling vat-tanks, kept in a dormant state. That single factorum must have held ten thousand inert bodies, or 'flesh units' as the magos called them. Darioq had coldly explained that while the Mechanicus was capable of creating its own vat-grown host bodies, it was time consuming and resource heavy, so most of these soldiers were from the other Imperial Guard units within the Crusade. They had suffered grave injuries, leaving them alive, but brain-dead. Others were criminals and deserters, and the punishment for their crimes was to be turned over to the Mechanicus.

They were destined to become battle servitors, all semblances of their former selves erased with mind-wipes and the removal of their frontal lobes. Indeed, Darioq had stated, the entire right hemisphere of the brain was removed from all but a few, those used as shock-troops and specialists, where a certain degree of adaptability and autonomous decision making, albeit severely limited in nature, was required.

Such concepts as creativity were clearly frowned upon within the Mechanicus and Laron had found this galling, for it was anathema to the way that the Elysians operated. Adaptability, being able to react to changing directives, objectives and situations, and the ability to operate effectively deep behind enemy lines with little or no direction from the upper echelons of command, were all favoured skills in the ranks of the Elysians. Those same traits were deplored as dangerous and heretical amongst the adepts of the Machine-God.

'Deep in thought, acting colonel?' asked a voice behind him and Laron turned to see the approach of the leather-clad figure of Kheler walking towards him.

'Commissar,' said Laron in acknowledgement. The commissar had been his shadow ever since Havorn had assigned him to watch over Laron and he had certainly not been lax in his duty. Wherever he turned, the man was there, watching and listening, waiting for him to slip up.

'Survived another day without getting shot then, acting colonel?'

'The day isn't over yet, Kheler.'

The commissar chuckled. It was insulting and belittling to have the man watching over him and the threat of his presence was obvious. His uniform demanded respect, yet he was a canny warrior and a highly capable officer.

The swiftness and the severity of his judgement was shocking. The commissar had been smiling and talking with one of Laron's men, but had executed that same man without a thought not an hour later when the trooper had turned to flee because his lasgun's powercell had run dry. A laspistol blast in the man's head had shown all the troopers that cowardice of any kind would not be tolerated.

'You do not flee the enemy under any circumstances!' he had roared. 'The Emperor watches over you! If your power cell runs dry, you pick up the weapon of a fallen comrade. If that runs out of ammunition, you draw your pistol. If you have no pistol, you fight with your knife. If your knife breaks, you fight with your bare hands. And if your hands are cut off, still you do not flee, you attack the enemy with any weapon that you have. You bite their damned kneecaps off if that's all you can do!'

That had got a scattered laugh and Laron had marvelled at the commissar's skill. The man had just killed one of their comrades and he had got them to laugh.

'But you do not flee!' Kheler had shouted severely, his eyes wide and threatening. 'Or I promise you, as the Emperor is my witness, I will gun you down like traitorous dogs.'

'Motivation,' the commissar had explained to Laron. 'That is what I provide to the regiment. The threat of a bullet in the back of the head is good motivation not to turn tail and run.'

The man switched from jocular comrade to ruthless executioner in a second. Even knowing this, Laron found it hard to dislike the man.

'Aren't you hot in all that get up?' asked Laron, motioning towards the commissar's long, black, leather coat and hat. The temperature over the last days had soared and any sign of the storms of the week before were long passed.

'Hot, acting colonel? Yes, I am damn hot, but do you think I would look such a commanding figure if I were stripped down to my undergarments? And besides, I look damn good in black. Dashing is a word that springs to mind.'

Laron snorted and shook his head.

'We are only flying to the front to see if the enemy truly are retreating into the plains, or if it is some ploy.'

'Must keep up appearances, acting colonel,' replied Kheler.

'Hold on to your hat, commissar,' said Laron as the dark shape of a Valkyrie approached overhead and the Elysian clicked his visor down over his eyes.

The screaming reverse thruster jets of the Valkyrie blew salt dust up into the air as they rotated towards the ground. Laron smirked as the commissar shielded his eyes with one hand while the other was clamped down on his leather hat to keep it from blowing away in the hot blasts of air coming from the engines.

The aircraft touched down onto the ground and its door slid open. With a nod to the men inside, Laron climbed aboard and turned to help the commissar. The man fell into his seat, blinking salt dust and grit from his eyes. Laron stood in the open doorway grabbing the overhead rail tightly as the Valkyrie left the ground and began a vertical ascent into the air, turning slightly.

The Imperial battle force was spread out beneath him. Lines of tanks rolled towards the front and tens of thousands of men marched in snaking columns over the rough ground below. Free of the constriction of the ravine, the army moved forward quickly and in good order. It was surprisingly tiring to organise the dispositions and lines of advance, but no doubt that was why Havorn had ordered him to do it, to test how he progressed.

It was certainly very different from being a captain. He had not thought it would be quite as difficult and exhausting as this. A lot of thankless organisational and logistical work required his attention, and he found that he was weary beyond words. He was far more tired than he had ever been when engaged on the front line, or even more than when he had been when engaged in deep missions on enemy territory. At those times he would snatch sleep when he could get it, an hour here, a few minutes there, but at least that sleep had been deep and restful, even if it was in the middle of a siege barrage. Now he felt as if he hadn't slept for weeks and when he did sleep he was still filled with concerns and worries.

There were a thousand and one jobs that needed his agreement, his sign-off and his input, and he had found it overwhelming. He was floundering and he couldn't see how he could get on top of it all. It was difficult at first to know what truly needed his attention and what could be delegated to his captains. His respect for Havorn had grown immeasurably as he realised the responsibilities of command that must weigh upon him. But he never showed it. He was always the tough old campaigner and none doubted his judgement.

*His* captains; it still sounded strange to him. He was no longer one of them. Now he was their colonel and the easy camaraderie he had once shared with them was long gone. He grinned at that. In truth, there had never been any easy camaraderie with most of the other captains. They had always seen him as an arrogant bastard, the "glory boy" captain of the storm troopers. And they were mostly right.

It felt good to be in the air again and away from the pressures of his position, and he hated slogging along on foot. That was grunt's work. He was a glory boy, damn it, and if they were going to say it anyway, he might as well live like one.

'You think the enemy is truly retreating, colonel?' asked the commissar, though Laron knew that he already knew the answer. This was for the benefit of the men around them. He noted that in the presence of other members of the 72nd the commissar left out the *acting* part of his title. No doubt that was something else to do with motivation. He was a clever bastard.

'It's been hard and we have lost a lot of good men, but the enemy are falling back. I just want to see the traitors fleeing with my own eyes. The Emperor is with us! We will make them pay for the deaths of the men of the 72nd.'

He saw a slight smile in the eyes of the commissar as he played along.

'Motivation is vitally important,' the commissar had said earlier, 'whether it comes from the threat of a bullet, the impassioned speech of an officer, or propaganda from the mouth of a commissar, it doesn't matter. All that matters is that your soldiers fight and that they have fire in the bellies. For some that comes from faith, for others it is from outrage. It doesn't matter. But you must never miss an opportunity to inspire your men. It's not much, but a word here and there goes a long way with the common soldiers.'

These conversations with the commissar had been playing on his mind and he had begun to wonder if that was another reason why Havorn had attached the commissar to his staff, to teach him the power of motivation in all its forms.

'By the Emperor's name, they will pay,' said Laron once more.

THE VIEW ON the grainy, black and white pict screen had been astonishing as Marduk's Thunderhawk made its approach into Shinar. It was almost unrecognisable from the original Imperial city. From this high in the air, nothing of it could at first be seen, bar the immense Gehemahnet tower that rose into the atmosphere. It was as if some astral deity had hurled a mighty spear into the planet, skewering it. It could be seen for thousands of kilometres all around when the air was clear.

Beneath the tower, lower in the atmosphere and hanging directly over Shinar, was a thick, oily, black smog. It was roiling and contorting as if alive and it was swirling around the tower that rose in its midst. The tower was the very centre of the gaseous maelstrom and the fumes were thickest there, the winds strongest.

Nothing could penetrate the thick, noxious smog cloud, not even the Thunderhawk's sensitive, daemon infused sensor arrays. Marduk knew that the Gehemahnet was creating a wide cone of warp interference that spewed out through the atmosphere and beyond. This interference would effectively make the entire side of the planet all but invisible to the enemy. Just as he thought of this, the Thunderhawk's pict-screen flickered and degenerated to static. The power of the Gehemahnet was indiscriminate in whose equipment it affected. The gunship was still around two hundred kilometres from Shinar, but had clearly entered the wide cone of disruption. The Thunderhawk had no need for concern – it did not rely upon technical arrays and its witch sight saw all the more clearly within the warp field.

Marduk felt the field close over him and his twin hearts palpitated erratically for a moment, his breath catching in his chest. It was joyous to feel the power of the Immaterium wash over him. He heard the whispers of daemons in the air. He felt his sacred bond to the warp strengthen and his power with it. The Dark Apostle was wielding some powerful faith to have created a warp field of such potency.

Movement flickered at the corner of his eyes and he felt presences brush past him. The barriers between the realms of Chaos and the material plane were thin. He could almost make out the daemonic entities straining from beyond to cross the thin walls and enter the physical world. Soon, he whispered to them. Soon the barriers would be stripped away like flesh from bone and then they would be able to take corporeal form and bring hell to this world.

He felt a certain amount of apprehension as he approached Shinar and the Dark Apostle. To wield such power! Never had he been witness to such a feat of strength from the holy leader as this. He had not imagined that Jarulek would have been able to create such a powerful Gehemahnet. He had believed that the Dark Apostle had long reached the apex of his rise and that his own rise would eclipse Jarulek's power over the next millennia. Could he have underestimated him?

An uncomfortable and uncharacteristic flicker of doubt squirmed within him. Could he wield such power? He knew that he could not, not yet, but he was certain that his powers would treble once he passed the full indoctrinations required to become a true Dark Apostle. He would take up that mantle and soon, no matter what the cost or sacrifice required. Long had he waited for his moment to arise and he would be damned before he saw his opportunity splutter and die out like a blood-wick before it had even begun to blaze.

He was rocked as strong winds buffeted the Thunderhawk. The engines screamed as they fought against being sucked into the swirling morass rotating around the Gehemahnet. The speed of the wind whipping around the tower must have been immense. Pushing these thoughts from his mind, he closed his eyes and let his spirit break free of his earthly body.

Invisible and formless, he soared from the Thunderhawk, passing through its thick, armoured hull and out into the atmosphere beyond. The powerful winds touched him not at all, and with a thought he hurtled across the sky towards the rising Gehemahnet, faster than any crude mechanical aircraft ever could. This was the way of the spirit and with his insubstantial warp-touched eyes he saw the world in a different light.

The material world around him was shadowy and dim, a pale and dull land. With his sight he saw not the light of the sun, nor the colours of the mundane world, all was but shades of grey, lifeless and monotone. There was movement all around, the movement of daemons separated from the mundane world by only a micro-thin layer of reality. He flew somewhere in between the two worlds, neither truly in the real nor the Ether, but he could perceive both.

He heard nothing but the scraping, garbled cacophony of noise that was the sound of Chaos. A million scrambled, screaming voices mixed with the roars and whispers of daemons. It was to Marduk a comforting, neutral sound in the back of his mind. It was too easy for the unwary or uninitiated to be forever lost in the sound. If you listened too closely, it would draw you into it and never let you have peace.

Marduk willed himself on, drawn towards the massive Gehemahnet tower that rose in both the material world and the warp. It existed in both planes and it was not a monotone shadow like the rest of the world he passed over. Far from it, for the Gehemahnet tower was ablaze with light and colour. Deep red and purple shades blurred across its surface amid flashes of metallic sheen, like those created by oil on water.

Tiny pinpricks of light, countless thousands of them, marked the soul fires of the mortal worker slaves who toiled over the physical construct of the Gehemahnet. They were like tiny burning suns. Some burnt bright and fierce, their spirits strong, while others grew pale and faltering. Carrion daemons of the warp clustered around each burning soul fire, along with an endless myriad of daemons of other bizarre and horrific forms. They clumped around the souls of the living like cold children around a campfire in winter, struggling against each other to be the closest to the blaze. The mortals were completely unaware of the attention that they received, save perhaps for an occasional feeling of coldness, or a flicker of movement in the corner of the eye.

The kathartes were there, clustered around the bright soul lights, and they raised their beautiful, pristine and predatory feminine faces at his approach. They kicked away from their vigils and soared towards him upon glowing feathered wings. In the Ether they were angelic and alluring – it was only when they breached the material plane that they became twisted hag furies.

As he drew nearer the pulsating Gehemahnet, he saw the soul fire of one of the slaves flicker and dim as the man gave up his hold on his mortal body. Instantly, the pale light of the spirit was set upon by the daemons huddled around it and its light was hidden amongst the dense ball of daemons that were wild in their ravenous feeding frenzy as they consumed the unfortunate soul.

The soul fire of one slave drew his attention, for it was different from the others. It was bright and fierce, with a grand cluster of over a thousand ethereal denizens of the warp around it, and Marduk could feel their expectation. This one was favoured indeed, he thought.

A sudden tug upon his spirit pulled at Marduk and he allowed himself to be drawn towards the calling. In an instant he had passed through the walls of the shattered palace of Shinar and hovered before the Dark Apostle. He was infused with light, a strong presence in the warp as in reality. He turned his earthly eyes to look at Marduk and smiled.

'Welcome, my First Acolyte. I thought I felt your questing spirit lurking nearby.'

*I wished to see the glory of your Gehemahnet with more than the limited faculties of my mortal being, my lord.*

'Of course. Its power waxes strong.'

*It does, my lord. It is nearing completion?*

'It is close, but I need your strength, First Acolyte, to complete the rituals of binding. This is why I recalled you from battle.'

*The battle fares poorly. It is shaming.*

'I would sacrifice the entire Host in order to fulfil the will of the Dark Council, if such was needed.'

*And the warrior-brothers of the Legion will lay their lives down if that is what is required of them.*

'Yet you struggle, First Acolyte. Why is that?'

*The Coryphaus must be punished for his failures.*

'Must? You would make demands of me, First Acolyte?'

*No, my lord.*

'I have faith in my Coryphaus, First Acolyte. To doubt his abilities is a reflection of your doubt of me, for he is my chosen representative in all matters of war. You would insult me in such a way, dear Marduk?'

*No, my lord.*

'Do not defy me, young one. You are no Dark Apostle yet, and I hold the key to your future within my hand. I can destroy you at my will.'

*It will be as you will it, Dark Apostle,* said Marduk, and took his leave. His spirit soared high into the upper atmosphere. Hundreds of daemons were drawn to him, feeding upon the hot emotions of hate and anger flowing from his spirit.

THE TENT FLAP was thrown open and Havorn stooped to enter the shelter. The air was heavy and cloying with the stale smell of sweat. It took a moment for his eyes to adjust to the gloom before he could make out the three medicae officers standing over the cot in the corner. One of them approached him, saluting, and he recognised the man as Michelac, the chief surgeon of the 133rd. His black rimmed eyes were tired.

'It's not good, sir,' he said.

'What the hell happened?' asked Havorn.

'Astropath Klistorman collapsed late yesterday afternoon, as you know. He was ranting and was suffering severe convulsions, and he was bleeding from the nose. I suspected an internal haemorrhage within his brain; such a thing could have been building there for months. But he seemed to regain his strength this morning and he seemed to have suffered no ill effects.

This afternoon, however, he has had a series of episodes. He is sleeping now, but they are getting worse.'

'There are other astropaths with the fleet. This is war, medic, and people die. Why did you call me down here?'

The medicae officer licked his dry, cracked lips.

'His ranting has disturbed me. He has spoken of things that chill my soul.'

'You fear possession?' asked Havorn sharply, his hand falling to his holstered weapon.

'No sir, not that, thankfully,' said the man hurriedly. 'But... I know that astropaths are powerful psykers, sir. I am no expert in such things, but I am of the understanding that they are able to see things that humble men like I cannot. In my opinion, that is not a blessing but a curse.'

'So what has he been speaking of?'

'When his words are decipherable, he has been speaking of some construction of the enemy. It will erupt with power when the "Red orb waxes strongest" I believe were his words. Given that there is a damned big red planet hanging in the sky, I thought that you might wish to know what he said.'

Havorn walked to the side of the cot and looked down upon his astropath. The man was skeletally thin, his skin ashen. He wore a metallic, domed helmet over his head and his eyes were concealed beneath it, though there were no eye slits or visor. Pipes and wiring protruded from the back of the helmet, disappearing beneath his high-necked, sweat soaked robes. He was bound with leather straps, holding him firmly upon the cot.

'I didn't want to remove any of his accoutrements. I feared that I might harm him, or me,' muttered the medic. 'I ordered him restrained so that he did not harm himself if he had another seizure.'

Havorn nodded.

'Did he say what would happen when this power he talked about was unleashed?' he asked.

'He was not particularly lucid, sir. Most of his words were gibberish. He did, however, talk of hell being unleashed and of this world being turned inside out.'

The astropath coughed suddenly, blood and phlegm on his lips, and then he began to go into severe convulsions. The muscles in his neck strained as his entire body went rigid and shook, and the medic pushed a piece of leather between his teeth to stop him from biting though his own tongue. He twitched spasmodically for thirty seconds before going limp, his breathing heavy and ragged. He spat the leather from his mouth and turned his sightless gaze towards Brigadier-General Havorn.

'It draws near!' he said in a coarse whisper, flecks of foam spitting from his mouth. 'As the red orb waxes strong, it will erupt! Damnation! It will awaken Damnation! Destroy it before the time comes. It is...' The man's words dissolved into unintelligible gargles as another fit took hold of him.

'See to him as best you can,' said Havorn and he took his leave. Walking out of the tent, he raised his gaze to the giant red planet Korsis looming overhead. He had been told that it would be at its closest to Tanakreg in five days time.

Five days to wipe the enemy clear of the planet before whatever it was that the astropath had seen would occur. He wished that he could discount the man's fevered words as those of a diseased mind, but he felt that there was something in them.

Damn it, was he getting superstitious in his old age?

His gaze turned towards the insane construction that rose like a needle into the atmosphere. It was hard to believe it was over a thousand kilometres away.

It had to be destroyed. Five days, he thought.

'I AM WITHDRAWING the Host back to the defensive earthworks and bunkers outside the ruins of the city, my lord,' growled Kol Badar. He squeezed the trigger of his combi-bolter and ragged fire ripped apart the chest of yet another enemy trooper. There were thousands of them advancing all along the battle front and the Coryphaus's armour was slick with gore and the foul, milky, nutrient-rich blood of the Skitarii.

'I cannot hold them at the mountains with the valleys destroyed and our numbers are too few to halt them on the salt plains,' he said as he gunned down more soldiers advancing relentlessly into the Word Bearers' fire. The ground was liberally littered with the dead, yet the enemy continued to advance, stepping over the bodies of their fallen comrades. Others were crushed beneath the rolling tracks of battle tanks and mechanised crawlers. Earth and bodies exploded around him as shells from battle cannons pounded the line. Searing lascannons silenced a Leman Russ tank, blowing its turret clear of its chassis and Kol Badar heard the roars of the Warmonger nearby as the revered ancient one relived some long past battle as it killed.

The voice of his master, the Dark Apostle, throbbed in his head.

*The time of the Gehemahnet's awakening draws near. Allow it to be interrupted and your pain shall know no bounds, my Coryphaus.*

'I would gladly give my life in sacrifice for my failures, my lord,' said Kol Badar as he stepped slowly backwards, snapping off sharp bursts of fire left and right.

'Seventh and eighteenth coterie, close ranks and give covering fire,' he ordered, switching his comm-channel briefly. 'Twenty-first and eleventh, disengage and back off.'

*You have a duty to perform, Kol Badar, and you will have no such release while it remains unfulfilled.*

'Burias, ensure they do not encircle us with their light vehicles. Engage and destroy them,' he ordered before closing the comm once again.

'My lord is merciful.'

*No, I am not. Your failure will not go unpunished, nor will it be forgotten. Allow none to assail the Gehemahnet. Sacrifice every last warrior-brother before you allow a single enemy to launch an attack against it. Do this and the Dark Council will be pleased. Fail again and eternal torment will be yours.*

'I will fight them every step of the way, my lord,' swore Kol Badar. 'I have ordered Bokkar and the reserve to strengthen the defences, preparing for the arrival of the Host. We will hold.'

*Succeed in this, my Coryphaus, and I will give you what you most desire. I will give you the First Acolyte, and you can finish what you once started.*

Kol Badar blinked his eyes in surprise. He clenched his power claw tightly, the talons of the mighty weapon crackling with energy as he slew another pair of enemy soldiers, his fire cutting through their mid-sections. He chuckled in anticipation and felt a savage joy fire within him.

'I will not fail, my lord. I swear it before all the great gods of Chaos. I will not fail.'

# BOOK THREE: ASCENSION

*'With victories over others, we conquer. But with victories over ourselves, we are exalted. There must always be contests, and you must always win.'*

– Kor Phaeron – Master of the Faith

# CHAPTER SIXTEEN

The Imperial Dictator class cruiser *Vigilance* moved soundlessly through the void of space as it rounded the war-torn planet, dropping into close orbit. The calculations had to be absolutely precise and the logic engines housed within the bridge had been working constantly to provide the complex algorithms calculating the exact moment for the barrage to be unleashed.

The area of jammed communications was broad; to risk the *Vigilance* entering the field was testament to the severity of the threat. All sensory equipment was rendered useless as soon as they entered the zone. Even the astropaths were unable to pierce the gloom projected up from the planet's surface. Once within the field, the *Vigilance* was utterly cut off from the outside world. The only guiding light was that of the Astronomican, which Navigators could still thankfully perceive.

Nevertheless, to launch an orbital bombardment essentially blind was highly unorthodox and the risks were high. However, the Admiral had been insistent and the cogitators had been consulted to predict the exact mathematics required to plan such an endeavour.

The approach of the cruiser was painstakingly enacted. If it were but a fraction of a degree off its angle of approach, if its speed was slightly out and the tip of the massive cruiser off by the smallest fraction then the bombardment would miss the planet altogether, or would fall far from the target. Worse, it could fall upon the Imperial Guard on the planet's surface far below.

With its holo-screens blank and its sensor arrays rendered inoperative, the Dictator cruiser advanced into position. Muttering prayers to the Emperor that the algorithms he had been provided with were accurate and that his team of logisticians had coordinated them exactly, the ship's flag-captain breathed out slowly as the gunnery master initiated the launch sequence. The port battery, housing hundreds of massive weapons that could cripple a battle cruiser, were activated. Thousands of indentured workers slaved to match the exact range and trajectory initiated by the gunnery crew as they readied to fire. The gunnery captain prayed that his barrage would fall against the target.

His worry was in vain, for the *Vigilance* never had a chance to unleash its orbital bombardment.

A surge of warp energy from the infant Gehemahnet surged from the tower, creating an opening to the Ether for the smallest fraction of a second. In that brief flicker, the darkness of space was replaced with the roiling, red netherworld, a place of horror where the natural laws of the universe held no sway, and the nightmares of those of the material plane were given form. It was filled with screams and roars and the deafening, maddening blare of Chaos. It lasted but the blink of an eye, but when it passed, the *Vigilance* had gone with it, dragged into the realm of the Chaos gods.

Without the protection of its Gellar field, which it had no time to erect, the cruiser was overrun with hundreds of thousands of daemonic entities, its structure turned inside out. The physical forms of those unfortunates within the Dictator cruiser were driven instantly insane at the exposure to the pure energy of the warp, their bodies mutating wildly as Chaos took hold. Their souls were devoured and their screams joined with those of countless billions who had been consumed to feed the insatiable gods of the realm. Within the blink of an eye the *Vigilance* was no more.

MARDUK WAS ROCKED as the fledgling strength of the Gehemahnet surged. Such staggering power!

Only once before had he witnessed the birthing of a Gehemahnet, for to construct one of the potent totems was a draining experience. Only the most powerful Dark Apostles would even attempt to create one,and the process would often leave them shattered wrecks, weak shadows of their former selves.

Jarulek's presence was evidence of the truth of this. Marduk had been shocked by the appearance of his master when he had arrived back at the ruined shell of the once prosperous Imperial city.

Jarulek seemed to have aged several millennia. His skin was sunken and wasted, and bones and spider-web lines of veins were clearly visible beneath translucent, script inscribed flesh. His lips were thin and drawn back from his teeth like those of a long-dead corpse. Deep, dark, sepulchral sockets surrounded his eyes, though they flashed with defiant strength.

He is weak, thought Marduk, licking his lips.

'You feel the awakening, First Acolyte,' said Jarulek.

'Yes, Dark Apostle. It is... astounding,' Marduk replied truthfully. 'It must have taken much of your strength to imbue the tower with such potency.'

Jarulek waved a hand dismissively.

'The great gods gift me with the power to enact their will,' said the Dark Apostle lightly, but Marduk could see that he was almost utterly drained.

Jarulek saw Marduk's narrowed eyes and raised an eyebrow on his skeletal face.

'You have something to say, First Acolyte?'

'No, my Dark Apostle,' he said. It would not be wise for Marduk to antagonise his master, not yet. 'I am merely in awe of the power of your faith. I aspire one day to reach such glorified heights.'

'Perhaps, but the path to enlightenment is a long and painful road. Many fall along the way to eternal damnation and torment, seeking that which they desire too quickly, or by taking up challenges that are far beyond their reach,' said the Dark Apostle evenly, his velvet voice enunciating the words carefully.

'With your guidance, lord, I hope to avoid falling prey to such temptations,' said Marduk.

'As I would expect, my First Acolyte. The Imperials draw near?'

'They do, my lord. The Coryphaus pulls the Host back from its advance.'

'I do not require the Host to hold them indefinitely. It is but day's until the conjunction. That is when Korsis will be largest in the sky and the seven planets of this system will be aligned. We need but hold them until then. The Coryphaus understands my needs.'

'To be pushed back at all is an insult to the Legion. It shames us all.'

'To expect the unattainable is foolish, my First Acolyte. I never asked Kol Badar to destroy the foe, it is unnecessary. He must merely hold them until the alignment and buy time for the Gehemahnet to be completed.'

'And it is nearing completion, my lord?'

'It is. That is why I have called you back from the front line, to aid me in the final stages of its summoning. This Gehemehnet is to be different from any other totem that has been constructed before, for I have called it forth not to turn this planet to a daemon world, but to shatter it utterly,' said the Dark Apostle with a smile on his face.

'My lord?'

'It must be complete for the alignment. When the red planet is high, the Daemonschage will toll, signalling the death of this planet, and a great treasure will be revealed, a treasure that will be unlocked by the Enslaved.'

'The Enslaved?'

'One who will come to us. With the secrets unlocked, we will launch a new era of terror upon the followers of the Corpse Emperor. We will take the fight to those we hate the most.'

'The arrogant, cursed offspring of Guilliman,' said Marduk.

'Indeed.'

'First Acolyte, a question.'

'Yes, my lord?' asked Marduk, frowning.

'Have any holy scriptures appeared on your flesh yet?'

'No, my lord. I bear none but the passage that you honoured me with,' he said, indicating his left cheek where the skin of the Dark Apostle had knitted with his own.

'Tell me immediately if words begin to form upon your skin, First Acolyte. They... they mark your readiness to proceed with your induction into the fold.'

'Thank you, my lord,' said Marduk, bemused. 'I will consult you immediately should such a thing occur.'

'THEY ARE PLANNING to pound us into the ground with their artillery,' commented Burias, standing atop the first defensive line and watching as the Imperials advanced slowly. 'Are we just going to cower back here and allow them?'

The salt plains were spread with Imperials as far as the eye could see. They advanced in a massive, sweeping arc towards the curved first line of the Word Bearers' defence. The first bulwark was wider than the other three that guarded the crumbled remains of the Imperial city and, but for the reserve led by Bokkar, every warrior of the Host stood upon it awaiting the enemy. Havoc squads hunkered down within those bunkers that were intact, placed at one hundred metre intervals.

Burias and Kol Badar stood side by side as they watched the advance of the foe. A mass of salt dust rose up behind the advancing army.

Kol Badar swung around, his one good eye staring coldly down at the Icon Bearer. His other eye, shattered by shrapnel, had been replaced with an arcane augmetic sensor by the chirurgeons.

'You question the orders of your Coryphaus, whelp?' he snarled.

'No, Coryphaus, but I feel Drak'shal raging to be unleashed.'

'Keep a rein on your daemon parasite, Burias. Its time will come soon.'

'I shall, Coryphaus.'

'They have more ordnance than we.'

'There is no sign of that Ordinatus machine, though.'

'No. Its range is not as great as their artillery's. If it advanced ahead of the main battle line, it would sustain damage. The methodology of the Adeptus Mechanicus is rigid. They deviate not at all from their ritual tenets and the modes of behaviour programmed into their mechanical heads. They will not risk damage to the machine.'

'You know a lot about the followers of the Machine-God, my lord?'

'I have learnt much from the Forgemasters of Ghalmek. And I fought alongside Tech-Priests of the Mechanicum during the Great Crusade, marching to battle alongside blessed Lorgar and the Warmaster,' he said, bitterness in his voice. 'And afterwards, I fought against them.'

'I am sorry to have dredged up painful memories, Coryphaus.'

Kol Badar waved away the words of the younger Word Bearers warrior-brother.

'Bitterness, anger and hatred is what fuels the fires within. If we forget the past then we will lose the passion to dethrone the False Emperor. To lose the fire is to fail in our sacred duty, the Long War,' growled Kol Badar. A thought struck him, was the Dark Apostle fuelling his own hatred of the First Acolyte to keep the fires within him stoked? He dismissed the thought instantly as irrelevant to the situation at hand.

The Coryphaus placed the talons of his power claw upon Burias's shoulder plate and exerted just enough pressure for the ceramite to groan.

'No, we do not attack just yet. But when we do, Burias, *you* will lead it,' he said generously.

'You do me much honour, Coryphaus,' said Burias, surprise on his face.

'You may be the lackey of a wretched whoreson, but you should not be held in the shadows because of it,' said Kol Badar.

Burias tensed and the warlord could see the daemon within flash in his eyes.

'The First Acolyte is on the cusp of greatness,' said Kol Badar, 'though it is a dangerous position and his fate is not yet determined. He may yet be deemed unworthy. Your precious master may fail at the last. Be wary, young Burias. Make sure you know where your loyalty lies, with the Legion, or with an individual.'

Burias stared at the Coryphaus for a moment before he gave a sharp nod of his head and Kol Badar released his crushing grip on the Icon Bearer's shoulder.

'Do well, and I will see you initiated into the cult of the Anointed,' said Kol Badar and he was pleased to see fires of ambition and greed come to life within the younger Icon Bearer's eyes. He had him.

'Go now. Gather the most vicious berserkers of the Host. I want eight fully mechanised coteries ready to roll out on my word. I feel that the enemy will bring the fight to us, and when they do, I want you ready to meet them head on.'

MARDUK WALKED WITH the Dark Apostle towards a small, twin-engine transport, the pair of holy warriors accompanied by an honour guard. Daemon heads spewed smoke as its engines were revved and the doors hissed shut behind the Word Bearers. Marduk saw the Dark Apostle's eyes close in prayer or exhaustion.

On the short journey to the base of the Gehemahnet, Marduk marvelled at how the Imperial city had been transformed. From a bustling city of millions, it had been rendered into a wasteland of industry. Every building had been levelled and the fires of the Chaos factorums blazed in the dim light, spewing fumes and smog into the roiling sky. The ground was black with oil and pollution, and lines of slaves, each a thousand strong or more, wound through the black detritus and slag piles like multi-legged insects. Huge pistons drove up and down, conveyor belts piled with rock and bodies fed into hissing, steaming vaults and furnaces, and chains with links larger than battle tanks wound around immense wheels, turning the machineries of Chaos. It was almost like an infant version of Ghalmek, the daemonic forge monastery world, one of the great stronghold worlds of faith and industry of the Word Bearers, deep in the Maelstrom.

Black dust was kicked up as the shuttle landed and the honour guard stepped to the ground, scouring the area for any threat before they stood to attention. Marduk allowed the Dark Apostle to alight first and his dark eyes followed the movement of the older warrior priest as he stepped out of the shuttle. Even his movements were stiff, he thought. Truly it seemed the Dark Apostle was drained almost to the point of exhaustion. He smiled to himself.

They marched across the blackened earth towards the vast doors of a roaring furnace factorum, ignoring thousands of slaves and overseers that dropped to the ground to grovel before their master. Gears and chains groaned as the sliding doors were dragged aside and a blast of intense hot air radiated out from within, making his vision shimmer.

Workers prostrated themselves on the ground as the Word Bearers entered the massive factory. Huge vats of liquid metal were being poured into a vast mould, along with other liquids that flowed from dozens of spiralling tubes and distillery pipes. The super-heated liquid metal was doused with blood and clouds of heady steam rose.

'Now this, this is what sets my Gehemehnet apart from any other,' said Jarulek, his eyes alight.

A dozen huge chains lifted the mould into the air and it swung across the factorum to hang overhead. With a nod from Jarulek, it was released and it fell with bone shaking force ten metres to the floor of the factory. The entire area shuddered as it landed. The floor of the factorum cracked beneath the impact and small, spider web cracks spread across the surface of the mould. Searing light spilled from the branching cracks. Without the benefit of its inbuilt reactive auto-sensors in his helmet, Marduk squinted his eyes against the glare. More of the miniscule faults appeared across its surface, spilling light in all directions, and the mould began to crumble into tiny granules, falling to the ground, smoking and hissing.

The black mould exploded outwards suddenly, spreading scalding hot granules across the factorum, and blinding light filled the area. Overseers and slaves screamed and recoiled as burning particles seared into their skin and their retinas were burned away.

Even to Marduk the glare was painful and he hissed as super-heated granules burned the skin of his face. Still, he did not flinch, for he was determined not to show any weakness before the Dark Apostle.

A towering, glowing shape stood in the middle of the factorum.

'You have made a bell,' he said dryly.

Jarulek laughed, though the laughter tailed off into a hacking wheeze.

'A bell, yes. With this Daemonschage the power of the Gehemehnet will be harnessed. When that power is unleashed, it will shatter the planet's core. Come,' he said, motioning Marduk forward.

The pair approached the glowing bell towering over them. The intensity of the light it projected was dimming, so that it was bearable to look upon, and Marduk saw that it was smooth and the colour of blooded steel. Tiny script-work wound around its circumference, covering most of the bell. Waves of hot emotion, hatred, jealousy, anger and pain emanated from the Daemonschage.

'Place your hands upon it,' ordered Jarulek.

Marduk moved a hand tentatively forwards and touched his fingers gingerly upon the metallic surface.

'It's cold,' he said and placed both his hands firmly upon its surface. There were presences there. A myriad of voices screamed painfully in his mind and he pulled his hands back sharply.

'I have already bound the Daemonschage with the spirits of over a thousand daemons.'

'Such hatred I felt,' said Marduk. 'This is a powerful binding.'

'The daemons are angered that they are within the physical realm, yet they cannot manifest,' chuckled Jarulek. 'But it needs more daemons bound within this prison before it is complete. My strength wanes. It falls to you, First Acolyte, to complete the ceremonies of binding.'

'You honour me, my lord.'

'The construction of the Gehemehnet is all but complete and that is where my strength is needed. The Daemonschage is to be transported to the top of the tower. You will complete the summoning there, Marduk, and then the Daemonschage will sound and this world will be ripped asunder.'

THE THUNDER OF ordnance was constant. The lines of artillery and siege tanks boomed one after another, billowing smoke covering their positions. The shells had been hurled relentlessly towards the traitor lines for almost three hours and the salt plains and earthworks were pockmarked with craters. It was impossible to gauge enemy casualties, though Laron guessed they were few. The armour of the enemy, together with the defensive bulwarks and bunkers, would most likely ensure protection against most of the incoming fire.

He was pleased however that the brigadier-general was pushing for the war to come to a head. A long, drawn out siege was not a war for an Elysian. Surgical strikes, lightning raids and daring attacks deep into enemy territory: that was how the warriors of Elysia were meant to fight and it seemed that at last they would have the chance.

Still, it would not be easy and the loss of the Imperial cruiser had been a shock, its destruction testament to the unholy power of the enemy.

'Looks like the brigadier-general has had a change of heart,' said Captain Elias. Laron had promoted the man from sergeant when the brigadier-general had given him the mammoth task of becoming acting colonel. He nodded his head.

'Shinar's air defences are famed throughout the sector,' said Elias. 'You were the one that reminded me of that, sir. Won't we be blown out of the air on the approach?'

'It *is* going to be bloody, no two ways around it, Elias, but the brigadier-general feels that such a risk is necessary. The threat the enemy poses is far greater than was first understood. It is not going to be pretty, but this is war and it is what the Emperor demands of us.'

That suits me fine, thought Laron. The frustrations and stresses of the previous week had built up, and he longed for the simplicity of leading his men into battle once again.

Elias was right though, they would be at the mercy of the enemy guns until those emplacements were silenced. He prayed that their objective was achievable, else the 72nd and the 133rd would be slaughtered.

## CHAPTER SEVENTEEN

The Gehemehnet rose almost fifty kilometres into the atmosphere. Black, oily clouds circling the tower far below hid the land from Varnus's eyes, making him feel dizzy and disoriented. The giant, red planet Korsis dominated the sky above. It hung so close that it was an intimidating, looming presence.

Hot vapours rose from the hollow shaft of the Gehemehnet in long, steaming exhalations. The breath of the gods themselves, the Discord had told him, and its touch was intoxicating. It came from deep within the planet, for Varnus knew that the shaft plunged far beneath the earth, into the fiery heart of Tanakreg.

He noticed that there were fewer than a hundred slaves atop the tower: those that had proven to have the strength and will to survive its completion. Each man was crouching on his haunches, accompanied by an overseer who stood just behind him. Looking around at them, Varnus felt sickened. They all looked like worshippers of the Chaos gods, far from the industrious servants of the Emperor that they had once been. Varnus knew that he too must look like one of the cursed, *blessed,* followers of the ruinous powers and he seethed.

He knew that he had changed. Outwardly, the change was obvious, but the most damaging changes had occurred within him. His blood ran thick with serums concocted by chirurgeons and his mind was filled with hateful visions of darkness and death. Voices spoke within him constantly, chattering maddeningly, and heretical thoughts plagued him. He wanted to embrace the gods of the Ether, to allow himself to succumb utterly to their will, and he knew that the last barriers of resistance were being eaten away.

The tower spoke to him, its voice soothing him.

A massive, black-girded construction was brought over the lip of the tower, held aloft by a trio of spider-legged cranes, and Varnus stared at it in wonder. Its shape was bewitching to the eye and it was swung over his head to hang over the top of the open shaft. It had eight black, iron legs, the first of them touching down on the stone only metres to Varnus's left.

It was an eight-legged armature that rose to a point, like the frame of a giant, triangular tent. That point was embossed with beaten metal the colour of blood,and thick, spiked chains swung from the legs, hanging down into the vast emptiness of the shaft within the tower. Seeing the chains made Varnus put a hand to his neck, feeling around the circumference of his collar. He realised that he no longer wore a chain around his neck, though he had no recollection of the overseers having removed it.

He felt the Gehemenhet beneath him tremble and the feet of the black frame sank into the stone as if it were made of quicksand. Varnus blinked his eyes, as if they were deceiving him. *He saw fields of the skinless dead beneath a burning daemon sky.* But the stone was once again solid, holding the frame tightly in place.

There was a trembling in the air and a feeling of anticipation built within him. He felt a rumbling bass note shudder through the tower and the ceaseless blare of the Discord began to blend into a monotonous chant that rose up loudly around him. His internal organs shuddered as the intensity of the volume rose and the black arms of the armature began to resonate with power, chains shaking and clinking.

Darkness spilled from the centre of the Gehemehnet, fingers of shadow clawing out over the top of the stones and questing out in all directions. The gloom engulfed Varnus and he began to shiver. He saw flickers of movement in the darkness, shapes clustered all around him, and he felt their hot breath on his neck. They whispered to him and their talons brushed against him, painfully cold and ethereal. He could see the blood-red glow of their eyes in the netherworld staring hungrily out at him and he felt nausea and disorientation.

A trio of Discords rose from within the Gehemehnet, rising up out of its hollow shaft, their tentacles playing out around them like gently waving undersea fronds, angelic voices blurring with daemonic roars and melancholic chanting that boomed from their speakers. Beneath the cacophony of voices was the rhythmic grinding of machinery, the pounding of metal drums and the deep reverberations of pipes. Varnus felt the hairs of his body rise with the potent sounds.

Behind the Discords came a red, armoured figure, arms outstretched to either side, appearing out of darkness like some devil arisen from its hellish realm beneath the earth.

Varnus was in no doubt that this was a priest of the ruinous powers and he felt awed and horrified in equal measure. Faith and power, these were the two things that the warrior-priest radiated. He saw the shadowy, insubstantial shapes of daemons circling the warrior. He could feel their excitement and relentless hate being strengthened by the priest's radiance.

The warrior was huge and his ornate, red armour was scarred from battle. He wore no helmet, but appeared to suffer no ill-effects from the scarce amount of oxygen. His eyes were closed as he chanted, his voice powerful and deep. Varnus did not understand the meaning of the words the priest spoke, but he knew them well, having heard them for weeks on end within the roar of the Discords.

The chains hanging from the black frame began to rise and their barbed tips began to wave around in the air like the searching heads of serpents. They reached out towards the slaves, who were all face down bar Varnus. The tip of one of the chains approached him and it hovered in the air. The barbed tip was the size and length of his forearm and he saw that the dark metal was covered in tiny script. It swung back and forth before him, mesmerising and moving gently in time with the rhythms of the Discords, as if held in thrall by some fell snake charmer.

With the speed of a striking serpent, the chains struck down into the backs of the slaves, driving through their bodies and ripping out through their chests. The slaves were lifted up into the air, transfixed upon the living chains running through them. The bladed tips of the chains coiled around and lunged again, stabbing again and again the bodies of the slaves impaled on other chains, until no body was pierced fewer than a dozen of times.

The blade hovering before Varnus hung in the air before him, waving back and forth before it too plunged forward, but not into him, instead it descended into the back of the overseer at his side. The black-clad slaver squealed horribly as the bladed chain tore back and forth through its body, and it was lifted high in the air, along with all the others, black blood showering Varnus.

The chains began to knit together, forming an intricate pattern within the eight-legged frame above the hovering priest, who continued on with his intonation, uncaring of the mayhem that had been unleashed around him. The chains bound together tightly until they resembled a giant spider web, complete with grisly trophies. The bodies of the slaves and the overseers hung impaled and wrapped within the chains, and Varnus was horrified to see that most of them were not yet dead. They twitched and moaned, and their life blood dripped down onto the Chaos Marine priest beneath them.

He stood atop the Gehemehnet walls, his limbs shaking as he realised that he stood alone. Every other slave and overseer was within the sickening chain-length spider web, dying. Only he had been spared.

The priest's eyes opened and fell upon him. He felt as though the warrior's gaze pierced his soul and he cowered before him. Though the Chaos Marine continued to chant his monotonous incantation, Varnus felt a voice throb within his mind.

*The Gehemehnet has chosen you to witness its birth. You are privileged, little man.*

SCREAMING SHELLS RAINED down upon the Word Bearers, throwing up great explosions of earth as they struck at the embankments. The bombardment had increased in tempo and they detonated across the entire length of the Shinar peninsula.

The Warmonger stood atop the battlements in the centre of the first line of defence, uncaring of the mayhem exploding around him. The enemy's pitiful shells could not harm him and he stood motionless in the midst of the bombardment, surveying the battlefield coldly.

The other war machines and daemon engines of the Legion had been pulled back to the second line. Their unarmoured attendants would have been slaughtered beneath the fury of the attack and the daemon engines would have stormed forwards across the plain, eager to get to grips with the enemy. They would have been uniformly destroyed. None bar the Dark Apostle would be able to restrain them.

The Dreadnought's augmetic senses pierced the fire and smoke that surrounded the first line, and he saw a series of detonations erupt further out along the salt plains, several kilometres away. This was no bombardment of the Word Bearers, and the Warmonger was momentarily confused. Not even the pitiful gunners of the Imperial Guard could be so inaccurate with their fire. A second line of explosions ran out along the salt plains, this time two hundred metres closer to the Word Bearers' lines. His senses could not pierce the vast clouds of smoke that rose from the detonations.

'Kol Badar, the enemies of the Warmaster are on the approach. They mask their advance with ordnance and blind grenades.'

'Received, Warmonger,' came the vox reply. 'Incoming aircraft have been picked up. Be ready.'

'The blessings of the true gods upon you.'

'Kill well, old friend.'

'THE ENEMY HAS made its move, Icon Bearer. Your time has come,' said Kol Badar.

Burias bowed his head to the massive, Terminator-armoured war leader.

'You do me a great honour, my Coryphaus,' he said.

'Remember it, Burias,' growled Kol Badar. 'Do the Legion proud. Do not make me regret giving you my favour.'

'You will not, Coryphaus,' said Burias, his handsome, pale face serious with devotion. 'My first kill will be dedicated to you, my lord.'

He could not gauge the reaction of his words upon the Coryphaus's face, hidden as it was beneath his quad-tusked helmet, but he thought the warlord's posture showed that he was pleased. Good, thought Burias.

He turned away from the Coryphaus with another bow of the head, to face the gathered warriors below him, on the off-face of the embankment. Explosions detonated around them, but the warriors were unflinching, their helmets turned up towards him, awaiting his order.

Burias slammed his icon into the ground and the warrior-brothers stood motionless in rapt attention.

'My brothers, the time has come for us to ride out and face the enemy head on,' he roared, the daemon Drak'shal giving his voice unholy resonance and power.

A huge roar of approval rose from the gathered, since many of their voices were also enhanced by the daemons lurking within their souls.

'The Coryphaus honours us with this sacred duty,' Burias continued, which was met with another roar from the gathered warriors.

'Do the Coryphaus proud, my brothers, and kill in the name of Lorgar!'

The gathered warriors roared the name of their daemon primarch, their voices mingling with Burias's bloodcurdling bellow, screaming to the heavens so that their lord might hear their devotion.

The gathered Coteries intoned prayers to the dark gods as they climbed into their transport vehicles. A pair of Land Raiders would lead the Rhino attack column and the assault ramps of the monstrous tanks hissed as they slammed open to receive the warriors honoured to be carried within. Engines revved in anticipation and the lascannon turrets of the Land Raiders swivelled as the daemon spirits controlling them expressed their impatience.

'The smoke the Imperials use blocks our sight, but it blocks theirs as well, Burias. Go forth. Tackle them head on. They will not see you coming.'

Burias snarled a wordless reply. Drak'shal was rising within him. With a final nod, he turned and jogged towards the awaiting Land Raider. Before the assault ramp had even hissed completely closed, the column of tanks roared forwards, climbing the steep embankment quickly amid the explosions of incoming barrage fire. Engines screamed as the massive Land Raiders reached the apex of the climb and rose over the lip of the embankment before the tanks thumped down on the other side. They rolled towards the enemy, hidden behind a wall of smoke and ash that was drawing closer with every falling barrage.

Drak'shal's daemon essence pumped strength through his veins and his muscles strained within his power armour.

To become one of the Anointed had been his dream since his inception into the Legion. He knew that his relationship with Marduk had kept him from being embraced into the cult, for his prowess was faultless. Long had it been a source of dishonour for Burias and he had at times hated the First Acolyte for it. He had no idea what had occurred on the moon of Calite, but the hatred between Marduk and Kol Badar had been palpable ever since.

Curse him and his feud with the Coryphaus! Burias thought. If the warlord would allow him to be embraced into the cult of the Anointed then he would relish the opportunity and grasp it with both hands.

The Coryphaus was right, the future of the First Acolyte was far from certain, and to throw his support behind Marduk without consideration of this would be foolish. No, he would wait for the right moment to make his decision about where his loyalties lay.

Such thoughts left him instantly as he heard the mechanised, insane whisperings of the Land Raider cease for a moment. The vehicle's machine-spirit had been merged with the essence of a daemon upon the factory world of Ghalmek, bound within the casing of the tank by the fabricators and sorcerers of the Legion with the aid of the chirumeks.

'Entering the blind cloud, Icon Bearer,' said the drawling twin voices of the Land Raider's operators, warriors who had long ago become one with the machine.

The daemonic, mechanised whisperings of the tank began again, the voices agitated and excited.

'COMMAND? COME IN! Damn it!' swore the Valkyrie pilot. He could make no sense of the garbled nonsense being broadcast through the vox system. His sensor arrays had turned to darkness minutes earlier and he was flying completely without their assistance. Now the vox-caster was playing up and he was completely cut off from the rest of the squadron, not to mention base command. Damn it, he couldn't even communicate with the drop-troopers behind him, for even the closed circuit comm-transmissions of the unit were spewing nonsense.

He knew that the other Elysians were trying to make contact, but their voices morphed into hellish, bestial screams and roars. He wondered if that was how his voice sounded to their ears.

The closer they got to the damned insane tower of the enemy, the more garbled and chaotic the sounds became. He switched the system off, reasoning that he would rather hear nothing than that hellish blare. Yet even with the systems disabled, his earpieces blared with the evil sound and he slammed his fist into his helmet in desperation to get the insane noise out of his head.

*You are all going to die,* the voice said to him.

The Valkyrie was ripped apart as it was struck by anti-aircraft fire and the pilot was certain that he heard laughter in his ears, even as the cockpit exploded into a billowing fireball.

TANK COMMANDER WALYON grinned as he stood in the cupola of his Leman Russ battle tank, the wind and smoke blowing in his face. The lowered visor of his helmet protected his eyes, not that there was anything to see as the tank thundered through the smoke.

He glanced out to either side. He could dimly make out only the closest tanks, but he knew that there were scores of vehicles spread out on each wing. He was at the point of the arrowhead, roaring towards the enemy, and his heart was racing.

He had been waiting for this day for decades. He knew that being a tank commander within the Elysian ranks was regarded as a dubious honour; all good Elysians dreamt of attacking via drop-ship, for that was the rhetoric drilled into the soldiers from day one. But tanks had always been Walyon's true love and he had accepted the post with relish. The tank company within the 133rd was regarded as little more than a joke; few Elysian regiments even had a tank company. The other officers regarded the position as a dead end and he knew they sniggered behind his back – promotion out of harm's way, they said. Waylon did not care, for within the ranks of the tank company he had found his home.

However, what had followed was years of boredom and resentment. Time after time the 133rd were launched into battle, but the armoured divisions were held back.

Finally, his time had come and he would be damned if he wasn't going to enjoy it. He smiled like a child given his first exhilarating trip on the harbour shuttle of his home city-hive of Valorsia, and he screamed with exhilaration into the whipping wind.

Somewhere far overhead the Valkyries were disgorging their living cargos. Drop-troopers would be falling through the atmosphere towards their target, the second line of the enemy's defences. Somewhere behind, the Gorgons of the Mechanicus were grinding forwards in the wake of his battle tanks.

An echelon of low-flying Thunderbolt heavy fighters screamed overhead, dull shapes in the haze, utilising the same cover of smoke as the battle tanks, and Walyon punched his fist in the air as they passed, willing them on.

He grinned wildly, feeling as though he were screaming through a vacuum of white smoke. The feeling was not unlike falling blindly through clouds on a combat drop, but this felt much more secure, for he had a giant battle tank steed beneath him. Excitement building, he pulled out his shimmering sabre and levelled it out in front. He felt like one of the daring cavalry marshals of history and he screamed wordlessly, glorying in the sensation of speed.

That was when he saw the massive, red shape looming out of the smoke ahead of him, and the next second of his life seemed to occur in horrifying slow motion. He dimly registered twin flashes of searing white lascannons and the battle tank to his right exploded in a rising ball of black smoke.

Walyon ducked back within the cupola as heavy bolter rounds ripped across the hull of his tank. The command tank's driver must have seen the Land Raider at exactly the same moment and the Leman Russ slewed to the side in an attempt to avoid the massive shape. The move was one of desperation and instinct and the Land Raider turned into it, smashing into the side of the Leman Russ at full speed.

The force of the impact slammed the battle tank onto its side with the sickening sound of crunching metal. The front of the Land Raider rose up into the air like a looming monster of the depths as the impact and its momentum lifted it. The Leman Russ rolled onto its top and the massive traitor tank smashed down upon it, engines roaring as its tracks spun wildly, gaining no traction.

Metal screamed as it buckled beneath the weight of the giant and Walyon was buffeted from side to side, smashing his head on the inside of the cupola, the hot taste of exhaust fumes in his mouth. The next moments of his life were a blur as the Leman Russ rolled wildly across the salt plain, flipping and finally coming to rest upright.

Dazed and shell-shocked, blood running from nose, Walyon called out weakly to the crew within the tank. Pulling himself upright, wincing and feeling as if every bone in his body had been smashed by the severity of the impact, he looked across the smoky void of the salt plains. He couldn't see far, but now that the Leman Russ engine was dead, he could hear the roar of engines, the chatter of gunfire, the heavy boom of battle cannons and the hissing scream of lascannons. Explosions rocked the earth and rising plumes of oily, black smoke and bright orange fireballs pierced the haze. He coughed painfully, spitting blood, and he closed his eyes against the burning pain in his ribs.

An enemy Rhino screamed out of the smoke and Walyon dimly saw Chaos Space Marines standing in the open top of the vehicle, weapons raised. His vision was blurring before his eyes and he barely saw the plume of white-hot plasma screaming towards him, nor the meltagun that blurred the air as it fired upon his beloved tank.

Walyon died, his flesh burning and liquefying, and a moment later the Leman Russ exploded violently, throwing the blackened hull into the air.

A BATTLE CANNON shell detonated on the flank of the Land Raider's hull, spinning the behemoth to the side, its momentum lost.

'Out!' roared Burias. 'Lower the attack ramp!'

Leading the coteries from the Land Raider, desperate to get to grips with the enemy, Burias swung his head from side to side as battle tanks roared past them. Snarling, he snapped off an ineffectual shot with his bolt pistol.

One of the tanks spun amid a rising cloud of salt dust as its track was blown clear by a meltagun shot and the coterie broke into a run towards the slowing vehicle, roaring to the heavens.

One of the tank's side sponsons screeched as it rotated and unleashed its salvo into the Word Bearers, ripping apart bodies. Burias leapt over the fallen warrior-brothers.

Drak'shal surged to the surface of the Icon Bearer's being and his shape blurred as muscles bulged within his power armour. Bunching his legs beneath him, he leapt through the air, landing atop the Demolisher tank. He gripped the hatch atop the cannon turret and ripped it clear of its housing in one brutal movement, wires and cables sparking as the metal was wrenched out of shape, and he hurled it aside. Thumbing a pair of grenades into his hand, he hurled them into the exposed interior before leaping from the tank.

The grenades detonated behind him, but his focus had fixed on something new, and he stared into the impenetrable smoke cloud, his nostrils flaring. A giant shape appeared, roaring towards the Word Bearers.

Larger than even a Land Raider, a super-heavy Gorgon transport vehicle loomed out of the smoke. A giant, angled assault ram of thick metal protected its front, and the gunfire of the coterie pinged off its surface. The metal turned molten beneath the touch of melta weaponry, but even that was not enough to penetrate the thick armour.

Chattering gunfire ripped up the ground around the Coterie and a spray of autocannon shells smashed Burias back a step. He felt his anger grow. Lascannons from the Land Raider pierced the metal side of the massive super-heavy vehicle, but it did not slow, and Burias once again tensed his leg muscles, making ready to spring.

With a roar, he leapt as the massive tank bore down on him and he landed on the upper side of the assault ramp, the force of the impact causing him to hiss in pain. A second later, the Gorgon slammed into the wreckage of the Demolisher, smashing the battle tank aside with contemptible ease, nearly crushing Burias. He pulled himself up over the lip of the giant dozer blade. The vehicle was open-topped and he snarled in pleasure as he saw the score of heavy battle servitors packed within. Several were borne upon large tracked units, while others were bipedal, easily as large as a Space Marine, held in place by large clamps around their waists. Autocannon fire slammed into one of Burias's arms, shattering the ceramite, and he lost his grip momentarily, sliding precariously. With a roar he pulled himself up and, kicking off with one foot, he descended into the midst of the heavy Praetorian battle servitors. They raised their massive inbuilt weapon systems towards him, though they were hampered by the tight confines of the Gorgon.

Spinning cannons screamed, the heavy calibre gunfire tearing armour and flesh from Burias-Drak'shal's body, but he was amongst them in an instant. The holding clamps hissed open, releasing the Praetorians. Their immense weight and solid construction ensured they did not lose their footing, despite the speed the Gorgon was travelling at. He ripped the augmented head from the shoulders of one of the warriors as he landed, and protein rich, sickly, white synth-blood, sucrosol, sprayed out, mixing with spurting oil and Burias-Drak'shal's sizzling, scarlet vital fluids.

Another three possessed Chaos Marines launched themselves over the side of the Gorgon, landing amidst the Praetorians, roaring their dedications to the Chaos gods. Chainaxes and power swords rose and fell in bloody arcs and their bolt pistols barked as they fired into the tight press.

The enemy was all around him and Burias-Drak'shal lashed out blindly, ripping mechanical arms from torsos and punching his talons through chests. The Praetorians were the most highly advanced servitors created by the Adeptus Mechanicus, fitted with neuro-linked targeting processors and enhanced combat brain-stem implants, as well as heavy weaponry and powerfully armoured shells. They were easily a match for an Astartes warrior-brother.

One of the berserkers was clubbed to the ground by a heavy blow from a chaingun, mechanics and augmetics whirring as they lent immense power to the blow. Placing a heavy foot upon the downed warrior's chest, buckling his power armour, the Praetorian levelled its cannon towards the Word Bearer's helmet, which was torn to shreds beneath the power of the burst of fire it unleashed. The headless corpse twitched as it died.

Burias-Drak'shal caught a swinging, metal arm in one hand and with a powerful twist ripped it from its mechanical socket. Lashing out with his other hand, he slashed his claws across the head of another, tearing its red blinking eye free and ripping away a chunk of skull and brain with it. A spinning cannon was levelled at his back, but he spun around, the daemon within him sensing the danger. He knocked the weapon to the side using the Skitarii's dismembered arm as a club. Gunfire burst from the barrels, tearing apart a pair of Praetorians.

A heavy blow smashed into his head and Burias-Drak'shal staggered to the side, straight into another swinging metal arm that smashed into his high gorget. He was slammed backwards, falling to the floor of the roaring Gorgon, and a multi-barrelled cannon swung around towards him. The barrels of the gun were shorn off with the sweep of a power sword and a burst of bolt fire knocked the Skitarii backwards, allowing Burias-Drak'shal the time to regain his feet.

He came up fast, the talons of one hand swinging up in a slashing uppercut, ripping the head from a Praetorian, even as the warrior-brother that had saved him was slain, a hole appearing in his chest as a burst of cannon fire ripped through him. Holy Astartes blood splashed over Burias-Drak'shal's face, congealing even as it landed on his pale skin, and he grabbed the rotating cannon in his hands as it swung in his direction. The barrels halted instantly under his daemonic, crushing grip. He wrenched the metal out of shape and smoke rose from the mechanics of the weapon.

With a barked roar, he slammed his fist into the Praetorian's head, pulverising its skull. Burias-Drak'shal hurled it into one of its comrades, slamming it against the thick metal interior of the Gorgon.

The next minute passed in a flurry of bloodshed and gunfire. Burias-Drak'shal alone stood on his feet. Every Skitarii had been ripped and hacked apart, and lay twitching and sparking on the floor of the super-heavy vehicle. His fallen brethren lay unmoving, their souls having passed on to the Ether.

Burias-Drak'shal reached out and gripped a heavy, metal hatch, the metal bending out of shape beneath his grip as he wrenched it from its hinges. A withered servitor was revealed, hard-wired into the cabin of the vehicle, its sightless eyes staring forward and its arms connected directly to the gearshift and steering column of the tank. He grabbed the wretch around its throat and ripped it out of the cabin amid a shower of sparks and pale, sickly blood. It was ripped in half, its lower torso still attached to the machine, and its mouth moved soundlessly as milky fluid rose in its throat. The super-heavy vehicle came to a halt.

Burias intoned the words of binding and Drak'shal was pushed back within, fighting against the strength of its master. The overgrown tusks that protruded from his mouth retracted painfully and his long talons receded back into his hands. His posture straightened and he was once again the elegant, controlled warrior, though his body was ravaged and exhausted, the after-effects of possession.

'Coryphaus,' he spoke.

'Speak, Icon Bearer,' said the vox reply.

'Met the foe, head on,' said Burias, breathing heavily. 'My warriors fought well. More have advanced around us. Beware the Gorgons.'

'Acknowledged.'

'You wish me to return to the bulwark, Coryphaus?'

'No. The enemy has committed to the attack. They may have left their command unprotected. Continue your advance. Drive through them and kill their commanders. Succeed and the Cult of the Anointed will embrace you, young one.'

Wiping blood from his face, his breathing having almost returned to normal, Burias nodded his head.

'It will be done, my Coryphaus.'

# CHAPTER EIGHTEEN

THE ANTI-AIRCRAFT BATTERIES tore the heavens apart overhead, but the Warmonger was focused only on the Leman Russ battle tank climbing the embankment towards him. The Dreadnought stood motionless as a battle cannon shell streaked past its shoulder and its armoured plates were peppered with explosive heavy bolter rounds.

The Warmonger stepped heavily to the side, into the path of the tank. As it breached the top of the battlement, its front lifting up into the air, the Dreadnought reached up with its massive power claw and brought the vehicle to a screaming halt. Servos groaned as it held the tank and its huge mechanical feet slid backwards beneath the vehicle's weight and momentum. Its underbelly was less armoured than its front and the Warmonger fired its weaponry, the rapid firing rounds punching through the undercarriage, shredding the weakling mortals within and tearing through the Leman Russ's vital systems.

The Chaos Dreadnought's servos whined as it exerted its strength and pushed the tank back the way it had come, sending it toppling end over end down the embankment to smash into the front of another battle tank.

'Kill for the Warmaster!' the Dreadnought roared as it re-fought the battle for the Emperor's palace in its damaged mind. 'Destroy the Emperor, the betrayer of the Great Crusade!'

BODIES FELL ALL around Kol Badar. Many of them were already dead, though their timed grav-chutes were in operation and slowed their descent mere metres above the ground. Still, thousands of living drop-troopers were landing all along the second tier and the open space behind the first, and he fired off controlled bursts left and right as he killed.

The attack had been well coordinated, timed to perfection. The first drop-troopers had landed just as the line of tanks had emerged from the cloud wall and just after a scything attack run by air that had cost him many warriors and war machines of the dark gods.

It was a well-organised attack, but one that was ultimately flawed. Given an inordinate amount of time, the enemy would prevail, for their numbers were great, but time was not on the Imperials' side. Even he, Kol Badar, who felt the touch of the dark gods only faintly, could feel the birth tremors of the Gehemehnet. He knew that the enemy would feel it too. They would be fearful and rightly so.

In the meantime, the enemy would die upon his warriors' blades.

THE HAEMONCULUS ATTACHED to Techno-Magos Darioq via aqueduct cables flooded his system with suppressants and holy vital fluids, filtering his veins and cables for viruses. Red robes hid the tumorous, cancer-ridden flesh of the stunted creature that had been bred in the nutrient tanks of Mars. It diverted the diseases and weaknesses of the flesh into itself so that they did not afflict him; such was its purpose in life.

He quoted the fifteenth Universal Lore to himself, 'Flesh is fallible, but ritual honours the machine-spirit', and he intoned a prayer to the Omnissiah as his system was cleansed.

Nevertheless, he recognised something amiss within the frail remnants of his flesh body and he opened up the cortex channels to the right-hand side of his brain in order to determine its purpose. Synapses sparked and he realised that what he felt were crude and fleshy emotions: tension, trepidation and anger.

Such base, human things, emotions, yet he found them intriguing as well as deplorable.

It had been a long time since last he had stepped foot upon planet c6.7.32, what the Elysians called Tanakreg. He accessed the hard memories of his secondary brain units and one of the myriad arrays of screens within the control centre of his airship flashed with data.

It showed his report to the Fabricator Tianamek Primus, dated over two thousand years earlier, though his current brain units had no record of him having scribed them.

*Access to primary expeditionary focus/purpose denied. Magos Metallurgicus Annonus unable to determine material make-up of structure. Impervious. Logis cogitator augurs recommended path – terraform c6.7.32 and dissemble discovery. Magos Technicus Darioq to fabricate auditory station, and post watch over c6.7.32.*

That was the source of the alien emotions of tension and trepidation that he had felt in the past two millennia. None had sought out that which he had been unable to breach, yet here was a powerful enemy of the Omnissiah on c6.7.32. It was imperative that they did not uncover the structure that he had gone to such pains to eradicate from all Imperial and accessible Mechanicus records.

But anger had nothing to do with the exploratory expedition he had led. That strange, hot temper had been brought upon him by the nature of the foe. He could feel the affront to the Machine-God in their essence, in the unholy constructions that they had defiled beyond all heresies.

Their machines, infused with the essence of daemonic warp entities, were the greatest corruption that the adepts of Mars could contemplate, a blasphemy that made all other blasphemies pale. All thinking machineries of the Mechanicus had souls within their flesh, for a soulless sentient machine is the epitome of true evil. And upon the battlefield, raging beyond the concealing clouds of blind-smoke, were machineries that had been polluted by their merging with the soulless entities of the warp. A soulless sentience is the enemy of all.

Such heresies were utterly wrong and Darioq was both revolted and horrified by how low the Legion of the Word Bearers had stooped. He shut off the receptors and synapses that synched his right brain hemisphere and the uncomfortable feelings instantly vanished. All that remained was the irrefutable fact that the enemy made use of sacrilegious, dangerous machineries that were an affront to his god and that they needed to be neutralised, their heresies eradicated and their hold over c6.7.32 removed.

His mechadendrites plugged into the central control column and, connected as he was to the delicate sensors on the outside of the hull, he registered the field of disruption that spread out in a cone from the enemy's tower. At his impulse, the command ship was lowered towards the ground. It was imperative for him to maintain contact and hence control over his thousands of Skitarii warriors. If he were cut off from them and his adepts then his entire army would grind to a halt.

Vast turbine engines rotated in their housings as the airship began to descend, the linking cable that connected it to the holy Ordinatus *Magentus* drawing it in towards the docking station on its upper deck.

One of the servo-arms of Darioq's quad-manifold rotated, whining softly, and its clamp-like jaws eased open.

'Enginseer Kladdon, open the hiemalis chamber and bring forth my blessed cogitation units.'

One of the red-robed junior priests behind him lowered the head of his power halberd in respect for his master's order and stepped towards one of the walls of the command centre. He spoke the words of awakening as he pressed the buttons of the hiemalis unit ritualistically, timing his speech to coincide with the correct sequence of buttons. With a blessing to the machine-spirit he gripped the sunken circular handle and, as he incanted the correct words beseeching the unit for its acquiescence, he pulled the drawer open.

Fog billowed from the unit as the ice-cold air within reacted to the heat outside. Held within a long shelf were over a dozen carefully stored bell jars. Within each jar was a blessed brain hemisphere held in static charged null-liquid. One of Darioq's servo-arms reached forward, hovering over several of the jars before the magos selected the required unit, and his servo-arm gently lifted it free.

Another servo-arm folded down and grasped the top of one of the bell jars protruding from the massive power generator he bore, and as he muttered the required intonations of supplication, mechadendrites whirred as he loosened the cog-shaped bolts fixing the bell jar to him. Needle-like incision spikes clicked out of the centres of other mechadendrite tentacles and were carefully inserted into the cog-shaped holes revealed with the removed bolts. They turned and with a hissing sound the bell jar was lifted clear. He felt the loss of information and processing power of the brain unit like a vague emptiness within him.

Swiftly and precisely he placed this brain unit within the gap in the hiemalis unit and attached the new bell jar to his core systems. Fresh information that he had not accessed for many centuries flooded through him, including memories and algorithms that had departed from him completely when he had disconnected the brain unit.

Much of the content of this brain unit would have been classed as heretical by some of the priesthood of

Mars, but Darioq had felt driven to re-synch with the hemispheres within the bell jar. This was the unit that he had utilised when he had been part of the explorator team that had first investigated planet c6.7.32, and it had none of the synapse burns that altered and neutered many of the right brain functions.

This was a *creative* brain unit. Only a few secretive and covert members of the priesthood would dare to access such a component. *The knowledge of the ancients stands beyond question,* the tenets said, and for him to utilise a creative thinking brain unit to make adaptations and improvisations to mechanics, as he had done in the past when wired into this particular bell jar, was at best the height of hubris and, at worst, heresy of the worst kind.

His devotion to the Machine-God, Deus Mechanicus, and its conduit manifestation, the Omnissiah, was unwavering. To deny the effectiveness of such a creative drive when prescribed methodology would fail was abject foolishness, but even as these thoughts ran through his mind, he recognised the danger inherent within them. He must not utilise this brain unit for long periods, or he risked his whole being. Such dogmatism is folly, he thought. I must retain my dogmatism, he thought. The conflicting impulses gave him pause, but the new addition was the more dominant presence.

'Tech-priests, go forth and ready the plasma reactors of the Ordinatus. And bring the void shields up to full power,' Magos Technicus Darioq said. The robed figures bowed their cog-bladed power halberds in compliance and left the command shrine.

His cogitator units had judged the potency of the weapons of the enemy and calculated the likelihood of damage to the blessed Ordinatus. Any moderate risk of damage was to be avoided, thus spoke the tenets, and he had previously determined not to advance the giant war machine until the enemy forces had been pushed back by 7.435 Mechanicus standard units, back to the third defensive tier.

Now he thought differently. He remodelled the algorithms of trajectory and manifest firepower, and a flurry of numbers scrolled down the screens lining the walls of the command shrine.

If the energy of the rear void shields was redirected to the frontal arc then the probability of success rose exponentially the more power that he diverted there. Such a thing may be deemed heresy, for the STC explicitly stated the correct shield levels and to alter them was to ignore the teachings of the elders. But if his mission on planet c6.7.32 was compromised then it would be of no matter. He deemed the minor heresy a lesser evil than what would occur if the enemy breached the walls of the xenos structure, and he began the complex calculations necessary to adapt the systems of the Ordinatus to his will.

SCORES OF VALKYRIES were being ripped apart by the relentless anti-aircraft fire that speared up through the roiling black clouds. Thousands of the Elysians drop-troopers were slaughtered as they plummeted down through the atmosphere at terminal velocity, but still others survived and Laron prayed that the other storm trooper platoons were amongst them.

It was a baffling experience, to be falling alongside something so massive. They had launched from their Valkyrie above the tower and he had been falling past it for the last few minutes. That such a thing could be so high was inconceivable, the engineering impossible, but there it was in front of his eyes. It made him feel physically ill and he could hear strange voices in his head. The thing seemed to exert a gravitational pull of its own and he angled away from it, so as not to be drawn too close.

'Keep your distance from the tower,' he said into his micro-bead, but the thing merely fed back a blare of roaring, horrifying sounds in his ears and he doubted that any heard his order.

He angled further away from the tower, hoping that his storm troopers would follow his lead, but even as he did so he felt something tugging at him, pulling him in closer, towards the hateful construction.

He muttered a prayer to the Emperor and felt the pull slacken enough for him to angle as far from the tower as was feasible while staying on target. The surface of the tower seemed to pulse and waver, and he felt hot blasts of air spilling from it, disrupting his descent, bustling him from side to side.

He was rapidly closing on the roiling, black smog clouds circling the tower and he was pleased to have his rebreather mask. As soon as he hit the smoke he felt terror rise within him. There were *things* within the oily cloud and they slashed at him with their claws, their red, glowing eyes burning fiercely in the gloom as he screamed past them.

Wind whipped at him, drawing him off course, and he cried out as something raked a series of deep cuts across his arms and chest. It was more from shock than pain, for his heavy carapace armour ensured the wounds did little real damage, but such an attack startled him. He had the impression of insubstantial creatures flying alongside him.

Pushing these thoughts from his mind, he turned into a steep dive, legs held together and arms clasped tightly to his sides, and prayed that he would escape the hellish clouds alive.

MARDUK CHANTED AS he held his hands out towards the Daemonschage. As he bound each additional daemon essence within its structure, another tiny line from the Book of Lorgar flashed into existence upon its surface.

The true names of the daemonic entities contained within appeared between each line of the holy script and the beings of the warp screamed in hatred as they were sucked from the Ether and sealed within. The bell was vibrating slightly, creating a low hum that would have been impossible to hear with mere human ears.

His hands shook with the power of the summoning,and a bead of sweat rolled down his forehead from the exertion. He was vaguely aware of explosions in the skies above and of dark shapes falling around him, but his entire concentration was focused upon the Daemonschage, and its complex binding incantations.

The pressure in his head increased and he felt the strength of the warp building within him. Still, his faith was unwavering and he bound the daemons of the warp to his will with the power of his word. The corners of his mouth rose in a smile as he incanted, relishing the feeling of sheer joy that came with control over the entities of Chaos.

VARNUS CROUCHED, UNMOVING atop the towering Gehemehnet wall, enthralled and horrified. The air at the top of the tower was electric and he could see dim, shadowy shapes of daemons being pulled screaming and clawing into the massive bell that hung over the endless drop of the tower's chimney. The corpses hanging in the chains twitched and convulsed, and he reeled backwards in shock as a body fell from the sky to land upon that spider web of chain, crashing amongst the corpses with bone breaking force.

The body jerked as the chains broke its fall and the man's back, and the body hung for a moment before it continued downwards, spiralling madly, down into the depths of the planet. A moment later, a roar of hot air was expelled up the hollow shaft, and Varnus saw more bodies falling around him. He decided that he must truly have lost his sanity, if he was seeing men falling from the heavens.

Still they fell, some tumbling down into the gaping maw of the Gehemehnet, as if it were drawing them to it, and others flashing past him, smashing into the outside of the tower. He jumped to his feet as a figure fell directly towards him, scrambling out of the way as it smashed into stone with a sickening sound. The man lay broken and very dead, his legs and arms bent beneath him, blood splattering out over the stones and across Varnus's legs. He stood, looking down at the helmeted corpse dumbly. It was Imperial!

Another figure landed beside him, though this one's descent was slowed by a tech-device upon its back. He landed awkwardly, one of his legs buckling beneath him with a sickening, cracking sound.

The figure cried out in pain and fell to one knee. He held a lasgun in his hand and Varnus could see his pale blue eyes behind his visor. He saw the twin-headed eagle symbol of the aquila pinned to the man's chest and he felt a surge of recognition. This was an Imperial Guardsman! The Imperium had come to liberate Tanakreg!

He shouted out in joy and dropped to his knees to help the man, but the man scrambled back away from him.

'I am a friend!' Varnus called out, holding his empty hands up, showing the man he was unarmed. 'I am a citizen enforcer of this planet! Thank the Emperor you have come at last!'

GUARDSMAN THORTIS CRIED out in pain and pulled the rebreather mask from his face. His leg was a shattered wreck beneath him, but he pushed back with all his force away from the vile figure. His heart was thundering in his head and his stomach churned with the absolute *wrongness* of everything around him.

Insane daemon speakers blared a deafening, evil cacophony of hatred and corpses were strewn up in chains. A devil Astartes chanted vile words that made his skin crawl and *things* unnatural and maddening flickered at the corners of his vision.

The wretched follower of the ruinous powers clawed at him, his eyes as red as a daemon's and a burning eight-pointed star upon his forehead. His mouth was nothing but a grilled speaker-box amidst a tight fitting, black mask, and he spoke in the foul language of Chaos.

Amid the hateful, guttural speech of the traitor, he heard the word *Emperor.*

'Speak not His name, enemy of mankind,' Thortis spat and levelled his lasgun at the hated foe.

THE SPOKEN WORDS of the Guardsman meant nothing to Varnus, the sound coming out of the man's mouth little more than a garbled mess of childish sounds to his ears. In confusion he saw the hatred burning on the man's face and he saw the lasgun lower towards him.

A flash of anger burned hot within him, and he felt his blood pounding in his head. He had offered his hand in aid to this soldier, and he was turning his weapon on him! The shock of betrayal quickly changed to anger and his hand flashed out, knocking the barrel of the gun to one side. The lasgun blast seared across his shoulder and he hissed in pain. Without thinking, his survival instinct taking over, he drove the fingers of his other hand up into the man's throat, crushing his windpipe. He stepped in close and slammed his elbow into his head.

The Guardsman fell heavily, choking, his pale blue eyes bulging, but Varnus hauled him back to his feet.

'I was trying to help you and this is how you repay me?' he roared, weeks of repressed rage and shame rising to the surface. Holding onto the man's jacket front with one hand, he thundered a punch into the man's face, splattering his nose.

'I curse you!' Varnus shouted and landed another punch into the soldier's face, ignoring the man's feeble attempts to deflect the blow. He pulled the helmet off the man's head with a sharp rip and threw it over the edge of the Gehemehnet tower. He saw that the man's hair was sandy blond, and for some reason even this made him angry. He saw nothing but red, felt nothing but rising hatred, loathing and rage, and gripping the man with both hands, he smashed his forehead into his face, and let him fall to the stone.

'I curse you,' he screamed once more, kicking the soldier hard in his side. He knelt down on top of the man and gripped his head in both hands.

'And I curse the False Emperor!' he screamed as he slammed the soldier's head into the stone.

LARON LANDED SMOOTHLY, rolling to his feet and flicking the release of the heavy grav-chute with one hand, while he blasted his hellpistol into the face of an enemy Chaos Marine. His ornate plasma pistol appeared in his other hand and he fired it into the chest of a second enemy warrior, the screaming plasma searing through ceramite, flesh and bone. Super-heated air vented from the potent weapon, hissing like an angry serpent.

Storm troopers were landing all around him, laying down a withering hail of fire from their overcharged, gyro-stabilised hellguns. All vox communication was jammed and Laron wondered how many of his soldiers had survived the drop even if their Valkyrie had not been gunned down on the approach.

Thousands of drop-troopers were descending through the hellish clouds above and falling along the ridge of the second enemy embankment, just behind the long first line. Some squads of Laron's storm troopers had been briefed to attack along the second tier, targeting the enemy's static war machines with melta weaponry, but the majority of his elite cadre were targetting the bunkers along the first battlement.

While Laron's squad laid down a protective curtain of fire, one of his men knelt and stuck a melta charge to the thick door of the bunker.

'Clear,' yelled the man, stepping back, and the charge detonated inwards, melting the thick metal to liquid.

A second storm trooper stepped forward, kicked the heavy, metal door open and filled the interior with a spray of roaring promethium from his flamer, before pulling back, allowing Laron to lead the hellgun-armed soldiers in.

The walls were scorched black from the flames and the advanced auto-sensor systems in Laron's helmet adjusted to the gloom instantly. He fired both his pistols into the massive shape of the first Chaos Marine and his soldiers' hellguns shot down the next, even as the enemy swung their weapons to bear.

A blast from a lascannon, blindingly bright in the confines of the bunker, ripped a head-sized hole through one of his men and tore the arm off another, before striking the bunker wall behind them. A pair of enemy warriors had thrown down their missile launchers and hurled themselves at the storm troopers, their armour blackened and still burning in places.

Laron ducked beneath the huge slashing knife of the first and fired his plasma pistol into the giant Chaos

Marine's groin, followed by a sharp double-tap from his hellgun into the traitor's head as he fell back.

Four hellgun shots slammed into the second enemy warrior, but it did not slow him, and he barrelled into the storm troopers with a daemonic roar. The traitor rammed two men back against the thick wall of the bunker with the sickening sound of breaking bones and swung his fist into the face of another as he rose, shattering the bones of the man's jaw.

The lascannon-wielding enemy swung the heavy weapon like a club, sending Laron flying into a wall. He slid to the ground gasping for breath. Raising both his pistols from his prone position, he fired into the chest of the Chaos Marine, who twitched and fell.

Laron pushed himself to his feet to see the last traitor fall to his knees. Even as the Chaos Marine died, he broke the neck of a storm trooper, before a trio of hellgun shots took him in the head.

Four of Laron's men were dead, but the bunker had been neutralised.

'Out,' he shouted. 'To the next one.'

CONCENTRATED HEAVY WEAPON fire ripped through the Imperial armoured advance and the embankment was littered with scores of motionless and burned out vehicles. Battle cannons roared and the heavy siege shells fired at close range, obliterated dozens of bunkers.

The south end of the embankment was overrun, armoured vehicles rolling up and over the defensive position. Hellhound tanks spewed sheets of flaming promethium, engulfing dozens of Word Bearers before heavy weapons pierced their fuel tanks and they exploded in rising balls of fire, sending the searing, flammable liquid spraying out in all directions.

Hulking, super-heavy Gorgon assault tanks roared up the steep embankment, their side-sponsons spewing flaming death and autocannon turrets raking along the ridge top.

Streaking lascannon beams and smoking krak missiles zeroed in on the Mechanicus vehicles, but nothing was able to halt their advance. As they reached the top of the tier, their huge assault ramps were dropped and the heavy battle servitors within surged out, chainguns spinning and multi-meltas hissing.

'The reserve is committed, my lord. Have engaged the enemy behind the second tier,' said the growling voice of Bokkar, Kol Badar's Anointed sergeant, across a closed vox-channel.

'Understood,' replied Kol Badar. The reserve had occupied the third tier, guarding against the enemy dropping in behind the main battle force of the Host.

THE KATAPHRACTOI FOLLOWED in the wake of the Gorgons, Skitarii warriors hard-wired into tracked units. They roared forward, heavy bolters barking and missile pods sending streams of self-propelled explosives towards the Word Bearers.

Echelons of Thunderbolts screamed through the air, flying low, tearing up the ground with their strafing gunfire. Several of the fighters were blown out of the sky, lascannon fire and anti-aircraft cannons tearing through wings and cockpits, and they smashed down into the ground, carving burning furrows through the earth and killing all in their path.

Still more drop-troopers fell from the sky, though for every soldier who landed ready to fight, another four smashed lifeless into the earth. Marauder bombers and Valkyries descended in flames through the wildly circling black clouds overhead to crash amid the chaotic battle.

Kol Badar grinned at the spectacle of carnage around him as he gunned down dozens of enemy Guardsmen as they landed. There would be no break in the fighting until victory was achieved and all his enemies were dead or dying upon this field of battle.

Flames washed over him, but he stepped through the conflagration and smashed the weapon out of a Guardsman's hands, placing the barrel of his combi-bolter against the chest of the soldier, relishing the look of terror on the man's face. He pulled the trigger and the man was smashed to the ground, his chest blown open.

'Captains of the Legion, pull your warriors back to the second tier.'

The evacuation of the first line of defence was methodical and organised. The Coryphaus had dictated his orders to his underlings and each enacted his designs with practised efficiency.

Under the covering fire of the restrained Dreadnoughts and war machines of the Host, the warrior-brothers pulled back. They walked with unhurried, measured steps as they laid down overlapping enfilades of fire against the combat servitors emerging from their transports, specialist weaponry destroying vehicles and tanks.

Kol Badar and his Anointed stood at the base of the second tier, clearing the area of incoming drop-troopers, their roaring weapons ripping easily through the lightly armoured foe. They were practically immune to the Guardsmen's fire and carved through them with ease, though the number of the foe was starting to clog the open space with bodies.

He saw the Warmonger stepping resolutely backwards, his roaring cannons ripping apart the foe, and the heavy flamer slung beneath his power claw engulfing dozens in flames.

LARON DROPPED OFF the stepped rampart of the embankment, snapping off shots with his pistols at the retreating enemy, before taking cover behind the wrecked chassis of a Gorgon. They were masterful in their order and precision. Each squad that backed off was supported by angled lines of troops firing their bolters in controlled bursts. It was like attacking a damned fortification. The lines of the enemy were angled like those of the greatest fortresses, with the strongest points, the 'towers', being squads bearing heavy weapons. The Guardsmen were naturally drawn towards the apparently weaker points, veering away from the heavy weapons, but this brought them into the deadly killing ground where the enemy's guns were able to assail them from both sides.

'Where is that damned infantry?' he snarled. He desperately needed the massed ranks of the Skitarii foot cohorts to arrive, for he had not the men to tackle the retreating foe, and the incoming Elysians were being cut down in swathes.

As if on cue, the first ranks of the tech-guard cohort appeared over the edge of the battlements, tracked weaponry rolling forward at their side. They began to fire as they marched resolutely forwards.

The tracked units of the tech-guard unleashed the power of their arcane construction at the Chaos Marines as they backed away. The air crackled with energy as coruscating lightning leapt from humming bronze spheres to strike the foe. The ground was ripped up as bizarre weapons fired, causing great rents to rip along the ground, tossing the enemy into the air. Heavy, quad-barrelled cannons pumped fire into the foe, but the traitors, recognising the new threat, began to target the tracked units of the Mechanicus with missiles and other heavy weapons fire.

Laron's eyes flashed to the timer counting down in the corner of the head-up display in his helmet and he swore. The second wave of drop-troopers was about to be launched and the anti-aircraft fire from the palace had not yet been silenced. The first wave had been devastated and it looked as though the second would face a similar barrage.

Time was running out.

# CHAPTER NINETEEN

BRIGADIER-GENERAL HAVORN cursed as the pict-screen before him flickered, the detailed map-schematic shorting out. The Chimera bumped its occupants about as it rolled across the salt plain in the wake of the tech-guard cohorts. Sweat was dripping down Havorn's face.

Bestial roars and screaming mixed with hissing static blared out of the vox-unit suddenly, replacing the relayed chatter of the senior captains.

'What the hell's all that?' Havorn snarled.

'I don't know, sir, but its been flooding the less powerful voxes for the past hundred metres or so,' replied his adjutant. 'I thought my set-up would be too powerful for it. Damn enemy's jamming our comms somehow.'

'Perfect. Looks like the rest of this war is going to be fought deaf, dumb and blind.'

'Your officers are good men, sir,' replied the man. 'They know their orders.'

'Move us up closer to the front, Kashar. I want to at least be able to see what the hell is going on.'

'Is that wise, brigadier-general? You would be exposing yourself to unnecessary danger.'

'What do you think is going to happen if we lose this battle, Kashar? We lose this battle and we are all dead men. Move us up closer. I want to be able to see the outcome with my own eyes.'

BURIAS-DRAK'SHAL HACKED left and right, smashing the Skitarii out of his way with sweeps of his spiked icon. At the Coryphaus's order he had remounted his Land Raider and led his warriors straight into the massed ranks of the enemy cohorts, meeting them within another of the slowly dispersing cloud walls. The vehicles had ploughed through the enemy ranks, crushing hundreds beneath their heavy tracks.

The Rhinos disabled by the foe were left behind, the warrior-brothers within abandoned to their fate. They would kill many before they fell. It was an honour to die for the Legion.

They had ridden deep into the heart of the enemy formation, until his Land Raider was finally brought to a halt, its hull pierced by countless melta-blasts, its tracks torn and ragged, and its engine reduced to molten metal.

Even then, Burias-Drak'shal refused to be slowed, leading his coterie of warrior-brothers out of the ruined vehicle, roaring and screaming their battle-cries. He pulverised the enemy in his path, shrugging off countless wounds and gunshots that would have killed any other warrior-brother within the Host. The Word Bearers carved a bloody swathe through the Skitarii cohorts, urged ever onwards by the Icon Bearer, following the frenzied warrior deeper into the enemy formation. These were the regular troopers of the Adeptus Mechanicus, indentured warriors who had only minor augmetic enhancements: eye-piece targeters, altered neural pathways, enhanced lungs and such, and they died easily beneath the fury of the possessed warrior and his battle-brothers.

Hissing ichor dripped from his wounds and his armour was cracked and blistering, yet Burias-Drak'shal continued on, ploughing through the enemy, bashing them out of his path. His warriors' chainaxes rose and fell, and bolt pistols blasted as they followed behind him.

Burias-Drak'shal blocked a swinging double-handed axe with the shaft of his icon and grabbed a hovering metallic tentacle attached to the red-robed Tech-Priest's spine, pulling the adept towards him. He leant forwards, snarling as the priest stumbled, and ripped out his throat with a bite, tasting putrid oils and blood-replacement fluids in his mouth. Knocking the priest to the ground he continued to run, impaling a gun-servitor upon the point of the icon and hurling it into the air as its heavy bolter armament ripped chunks out of his shoulder pad.

He saw armoured personnel carriers through the press of bodies up ahead and roared as he sensed that the prey was close, sprinting on with renewed vigour. With a flick of his talons he decapitated another foe, and smashed another out of his way with the return blow, a brutal backhand swing that almost ripped the head of another Skitarii from its shoulders.

THE FIGHTING BETWEEN the first and second tier was brutal and bloody. The daemon engines of the Word Bearers unleashed countless barrages of warp infused shells into the no man's land, killing thousands. The Skitarii warriors marched in perfect unison into the guns of the Word Bearers protected behind the fortified bulwark of the second embankment and hundreds of them were torn apart by the concentrated fire.

'Ancients of battle,' roared the Warmonger, 'be released from your shackles and kill once more in the name of Lorgar!'

Thirty Dreadnoughts roared and screamed wordlessly, straining against the inscribed chains that bound them. The chains were suddenly released and the bloodthirsty machines, all semblance of their sanity having long abandoned them, were unleashed on the enemy as they pushed up the second tier.

They surged over the parapet, their ancient weapons roaring and booming, and they slammed into the enemy, hurling them into the air with great sweeps of their power claws and piston-driven siege hammers. Multi-bladed power gauntlets scythed through the front ranks of the foe, cleaving men and Skitarii in half, and screaming chainfists the length of two men carved down through the bodies of others, throwing blood and chunks of flesh in every direction.

Dreadnoughts stood atop the bulwark, missiles firing from their inbuilt weapon systems, detonating amongst the foe in fiery blasts. One Dreadnought, screaming insanely, turned its rapid firing autocannons upon power armoured warrior-brothers, his ability to distinguish between friend and foe lost in the madness of battle.

The Warmonger strode towards the machine and struck it to the ground with one mighty sweep of its arm. It kicked and screamed madly as it tried to right itself, and the Warmonger unleashed the power of its guns into the sarcophagus casing of the Dreadnought, seeking to put an end to its struggles. Its kicking ceased and its screams became a gurgled hiss. A cadaverous, jawless head could be seen within the cracked sarcophagus, the skull malformed and covered with bony, spiny growths coated in sickly pus.

'You are released from your bondage, warrior-brother,' intoned the Warmonger before it turned its guns once more towards the numberless enemy swarming over the barricade.

'CORYPHAUS, THE SMOKE-WALL is abating. The Ordinatus is come,' said Bokkar.

'What?' growled Kol Badar. 'The Mechanicus would never risk the war machine until its safety was assured.'

'Nevertheless, it is advancing across the salt plain, my lord. It will be in range of the daemon engines within the minute and will be ready to fire upon the palace within ten.'

'A curse upon them! Pull out from combat, Bokkar. Take a Thunderhawk and slow the damned thing down! Get the daemon engines to target it.'

'As you wish, Coryphaus.'

* * *

MY LORD JARULEK, *it is done. The Daemonschage is ready.*

*Good, my acolyte,* Jarulek replied. *Everything is set in motion. I will join you shortly.*

Jarulek opened his eyes from the deep trance. He sat in the restoration chamber, blinking against the thick, viscous liquid that he was immersed in. His arms were bare, the script-covered, pale and heavily muscled limbs pierced by dozens of pipes and needles, pumping him with biologics and serums. He had no wish for his underlings to realise just how taxing the creation of the Gehemehnet had been on his system, but the last twelve hours in the tank, deep in a trance and communion with the higher powers, had rejuvenated him.

The thick liquid evacuated from the chamber, sucked into gurgling pipes, and he sank to his feet. Chirumeks clustered around him, pulling free the tubes and pipes inserted into his veins and muscles, and he flexed his fingers. The time to rejoin the Host had come. It was mere hours until the alignment of planets took place, until the Gehemehnet awoke.

TECHNO-MAGOS DARIOQ stood impassively upon the secondary gantry deck of the Ordinatus as heavy-calibre anti-aircraft batteries directed fire towards the Thunderhawk. The enemy's barrages had been as nothing to the Ordinatus, the incoming ordnance soaked up by flashing void shields, and its return fire darkened the air, overloading the gunship's shielding with ease.

The critically damaged Thunderhawk turned towards the Ordinatus, its pilot clearly fighting with its controls to guide it towards the target. It passed through the giant vehicle's void shields as its left wing tore loose, sending the gunship spinning, and the concentrated, servitor aimed quad-cannons ripped the hull apart, tearing the bulky aircraft in two. The rear half was engulfed in flames and exploded as the fire reached its fuel lines. The front half of the gunship fell from the sky, plummeting towards the Ordinatus, propelled by its velocity and the force of the explosion.

Techno-Magos Darioq calculated the trajectory and velocity of the incoming debris from his position and stood stone still as it slammed into the upper deck above. The metal grid was smashed asunder by the massive incoming weight and it skimmed along the metal, raising a shower of sparks as it ploughed through barricades and crane-structures. It screeched through one of the cannon batteries, instantly crushing a pair of ogryn servitor loaders, before careening off the edge and falling to the secondary gantry where Darioq stood.

The front section of the Thunderhawk screeched across the metal latticework towards him, but he did not move, and it ground to a halt just metres from him, as he had calculated.

Servitors rolled forwards on tracked units, dousing the flames with foam.

'Life signs remain,' said Darioq as he scanned the Thunderhawk, and the servitors retreated from the wreckage instantly. Heavy combat servitors rolled forwards, weapons raised, scanning for the enemy.

Red-armoured Chaos Marines emerged from the flames and the servitors fired upon the survivors. Several of the servitors were ripped apart by bolt fire, but others rolled forwards even as their fallen comrades were dragged aside by tentacled scavenger servitors for re-manufacture.

Darioq's four servo arms unfolded like the legs of a gigantic spider, the weapons systems built into their design humming into activation. Four of the enemy warriors were ripped apart by the fire from his potent weaponry.

With a roar, a bulky shape emerged from the wreckage, smashing through twisted, burning metal. Flaming promethium from this warrior's heavy weapon system engulfed the servitors, turning their flesh to liquid and detonating their ammunition drums.

BOKKAR ROARED AS he smashed his way towards the magos. Plasma pierced the reinforced plasteel plating of his Terminator armour and heavy bolt-rounds tore through his chest plate.

He unleashed the fury of his heavy flamer and roaring promethium engulfed the magos, hiding him from view. As the inferno dissipated, Bokkar could see that the flames had washed harmlessly over a bubble of protective energy surrounding the cursed Mechanicus priest, and he powered forwards, intent on smashing the magos apart with the force of his chainfist.

Bokkar stepped within the boundaries of the tech-priest's protective field and swung his chainfist around in a murderous arc. The blow never landed, as one of the servo-arms, hanging over the magos's shoulder like the barbed tail of a scorpion, snapped out and grabbed his arm, halting it mid-swing.

The servo-arm over the other shoulder grabbed his other arm, and he felt his blessed Terminator armour crack beneath the immense pressure that the whining arms exerted. The servo arms pulled out to each side sharply and both of Bokkar's arms were ripped from his body, spraying blood out in both directions.

He stared down dumbly at his armless torso and was cut in half by the magos's swinging power halberd, the cogged blade hacking through his midsection. He fell to the metal lattice floor.

He had failed his Coryphaus, failed his Legion and only damnation awaited him.

THE AIR TURNED electric as the massive plasma reactors roared to full power in readiness to fire. Fashioned from the same STC templates from which the grand Ordinatus Mars was constructed, the giant weapon's humming increased to painful decibels as it drew the reactors' energy into its power drums.

The pitch of the weapon rose beyond that of human hearing and the entire colossal structure of the Ordinatus began to shudder.

'Dispose of this in the inferno chambers,' said Darioq as he dropped the severed arms of the traitor Terminator beside the severed torso. The armour had been constructed by Mechanicus Forge Worlds over ten thousand years ago and he was loathe to destroy such a revered piece of artifice, but the enemy had long tainted it with its corruption.

He registered the rising pitch of the sonic destructor cannon, and reran the trajectory algorithms. Satisfied, he waited until the warning beacon began to flash within his inner systems, indicating that the Ordinatus was ready.

'Targeting locked, magos,' said the mechanised voice of one of his Tech-Priest subordinates.

'Initiate firing sequence,' Darioq intoned.

THE PALACE THAT had stood upon Tanakreg since it was populated two thousand years previously shuddered as the focused sonic beams ripped through it, shattering its structure at a molecular level. Fully three kilometres long from one end of the structure to the other, and rising hundreds of metres above the low-lying salt plains, the structure began to vibrate as its rocky substructure was rent with hundreds of cracking faults and weaknesses.

One section of the palace collapsed with a thundering roar that echoed across the battlefield as the cliff walls beneath it gave way. The fortified battlements atop the sprawling defensive structure were shattered and the anti-aircraft turrets and batteries ripped from their plascrete housings as more of the palace collapsed.

The whole mountainous outcrop from which the palace was carved disappeared beneath a rising cloud, and the thunder of its collapse made the earth beneath the feet of the battling armies shudder. The potent guns of the palace were silenced as the entire structure smashed to the ground.

A subterranean explosion rocked the earth and Darioq's delicate sensors picked up the faint hint of radiation as the plasma reactor buried deep beneath the ground was breached. A secondary subterranean explosion roared as the palace settled, and rock and debris was hurled hundreds of metres into the air.

A shockwave rippled out from the detonating plasma reactor, hurling tanks and men into the air as it whipped across the land before its power was spent.

The enemy's giant tower shook, dried mortar cracking and slipping from between its massive stone bricks, and a shudder ran up its length. Yet, denying the laws of the physical universe, it remained standing.

'What in the Emperor's holy name was that?' asked Havorn as the Chimera ground to a halt. He scrambled out of the command tank, his blinking advisors and adjutant at his side, and the ever-present bulk of his ogryn bodyguard behind him.

Putting his magnoculars to his eyes, he saw the rising dust cloud where a moment before the towering presence of the palace had been located.

'Emperor be praised,' he exclaimed.

He laughed out loud in surprise and astonishment.

'When's our second wave of drop-troopers inbound?'

'Now sir, they should be falling as we speak,' answered his comms officer, who had been staring blankly at his useless machines since his vox communication had been silenced.

'And now they are safe from the wretched fire from those air turrets,' exclaimed Havorn's young adjutant. 'This is a good day for the Imperium indeed! Victory is assured!'

'Victory is never assured,' said Havorn as his eyes fell on the red-armoured Chaos Marines fighting their way free of the tech-guard cohorts. His augmented, ogryn bodyguard growled menacingly and took a step in front of the brigadier-general.

'Quick, sir!' said his adjutant, urgently.

'We have not the time,' said Havorn flatly, seeing the enemy carve a bloody exit from the mass of bodies and begin hurtling across the salt plain towards them. He pulled his gold-rimmed plasma pistol from his holster.

His entourage raised their weapons and sprayed the approaching warriors with gunfire. The ogryn roared as it planted its heavy feet and empty shells streamed from its ripper gun as it fired the weapon wildly. The Chimera behind them rotated its turret and multi-laser fire peppered the traitors, cutting several of them down. Only six Chaos Marines reached the brigadier-general's command group, but it was enough.

The first Chaos Marine ducked under the ogryn's heavy swinging arm and leapt forwards, smashing its tall, spiked icon into the head of Havorn's adjutant, pulverising his skull.

A burst of fire tore apart another of Havorn's men and the brigadier-general fired his plasma pistol in response, knocking back a chainsword wielding foe as the shot took him in the shoulder. He fired again quickly and despatched the traitor, streaming plasma engulfing his helmet.

This was the end, he thought. An ignominious end to his thirty-seven years within the Imperial Guard, hacked apart by brutal warriors behind his battle lines.

'Damn you, you traitorous whoresons!' he muttered and fired his pistol twice in quick succession, felling another of the two and half metre behemoths.

Two more of his entourage were hacked down and he backed further away.

He saw the loyal ogryn fall to the ground with a bestial roar. He wasn't a sentimental man by any stretch, but he felt pain as his faithful bodyguard fell to the ground, coughing blood from his lungs.

Havorn fired his pistol again and again, and felt the rising pain beneath his hand as the pistol overheated, venting super-heated air. With a snarl, he hurled it to the ground and drew his long bladed combat knife. It had been more than twenty years since it had tasted blood, back in the days when he was a captain of the storm troopers.

Only two of the enemy remained standing and they stalked towards him, wordlessly stepping away from each other to take him from both sides.

Havorn kept his eyes on the foe so as not to attract their attention to the massive form of the ogryn picking itself up behind them, blood running from the wounds on its arms and chest, and spilling from its mouth.

With a roar, the ogryn picked up one of the traitors, one massive hand upon the enemy's backpack and the other between his legs. It lifted the Chaos Marine high into the air and slammed it head first into the ground, cracking its neck.

The second traitor turned with a snarl and swung its icon two handed into the ogryn's legs, driving it to its knees. Releasing his grip on the haft of the hateful symbol of Chaos, the Chaos Marine leapt at the ogryn, its long talons extended for the killing blow.

Havorn cried out and surged forwards, but he was too slow and he saw the bodyguard fall, its throat ripped completely out, blood spurting from the fatal wound.

He drove his combat knife through a crack in the traitor's ceramite back plate, the blade sinking deep. Blood spurted from the wound, burning through Havorn's leather glove, and the enemy spun, his fist smashing into the brigadier-general's cheek, shattering the bone.

Pain exploded in his head and he fell back from the force of the blow. He saw the ogryn's large, mournful eyes as it tried desperately to aid its master before the Chaos Marine reached down and broke its neck with a brutal twist.

'Traitorous hellspawn,' spat Havorn.

'Hellspawn yes. Traitor, no,' replied the hateful, possessed traitor, his fang-filled maw forming the Low Gothic words with difficulty. The fangs retracted and the warrior shook his head, his daemonic visage melting away to leave a cold, pale handsome face.

'The Word Bearers Legion, blessed of Lorgar, are no traitors, wretched fool,' growled the warrior as he stalked towards Havorn.

'You and your wretched kin turned your back on the glorious Emperor and all of humanity to embrace damnation,' said Havorn, crawling back towards his fallen adjutant and the dead man's laspistol.

'The Emperor turned his back on us!' raged the traitor. 'Only through the unified worship of *true* divinities can mankind be saved. Your False Emperor is nothing more than a rotting corpse perched atop a golden high-chair, a puppet for bureaucrats and taxmen. And you pathetic humans pray to him? You are the lowest of scum, ignorant and embracing that ignorance.'

Havorn's hand slid behind him and closed on the grip of the laspistol.

'Your soul will be damned when you leave this world, while I will go to the blessed Emperor's side in glory and light,' said Havorn, trying to keep the bastard distracted.

'I say my soul is already damned in *this* world, and that there will be nothing but hell waiting for *you*,' said the traitor.

'I'll see you there,' said Havorn and he swung the laspistol up, firing it straight into the face of the Chaos Marine. The traitor fell backwards with a cry of anger and pain, and lay still.

Havorn pushed himself to his feet, pain throbbing from his shattered cheek-bone, and he began to stagger away.

A clawed hand wrapped around his neck from behind, and he was lifted into the air and turned to face the traitor. The wound on the traitor's forehead was closing as he watched, the bone knitting together and flesh re-forming over the bullet hole, leaving not a scratch upon the traitor's darkly handsome face.

'YES, I WILL see you in hell, human,' said Burias-Drak'shal as he plunged his clawed hand through the brigadier-general's chest. With one decisive wrench, he pulled the Elysian commander's still-beating heart from the old man's broken ribcage and watched as the life left his eyes. He held the beating heart to his mouth, tasting the sweet, warm blood, and threw the lifeless corpse dismissively to the ground.

The Chimera slammed into Burias-Drak'shal with shocking force, sending him flying out in front of the armoured personnel carrier. As he tried to rise to his feet it slammed into him again, and he disappeared beneath its whirling tracks, sixty tonnes of Imperial tank rolling over him.

A RIPPLE OF movement spread out from the base of the Gehemenhet, the blackened earth around the tower shimmering and wavering. Electricity coalesced down the tower and surged across the surface of the ground before dissipating. Glowing light began to spill from the mortar between the massive stone blocks, which began to bulge and warp like molten rubber. A daemonic, fanged face appeared within the stone, pushing outwards, straining to break into the mortal realm.

'Not just yet, precious,' said Jarulek, caressing the daemonic manifestation. Claws appeared in the stone, reaching out towards the Dark Apostle and he chuckled. He spoke a word in the language of the daemon and the creature recoiled, its face a mask of childish, shamefaced repentance.

'Not just yet,' he repeated and the daemon retreated back within the Gehemehnet.

# CHAPTER TWENTY

FOR A DAY and night the Chaos Marines held the Imperials at bay, though they were driven slowly back, unable to contain the sheer numbers of the foe advancing against them. There were moments of brief respite in the action, as the Elysians gathered themselves for another push forwards, but always there were skirmishes and minor actions. The Skitarii tech-guard cohorts advanced tirelessly. Without the threat of the potent air defences that had been housed within the palace, the heavens were filled with Elysian and Imperial Navy aircraft, and Elysian drop-troopers descended through the darkness above to fall behind the enemy lines. Laron felt a touch of admiration and awe for the enemy, for they fought without rest as never-ending waves of the Imperials attacked, and they resisted every push and new attack with great fervour. He dismissed the thought as soon as it formed. To even think such a thing bordered on heresy.

Arcs of lightning reached out from the tower to ensnare Valkyries, Thunderbolts and drop-troopers that strayed close, and they were dragged through the air into its sheer stone sides. Pilots fought with their controls as the circuitry of their aircrafts was fried and they were drawn in towards the tower. There were no explosions, however; they merely disappeared as they should have struck stone, sucked into the Ether, to be fed upon by the army of daemons waiting just beyond the thin membrane separating the physical world from the warp.

Missiles screamed from beneath the wings of fighters, detonating explosively into the side of the daemon tower, and keening, high-pitched, maddening screams echoed across the skies. The attacks caused great rents to appear in the side of the tower and dark blood seeped from the wounds, thick and glutinous. Bombardment from the advancing Imperial line joined with the attack and battle cannons and siege ordnance were directed towards the giant tower as they too came into range, and bleeding pockmarks appeared across the sheer walls of the tower.

The tower's pain resonated within the soul of every warrior on the battlefield. The traitorous enemy seemed to become enraged by the power of the cries and they attacked with renewed fury. Laron staggered beneath the twisting power of Chaos that burst in waves from the tower, his head spinning and nausea making bile rise in his throat, and he knew that every Elysian on the field of battle suffered. Even the tech-guard warriors of the Adeptus Mechanicus seemed affected, pausing mid-battle in confusion at the unwholesome stimuli washing over them.

The Ordinatus continued its relentless, unstoppable advance and it levelled great sections of the Chaos defences with every titanic blast from its sonic weapon. Laron swore as enemy warriors and Elysians alike were caught in the blasts, their internal organs exploding and their bones shattering as the resonating blast ripped through them. The foes' ancient ceramite power armour shattered into millions of tiny shards beneath the potent Mechanicus weapon.

Clearly recognising the threat that the Ordinatus posed, the Chaos Marines hammered thousands of rounds of fire into its void shields, overriding them completely several times. Little damage was sustained by the behemoth before dutiful Tech-Priests and the army of servitors that swarmed over the machine restored the shields and it continued its relentless advance. Soon it would be within range of the cursed daemon tower. Laron prayed to the Emperor that the war machine would fell it.

The enemy was pushed back to the third tier and then back to the fourth. Here it seemed that they had determined to make their stand. They would hold the fourth tier or they would be slaughtered to a man. That suited Laron just fine. It was brutal, gritty fighting, but he took heart in the fact that they *were* grinding the enemy down, though it was a slow process. The enemy were being beaten, individual by individual, even though Imperial losses were horrific.

Communications remained completely inoperative and Brigadier-General Havorn's corpse had been found behind the tech-guard cohorts. Colonel Laron had donned a black armband in mourning for the old general, but he had taken over as the overall commander of the Elysian 72nd and 133rd with some reluctance. He set up crude communications using runners, flags, loudhailers and searchlights to organise attacks and retreats across the peninsula. Commissar Kheler proved an admirable and forthright advisor. Kheler tempered Laron's more foolhardy attitudes and the acting colonel developed an appreciation of Kheler's uncompromising expectations of the captains of the regiments. He allowed no talk of retreat and shot any man who showed the slightest sign of doubt or reluctance to perform his duties.

It will all be over soon, thought Laron. The enemy could not hold out for longer than hours at most. They would be victorious and they would return to the Crusade bearing Havorn's body with full honours.

This was the final push. They just needed to break the enemy from the fourth tier of defence and that would allow the Ordinatus to begin its barrage upon the cursed tower. It was unholy, the massive thing that rose up and pierced the skies over head. It must have been over a kilometre in diameter, and the aura of *wrongness* that it exuded made him feel physically sick. It must be destroyed.

If there was a portal to hell, it was surely this damned tower. With a nod to his subordinates, he indicated the commencement of the final push against the enemy. Flags were raised and powerful spotlights flashed the signal along the Imperial line.

The final chapter of the war would be played out in the next hours of engagement, for better or for worse.

VARNUS PACED BACK and forth behind the picketed slaves, a lasgun in his hands and his mind seething.

Blood filled his thoughts, anger and bitterness infusing him.

A hundred thousand workers, the last remaining Imperial subjects enslaved by the Word Bearers, had been herded together and picketed along the top of the third tier. Their chains were bolted into the plascrete battlements atop the earthen bulwark. There they stood, forming a living shield of bodies.

The red-armoured priest had dragged him there. Varnus's thoughts were confused and tormented. He had not realised at first what was going on. All he could hear were the voices of Chaos in his head and the pounding of blood, and he had stared at his bloody hands in dumb incomprehension.

A small shuttle had risen to the top of the Gehemahnet tower and a glorious, terrifying figure had emerged. Without any conscious will, he had dropped to the ground before this warrior-priest, screwing his eyes tightly shut and trying desperately to maintain control of his bodily functions. The figure radiated power and the essence of Chaos and Varnus found his insides twisting within him, his skin crawling and his head aching. He felt as if he was being turned inside out and pain wracked his body before he passed out.

He had awoken to find the first warrior-priest dragging him across the earth and he was deposited at the top of the fourth defensive line with the other slaves.

The warrior had left him without a word, going to join in the raging battle.

The overseers had tried to chain him with the others, but they soon backed away from him after he had killed two of them and turned their needle-fingers upon them. Some of the slaves had cheered at that, but their cries died in their throats as Varnus looked at them. Perhaps they saw the same thing that made the overseers back away.

And so he had waited with the slaves, unchained but bound there nonetheless. To go forward was to die, but to go back would only be to lengthen his torment. No, this was the battlefield where his eternal fate was to be determined and he waited whatever was to come with little care of the outcome. He stalked back and forth, letting his anger and bitterness build.

He raged as he felt the pain of the Gehemehnet and cried out in anguish as each shell screamed over his head to strike against it. The child was strong and it would take more than humble shells to destroy it, but still he roared with anger at the pain it endured.

Even here on the battlefield, the Discords blared at the slaves and Varnus knew now that they spoke the truth.

The Emperor was no god; he was a shattered corpse that clung to a last vestige of life by feeding off the deaths of those dedicated to him, and he cared not at all for Varnus or any of the other wretched, deceived slaves that invoked his name in prayer.

But there were true gods in the universe, ones that took an active interest in the lives of mortals: gods that granted strength to their followers and brought ruin upon their foes.

He had been blind, but now his eyes had been opened wide. He didn't hate the Imperial Guardsmen for their ignorance, for he too had been duped into believing the lies of the Ecclesiarchy. He hated them for betraying him and all these poor chained-up individuals. They had waited for liberation, enduring hell at the hands of their captors, and now they were being killed by those they had waited so long to save them.

He had picked up a lasgun from a corpse and he stood waiting for them to come to him. He would damn well kill as many of the bastards as he could before he was overcome. It would not be long before the fighting was upon them once more. The Chaos Marines were even now pulling back towards the fourth line and it was time for the slaves to do their part.

The overseers had attached the slaves' chains to dozens of massive living machines of horrific power and brutal will. These daemonic, infernal creations roared as they fired their ordnance into the advancing Imperial ranks and the closest to them were deafened by the sound. Scores more slaves were killed by the daemon engines, dragged beneath their claws and within reach of snapping mouth-tentacles of flesh and metal.

Varnus could feel the ceaseless anger of the daemon essences bound within the vehicles and he felt somehow akin to them. At some unheard command, the daemon engines were released from their bindings of words and shackles, and they surged over the barricade of the fourth and last defensive line, dragging the slaves forward between them.

Varnus screamed his hatred and pain, and followed, clutching his lasgun.

MARDUK STOOD ATOP the fourth and final embankment, watching as the enemy began its final push. The bombardment of artillery began afresh and the lines of the Host were hidden beneath plumes of smoke and flame. An endless wave of enemy troops and tanks spilled down into the open ground between the third and fourth lines of embankments, the intensity of gunfire lifting dramatically as they came into bolter range.

'The end is nigh,' commented Burias.

'It will be a close run thing. This will be the final battle' said Marduk. He glanced over at the Icon Bearer. 'Watch out for your nemesis, Burias. Fear the dreaded Chimera.'

Burias laughed out loud and rubbed his unmarked head with one hand.

'Damn thing hurt,' he said. He had returned to the lines of the Word Bearers, driving a battered enemy tank through the ranks of battle servitors, crushing them under its tracks, but they did not target it. It was an Imperial tank and it was not in their programming to raise a weapon against it. As it drew near the Host's lines a missile had sent it spinning into the air. Burias had crawled from the flaming wreckage and told a laughing Marduk of his tale.

He had gripped onto the tank as it thundered over him and had crawled across its hull before ripping away a hatch and slaughtering the occupants. Then he had ripped the driver's seat from its housing so that he could fit his bulk into the compartment before driving back towards the lines of the Host.

'I saw you speaking with the Coryphaus,' said Marduk.

Burias looked over at him and Marduk raised his eyebrows.

'Yes, First Acolyte.'

'Of what were you speaking?'

'Things of little consequence,' said Burias. 'The deployment of our Havoc squads, the use of the slaves.'

Marduk narrowed his eyes. The Icon Bearer was concealing something. He was a conniving snake, and Marduk had no doubt that he would turn on him if that would benefit him.

'The Dark Apostle comes!' Marduk heard one of the warrior-brothers exclaim, and he turned, his thoughts pulled away from Burias, inclining his head to witness his lord's arrival.

He floated out of the roiling, black, lightning filled clouds, surrounded by a glistening nimbus of light, descending gently towards the battle like a glorified angel. He was borne aloft upon a disc-like daemon pulpit, one hand upon the spiked railing at its front. Daemons swirled around him, filling the air with their keening screams as they scythed around the Dark Apostle in intricate weaving patterns.

They were daemons blessed by Tzeentch, the Great Changer of the Ways, and their bodies were long and smooth, rimmed with thousands of jagged barbs. Hunters of the Ether, they resembled the ray-fish that existed in the oceans of countless worlds, sleek and deadly. Their bodies were ovular in shape and long barbed tails swished behind them as they cut through the air, fleshy wing tips rising and falling deceptively slowly. Colours played over their dark hides, glistening patterns of iridescent shades. Each was the length of three men and they cut through the air in a deadly dance, spiralling down in steep dives before turning into climbing corkscrews, interweaving with the paths of others of their kind.

Smaller versions of the screaming daemon-rays, no larger than a hand span across, whipped around the Dark Apostle, spiralling around him like a dense shoal of frenzied fish.

Jarulek held his crozius of the dark gods high before him and a roar rose up to greet him from the assembled Host.

He certainly knew how to make an entrance, Marduk thought wryly.

'The way you appear to the Host is paramount, First Acolyte,' he remembered Jarulek lecturing him. 'Always you must project an aura of authority and religious awe. We are beyond the warrior-brothers of the Legion, we are the chosen of the gods, exalted in Lorgar's eyes and raised beyond the morass of the lower warrior. Our warriors must worship us. And why? We must appear glorified and exalted so that always we can inspire utter devotion in the Host. A warrior fuelled with faith fights with twice the hatred and twice the strength of one that does not, and he will fight on past the point when he would otherwise give in to death. A Dark Apostle must always inspire such devotion in his flock,' said Jarulek, his eyes filled with passion and belief.

'That is the reason that we need a Coryphaus, Marduk. The Dark Apostle must be separate and aloof from the Host to maintain the utter devotion of the warrior-brothers. He must not be one of them, he must be beyond them. The Coryphaus is the war leader of the Host, but he is also the conduit through which the Dark Apostle can gauge the feeling of the Host. For once you take on the mantle of Dark Apostle, you must be one apart from the Legion. Always you must project a holy aura that will inspire utter, fanatical loyalty and devotion.'

The full power of the Dark Apostle's words were driven home to Marduk as he felt the spirit of the Host rise as Jarulek made his descent upon the back of the hellish daemon construct.

The daemon pulpit was a work of mad genius, formed from the lucid dreams of the Dark Apostle's mind and birthed in the Immaterium before it had been dragged into the material realm to serve his will. Its skeleton was of blackest iron and the ribs of the metallic frame formed an eight-pointed star beneath his feet. Between these was living, red-raw flesh and muscle, and it was upon this that the Dark Apostle stood.

The whole daemon construct was disc shaped and razor sharp barbs of black iron lined its edges. Black, iron rib work rose up at the front of the pulpit, curved to either side of the Dark Apostle like a chariot of old, and living, bloody flesh filled the gaps between the struts. An ancient book bound in human leather was open before him and a pair of burning braziers trailed oily, black smoke in his wake.

He held his arms out wide to receive the praise of the Host, a rapturous smile upon his upturned face. He glided down until he was hovering just above the heads of the warrior-brothers and his velvet voice swept out before him as he spoke.

'Let the infidel worshippers of the Corpse Emperor witness the power of true gods!' he said, his words carrying easily over the throng of battle, though he seemed barely to raise his voice. 'Show them the power of the warriors of true faith! Let them not defile the sacred monument of the Gehemahnet! Slaughter them with the words of blessed Lorgar upon your lips! Feel the power of the gods surge within you! Kill them, my warriors! The gods hunger for sacrifice!'

The Dark Apostle lowered his defiled crozius arcanum in the direction of the enemy and his daemon pulpit began gliding forwards over the heads of his warriors. The scything daemon rays of Tzeentch screamed ahead of him, weaving deadly patterns and glowing with iridescent light.

The explosions of incoming shells erupted around the Dark Apostle, but he emerged unscathed, protected by a nimbus of light that surrounded him.

As one, the Host of the Word Bearers gave a roar of devotion and hatred, and surged forwards. The Gehemahnet rumbled behind them and Marduk could feel the presence of thousands of daemons struggling to enter the physical realm. Its time was almost upon them.

There was no glory to be had in waiting behind walls for death to come. No, the final battle would be a full attack against the enemy. Havoc squads would hold position upon the fourth tier, but the remainder of the Host was to attack in one powerful wave and engage the enemy in the open.

Marduk lifted his daemon weapon, feeling its power building as the Gehemehnet neared its awakening, and he leapt the barricade.

'Purge them of their heresies!' he roared. 'Death to the followers of the Corpse Emperor!'

The Host surged towards the enemy behind the advance of the slaves, bolters barking. Marduk was pleased to see that many of the slaves picked up weapons from fallen enemy soldiers and put them to use, shooting at their erstwhile allies. Some turned these weapons back to shoot at the Word Bearers, but they were few, and they were clubbed to the ground and murdered by their fellow slaves.

Marduk always found it pleasing to seeing former heathen worshippers of the False Emperor turn to Chaos, embracing the truth and becoming true converts, proselytes of the true Gods. The corruption of the innocent some would say, but he knew that it was something far more worthwhile. He was seeing enlightenment come to those who had been exposed to lies and falsehood for their entire lives. It was liberation and it was salvation.

The daemonic war engines that the slaves were chained to bellowed and roared as they clawed up the earth beneath them and filled the air with sprays of shells, flame and missiles. They smashed into the enemy foot soldiers and began ripping them apart and crushing them beneath their weight. Hundreds of slaves were injured as they were dragged into the fray and their chains snapped tight between the machines, entangling them with the foe.

The Host followed closely, firing into the mayhem, not caring who they killed. Thousands dropped beneath the roar of bolters, and as chains were driven into the ground and snapped, the Host broke into a run. They fell amongst the slaves and enemy, hacking and cutting with chainaxes and swords, bludgeoning with bolters and burning with roaring flamers.

Marduk saw Jarulek enter battle ahead of him, shooting down from his floating pulpit with a monstrous, daemon-bolter that caused hideous mutations in those it struck. The screaming daemons of Tzeentch scythed through the enemy, their razor-edged forms cutting limbs from bodies and cleaving through heads. The smaller daemons whirled around the Dark Apostle, eviscerating anything that came close.

Marduk saw a warrior raise a hand to hurl a grenade at the Dark Apostle, but his forearm was cleanly severed as he pulled it back for the throw. It fell to the ground as his feet. Marduk laughed as he saw the look of frantic panic on the man's face before he was hurled through the air by the force of the explosion. A pair of screaming ray-daemons cut through the air and sliced into the flailing body as if playing with a new toy and he fell to the ground in pieces.

*Give them a taste of the power of Chaos that will soon come,* said the voice of Jarulek.

Marduk fired his bolt pistol into the face of an enemy as he formed the complex words of a passage from the *Enumeration of Convocation,* an inspired work that blessed Erebus had crafted in the language of the daemon. He spoke the difficult words easily, his chainsword hacking into flesh and his bolt pistol blasting through bone.

A searing beam of white-blue energy from a Skitarii weapon caused the flesh and blood of several Word Bearers to boil within their power armour, and Marduk rolled to the side as the beam swept towards him, almost stumbling over the words of the complex enumeration. The results of such a slip could be catastrophic, but he picked up the incantation smoothly once again as he rolled to his feet, cleaving his weapon across the throat of another foe.

He barked out the guttural words of the enumeration, feeling the power of Chaos building, tapping into the excessive amounts of energy waiting to be released. Burias-Drak'shal's horned head lifted as the possessed warrior crouched over a kill, nostrils flaring as it scented the build-up of warp energy.

With a wave of his chainsword, Marduk ordered the warriors around him to form a circle, with him as its centre. The power armoured Chaos Marines of the Legion planted their feet, facing outwards, mowing down any that drew near their First Acolyte.

Burias-Drak'shal stalked through the maelstrom of battle. His whole posture was altered once the change had taken him. From a tall, proud and graceful warrior, he became a hulking, stooped, feral creature that oozed power and barely suppressed rage. He roughly shoved a Word Bearers warrior-brother out of his way to take his place beside the First Acolyte, who was drawing near the end of the enumeration, and planted his icon firmly into the ground.

Reaching out with one hand, Marduk gripped the icon, directing the building power of Chaos through its black metal. He gripped the icon tightly and closed his eyes, still speaking in the contorting language of the warp. When he opened his eyes they were as black as pitch.

He barked the last words of the enumeration and, in the moment of silence that followed, he and Burias-Drak'shal raised the icon high before slamming its butt down into the ground, steam rising from where it touched the earth.

The air around the icon shimmered as if with the heat of a star-engine and the long, spiked haft began to vibrate. A swirling vortex of darkness suddenly opened, and the surrounding air was sucked towards it. The kathartes screamed into reality from within the portal. Scores of them hurtled up into the sky from the rift in real space.

Their exposed muscles were slick with blood and they beat their powerful, flayed wings as they coiled overhead before descending upon the battlefield. They plummeted into the Elysians, talons curled forwards like those of an attacking bird of prey, hooking and ripping into flesh. Some men were grasped by the shoulders and lifted into the air before other kathartes screamed into them, ripping at them and squabbling over the pickings. Guardsmen were torn apart as the kathartes fought, and Marduk could feel the rising terror and fear of the soldiers, their resolve wavering.

'Fear not the devils! Faith in the Emperor will protect your souls!' came a shout from a leather-clad individual with wide, mad eyes and Marduk laughed at his folly. The man screamed an oath to the Emperor and shot down one of the katharte daemons. The shot broke one of its wings and it fell into the crush of men.

Marduk roared and leapt towards the figure, smashing aside those in his path, but the black-clad commissar was lost amongst the melee. Marduk swore in anger and continued to slaughter those around him.

* * *

LARON SMILED AS he saw the enemy surge forward. This was the moment he had been waiting for. He commanded his signal communicators to order the attack. They had stormed forward from their final defensive line. Now the sheer weight of the Imperials must surely prevail.

Laron raced back down the embankment towards the waiting Valkyries. He leapt aboard the closest aircraft and hooked himself onto the rappel line attached just inside the open bay door, nodding to Captain Elias. The aircraft's engines roared as it took off and the flight of thirty Valkyries rose just high enough to clear the embankment of the third defensive line before screeching over the heads of the frantically battling combatants in the no man's land below. The crewmen manning a pair of secured heavy bolters opened fire as the Valkyries swooped low over the field of battle. Laron's storm troopers, kneeling in the open doors and secured with rappel lines, fired their hellguns down into the melee, picking out targets amongst the chaotic battle surging below.

A hellish shape burst through the open bay door, ripping with daemonic claws, and blood splashed across the close interior of the Valkyrie. The stench of the creature was foul and it slashed around frenziedly, ripping at the storm troopers and hacking through rappel lines as if they were twine. Two storm troopers fell from the aircraft as it roared across the battlefield, jinking from side to side to avoid incoming fire. They fell into the mayhem below, and another's face was ripped off as the creature's tri-hinged jaw snapped.

Laron clubbed the hateful thing in the face with the butt of his pistol. Its head swung towards him, eyes burning with flames and steam emanating from the twin gashes that marked where a nose should have been. Its foetid breath made him gag and he saw that its tongue was made up of a thousand wriggling worm-tentacles as it reached for him. He jammed his melta-pistol into the daemon's mouth and pulled the trigger. The thing was lit up from the inside before it broke up into a million tiny pieces of ash and was blown out of the aircraft.

Laron grimaced as he spat the foul ash from his mouth, before grinning at the surviving storm troopers.

The Valkyries carried large cases packed with explosives. The Ordinatus might well destroy the tower, but he wasn't taking any chances and he didn't like the idea of their victory relying upon the disconcerting Adeptus Mechanicus magos. This might have been an old-fashioned way of blowing something up, but sometimes that was the best way.

'HAVOC SQUADS, SHOOT them down,' ordered Kol Badar as the Valkyries appeared over the ridge, flying fast and low over the top of the raging battle, fire pumping from their forward-mounted guns and from their open doors.

Shells smashed down along the defensive tier as carefully timed and targeted artillery fire was unleashed, and an echelon of thunderbolts screamed along the line, peppering the heavy weapons teams with their intense strafing runs. The Havoc squads took down over a dozen of the Valkyries, but the relentless attacks forced them to take cover, and the remaining Valkyries screamed overhead, past the fourth defensive line, heading towards the base of the Gehemehnet.

'Rearguard, incoming,' Kol Badar said as he ripped through a pair of enemies with his combi-bolter.

'Acknowledged, Coryphaus,' came the response.

VARNUS COULD SEE nothing but red as his rage lent him strength and he swung his lasgun into the face of the Elysian, smashing his visor. He leapt upon the Guardsman as he fell and smashed the butt of his lasgun into his face again before rising from the kill and gunning down another.

Something struck him from behind and he was thrown forwards, falling at the feet of a man dressed in black. A commissar, he recognised dimly, seeing the man level a pistol at his head. He stared back at the commissar hatefully, awaiting the shot that would end his life.

But it never came. The commissar's hand was hacked off by a chainsword and Varnus surged to his feet.

'This one is mine!' he roared and the Chaos Marine towering over him turned its helmeted head in his direction. With a dignified nod of its head, it left the wounded commissar to Varnus and leapt back into the fray, its twin chainswords whirring.

Varnus stood on the one good hand of the commissar as he scrabbled for a weapon and the man turned his face towards him, twisted in hatred and pain.

'Where is the Emperor now?' asked Varnus in a language the commissar could not understand. 'He has abandoned you, just as he abandoned me.'

Varnus placed the barrel of his lasgun against the commissar's forehead. The man's eyes were defiant till the last and Varnus pulled the trigger. He watched as the life faded from his eyes and a pang wrenched inside him. He dropped to his knees over the dead figure, confused and lost. The anger drained from him and was replaced with self-loathing, guilt and anguish.

He caught the sight of his own reflection in the highly buffed, silver pin on the commissar's hat and he lifted it up, staring at his own hate-filled visage.

What had he become? This was the face of the enemy. *The False Emperor is the enemy!*

He looked upon the two-headed eagle symbol upon the black leather hat he held in his hands and he felt duel emotions: hate and sadness. *They betrayed you! The worship of the False Emperor is a lie!*

Maybe it was a lie, but was this a better alternative? This embracing of evil and slaughter?

*Slaughter is the holy sacrifice that the gods demand.*

The madness was descending upon him again and he had not the strength to fight it any longer. He would continue to fall into damnation. No, he would not fall, he would embrace it. He felt the rage building within him and it terrified him that it was not unpleasant. He would be lost and he would not care that he was lost.

With the last vestiges of himself, he lifted the pistol from the commissar's hand and raised it to his head. Emperor, save me, he thought. Before the unrelenting rage descended upon him once again and he was completely lost, he pulled the trigger.

At last he had found release from the sound of Chaos in his mind.

* * *

'GET THOSE DAMNED explosives set! We ain't got much time!' shouted Laron as he hunkered down behind the Valkyrie. His storm troopers were firing on the incoming enemies, but they would be on them in a moment. Bolter rounds impacted against the aircraft, and the crewman operating the heavy bolter flew backwards as a bolt shell detonated in his skull, splattering Laron with blood. He swore and took the man's position, swinging the heavy weapon towards the enemy. A missile slammed into one of the other Valkyries, which detonated explosively, throwing flaming debris in all directions.

Laron pressed the twin thumb triggers of the pivot mounted heavy bolter and fired a spray of heavy calibre rounds towards the incoming foe, dropping several of them. Rhinos could be seen cutting towards the storm troopers from further off, and Laron swore.

'Set the damned timers! Move it!' he roared in between bursts of fire.

'Sir, we have incoming hostiles from the east,' said a wounded storm trooper as he pulled a piece of metal from his shoulder.

'Just great,' muttered Laron as he gunned down another enemy.

'All set,' Captain Elias shouted.

A sudden scream from the base of the tower made Laron glance around and he did a double take as he saw the scene unfolding. A long, spined arm had reached out of the stone of the tower, grabbed one his men around the throat and was dragging him towards the wall. Another storm trooper was hacking at the arm with his knife, and hissing ichor dripped from the wound. Fleshy, hooked claws burst from the wall and latched onto another man. He was pulled off balance and tumbled into the wall. He half disappeared into the surface of the stone, and tentacles and claws gripped his armour and hauled him fully inside as he screamed.

The storm troopers backed away from the wall and began firing at the things materialising out of the stone surface. Hissing, fanged faces pushed out, bulbous, mutated eyes opened up all over the stone. A flickering figure of a huge, horned daemon with a twisting blade of fire in its hand strained to escape the stone, and hellguns blasted as the soldiers targeted the emerging monster.

'Back! Get back to the Valkyries!' shouted Laron, ducking down behind the heavy bolter as rounds of incoming fire peppered the aircraft.

One of the storm troopers shot their comrade who was still being pulled into the tower. It was a mercy killing, to end whatever cruel fate had awaited him.

A heavily muscled humanoid figure pulled free of the wall and ran at the storm troopers, hefting a heavy, archaic broadsword in its muscular red arms. With one sweep of the blade it carved a man in half from shoulder to waist, and it roared, flames spilling from its eyes and throat.

Laron swung his heavy bolter around and unleashed a long burst of fire into the daemon's chest. It was driven back several steps by the impacts, though it appeared unharmed. It turned its snarling head towards Colonel Laron and began to advance through the barrage.

'Go!' he shouted to the pilot as the surviving storm troopers scrambled aboard, and the Valkyrie lifted straight up into the air, its powerful vertical thrusters roaring. Boltgun fire ripped through the undercarriage of the aircraft as it lifted and several men were killed, their blood spraying the roof.

'The charges blow in ten, sir!' shouted one of his men, and Laron nodded as he fired upon the Chaos Marines below. More things were emerging from the walls of the tower.

The Valkyrie turned steeply, and a missile destined to smash into its side flew through the open doorway, screaming over Laron's head and miraculously passing straight out of the other open doorway, filling the interior with the smoke of its propulsion.

Open-mouthed, Laron turned.

'The Emperor protects!' shouted Elias, laughing at the sheer improbability of the occurrence.

'It certainly seems that way,' agreed Laron, shaking his head in utter disbelief.

He didn't see the hulking, winged daemon pushing out of the wall behind the turning Valkyrie. Nor did he see it leap towards the aircraft, nor hear the power of its roar over the screaming engines. But he felt the impact as it struck.

The tail of the Valkyrie tipped earthwards with the sudden additional weight, and the pilot struggled to keep it airborne. The head of a giant axe slammed through the raised rear assault ramp, smashing it asunder. The ramp was ripped from the aircraft as the axe was pulled free, and it tumbled end over end to the ground below.

The daemon roared as it pulled at the tail of the Valkyrie, its wings beating furiously and its infernal muscles straining to bring the aircraft down to the ground. It was thrown off as the Valkyrie's jet turbines kicked in, but with a beat of its powerfully muscled wings it turned in the air and its whip flicked out, wrapping around the tail of the aircraft, pulling it sharply downwards.

With its engines roaring, the Valkyrie screamed up into the air as its tail tipped beneath it, and the pilot lost control. The aircraft slammed into another Valkyrie before flipping upside down and plummeting to the ground. Laron leapt from the aircraft as it slammed into the earth, rolling into the dust.

The daemon landed atop the flaming wreck, its massive hooves twisting the metal beneath it. It seemed impervious to the flames, and Laron scrambled backwards as the malevolent thing stepped out of the inferno, its burning eyes fixed upon him.

It was over twelve feet tall and it seemed to flicker as if it were not fully there. Its skin was as black as pitch and a burning symbol was emblazoned on its chest, the mark of one of the ruinous powers.

'Emperor, protect my soul,' whispered Laron.

The charges exploded. Both man and daemon were ripped apart by the force of the detonations.

But the tower still stood.

THE ORDINATUS FIRED upon the Gehemehnet, enormous amounts of energy focused into a deadly frequency that held the power to shatter mountains and crush bones to powder. The air shimmered as the ultra-high and ultra-low frequencies screamed over the top of the chaotic battle and roared towards the fifty kilometre high structure. It struck the side of the tower some forty metres up, and stones were ruptured from within as they were shaken apart. They exploded into sand and were blown out of the other side. A hole the size of a building was driven through the tower.

Impossibly, the tower still stood, despite the lack of integrity holding it together, for it was no longer bound by the rules of geometry or gravity. The tower was a gateway to the warp beyond, and through the hole blasted in its side the roiling darkness and liquid flame of the Ether could be seen.

With a roar that came from the throats of a million infernal entities the Gehemehnet awoke and the barrier between the realm of the daemon and the material plane was stripped away. Energy roared outwards from the Gehemehnet, throwing dust up into the air and hurling men to the ground. It made the black seas beyond the Shinar peninsula rise in a giant tidal wave that roared out from the tower, and lightning tore apart the heavens. Rumblings shook the ground, and daemons screamed into being.

They emerged from within the tower, thousands of straining hellish entities clawing out of living stone, and they roared their pleasure as they manifested. Thousands of others flew from the rent in the tower's side, held aloft by pinioning wings or twisting, contorting winds of fire. Screams and roars thundered across the Shinar peninsula and tens of thousands of daemons poured from the gateway, descending on the mortals.

The Ordinatus machine fired again, but this time the force of its attack seemed to rebound from the tower and it hurtled back towards the behemoth, smashing into its void shields and ripping them apart, the fury of its own power turned against it. The void shields crumbled one by one beneath the onslaught, robbing the energy of its force, but still enough power hurtled into the Ordinatus to rip it apart.

The Ordinatus was rocked by the force of its own weapon, though even this was not enough to destroy it completely. Plumes of smoke wreathed its iron sides, and metal scaffolds and gantries were shattered. The great weapon housed upon its back, greater than even those of a mighty Titan, was torn from its housing and collapsed beneath its own weight. Blue fire spurted from breaches in the plasma core powering the machine and tech-priests wailed as the machine-spirit groaned in agony.

Daemons streamed across the battlefield, hacking, slashing and ripping. Thousands of mortals were slaughtered in the first moments of the insane combat, their limbs hacked apart by brutal hellblades, their bodies turned to liquid by blasts of yellow and pink unearthly fire and their souls ripped from their still warm bodies by lascivious, hateful daemons.

The clouds overhead were sucked suddenly inwards, towards the Gehemehnet, and fierce winds pulled at everyone battling upon the plains. Tanks slid across the ground under the force of the sudden gale and men were sent flying through the air.

As suddenly as they came into being, the daemons of the warp were sucked back towards the Gehemehnet, screaming in rage as the fabric of their beings was stripped away like melting wax, and the energies that composed them was drawn back into the tower.

The heavens were cleared of darkness and the great orb of the red planet Korsis could be seen large overhead.

'The conjunction comes,' muttered Jarulek in awe, down on one knee as he strained to resist being pulled back by the roaring gale, his daemonic pulpit having been sucked back to the Gehemehnet by the force of the Daemonschage. He put a hand out to break his fall as the wind stopped abruptly and silence descended across the peninsula, except for one sound.

At the top of the Gehemehnet, the Daemonschage bell tolled as the twelve planets of the Dalar system drew into line and the energies of the ten thousand daemons contained within the tower were propelled down the shaft into the core of the planet.

The dense rock that formed the mantle surrounding the absolute centre of Tanakreg was ripped apart by the unholy power and the land above was shattered.

Massive fault lines ripped up the continents as tectonic plates shifted and smashed into each other. New mountains were instantly formed as shifting rock plates collided and were thrown up into the sky, and existing mountain ranges disappeared as they sank into the vast chasm opening up beneath them.

Earthquakes rolled across the planet, throwing up giant tidal waves that roared across the earth, destroying everything in their path and creating new oceans as plains were overrun with the deluge. New continents were formed as the oceans roiled and great up-thrusts of rock climbed into the sky.

Volcanoes spewed lava and ash into the atmosphere, and acidic seas boiled away as they were exposed to rising streams of liquid iron from the planet's core. Deep, subterranean avalanches at the core mantle boundary, far below the planet's surface, disrupted the planet's magnetic field, and the integrity of the planet as a whole wavered.

The gravitational pull of Korsis strained at the weakness of the planet and Tanakreg was tipped off its axis, sending a new shockwave through it, and triggering a second wave of earthquakes.

Great cracks appeared across the Shinar peninsula and the mountains to the east were lost to oblivion as the continental plate sank. The peninsula was lifted up into the air, throwing the Gehemehnet off at an oblique angle, though it still stood. Water rushed across the plains as it vacated the seas below the peninsula, boiling and rising into scalding steam as it touched the rising lava spilling up through the cracks in the earth.

Ash, dust and gases filled the skies, covering the hot, white sun and obscuring Korsis once more.

The Ordinatus slipped into a giant chasm that opened up beneath it, falling into the molten magma rising from below, even as the airship docked upon its back lifted off and rose into the air, smoking and labouring to stay airborne. It drifted sluggishly through the air, hanging heavily to one side where its gyro-stabilisers had been destroyed, passing over the shattered battlefield. Missiles impacted with the undercarriage of the airship and it dived down over the edge of the cliff, flame and smoke spewing from it.

The Word Bearers backed towards the base of the Gehemehnet, though scores of their vehicles and daemon engines were lost as they fell into chasms that opened beneath them, or were swept away by the black acid sea.

At last the continents settled.

And there below the peninsula where the Gehemehnet had been built, deep in an abyssal channel that just moments before had been hidden beneath kilometres of inky black, acidic waters, was a structure.

It was a black-sided pyramid, its sides perfectly smooth and gleaming. The burning, shattered airship descended into the chasm before smashing upon its floor.

'And that,' breathed Jarulek as he stared down at the structure hungrily, 'is what I have come to find.'

# CHAPTER TWENTY-ONE

The Cult of the Anointed stood to attention upon the deep, abyssal chasm floor. The glossy black sides of the pyramid rose up some two hundred metres behind them. Nothing upon its sides gave any indication as to its origin and it was unmarked by scratch or blemish.

The Dark Apostle strode imperiously down the assault ramp of the Stormbird, flanked by his First Acolyte and the Icon Bearer. He wore his ceremonial cloak of skin, the inside lined with golden thread, and his head was held high, for this was the moment of his success.

Twenty of the Anointed formed a corridor that the trio strode along, each slamming a heavy foot down onto the earth as they passed. They advanced towards the bulky form of Kol Badar, standing at the head of the two hundred Terminators arrayed in serried ranks, who awaited the arrival of their lord in silence. All two hundred warriors stamped their feet into the ground as the Dark Apostle halted before them.

The Coryphaus spread his arms wide, palms up, the power claw on his left arm dwarfing the right, as he intoned the ritual greeting.

'The Cult of the Anointed greets the revered Dark Apostle with open arms and beseeches the Dark Gods to bless him for time eternal.'

'And the blessing of the Ether upon you, my loyal Anointed warriors,' said Jarulek, concluding the ritual.

'My lord, we have secured the area and I have inspected the outside of the structure. There appears to be no entrances to its interior.'

'The door shall be opened to him of pure faith,' said Jarulek, a knowing smile on his face.

'Yes, my lord,' said the Coryphaus, bowing his head to Jarulek's proclamation. 'Our auspexes and sensors are unable to scan within. It gives off nothing, my lord.'

'And what of that?' asked Jarulek, pointing towards the black smoke rising in the distance that marked where the airship of the Mechanicus had gone down. 'Did you ensure it was destroyed?'

'I did, my lord. There was a survivor from the crash. I brought it back alive, for I thought it would interest you.'

'Master of the cog will come in chains and tattered robes, to become Enslaved,' quoted Jarulek, a smile upon his script covered, pale face.

'And so, the prophecy comes to fruition.'

* * *

JARULEK STRODE FORWARDS, raising his cursed crozius arcanum high into the air as he neared the base of the black, flawless structure. Not a mark could be seen upon the pyramid's slick surface, not a crack or a join – it was as if the whole structure had been carved from one gigantic piece of some midnight, glossy mineral.

As he neared it, a green light began to glow, dimly at first and then more fiercely. The light coalesced into strange symbols running vertically down the surface in front of the Dark Apostle, hieroglyphs the likes of which Marduk had never seen before. It appeared to be a form of early picture writing, consisting of circles and lines, but it was utterly alien in design.

The green light grew in intensity until the glare spilling from the strange glyphs was almost blinding. More light began to appear upon the surface of the pyramid and Marduk clenched his hand around the grip of his daemon-blade, feeling the reassuring connection as the barbs of the grip pierced his armour andd flesh.

A circular symbol appeared, and lines that could have been representations of sunbeams spread from its circumference. Without a sound, the circle sank into the black surface of the stone and the panels created by the 'sunbeams' slid to the side, revealing a dark entranceway within the structure, almost five metres in height. Air was sucked into the open gateway, as if the inside of the structure was a vacuum, and icy coldness exuded from within.

The Anointed moved up protectively around the Dark Apostle, combi-bolters and heavy weapons swinging towards the open gateway. Jarulek turned towards Marduk, a smile upon his lips.

'Come, my First Acolyte. Our destinies await us.'

Allowing a dozen members of the Anointed to take the lead, Marduk and Jarulek entered the ancient, alien pyramid.

A searing pain flared on Marduk's head beneath his helmet as he crossed the boundary into the pyramid, and he dropped to one knee, eyes tightly shut. It felt like someone had pressed a red-hot brand against the flesh of his forehead.

'What is wrong with you?' snapped Jarulek.

Marduk concentrated hard, mouthing the scriptures of Lorgar to shut off the burning pain, and pushed himself back to his feet.

It felt as though his skin was being melted away from the bone and he gritted his sharp teeth as he mouthed the sacred words.

He knew what the feeling was – it had been described to him – and he had read of it in countless accounts of Dark Apostles.

Jarulek's words came back to him.

*Have you had any holy scriptures appear on your flesh yet?*

He pushed the pain deep within him, feeling a surge of pride. He could still feel the searing pain, but it would not dominate him. He rose to his feet.

'Nothing, Dark Apostle,' he said, and the Word Bearers pressed on into the alien pyramid.

'THERE IS NOTHING here,' said Kol Badar. They had been walking through the darkness for what seemed like hours, passing through endless, smooth corridors flanked by columns of obsidian, descending deeper into the stygian blackness. They must have been far beneath the ground, thought Marduk. How large a structure was this unearthly, black pyramid?

'That which I seek is here,' said the Dark Apostle. 'I have seen this place in my dream visions.'

Marduk could sense something, but what it was he didn't know. His skin prickled with vague unease. He ran his hand along the smooth, black stone, feeling the icy chill within.

The corridor was wide enough for four Terminators to walk side by side, and the Dark Apostle was flanked by warriors who formed a shield of ablative armour around him. They had passed dozens of other corridors and passages that bisected their own, but Jarulek had never once paused to consider the way forward. He strode onwards, his head held high, as if he had been here before.

'This place is ancient,' said Marduk. 'What manner of xenos created this structure?'

'Creatures long dead,' said Kol Badar, his deep voice ringing out from the speakers concealed beneath the quad-tusks of his helmet.

'Maybe,' said Marduk, but he was not so certain. This place certainly felt dead, but unease nagged at him.

'DRAK'SHAL IS WRITHING within me,' snarled Burias. His eyes shone with daemonic witch-sight, like silver orbs in the gloom.

'Keep control of yourself, Icon Bearer,' replied Kol Badar sharply.

'The daemon is... repelled by this place,' said Burias.

A whisper of air brushed past Marduk and he swung his helmeted head to one side, scanning for movement or heat signals that would indicate an enemy presence. There was nothing. Another wisp of air shadowed by him and he raised his bolt pistol, scanning to the left.

'Something is in here with us,' he hissed.

'Anointed, be vigilant, possible hostile presence,' said Kol Badar, his words carrying to each of the Terminators through their internal comm-system. The Terminators turned left and right, weapons panning.

There was a sudden shout and the darkness was lit up as combi-bolters roared. There was a crunching sound followed by a wet splash and more bolter-fire barked.

Marduk felt a shadow rise behind him and he spun to see a towering shape looming out of the gloom, something that did not register on any of his heat or life sensors. Even with his advanced vision and the keen autosenses of his helmet, the shape was still little more than a shadow, a tapering coil of darkness that rose up to a hunched pair of shoulders. Skeletally thin arms whipped out, plunging down into the body of an Anointed warrior-brother, skewering him, and blood splashed out across the slick, black walls.

With a shout, Marduk fired his bolt pistol into the shape and he saw a shadowy face turn towards him, pinpricks of green light marking eyes amidst the darkness. With inhuman speed the creature was gone, leaping straight into the smooth, black wall, its tapering shadow tail whipping behind it as it disappeared.

The Anointed warrior fell to the ground, dead.

'They are coming out of the walls,' roared Marduk, spinning as he felt another shadow flash past him. He thumbed the activation rune of his daemon-blade to life and the chainblades roared.

Shouts and gunfire erupted as more shadowy forms appeared all along the corridor, plunging their long arms into the bodies of the Anointed, killing and rending, before disappearing like ghosts.

A pair of green, glowing eyes appeared as a shape rose out of the floor before Marduk, and he swung his chainsword towards it. He saw a dark, metallic, skeletal face as the thing opened its mouth in a soundless hiss. It reared back out of range of his attack, its shadowy torso held aloft upon a long, flexible spinal cord that tapered into darkness.

He fired his pistol towards the thing's head, but the bolts passed through it as it turned to black smoke. In an instant, it had regained its metallic, physical form and lunged at him, preternaturally fast arms plunging down to impale him. He lashed out with his chainsword and threw himself into a desperate roll beneath the descending ghost creature, feeling the teeth of his weapon bite against something solid. As he came to his feet, the creature was gone.

The Terminator to his left staggered to his knees as shadowy blades punched through his head, and Marduk lashed out with his chainsword once more, the blade passing harmlessly through the shadowy, serpentine spinal cord of the creature before it disappeared back within the sanctity of the black walls.

'We have to get out of this corridor, we need more space!' yelled Burias, flailing to defend himself against a shadow that emerged to his right.

'Warriors of Lorgar! Advance, double time!' roared Kol Badar.

Marduk saw a creature descend from the darkness above, coiling down to impale another warrior upon its skeletal arms, and the man was lifted up into the air, legs kicking.

'Gods of the Ether give me strength,' Marduk heard the Dark Apostle spit, and he saw him smash his cursed crozius into the enemy. A burst of hot electric energy crackled over the dark shape as the weapon made contact, and it was smashed to the ground, its metallic limbs and long, serpentine spine thrashing feebly. The skull of the creature caved in with the Dark Apostle's next blow and the green glow of its eyes faded to darkness.

'Move out! Protect the Dark Apostle,' roared Kol Badar as he turned to give covering fire to those warriors behind him. More of the Anointed were slain as wraiths appeared out of nowhere and drove their bladed, shadow-arms through armour and flesh.

One warrior, walking resolutely backwards, his reaper autocannon roaring, caught one of the shadowy creatures in a blast of heavy fire and it was ripped apart by the awesome force of the weapon.

'Enkil, turn!' roared Kol Badar as a wraith dropped down from the darkness behind the warrior. The Coryphaus stepped forwards, pumping fire towards the dark shape looming over the warrior, but the shots passed straight through the creature. Enkil turned, swinging his heavy weapon around to bear, but the shadow was too quick and it drove twin-bladed arms through his body. He fell to his knees, blood pumping from the wounds. Kol Badar roared as he stepped forwards, his combi-bolter barking as the injured warrior tried to push himself to his feet. Three wraiths appeared around him like looming spectres of death, their arms raised, poised for the kill.

The Coryphaus took another step towards the fallen warrior, but a hand on his arm halted him.

'Coryphaus, we must leave this place,' said Burias, his eyes glittering like molten silver.

With a snarl, Kol Badar shook off the Icon Bearer's hand, but nodded his head.

'The gods be with you, Enkil,' he said, firing a final burst towards the gathered wraiths as they killed the warrior. He turned and moved as swiftly as his armour allowed him, passing the rearguard walking steadily backwards, fire barking from their weapons.

MARDUK RAN AHEAD of the Anointed warriors, unencumbered by the bulky Terminator armour they wore, and the corridor gave way to a vast open area. Steps rose to a large circular dais that dominated the room, surrounded by dozens of columns glowing with green hieroglyphs. A black-sided pyramid stood in the centre of the dais, a miniature replica of the structure they were within, some ten metres in height.

He scanned left and right as he ran, seeking out any sign of the enemy, and he leapt up the steps and onto the circular dais. He circled and realised that dozens of corridors similar to the one he had just exited,branched off this large, circular room, spaced evenly around the perimeter. Darkness, impenetrable even to his eyes, was beyond these corridors, but he had the impression that they all led back up towards the surface. Everything was perfectly symmetrical and it made sense that none of these corridors led further down. The circular room rose up high into darkness – no ceiling could be seen – and the cylindrical open space projected straight up what Marduk guessed was the centre of the structure.

He approached the central pyramid warily, weapons ready. It began to silently rise, green light spilling from beneath it. Whatever mechanism or sorcery lifted the massive weight was powerful indeed and the smooth black pyramid rose high into the air, steadily and silently. He realised that it was not a pyramid at all, but rather was an immense diamond shape, and he squinted against the green glare that spilled from beneath its bulk, his bolt pistol scanning for movement.

'The gateway to the ancients,' breathed Jarulek as he came up beside Marduk. There was nothing holding or supporting the giant, black diamond shape as it rose, neither above nor below. It lifted higher and higher into the vast empty space above them, hanging suspended in the air.

The Coryphaus entered the room, Burias at his side, and Marduk's eyes narrowed.

'We hold here. We are right where we are meant to be,' ordered Jarulek.

With a nod, Kol Badar quickly ordered the Cult of the Anointed into positions around the edge of the circular dais, guarding the corridor entrances, forming a protective circle around the Dark Apostle, facing out.

'The shadow wraiths seem unable or unwilling to enter this room,' said Marduk.

The Dark Apostle made no response, his eyes fixed on the expanse vacated by the diamond that had come to a halt, hanging ten metres above them. The green light had dimmed and from from the smooth, black sides of the angled hole that the diamond fitted perfectly into, wide steps appeared out of the seamless, black stone. A section of the black stone sank away and a gateway was revealed at the foot of the steps, green light spilling from the same sun and light-beam icon that had appeared on the outside of the pyramid.

There was a shout for silence from the Coryphaus, and Marduk ripped his eyes away from the newly exposed gateway. A dim, rhythmic and repetitive sound could be heard in the silence that followed, something akin to metal striking stone. He realised that it was getting louder and he turned around, trying to get a lock on where the sound was emanating from. It seemed to be coming from all around.

'What in the name of the true gods is that?' he said.

'Something comes,' hissed Burias.

He could see nothing at first, but then he saw green lights, eyes of the enemy, appearing within the darkness of one of the corridors, no, from *all* of the corridors. They were completely surrounded. His first thought was that the shadow wraiths had returned, but these creatures were not ethereal shadows; their bodies were very real.

They were the walking dead and Marduk jolted as the force of his recurring vision entered his head. *Assailed by the dead, long dead, and they claw at my armour with skeletal claws.* This was his vision come to life.

But it was different. These creatures were not formed of bones held together by desiccated, dried skin. Their skulls glinted with a metallic sheen and their eyes glowed with baleful green light. That light matched the coiling, green energy that was contained within the enemies' weapons, held low in their skeletal hands as they trudged forward. The creatures were formed of dark metal and the green glow spilling from their weapons was reflected upon their ribs and bony arms.

The first were smashed apart by the guns of the Anointed, falling silently to the floor where they were stepped over by others of their mechanical kind. There were scores of the creatures spilling from each corridor, marching in perfect unison, shoulder-to-shoulder, silent except for the sound of their metal feet clanking rhythmically on the stone floor.

On and on they came, walking slowly into the torrent of gunfire laid down by the Anointed, and still they did not raise their weapons. Marduk saw one of the fallen creatures, its head shattered by autocannon rounds, begin to rise to its feet once more, its eyes, which were black moments before, glowing once again. The damage done to its cranium repaired before his eyes, the metal knitting back into shape. Its skull was smooth and immaculate, and it stepped back into line with its companions.

Liquid promethium from heavy flamers roared as it was unleashed, as the walking corpse-machines drew ever nearer to the Terminators, but the flames did nothing to halt their progress.

As one, the front rank of the corpse-machines raised their weapons and blinding, green light roared from their barrels. Marduk saw the thick Terminator armour of one warrior-brother flayed instantly to nothing beneath the searing light. Skin was torn away, exposing first muscle tissue then inner organs then nothing but bone, before even that was seared away.

Several of the Anointed fell beneath the blasts, though return fire smashed the first line of the foe away. The second line stepped forwards, lowering their weapons, and a second barrage of green light spewed from the barrels of their potent weapons.

'First Acolyte, we are entering that gateway. Hold them here, Kol Badar,' Jarulek said into his comm unit.

Kol Badar broke away from the circle of Terminators and approached the Dark Apostle, the armour of his left shoulder pad sheared away from a glancing shot, exposing servos and insulation beneath.

'My lord, the Cult warriors can hold here. I shall accompany you,' said the Coryphaus.

'No, you will not,' said Jarulek, stepping close to the big warrior.

Marduk turned away from the pair, scanning the area. There seemed to be no end to the undead warrior-machines entering the room. The Anointed were the finest fighting force within the Host, but he could see that even they would eventually be slaughtered by this relentless foe.

This will be our tomb, he thought.

'My lord?' said Kol Badar. Always he had fought at the side of the Dark Apostle. He was his champion, his protector. To allow the holy leader to face some unknown enemy without him was unthinkable. The life of a Coryphaus who allowed his master to fall in battle was forfeit. The Council would see him dead were Jarulek to fall.

'What I go to face is not for you to be a part of,' hissed Jarulek, his voice low, his eyes resolute. 'This is one battle that you cannot win, Kol Badar, and it is one foe that you cannot face.'

Doubt plagued the Coryphaus.

'My place is at your side, my lord,' he said. 'You would take the wretched whelp with you, but not me?'

'I am telling you that, for now, your place is not at my side. Hold the line here. The Anointed need you. This battle will not be easily won. Await my return.'

'As you wish, my lord,' said Kol Badar, fuming. The Dark Apostle stepped in close to him, looking up at him with eyes ablaze with faith.

'If we both return, then you may kill Marduk, my Coryphaus. Your honour will be fulfilled.'

A surge of pleasure ran through Kol Badar at the Dark Apostle's words and he smiled beneath his quad-tusked helmet. At last his hand that had once been stayed was free of constraint. At last, he would kill the whoreson whelp, Marduk.

'We shall hold, my lord. I await your return with great expectation.'

'The blessings of the dark gods upon you, my Coryphaus.'

'And with you, my lord. May the gods be at your side as you walk into darkness.'

Kol Badar watched as the Dark Apostle and the First Acolyte descended the stairs. The panels of the gateway slid aside soundlessly and the pair of Word Bearers stepped inside, disappearing into the inky blackness as if consumed. The panels flicked back into place. There was no way of following them now, he thought. He just had to wait and hold off these forsaken corpse-machines long enough for him to be able to kill Marduk.

He rejoined his warriors, racking the underslung mechanism that activated the meltagun attached to his bolter.

'They are gone, Coryphaus?' asked Burias as he fired his bolt pistol into the head of an enemy, knocking it back a step.

'They are, Icon Bearer. The fate of the Host hangs in the balance.'

# CHAPTER TWENTY-TWO

THE PANELS SLID shut behind them, cutting off all noise of the raging battle, and they stood in absolute darkness. Not a sound pierced the pitch-black night that descended on them. The silence was heavy, claustrophobic and dense. Marduk was utterly blind. Never before had he experienced such all-encompassing darkness.

He felt lost, adrift, his connection to the warp severed, and he panicked for a moment as his head reeled as if with vertigo, though it was impossible for him to experience such a sensation.

Marduk wobbled, though his senses came back to him in an instant, and his faculties returned. He saw a dim light, though perhaps it had only just begun to shine. It reached out towards them from below, a slowly pulsing beam.

He looked at Jarulek beside him, whose face showed tension and wariness.

'It felt as though we just travelled an infinite distance in the blink of an eye,' said Marduk quietly, unwilling to break the oppressive silence. The gateway they had come through was sealed shut, though the sun icon emblazoned upon it glowed dimly with light. He pushed against it, but it would not budge. As the pulsing light increased, he saw that the black stone wall in which the gateway was positioned rose impossibly high above them. They stood on a bridge of black stone that seemed to hang in the air. There were sheer drops to either side, and it was joined by dozens of black staircases. These in turn were linked to other bridges, gantries and platforms, all formed of black stone and all hanging in the air without any clear support.

'This place is insane,' he hissed. 'It is madness.'

Marduk had encountered many landscapes and worlds that most would consider maddening within the warp, where the rules of the physical world held no sway, but here he felt no touch of Chaos. Far from it, this place felt like it actively kept Chaos out. It was sterile and lifeless, devoid of any touch of the warp.

'Is it some trick of the Changer?' asked Marduk, speaking of Tzeentch, the lord of the twisting fates and one of the greater gods of the Ether. He knew as he spoke that it was not, for even the great Changer of the Ways would surely be unable to create such a place, so cut off from the essence of magic.

'Far from it, First Acolyte,' said Jarulek. 'This is the antithesis of the Great Changer and indeed of all of Chaos.'

'And what you seek is here, in this place? It would seem that anything here would be better destroyed than utilised.'

'Much can be tainted and changed by Chaos, Marduk. Turning an enemy's weapons against them is the greatest strength that we have.'

'And you have foreseen this place in your dream visions?'

'This place, no. It has always been hidden from my sight. I foresaw our entrance through the gateway, but never what transposed beyond it, only what occurs afterwards.'

'You have seen our return from this place?'

'Sometimes. The future is fickle and unclear. In some twists of what may come to pass we return with our prize. In others, we do not and the Anointed are destroyed. The guardians assailing them return to their eternal rest. In others I have seen just myself return. In others, just you.'

'I would not abandon you here, Dark Apostle,' said Marduk. Jarulek chuckled.

'We need to move,' he said.

'Which way?'

'Down.'

It seemed that they had been walking for days on end, or perhaps it had been but minutes. Marduk was not sure anymore. This place was maddening in its power to disorient, and he had long since lost a sense of his bearings. They had walked down stairways only to find themselves walking up, had crossed straight walkways only to find themselves somehow turned around and walking back the way they had come, and more than once they had descended staircases only to find themselves higher up than they had been before the descent.

'This place affects our connection with the blessed Ether,' said Jarulek.

'It does,' replied Marduk. 'It is as though this place muffles it. I can still feel it, but it is distant, and faint.'

'It is an unholy place,' said Jarulek. 'What do you feel from your daemon-blade?'

'I feel... nothing,' said Marduk, placing his hand around the thorn-covered hilt of his chainsword. There was none of the tingling sensation that usually announced the essence of the daemon Borhg'ash merging with his own. There was no indication of its presence at all.

'It is as though the daemon has escaped its binding, but that is not possible.'

They continued their descent towards the slowly pulsing light below. After what seemed an age, they could discern a circular platform beneath them, though it was certainly not the bottom of the expanse. Marduk wondered if there truly was a base to this maddening place, or if it extended forever. Or perhaps if they continued down they would find themselves back where they had started.

Shaking his head, he concentrated upon the circular platform. It seemed that it was covered in silver waters that rippled with movement. As they descended, he realised that it was not liquid.

THOUSANDS OF TINY, crawling insect creatures swarmed away from the Word Bearers as they stepped down from the last of the maddening steps onto the slick, black, circular platform. The creatures scuttled away on metallic, barbed legs, making a sound like gentle ocean waves crashing, as their metallic carapaces scraped and millions of tiny metal legs scrambled for purchase. Their glistening carapaces were dark and the smallest of them was no larger than a grain of sand.

Marduk bent and grasped one of the larger, scuttling beetle creatures, lifting it up between his thumb and forefinger for closer inspection. Dozens of glowing green eyes were arrayed upon its segmented head and its wickedly barbed mandibles clicked as it tried vainly to bite him. Its eight-spiked legs kicked and pushed at him, surprising him with their strength as it tried to get free. Its carapace was of dark metal and a golden emblem, the now familiar sun circle with light beams streaming from it, was emblazoned across it.

He turned it over in his hand to get a look at the creature's underside, but its sharp mandibles bit into him, gripping onto the ceramite protecting his finger. It could not pierce his armour, but it would not let go. He flicked his wrist as he lost interest and patience with the creature, sending the mechanical bug flying. It unfurled wafer-thin membranes of metal from beneath its thick carapace and flittered through the air to join its fleeing companions. It landed amongst the scuttling mass of creatures moving like a living, metal carpet away from the intruders who had entered their realm. They streamed towards a sunken, circular pit that lay before the pair, crawling over its lip and down into its protective darkness.

There must have been tens of thousands of the creatures, and they swarmed towards the pit from all directions. Marduk stepped forwards and the living mass of mechanical insects surged away, parting before him.

Stepping to the edge of the hole, he looked down into the darkness. It was impossible to guess its depth.

He felt a presence behind him and quickly turned, moving away from the edge of the abyss, seeing Jarulek smirk at his discomfort. Marduk glared hatefully at his master from within his helmet. Not long, he thought.

The pair of unholy warriors stalked warily around the edge of the pit. Curved walls rose up around the platform, rising high into the air above. The floor gave way a metre before the wall and it fell down into darkness. They walked carefully around the ring of stone towards the pulsating light throbbing from an adjacent chamber.

A short, enclosed passageway linked the two rooms, and the Word Bearers stepped along it warily. Marduk was uneasy, but it was good to feel solid walls on each side rather than an empty expanse. The second chamber was small and its glossy, black walls reflected the glaring, green light of the glowing object suspended in mid-air in the centre of the room. Pulsing light spilled from it as it spun slowly, floating above the tip of a metre-high black pyramid set in the floor. Light rose in a shaft from the tip of the pyramid, encasing the spinning orb in its beam.

It was a captivating piece of mechanical artistry of utterly alien design, and it revolved slowly. Its centre was a glowing ball of harnessed energy, around which revolved a series of metal rings that spun in all directions around the sphere in a complex weave. The rings overlapped and swung around the glowing centre of the sphere, forming intricate and mesmerising patterns. Marduk could not be certain exactly how many rotating rings there were and he saw that glowing, alien hieroglyphs shone across their flat surfaces. He thought he could see something solid within the ball of energy, but the light was too intense for him to be sure.

He was pulled away from the fascinating object by a hand on his shoulder and he snapped his gaze away, a dull pain in his head.

'Do not look too closely,' warned Jarulek. 'It will ensnare you.'

Marduk nodded, his temples throbbing.

'This is the object you have come to find,' he said finally.

'It is. This is the artefact spoken of in the third book of the *Oraculata Noctis*.'

Marduk's eyes widened.

'And with the Nexus Arrangement one shall wield great force, and he shall open and close the portals to the netherward and become Gatemaster,' quoted Marduk. 'You believe that *this* is the... the Nexus Arrangement?'

'It is,' said Jarulek, his eyes alight with faith and passion. 'And long have I waited for its discovery.

'The Nexus Arrangement is the tool, it is said, that will usher in a new age of destruction. But it is unclear about the destruction of *what*, or of *whom*.

'It is the same as any weapon. It has no will of its own, but is directed by he who would use it. A boltgun is indiscriminate in who it kills, the one who pulls the trigger is the killer. It is a holy weapon to those who use it as such and it is a tool of the great enemy.

'But *this*... this is something far more potent. With this, we will be able to strike at our enemies without fear of reprisal.'

'Open and close the portals to the netherward?'

'That's right, my First Acolyte,' laughed Jarulek. 'Entire systems could have the warp closed off to them, allowing nothing to pass in or out of the region. Imagine it: systems unable to receive reinforcements, communications, supplies, munitions. Imagine, if you will, if this were activated near ancient Terra,' said Jarulek, an evil grin upon his face. 'Terra itself, closed to the warp, the cursed light of the False Emperor effectively kept in shadow, his ships, blind and lost in the turmoil of the Immaterium...'

'This could bring about the end of the Imperium,' Marduk breathed, awe and lust in his soul.

'And it is foretold that it may only be removed when in the presence of a master and an apprentice, holy warriors of Lorgar both. Our being here was prophesied and now that prophecy is complete.'

The Dark Apostle whispered an entreaty to the dark powers and reached his hands slowly forwards, into the light projecting up from the top of the pyramid, reaching towards the revolving sphere. Instantly the light from the pyramid dimmed, plunging the room into darkness, but for the green light emanating from the glowing sphere.

Holding his breath, Marduk watched as the Dark Apostle's hands neared the spinning rings, reaching underneath the orb to cup it. The spinning rings began to slow. Each pulse of light was timed with the revolutions of the rings. There were seven rings, he now saw as they slowed to a standstill, and they seemed to melt together, their edges merging, so that within seconds all that remained was what appeared to be a solid sphere of dark metal. The green hieroglyphs faded away and darkness descended. The blackness was not complete, for now that the glare of the room had faded, a dim light could be seen emanating from the pit in the adjacent chamber, where the scarabs had retreated.

Jarulek lifted the metal orb out from where it hovered above the black pyramid, awe upon his face.

It was the size of grown man's heart and he cradled it in his hands like a newborn child.

Marduk felt greed and desire rise within him. He licked his lips and toyed with the activation rune of his chainsword as he stared at his master. As the Dark Apostle had said, the prophecy had been fulfilled.

A flicker of movement in the corner of his eyes drew his attention and he spun towards it.

A dark shape was rising from the circular pit in the adjacent chamber and Marduk thumbed the activation rune of his chainsword, snarling. His gazed shifted between Jarulek, who was focused on the sphere in his hands, and the rising shadow that blocked their retreat.

The shape was roughly humanoid, though it was covered in thousands of the metallic scarabs, or more correctly it was *formed* from them. They skittered over the humanoid torso, rising slowly and silently from the pit, their body mass creating the shape of a man.

'Jarulek,' he hissed. The eyes of the Dark Apostle flashed with outrage that he dare use his name, but then he too saw the rising shape.

As they watched, the skittering bugs came to rest as they aligned in their appropriate positions, and their bodies merged, like droplets of water that were sucked together to form a greater mass. Thousands of metallic insects blurred together, their individual shapes and limbs moulding like liquid metal to form the immaculate and perfect form of a skeletal torso, gleaming silver.

Black, carapaced scarabs gave up their physical uniqueness, forming a black chest-plate over the silver ribs of the cadaverous, ancient lord rising up out of the light below. A golden sun gleamed on the centre of the black, lustrous armour plate, golden lines representing the sun's rays spilling from it. The corpse-machine's head was down, its chin lowered, and its eye sockets were dark and hollow.

A long-hafted weapon was formed in the creature's metallic hands, as hundreds of scarabs gripped each other with claw and mandible to form a solid shape. They blurred as they melted together, creating an arcane and impressively sized weapon, a pair of curving blades at each end of a long shaft.

Marduk and Jarulek raised their weapons as one, the Dark Apostle supporting the heavy weight of his archaic bolter on his forearm, the orb still held in his hand. They unleashed a salvo of barking shots towards the forming corpse-machine. Bolts smashed into its gleaming, silver skull, blasting chunks of metal away, and others caused chips of black stone to crack from its chest-plate.

These pieces of metal and stone landed on the black, glossy surface of the floor and immediately returned to their metallic scarab forms. They skittered about for a second before launching themselves into the air, wafer-thin metallic wings clicking out. They hovered over the deathly machine before settling on the damage done by the guns of the holy Word Bearer warriors. The metallic insects disappeared as they melted into the metal body of their master, leaving no appearance of the damage that had been caused.

'The Undying One,' said Jarulek.

A scarab with a gleaming, golden carapace skittered over the skull of the forming creature, and it melted to become a shining circlet upon its forehead, glittering with intricate, alien line work. It was an alien yet clearly regal device, and Marduk was left in no doubt that this was some lord of the undead, living machines.

Swarms of smaller insects, some barely large enough for the eye to discern, glided over the silver bones of the creature and blurred together, forming a semi-opaque, wafer-thin, billowing shroud that whipped around the skeletal form. This cloak had a dark, metallic sheen as if it had been woven of infinitely fine mesh, and it shimmered like liquid metal. It fluttered as if caught in a breeze, though there was no movement of air. From beneath the deep hood, the darkness of the creature's eye sockets began to glow a baleful green and it raised its chin to look upon the interlopers trespassing on its ancient realm. A feeling of dread washed over Marduk. He gritted his sharp teeth in anger at the unwelcome and uncommon feeling.

The creature rose higher out of the pit, accompanied by a rhythmic humming noise, and the light beneath it grew stronger, throwing its skull into deeper shadow beneath its billowing shroud. Rather than ending in hips and legs, the metallic spinal column of the creature merged into a bulky shape that was not dissimilar to the armoured carapace of one of the diminutive scarabs, though on a colossal scale. Thousands of teeming insects scrambled over each other and moulded together to form this lower body, and eight barbed legs hanging beneath the bulk of its armour took shape. The light filling the room came from beneath this carapace, shining out below it and throwing its upper body into gloom.

The creature rose into the air, hovering above the open pit as it awoke, its silver, insect legs curling and clicking beneath it, the humanoid torso flexing as the ancient, unliving being rolled its shoulders. It did not move in the same manner as the skeletal machines guarding the upper chambers of the pyramid. Where they were mechanical and jerky in movement, this creature was fluid and supple, its limbs moving smoothly and in perfect balance.

It spun the staff before it, the twin blades humming through the air. It seemed ignorant or uncaring of the Word Bearers as it went through a series of lithe movements with the double-headed blade, spinning the haft of the weapon around in its metallic hands with consummate ease.

Intent on the monstrous creature, Marduk failed to see Jarulek raising his ornate bolter towards his head.

'And this, my First Acolyte, is where your education comes to an end,' breathed the Dark Apostle, and pulled the trigger.

# CHAPTER TWENTY-THREE

Marduk threw himself to the side, servo-muscles straining, but he could not avoid the burst of fire at such close range. The mass-reactive tips of the bolt-rounds impacted with the side of his helmet as he dodged and their explosions tore the right side of his helmet and face apart in a gory mess of blood and sparks.

He fell, smashed to the ground by the impact. The inside of his helmet was awash with blood and he ripped it from his head, hurling it away from him as he staggered backwards on the floor.

He could feel that the left side of his skull was shattered and he could not see from his left eye. He felt fragments of bone and tooth in his mouth, and he spat them to the floor amid blood and saliva. He tongued the inside of his mouth and felt that the teeth on his left side had been shattered, and where he should have felt the inside of his cheek, he felt nothing. The flesh had been completely blown away. He heard a chuckle.

*'One shall fall, he of lesser faith, he unmarked by godly touch,'* Jarulek said. 'Did you think that I did not notice your treacherous intent, whelp? Your usefulness passed as soon as you fulfilled your role in the prophecy.'

Marduk blinked blood from his working eye. He scrabbled on the ground around him, but realised that he had lost his grip on his bolt pistol and it lay out of his reach. He felt dizzy and disoriented.

Jarulek stood with his bolter pointed at Marduk. The metal sphere was still in one hand and the bolter was supported upon his forearm. He stared down the stylised daemonic maw that was the barrel of the archaic weapon and Marduk knew that he was too far from the Dark Apostle to be able to rush him without taking a full clip of bolts.

'What damned prophecy?' he spat, his jaw not working properly, spraying blood.

'Why, the Prophecy of Jarulek, dear Marduk: the prophecy that appears on only one page: my flesh, the prophecy that I have lived with since the fall of the Warmaster. The prophecy says that only one of us will leave this place and I intend that to be me.'

Marduk tensed himself to leap. He wiped the blood from his face quickly with his free hand and he saw Jarulek's eyes widen in shock.

A searing beam of green light slammed into the back of the Dark Apostle and ripped through him, boring a fist-sized hole from abdomen to lower back.

The bolter in Jarulek's hand barked as Marduk leapt from the floor, bolts ricocheting around the chamber. With a roar of pure hatred, Marduk swung the blade of his chainsword towards the staggering Dark Apostle, but Jarulek managed to bring his arm up before him and swipe the blade away, though it tore a chunk of armour and flesh from his arm. Marduk felt the faint presence of the daemon Borhg'ash rouse within the weapon as it tasted the sacrosanct blood, and it lent him strength.

'The mark! This cannot be!' screamed Jarulek, his eyes locked to Marduk's forehead, where pain still seared him.

Another blast of green light speared towards the pair and Marduk rolled to the side to avoid it, coming to his feet quickly, positioning himself so he could see both enemies with his limited vision.

The skeletal, ancient xenos lord was hovering towards them, its dark shroud whipping around it furiously. The tips of its double-bladed staff were glowing with power and it thrust one end forwards, a searing beam lancing from the weapon. Marduk swayed to the side, the blast just grazing against his chest-plate, searing a groove along it as the super-hard ceramite was stripped away.

Bolts impacted with his chest a millisecond later, slamming him back against the wall. He snarled, his attention swinging towards Jarulek.

'I'm going to rip you apart, you whoreson,' he spat.

'Not the way one should speak to his holy leader. Mark or no mark, you are dying here,' said Jarulek. Seeing movement, he turned and fired a burst towards the advancing alien machine-creature, the bolts making its head reel back, but not slowing its advance.

Marduk rolled as another green lance of light streaked towards him, and came up in front of the Dark Apostle. His chainsword roared and he ripped it up in a murderous arc as he rose, carving it between Jarulek's legs. Pre-empting the attack, but with nothing to defend against it, the Dark Apostle released his grip on his bolter and grabbed the whirring chain-blades with his hand, halting its progress before it struck.

Blood and ceramite sprayed as his hand was ripped apart, but the move had taken Marduk by surprise, and the Dark Apostle slammed a kick into the outside of his knee. The leg collapsed beneath him. Jarulek followed the attack with a thundering elbow that struck Marduk in the head, cracking the bone, and he fell heavily.

Switching the precious sphere into the crook of his other, now handless, arm, Jarulek swept up his discarded bolter with his left hand and fired towards the closing skeletal alien, hefting the kicking weapon with difficulty in one hand. Bolts hammered into the creature's arm, sending its next shot wide. The Dark Apostle hurled the bolter aside, its ammo spent, and pulled his crozius arcanum from where it hung on his hip, the spiked head of the holy weapon crackling with energy as it came to life. He sprang directly towards the hovering, monstrous creature, a curse on his lips.

Marduk scrambled to his feet, swept up the Dark Apostle's discarded bolter and slammed a new clip into its base. He looked up to see the hovering, skeletal machine fire a blast of green energy towards Jarulek, who swayed to the side with nigh on preternatural speed, and leapt forwards with a shout, swinging the crozius towards the foe.

The enemy lowered itself towards the ground, so that it hovered less than a metre above the floor, its claws clicking and flexing beneath it. Its shimmering shroud whipped around it and it flashed out with its double-bladed staff, blocking Jarulek's attack with a screech of sparks and crackling energy. The other end of the staff swept around, its long curved blade slicing towards his throat. The Dark Apostle swayed beneath the lightning quick repost and swung his crozius again. The heavy blow was deflected easily and he stepped to the side, moving further around the flank of the creature and closer to escape.

Marduk broke into a run, invoking the gods of Chaos, and fired the bolter one-handed. If the Dark Apostle escaped then his life was forfeit. The bolts slammed into Jarulek's lower back, pitching him forwards. He roared in despair as he lost his grip on the metal sphere, and it flew through the air away from him.

The hovering corpse-machine swung its weapon in a wide arc as the Dark Apostle fell, the blow carving through the chest armour just below the fused ribcage. Blood sprayed from the wound and from the blade as it passed through the Dark Apostle's body and out the other side, severing his torso. Jarulek flailed frantically for the spilled sphere as he fell to the ground in two pieces, his lifeblood flooding the floor beneath him.

Marduk leapt, landing with his right foot on the carapace of the enemy and hacked his chainsword into its head. Chunks of metal were torn loose by the whirring chainblade, turning almost instantly into tiny, metallic flying scarabs, and the death's-head visage of the foe was snapped back by the force of the blow. Pushing off with his other foot, Marduk leapt through the air, his good eye focused on the falling sphere, and his hand reaching out vainly to catch it.

The metal ball slipped beyond his reach and hit the ground with a heavy, reverberating thud. It did not bounce, but began to roll straight towards the pit from which the cursed alien creature had emerged. Marduk hit the ground and slid after the ancient artefact. His hand closed on it just as it rolled clear of the edge and the unnatural weight of it almost took him with it.

He saw Jarulek's eyes glaring at him, filled with bitterness and hatred. The Dark Apostle clawed his way towards him, pulling his legless torso across the blood-slick floor.

*'He unmarked by godly touch,'* spat the Dark Apostle. 'You deceived me, Marduk. Somehow, you kept that mark concealed.'

Jarulek was silenced as his head was skewered upon the blade of the massive skeletal creature. It lifted his severed torso high into the air and the dark crozius slipped from dead fingers to the floor. The Dark Apostle was hurled through the air, thudding wetly against the curving wall of the chamber. He slid down its slick surface and disappeared into the abyssal darkness.

Marduk attached his daemon-blade to his waist and staggered forward to retrieve the fallen crozius. He raised it before him and it crackled to life, arcing blue electricity shimmering over its spiked head.

He felt the baleful gaze of the enemy fall towards him and he turned and ran.

MARDUK STAGGERED FROM the gateway, falling to his knees, the ice-cold sphere cradled under his arm.

Had the Undying One allowed him to leave its realm? No, he told himself, my faith brought me back from that ungodly place.

Gunfire blared around him and he stumbled up the black steps to the top of the dais. The Anointed, their ranks more than halved in number, had fallen back, forming an ever-tightening circle of warriors.

Kol Badar spun as he saw the First Acolyte rise from the steps, and took a few paces forward, lightning crackling across the talons of his power claw, but he slowed his advance as he drew nearer.

'Where is the Dark Apostle?' he thundered.

'Dead,' spat Marduk. 'He sacrificed himself that I may escape to lead the Host.'

'That is a lie!' roared Kol Badar, stepping forward to smash Marduk with his powerful fist. He halted his movement as Marduk lifted the crozius up between them.

'The Dark Apostle gifted me this, his sacred crozius arcanum,' said Marduk, his voice raised loudly to carry to all the Anointed. 'He told me to lead the Host to Sicarus, to see me sworn in as Dark Apostle. He sacrificed himself that I could escape with that which we have fought so hard, my brothers, to attain. Come,' he said, as more of the Word Bearers were cut down by the scything green flashes of the xenos weaponry, 'we must vacate this world.'

Kol Badar clenched his fist but did not move. Did he know that Jarulek had always intended to see him dead, pondered Marduk? Most probably, he surmised.

'The Host must honour the Dark Apostle's last wishes, else his sacrifice has been made in vain,' said Marduk loudly, a smile curling the right side of his mouth. The left side of his face was a mess of torn and missing flesh. 'Come, Coryphaus, we must leave here.'

Kol Badar's face twisted in anger and hatred, and he lashed out violently with his power claw, the talons curling around Marduk's neck, crushing the ceramite of his gorget and lifting the smaller Word Bearer up into the air before him like a child. The muscles of his neck straining against the immense grip, Marduk still managed a crooked smile.

'Just like our encounter upon the cursed moon so many years past, Coryphaus, 'and all because I killed your worthless, heathen blood-brother.' Marduk's face turned red as Kol Badar tightened his grip. 'He was a worthless dog, not fit to be named Word Bearer,' gasped Marduk. 'He brought nothing but shame to the noble Host. Lorgar himself would have done as I did that day.'

'Your words are poison. They mean nothing to me,' snarled Kol Badar, exerting even more force, hearing the enhanced muscles and vertebrae of the First Acolyte groan in resistance to his pressure.

'You would try to kill me here, Kol Badar?' snarled Marduk, his voice strained.

'You wouldn't be able to stop me,' growled the big warrior.

'No,' said Marduk, with difficulty, 'but *he* would.'

Kol Badar glanced to his side to see Burias-Drak'shal's hulking form beside him, staring at him.

Great horns rose from the possessed warrior's forehead and his corded muscles were tense. His massive clawed hands clenched and unclenched as he stared at the Coryphaus with glittering, daemonic eyes filled with bestial rage.

The possessed warrior rose to his full, towering height, his chest rising and falling heavily as he drew breath, steam billowing from his flared nostrils. He was quivering with anticipation for the kill, veins bulging within his hyper-tense muscles.

'You would stand against me, Icon Bearer?' growled Kol Badar.

'I would not stand against the holy leader of the Host,' replied Burias-Drak'shal, forming the words with some difficulty, his jaw having altered in form to contain his thick, tusk-like teeth.

'And this is not he!' thundered the Coryphaus.

'The Dark Apostle entrusted me with his holy writ,' said Marduk. 'Go against me and forfeit your life. Choose your words carefully.'

The Coryphaus was silent. The sound of bolters firing echoed from the glossy black walls, accompanied by the death groans of falling Anointed warriors.

'We cannot leave this place without the Dark Apostle,' Kol Badar said, at last.

'He is dead!' snarled Marduk.

'Then we must bear his holy body back to Sicarus,' roared Kol Badar, his grip around Marduk's neck tightening. Burias-Drak'shal hissed and grasped Kol Badar's arm, his claws digging deep, cutting into the thick armour. Their strength was evenly matched.

'You would dare put hands upon me,' Kol Badar growled. Burias-Drak'shal snarled, digging his talons in deeper, blood pooling around them and flowing over the Coryphaus's sacred Terminator armour.

'And you would dare defy my command?' asked Marduk. 'Your life is on tenterhooks, Kol Badar. We leave this place, *now*. Choose your path. Follow me, or die here in this tomb. Your name will be cursed by the Legion for time immaterial, a traitor to the Legion and a traitor to Lorgar.'

Kol Badar stared at Marduk, who returned the glare, staring back at himself in the eyes of the Terminator's helmet.

'Choose swiftly, Kol Badar. The warriors of the Legion are dying.'

'This is not over,' growled Kol Badar, releasing his grip around Marduk's neck with a shove. 'Remove your hands, Icon Bearer.' Burias-Drak'shal looked to Marduk, who nodded, and the possessed warrior released his grip, blood upon his talons.

Kol Badar swung away, shouting orders.

'We leave, now!' he roared. 'Form up!'

'Your forehead,' growled Burias-Drak'shal. 'You bear the mark of Lorgar.'

The burning pain on his forehead was as nothing to the pain covering the rest of his head, but it was worth the feeling of satisfaction that he felt as he looked upon the crozius in his hands.

'Let us leave this forsaken world,' said Marduk. 'It has served its purpose.'

AT MARDUK'S PSYCHIC call, the *Infidus Diabolus* returned to the shattered wreck of Tanakreg, tearing a rift in reality as it emerged from the warp to meet the

Thunderhawks, Stormbirds and other landing craft streaming up from the planet's surface.

The Imperial ships that had remained in orbit around the planet moved to engage, though they were sluggish to respond to its appearance. Their astropaths' senses were dulled by the warp field projected by the Gehemehnet and they had no warning as to the strike cruiser's sudden appearance. The Imperial ships kept a respectful distance from the field of unbridled Chaos energy that the tower continued to project into the outer atmosphere. Flights of fighters swarmed from the bowels of the *Infidus Diabolus* to slow the enemy's approach, though the Chaos ships were outnumbered and outclassed by those of the Imperial Navy.

Several transportation craft were destroyed as they sought to dock with the *Infidus Diabolus* and the powerful strike cruiser took damage from incoming torpedoes fired from an Imperial Dictator class warship.

The Host had suffered heavy casualties and many of the holy suits of armour worn by the Anointed had been lost in the xenos pyramid. The revered religious leader of the Host had fallen, and long would be the requiem services dedicated to his honour. The First Acolyte, mourning the loss of his master and spiritual guide, would lead these ceremonies of lamentation and grievance.

The *Infidus Diabolus* returned to the roiling seas of the Ether, forging a path towards the Eye of Terror and Sicarus, the world claimed by the Daemon-Primarch Lorgar, and the religious seat of the Council of Apostles. There Marduk would face trial, to prove his worth to be embraced into the fold and become a true Dark Apostle of the Word.

# EPILOGUE

THE TWITCHING MAGOS was held against the back wall of the cell, deep within the *Infidus Diabolus*. His legs had been sheared off above the knees, and he hung suspended by dozens of chains. His wasted arms, covered with cancers and black malignancies, were outstretched and clamped with spiked manacles attached to further chains. Those arms had not been moved or utilised for centuries, and they were little more than canker ridden, skin-covered bones. They had broken as they had been pulled away from their position across the magos's chest, where they had been held unmoving for countless centuries.

Marduk moved beneath the sole, flickering glow-globe that buzzed overhead. The entire left side of his face was covered in augmetics and the skin around these bionics was puckered and a deathly shade of blue. His left eye was an angry, lidless, red orb, the pupil slender and slitted like a cat's. He had rejected the bionic eye replacements that the Chirumeks had offered, instead demanding this daemonic flesh hybrid, and he was pleased with the chirurgeons' efforts.

The sparking stubs of four mechanical servo-arms flailed spasmodically from the priest's shoulders and the remnants of mechadendrites quivered. Most had been ripped from the magos's spine and those that remained were little more than shorn off, useless protuberances. The haemoncolyte that had been attached by umbilical tubes to the machine priest had been severed from him and its repulsive, diminutive form opened up by the chirurgeons for study. It had squirmed as their knives had cut into its cankerous flesh. Large bell jars filled with viscous liquid protruded from the hunched back of the magos, though several of them had been smashed open, leaking pungent green-blue liquid, and sparking electricity flashed from within them occasionally. The contents of the jars had been placed under close scrutiny to try to tease the secrets from the preserved, ancient brains.

The red robes of the magos had been stripped from his mechanical body, and without its all concealing hood, the priest's head was exposed. Little human flesh remained of its face, and what existed was corpse pale and twitched uncontrollably. Tubes and pipes fed via thick needles had been shoved into his exposed flesh, pumping him with serums and foul secretions.

'It would seem that it has some kind of protective field generator around it,' Kol Badar had explained when the magos had first been discovered amongst the wreckage of the crashed airship.

'I would presume that this is what enabled it to survive the crash,' he had said. 'Allow me to demonstrate.'

The Coryphaus had fired a burst of fire from his combi-bolter towards the magos and an energy bubble surrounding the priest of the Machine-God shimmered as it absorbed the momentum from the incoming bolt-rounds, slowing them enough for them to fall harmlessly at the magos's feet.

But this device did not protect him any longer. No, the device had been prised from his flesh and the Chirumeks of the Host were even now examining its workings. Marduk could do whatever he wanted to the magos, who now had no defence.

'Greetings Magos Darioq.'

'I will not aid you Marduk, First Acolyte of the Word Bearers Legion of Astartes, genetic descendant of the traitor Primarch Lorgar. My systems are failing. This flesh unit is dying and I shall soon become one with Deus Machina.'

'You *will* aid me, and you will *not* be granted release. Yes, your flesh is dying since we removed your filthy dwarf clone, but soon you will be... changed. A daemon essence is being nurtured especially for you; you should feel privileged. Soon it will merge with you. Daemon, human and machine will become one within you. You will become that which your order loathes.'

Marduk smiled, the buzzing glow-globe lighting his face daemonically.

Soon you will be a puppet, dancing to my words, thought Marduk, and then you will beg to do my bidding. You will unlock the secrets of the Nexus Arrangement and a new era of destruction will be unleashed upon the Imperium of Man.

## ABOUT THE AUTHOR

After finishing university **Anthony Reynolds** set sail from his homeland and ventured forth to foreign climes. He ended up settling in the UK, and managed to blag his way into Games Workshop's hallowed Design Studio. There he worked for four years as a games developer and two years as part of the management team. He now resides back in his hometown of Sydney, overlooking the beach and enjoying the sun and the surf, though he finds that to capture the true darkness and horror of *Warhammer* and *Warhammer 40,000* he has taken to writing in what could be described as a darkened cave.